Also by SHELBY BACH

The Ever Afters: Of Witches and Wind

THE EVER AFTERS

OF GIANTS AND ICE

SHELBY BACH

Simon & Schuster Books for Young Readers

NEW YORK   LONDON   TORONTO   SYDNEY   NEW DELHI

SIMON & SCHUSTER BOOKS FOR YOUNG READERS
An imprint of Simon & Schuster Children's Publishing Division
1230 Avenue of the Americas, New York, New York 10020
This book is a work of fiction. Any references to historical events, real people, or real places are used fictitiously. Other names, characters, places, and events are products of the author's imagination, and any resemblance to actual events or places or persons, living or dead, is entirely coincidental.

SIMON & SCHUSTER BOOKS FOR YOUNG READERS is a trademark of Simon & Schuster, Inc.
For information about special discounts for bulk purchases, please contact Simon & Schuster Special Sales at 1-866-506-1949 or business@simonandschuster.com.
The Simon & Schuster Speakers Bureau can bring authors to your live event. For more information or to book an event, contact the Simon & Schuster Speakers Bureau at 1-866-248-3049 or visit our website at www.simonspeakers.com.
Also available in a Simon & Schuster Books for Young Readers hardcover edition
Book design by Chloe Foglia
The text for this book is set in Usherwood.
Manufactured in the United States of America
0413 OFF
First Simon & Schuster Books for Young Readers paperback edition May 2013
2 4 6 8 10 9 7 5 3 1
The Library of Congress has cataloged the hardcover edition as follows:
Bach, Shelby.
Of giants and ice / Shelby Bach.
p. cm.— (The ever afters)
Summary: Eleven-year-old Rory, daughter of a famous actress and a famous movie director, finds herself becoming a celebrity in her own right as she helps create a new fairy tale as a participant in the after school program, Ever After School.
ISBN 978-1-4424-3146-1 (hc)
[1. Characters in literature—Fiction. 2. Magic—Fiction. 3. Fairy tales—Fiction. 4. Adventure and adventurers—Fiction. 5. Dreams—Fiction.] I. Title.
PZ7.B1319Of 2012
[Fic]—dc23
2011029781
ISBN 978-1-4424-3147-8 (pbk)
ISBN 978-1-4424-3148-5 (eBook)

*To Mom and Dad,
who always picked me up on time
and encouraged me to go on every adventure,
especially this one*

n my first trip to Yellowstone National Park, I threw a rock at a dragon. It wasn't my smartest idea.

I'm not telling you this to brag, or to scare you away from national parks and their fire-breathing inhabitants, but you need to know: at some point in your life, you stop acting like a side character in someone else's life story and start being the main character in your own.

Look. If you're like me, you've dreamed of it already—your real life, I mean. Maybe it happens when you scan the whole carpool line and realize that no one has come for you. Or maybe when your parents are shouting at each other so loud you can hear them three rooms away. You look out the window and wonder when the good stuff happens—when your life gets jump-started. You might not be sure what that real life will be, but you know that this really isn't it.

Well, you're right. It's not. Just around the corner lurks the beginning of your story.

And I'm here to tell you: It won't be much like you think it'll be. It's always more terrifying and more awesome than you can ever imagine.

My life story, for example, started when I threw a rock at a dragon.

Of course, I didn't know it at the time. I was kind of busy running for my life.

You might not recognize yours, either.

No one could give this presentation to a bunch of sixth graders and get away with it. Maybe to grown-ups, but not us.

"Ever After School offers a wide range of activities between three and seven every afternoon. You can do your homework in our reading room, hang out with your friends, or even take a special afternoon class—all without the hassle of a babysitter or a nanny."

A few of my classmates snickered.

Definitely a mistake to bring up the nanny.

Ms. White, the representative from EAS, slammed her briefcase on our teacher's desk so hard that the students in the front jumped.

"I have handed out an application form for those of you who are interested," she said. "Please complete it with your name, physical address, e-mail address, and phone number, and bring it to the front when you're finished. Are there any questions?"

I watched it all from my desk, a row from the back, against the wall farthest from the window. That part of the classroom attracts the least amount of attention. (Trust me, I know. I had avoiding attention down to an art form.)

Then one kid raised his hand. "Can I go to the bathroom?"

"Yeah, me too," said his buddy, seated behind him. "I have to go too."

They both struggled to keep a straight face. A clear sign that they wanted to goof off out of class.

Ms. White wasn't fooled. "No, but I will speak to Mrs. Coleman about the next student who wastes my time," she said in a cold voice. "She can send you to the principal."

After that, all my classmates bent over their papers silently. Even if the only thing they did with the form was make a paper airplane.

I had only been in Mrs. Coleman's class for a week and a half, but I had met plenty of recruiters before. They were usually friendly people who introduced themselves and whatever program they promoted in a ridiculously upbeat voice.

Not Ms. White. For one thing, she was beautiful in a scary way— with very pale skin and dark hair and bright red lipstick. With one sharp look, she had sent Mrs. Coleman scurrying to the teacher's lounge of Ridgefield Middle School. Then Ms. White passed out a stack of photocopies while silently and creepily glaring at us all. She obviously didn't even *like* kids.

She also kept weird things in her purse. After threatening us with a visit to the principal, she pulled out a mirror—not even a whole mirror, just a shard about the size of her hand, diamond-shaped with jagged edges. She laid it carefully at the edge of the desk.

That mirror convinced me I was seeing things.

I filled my form out politely. When I finished, I took it up to the front like Ms. White had asked and placed it on top of the stack.

The mirror's reflection caught my eye. It had a girl's face in it, but not *my* face—someone older and very pretty. Long hair fell over her shoulders, a blond so pale that it looked almost silver. She stared into the mirror, like she was waiting for something she wanted very badly and couldn't decide if our classroom could help her get it faster. She also wore a crown made of towering icicles, which made her even weirder than Ms. White.

I glanced over my shoulder toward the door.

No one was there.

I looked back at the mirror to check again, but the picture had changed: Now a wrinkled man in spectacles struggled to open a leather-bound book. He was either a very small man, or it was one enormous book. I didn't bother to look behind me this time, because once the book was open, the picture in the mirror changed again. It centered on the man's face like a camera zooming in during a movie. The man's mouth moved, and even though there was no sound, I was sure he said, "Rory Landon." My name.

I jumped away, rubbing my eyes.

The entire room stared at me. Even Ms. White. I felt my face heating up, like it always did when I was the center of attention.

I glanced at the mirror one more time, but now it only showed the speckles on the ceiling tiles.

"Are you feeling all right, Rory?" Ms. White asked.

"Fine." I hurried back to my seat. It was hard enough being the new girl in April. I didn't want to also become the girl who started hallucinating after one too many fish sticks in the cafeteria. Especially if it might end up in a tabloid someplace. People were still looking at me, so I added, "I, um, thought I was going to sneeze."

A couple kids snickered, but Ms. White just turned to the rest of the class. "Any more forms to turn in?"

By the time school ended, I had let the whole mirror incident slide. The weirdest thing that happened after Ms. White left was Bobby Fuller getting a bloody nose during P.E.

Then, after the bell rang, I turned my phone on and found two messages.

My heart sank. Getting voice mail ten minutes before you're supposed to be picked up is *never* a good sign.

"See you tomorrow, Rory Landon," someone said behind me.

I turned. Two seventh graders passed by, in cleats and shin guards, on their way to soccer practice. They had the exact same hairstyle— blond in a high ponytail—and I had no idea who they were.

I saw the faraway glaze in their eyes, and I knew they were thinking of my parents, maybe remembering Mom's Oscar acceptance speech or the poster for Dad's latest film.

"See you," I said with an awkward half-wave. I could pretty much guarantee that before they started practice they would tell at least three separate people that they'd talked to the daughter of the famous Maggie Wright and Eric Landon. I tried to look busy listening to my voice mail so no one else would talk to me.

"Hi, sweetie! It's Amy."

Amy, my mother's assistant, always tried to sound cheerful when she told me bad news. I braced myself.

"I'm so sorry. We're running a little late today. The director changed the shooting schedule around. I don't think we'll be able to pick you up until maybe six o'clock."

I sighed. That was *hours* later than usual.

"You can hang out in the library. I'll call you if we can get there any earlier. I *am* really sorry, honey." It sounded like she really meant it.

Okay, so maybe this part wasn't weird.

When people found out Mom was an actress, they usually thought my life was pretty glamorous, but most of the time, it was like this.

I was a practiced new kid. I was practically a professional.

I'd been to ten schools in the last three years. We started moving a lot after my parents divorced and my mom got tired of running into my father in L.A. Since then, Mom focused on making movies that shoot only on location.

It wasn't really so bad, but I was tired of getting picked up late.

The other message from Amy was the strange one.

"Hey, Rory. Me again! I bet you're sick of the library, so maybe you could try out that Ever After School thing. Ms. White called this afternoon to offer you a place in their program."

First of all, my mom never placed me into any program without speaking to every teacher, principal, and guidance counselor I might meet. She liked to be "involved," as she called it. I usually called it "overprotective."

I was glad that she cared, but it also meant that the whole school knew who my parents were before my first class. Which kind of led to kids like those seventh graders talking to me for reasons that have nothing to do with *me*.

Just once, I'd like to walk into a school and not hear "Maggie Wright" and "Eric Landon" whispered as I passed.

Not that I had ever mentioned it to Mom or Dad.

"She spoke to your mom. She seems very nice," Amy continued.

"Nice" didn't seem like the right word to describe Ms. White.

"Very professional." That sounded a lot more fitting. "Ms. White said that if you wanted to do a test run this evening, you could walk there. To the right of the school, three houses down, the red door. She said you can't miss it. What do you think?"

It couldn't be worse than two and a half hours in the library. The kids' shelves at this branch were pretty picked over, and surfing the Internet for that long made my eyes hurt.

"Who knows? You might make some friends," Amy added slyly. "Anyway, I'll pick you up there at six. See you soon!" That meant she and Mom had made the decision for me.

• • •

The red door belonged to an ordinary brick house. The lawn was a little overgrown, and I didn't see any other kids going in. When I noticed a JUST SOLD! real estate sign hidden behind the bushes, I thought I might have the wrong place.

But the plaque on the door read *Ever After School* in curly script. Someone had added a little blue Post-it that said: *Welcome, Rory!*

Sketchy was the word that came to mind. My mom would've wanted me to back out and head to the library instead.

I knocked.

The door opened. A woman about Mom's age came out, smiling. Her brown hair was very frizzy, and she wore a blue and white apron around a thickening waist. "You must be Rory Landon. Come in! I'm Ellie. I'm so sorry that the Director couldn't come meet you herself. A minor emergency has come up that requires her immediate attention. You know how it is. Always putting out small fires."

Laughing a little to herself, she bustled through a dim hallway, but she didn't give me time to look around. At the far end, she held the door open to the backyard. "Everyone's so excited to make your acquaintance. Snow has told us so much about you."

"Snow?"

"Ms. White, dear," Ellie explained.

"Snow White?" I said, in disbelief.

With a sinking feeling, I realized that this was probably one of those *themed* day care centers. I hadn't gotten stuck at one of those since I was seven. I glanced back. Maybe there was still time for me to pretend I had tons of homework and escape to the library.

If Ellie noticed, she pretended she didn't. She closed the door behind us. It was as red as the front door with a red crystal doorknob. "This is the ruby door, my dear. Remember that for when it's time to go home. This way, now. You're just in time for the field trip."

The backyard looked like a formal courtyard. An enormous tree stood in the middle of the grass, almost three stories tall, with branches dipping to the ground and twisting up again into the sky.

Underneath the tree, a crowd of kids had gathered around a woman standing on a podium. Blond hair fell to her waist and curled girlishly. Her velvet dress was *way* old-fashioned. The last time I had seen one like it was when Mom played a medieval queen in a historical drama. The blond woman wore it like a uniform. Which meant that EAS was definitely into the themed thing.

"That's the Director," Ellie whispered. "She's explaining today's trip. The sixth graders are over there." She pointed out half a dozen kids my own age. One of the boys stood on the lower branches of the tree, leaning against the trunk, his arms crossed over his chest. A girl in a green silk dress took in his every move with a small smile.

If the kids had also been dressed in costumes, I might have turned and made a break for it. Instead, I dropped my backpack and crossed the courtyard. A few people noticed me, but most just listened to the Director as I crept around the trunk.

If you're like me, an only child whose mom's job forces you to change schools three times a year, you develop a system for making friends. The first step in mine was to identify possible candidates, attracting as little attention as possible.

The girl in the green dress tossed her long blond hair and moved away from me, nose up. Friendship with her didn't seem likely—or very appealing.

So I stood by a girl sitting on the roots of the tree, bent so low over a book that the beads in her braids touched the page. She read really fast, turning pages every few seconds and tapping her dark brown fingers on the spine nervously. It didn't look like it, but I had the feeling that she was listening to every word the Director said.

"Rangers have reported five fires in the park area." The Director gestured to a map behind her, but it was too far away for me to read. "Four have been extinguished, and the park is allowing one to smolder in order to clear out the underbrush. Our objective is to stop the source before the problem gets out of hand."

She surveyed the crowd like a general sending troops into battle. When she saw me, she smiled. I froze, all my plans for keeping a low profile going up in smoke.

"Ah, Rory—so glad you could join us."

Over a hundred heads turned toward me. A flush crept hotly across my cheeks, and trying to smile, I swallowed around a lump in my throat.

"Everyone, this is Rory Landon. She's new to Ever After School, so it would be best if you could watch out for her," the Director said.

My face grew even hotter, and I knew I was doing a great impression of a human traffic light.

"Please join me in welcoming Rory."

Everybody around me applauded dutifully, and looked me over a second too long to be normal, even the boy in the tree. I waited for them to start whispering about my actress mother or director father, but they didn't.

"And Chase Turnleaf, let me remind you that we do *not* climb the Tree of Hope," the Director added sternly.

When everyone turned to him, the boy grinned carelessly, as if it didn't matter whether he was in the Tree or not. He jumped down and landed as lightly as a cat.

"And let me remind you *all* of the rules for today's excursion," the Director said. "Only high school EASers are allowed to approach the problem directly."

Surprised, I looked into the crowd more carefully. At least half the kids were *definitely* too old for day care. I started to worry that Ever After School was one of those role-play programs, where they stage mock battles with elaborate point systems.

And I left all my armor at home.

"Those of you in middle school are attending purely in a scouting capacity," the Director added.

Even weirder, I didn't recognize any of the younger kids. Considering that we were so close to *my* school, you would think I would see one or two familiar faces. Maybe it was just because I was new to the area.

"Do you guys go to Ridgefield too?" I asked. (This is another friend-making tactic—finding out who answers questions nicely, and who doesn't.)

Chase Turnleaf frowned, as if this was a really weird thing to ask. The girl in the green dress said, "No. Millstone."

From the snotty way she said it, I guessed Millstone was exclusive—maybe even private. If most of the girls were like her, I was really grateful Mom hadn't sent me there.

"Hansel has led the juniors and seniors ahead," the Director continued.

"Hansel? As in Hansel and Gretel?"

I hadn't meant for anyone to hear me, but without looking up, the girl sitting on the roots answered, "Yes."

"Now, follow me. We'll need to hurry if we're going to get back in time." The Director rushed down the foot ladder behind the podium and led us across the courtyard, her skirt raised in both gloved hands. The train of her dress dragged behind her over the grass. It was embroidered with a flame-colored bird. "Don't forget to take a flare as you enter the passage."

They were taking this a little far. "Who's she supposed to be? Cinderella?"

"No," said the same girl. She stood up, still flipping through pages in her book, *Dragons for Dummies: Dos and Don'ts*, as the crowd meandered across the courtyard. Her thick, old-fashioned glasses made her brown eyes look huge. "Ellie's Cinderella. The Director is Sleeping Beauty."

I laughed a little, but the girl gave me an odd look.

As we lined up, she read one final page, closed her book, and tucked it behind a box holding open a yellow door. Then she held out her hand with a smile. "I'm Lena."

"Rory." I shook her hand, relieved that she'd made the first move.

The hallway we walked down was dark, lit only with strips of tiny lights on the floor like you see in airplane cabins and movie theaters.

"We *know* who you are," said a boy walking behind us. It was Chase. His blond hair hung in shaggy curls around his ears, and he looked a lot taller up close. "Ms. White came back from your school and dragged Rumpy into a conference about you for two whole hours—"

"Don't call him that." Lena glanced back nervously.

Chase ignored her completely, which I didn't like much.

After being the new girl so many times, I'd gotten better at figuring people out. Chase seemed like he couldn't decide what he wanted to be exactly—the class clown or the school bully. It was probably better to avoid him until he made a decision.

So I turned to Lena. "Why were they talking about me?"

Lena sighed. "We were hoping you could tell us."

"Was it because of my parents?" It would *not* be a good sign if even the adults running Ever After School got excited over Mom and Dad.

"Why?" asked Lena. "Are they Characters?"

I stared at her blankly, wondering if "Character" was a code word in role-play speak.

"Your dad's not an Aladdin, is he?" Chase asked darkly.

That had to be the single weirdest question anyone had ever asked me about my father.

"His name is Eric," I said hesitantly.

"That name sounds familiar. . . ." Lena said. For a second, I thought she would make the connection and ask, *Eric Landon, the director?* But she just looked thoughtful.

Maybe, just maybe, nobody here knew anything about my parents.

Most people couldn't tell just by looking at me. Everyone recognized Mom. She was the petite, elegant blonde they'd seen on magazine covers. I looked more like my dad—athletic and on the tall side, with wavy brown hair so thick that it went everywhere no matter how tight my ponytail was. The only part of me that came from Mom was my eyes—hazel with dark, arching eyebrows.

"Sometimes parents don't talk about it," Lena added with a sympathetic smile. "They don't want to get your hopes up—in case you don't turn out to be a Character."

But if these kids didn't know— Well, it made this role-play deal look a lot more promising.

I wanted to ask what a Character was, but then Chase nodded to his left where three boys with light brown hair and brown eyes walked with flashlights. "These are the Zipes brothers—Conner, Kyle, and Kevin."

"Nice to meet you," one of them said.

"We're triplets," said another.

"Fraternal," added the last.

"So you can tell us apart," said the first.

"Great," I said. Maybe it was the dim light, but they all looked identical to me—except that maybe one was a little taller and one had darker hair.

Triplets were tough. I had been friends with identical twins a couple schools back. Erna and Erma were always nice to me, but every once in a while, they would completely forget I was there and start talking like they had a secret language. If these guys were fraternal, they might not be like that, but I would have to wait until I could tell them apart to be sure.

Lena pointed to the girl in the green silk dress, who was walking ahead of us and hadn't once looked back. "And that's Adelaide."

"Charlotte Adelaide Eleanora Radcliffe," Adelaide corrected.

"What's her problem?" I whispered to Lena.

"Her grandmother is a grand duchess or something, so she thinks she can act like a princess." Then Lena rolled her eyes so hugely that I saw it even in the dark, and we both grinned.

I liked Lena.

That hallway seemed longer than hallways in a building should be, but maybe it only felt that way when it was crowded with students shuffling along in the dark.

My elbow brushed the wall, which was cold, like wet stone, and it smelled a little like rotten eggs. I wasn't the only one who noticed.

"All right, own up," said an older boy. "Who farted?"

"That's sulfur, dummy," replied one of his classmates, and several people laughed, including Chase.

Lena shivered and started counting on her fingers. "Besides fire, weapons include teeth, claws, tail—"

She seemed way more into the role-play deal than I was. I sighed, but another step in making friends was developing shared interests. "So, where are we going again?"

"Yellowstone National Park," said Chase.

"Oh. I've never been there." Yellowstone was thousands of miles across the continent, not just a short walk down a creepy corridor, but I played along anyway. "Are there other rules I should know before we start the game?"

"Uh-oh." Lena stared at me. "You didn't have your orientation yet, did you?"

"There was an orientation?"

Lena gasped. "Oh, my gumdrops."

"This should be fun," said Adelaide.

The triplets behind us laughed.

I ignored them. Lena looked like she might have a panic attack any second. "What problem are we supposed to be looking for?" I asked.

"Nobody tell her," said Chase quickly. "It'll ruin the surprise. Who wants to bet we have a screamer?" Someone patted my head in the dark.

"Hey!" I swatted at the hand. The other kids were really laughing now. My hands curled into fists, but I didn't lose my temper. I just told myself that this was better than the usual gossip, even if I wasn't totally sure that was true.

"I don't think I'll tell you either," Lena said, more worried than teasing. "You'll either freak out or not believe me." There was a light up ahead. We were almost outside. The air felt cooler than it had in the courtyard. "I just hope that we don't see anything bigger than a buffalo."

We stepped out into a forest. I blinked in surprise. It looked nothing like the woods outside my school. No oaks, no maples, no roads, either—just hills covered in pines as far as I could see.

"None of them waited?" Lena said, horrified. "The Director specifically said that someone would be stationed outside in case we had any problems."

"I'm sure it'll be okay," I said, a little distracted by the exit. It looked a lot like the mouth of a cave.

Lena pulled me to the side. "We'll just wait here."

"Do what you want," Chase said, leading Adelaide and the triplets over a small stream. Part of me wanted to ask who put him in charge, but I bit my tongue.

"Wait!" Lena called after them, but none of the sixth graders looked back.

Apparently, it was also against the rules to stay there alone.

Tagging along behind the others, Lena comforted herself by repeating all the rules that the Director had told them before I arrived. I tried to pay attention, but I couldn't stop staring at the tall, skinny pines and the yellowish hills with hidden pockets of melting snow.

"Travel in squadrons of no less than seven," Lena said, huffing a little as Chase started up a ridge. We passed a sign that said OLD FAITHFUL—15 MI. Ever After School really went all out with this role-playing deal. "If we see any signs of the beast, we're supposed to send up a flare and wait for one of the high school squadrons to reach us."

One of the triplets pointed over the ridge. "There's one."

"Where? Is Hansel with them?" Lena rushed up to look.

When I saw the drop, bile rose to my throat. I stumbled back behind the others, hoping that no one could tell that I'd broken out in a cold sweat. Heights aren't my favorite thing in the world.

After a few steadying breaths, I made myself peer over the ridge with everyone else.

A hundred feet below us, a herd of buffalo grazed on a plain of short yellow grass, steam billowing around them. Smaller figures—the teenage squadron—passed just beyond them. One of them playfully swung a long, pointy thing that looked suspiciously like a sword. "What's that he's carrying?" I asked.

"One of these." Chase lifted a short silver sword. It had a blue-colored jewel on the hilt and his name etched on the blade.

The triplets looked impressed—and kind of jealous.

That was about the time I started to feel like I was dreaming.

"Oh," I said. A bald eagle soared in and landed directly opposite us in the top branches of a pine tree.

"You weren't supposed to bring that!" Lena cried.

Chase shrugged. His grin took up half his face, and he had a dimple in his right cheek.

Mom always said to be careful of someone with dimples. They usually know how cute they are, and they're used to getting away with stuff. Of course, my dad had a dimple too, on his chin, and since the divorce, she'd been a little biased.

"Need to be able to defend any damsels-in-distress." Chase looked over at Adelaide and me.

Adelaide smiled in a syrupy way, and I liked her even less.

Lena eyed Chase's sword like it was going to come to life and bite somebody. "The Director said that we aren't supposed to attack it ourselves. She said if we—"

"Shut it already." Chase slid his sword back in its sheath. "We were all there. We know what she said."

Lena looked hurt. If we were going to be friends, I couldn't let anyone talk to her like that.

So, even though I was kind of tired of hearing about it too, and even though I felt the blush creeping up again, I said, "Well, I missed it. And I think it's important to know what's going on."

Chase only rolled his eyes and started over the next ridge, but Lena smiled gratefully. "Signs of the beast include fire, fewmets, scales—"

The tallest triplet pointed up ahead. "Does smoke count as a sign?"

A dark gray cloud rose in a plume to our right, and everyone perked up.

"Where there's smoke, there's fire." Lena stopped walking. "Quick—who has a flare?"

Chase shook his head and hurried toward the smoke. "The Director also said there have been a bunch of fires already. You don't want to send up a false alarm, do you?"

Lena was obviously torn, but she kept quiet as we approached the smoldering tree—a smaller pine, charred gray. A little orange flame danced on one of the bottom branches, the only part still burning.

Chase blew it out.

"Well done," said one triplet.

His brother examined the golden embers glowing through the trunk. "That fixed it."

"Hey. Only *we* can prevent forest fires," Chase said, and they all cracked up. Even Lena smiled tremulously.

I stared at the smoking tree. If this wasn't a dream, and if Ever After School was setting fire to trees, then they took the role-play game *really* seriously. I could get in a lot of trouble. If the wrong people found out about it, I could get my *parents* into a lot of trouble. I edged away, wondering if I could find the way back by myself.

My foot found a hole in the ground, and I almost tripped. It was about the size of a manhole, but it had five jagged points, like claw marks. A few feet away, there was a groove in the yellowish chalky soil.

Lena noticed it too. "The Park digs trenches to contain the forest fires."

"But aren't they supposed to be bigger than this?" The groove was only a foot deep and a couple feet wide, but it stretched from the burning tree all the way across the ridge and down the slope.

"Look," I said, pointing.

Beyond the spot where the groove disappeared over the hill, smoke rose in another cloud, much bigger and darker than the one above us.

Maybe it would've been smarter to make a hasty escape, but I was curious. Chase sprinted toward it, and I ran after him.

"Flares! Who has the flares?" Lena shouted.

"The Director would want visual confirmation of the target, Lena!" Chase yelled back, just as we reached the top of the hill.

I took one look into the valley below and screamed.

Called it!" Chase smirked as the others joined us.

I froze dead in my tracks and stared below us, too stunned to be annoyed.

Below the smoke, there was a dragon—or at least it *looked* like a dragon. It *had* to be a robot or something, but it seemed so real. It stalked two hundred feet away against a backdrop of burning trees and black smoke. One of the giant pines cracked and fell in a flaming arc. It landed across the dragon's back, but the robot thing shook it off like a twig.

"Smaller than the one last fall," said Adelaide.

"I don't know—I think it's about the same size," said one of the triplets.

"We're bigger though," said his tallest brother.

"No wings. We're in luck." Lena's voice quivered a little bit, but she seemed calmer now that we had found what we were looking for. "We don't need to worry about it flying away before the others find our position."

"So, who *does* have the flares?" Chase asked.

No one answered.

Okay, role-play didn't cover it. This was insane. And these props and special effects were good enough for one of Dad's movies. I had no idea how an after-school program could afford them. The dragon lumbered in our direction, dragging its tail on the ground. It didn't see us, but as we watched, it blew a long thread of fire. Another tree went up in flames. Watching it burn, I felt a little hypnotized. Pyrotechnics, maybe?

"Flares? Anyone?" Chase said. When nobody spoke up, he added, "Did *anybody* think to grab one?"

"I thought you were getting it," one triplet said to the tallest one.

The tallest triplet looked at the one with darker hair. "I told Kyle to take one."

"Don't look at me," said Kyle.

"Wow," Adelaide said. "Great teamwork, everyone."

My brain kept telling me that robot or not, I should be freaking out. But no one else seemed that upset, so the dragon thing had to be fake, right?

"It's fine," Chase said. "We're far enough away that we can watch it without getting in danger. We'll split up. Half of us will keep an eye on the dragon, and the other half will go find a group that actually remembered their flares."

The others nodded, but Lena repeated, "Travel in squadrons of no less than seven."

"Come off it, Lena," Chase said. "Now, who wants to—"

Then someone else screamed. It wasn't one of us—it came from the valley below, but it made me feel a little better about screaming myself.

"Oooh, is it the fifth graders?" Adelaide said, scanning the horizon.

"I don't see anyone," said one of the triplets.

She screamed again, and I saw her—a girl down there, about fifty feet from the dragon and a hundred feet from us. Her legs were tangled in a mass of hot pink. She tried to stand, but she couldn't shake herself free of the neon canvas.

"Wow," said one of the triplets. "That's a really bright tent. How did we not see that?"

"Do we know her?" Chase asked.

"I don't think so," said Lena. "That's a campsite."

The dragon took a few steps closer to it.

I swallowed hard. "Um, Lena . . . there's like a remote or something to stop the robot, right? To make sure that no one gets hurt?"

The other sixth graders glanced at each other uncomfortably.

"Rory, it's *not* a robot," Lena said, slowly and carefully. "The Director sent us to find the dragon before it burned down Yellowstone—well, more of it, anyway."

If it had been anyone besides Lena, I would have thought that she was pulling my leg. I wanted to believe her—it just didn't make sense.

"But—" I said stupidly. "How did we get to Yellowstone?"

The dragon was even closer to the girl now, head to the ground. It looked like it was smelling her out. I was suddenly sure it would eat her if it found her, and the thought shook me out of my daze. "Shouldn't we *do* something?" I said.

Everyone looked at Chase, like he was supposed to know.

"Uh." Chase sounded nervous for the first time since I'd met him. "Hope the dragon doesn't notice her?"

The girl screamed again, and this time, the dragon spotted her. It blew another stream of flame triumphantly and walked forward.

If someone didn't act fast, we were going to watch this girl die.

"Oh, my God," Adelaide said horrified.

And without really deciding to move, I started to run.

Down the hill.

Toward the dragon and the trapped girl.

This is why my mom says I don't think before I do stuff.

Lena shouted, "No, Rory!"

Chase rushed after me, yelling, "Wait!"

But I didn't stop until I reached the campsite. Half the trees around us were already burning. I was so close that all I could see of the dragon was a giant green backside, a tail covered in gold and green scales, and black blood streaming out around a spearhead stuck in its rump. The girl noticed me first. Her eyebrows rose, and her mouth opened.

This was where the rock came in.

It hit the dragon in the back of its head.

It whirled away from the teenager it had been about to barbecue. Which was a plus, considering that was what I hoped it would do.

Unfortunately, it turned toward me, which was not so good.

It looked me up and down with yellow eyes, each as big as my head, and let out a long, hot breath. The smell of sulfur seared my nostrils. I took a step back and stumbled on a loose rock.

"You idiot," Chase said behind me.

Then the dragon opened its jaws, showing off teeth half a foot long, and let out a noise like twenty Mack trucks honking at the same time.

"Run!" Chase yelled.

I didn't have time to be afraid.

We turned and sprinted back. Seeing us head their way, the others at the top of the ridge took off in five different directions. Lena was the fastest of all, which made me rethink that try-to-be-friends thing.

A ball of fire sailed over Chase's head, and the trees in front of him ignited in a swirl of blue and orange, cutting us off.

We weren't going to make it. We could never run up the incline fast enough.

I turned a sharp right and dashed through a dark opening at the bottom of the cliff.

"Not here!" Chase ran in behind me. His voice echoed around us.

For a second, while my eyes adjusted to the light, I had no idea what he meant. Then I saw what was inside—mounds of glittering gold, taller than Chase and me combined. Crowns were scattered around the cave like dirty socks in a kid's bedroom. Gold dishes, silver shields, and armor encrusted with jewels lined the cavern walls.

An enormous shadow crossed the entrance behind us. The dragon had followed us. Then it inhaled in a way that sounded even more threatening than the roar.

"Move!" Chase shoved me forward. We ran up a mound toward the back of the cave, because there wasn't anywhere else to run.

An orange fireball hit the coins right behind us. Steaming gold ran down the pile in rivulets and crept across the cave floor.

"We are in a dragon's lair," Chase muttered, mostly to himself, sounding as nervous as Lena. "We are messing with its hoard. Do you have any idea how mad that makes them?"

We reached the cavern wall. There wasn't any more room to run. We turned around, breathing hard. We were trapped.

The corners of the dragon's muzzle curled like a dog's grin, showing even more teeth. It stalked our way leisurely.

"It's not mad. It's *playing* with us," I said, annoyed.

The dragon stopped, only twenty feet away. It raised its head on its long neck, like a snake getting ready to strike.

I looked around for a shield, a spear, anything.

"Does that make it any better?" Chase said, exasperated. A

sword stuck out of the pile of coins he stood on, the wirework on the hilt just visible. "We're about to become Chase and Rory flambé."

But the dragon didn't breathe fire this time.

Its head whipped toward us, jaws open, just as my hand closed around the hilt. I threw my body to the side and slashed wildly. The sword connected. The dragon screamed and reared.

"Out! Now!" Chase grabbed me and hopped on a giant golden plate like it was a sled. We rode down the side of the mound. Chase hit the cavern floor running, dragging me along with him. We hopped over the scaled tail and raced out of the cave before the dragon's feet reconnected with the ground.

The dragon came after us so fast that it took out one of the stalagmites at the cave mouth.

"Wow," said a voice above us. "You weren't kidding, Lena."

Chase and I twisted until we could see them—two figures standing on a ledge above the cavern. One was Lena. The other was an older boy who looked a lot like her.

"I don't joke around about dragons," Lena said, her hands on her hips.

"George!" Chase shouted, still running and pulling me along. "It's blinded on its right side."

That didn't mean anything to me, but George apparently understood. The dragon realized we were looking at something above it, and it started to raise its head.

George jumped. A sword flashed once, and the dragon's head tumbled from its neck, rolling straight past Chase and me.

"Whoa," Chase said, skidding to a stop.

It was all over. We were out of danger.

"Are you two all right?" The boy ran toward us.

Well, almost.

The dragon's body crumpled and hit the ground with a heavy thump I felt through my shoes. I stepped toward it for a closer look, but the boy named George grabbed my shoulder.

"No, back up. Fast."

It was a good thing we did. Flames erupted over the scaly hide so quickly that I whirled around, looking for another dragon spitting fireballs.

Chase rolled his eyes. "There was only *one*. They don't roam in packs."

"It's the flammable gases in the stomach." Lena hopped down from the rock ledge and jogged over to us. Her voice sounded tinny and distant, like she was reciting something. "The dragon's body keeps them in a delicate balance, but only while it's alive. The corpse bursts into flame between thirty seconds and ten minutes after death."

"Oh," I said, still out of breath. My heart thumped so hard that I could hear the blood pounding in my ears.

"I read about it this afternoon," Lena added.

"Who took out the dragon's eye?" George asked Chase. "You?"

Chase hesitated and glanced toward me, not looking exactly pleased, and then George noticed which one of us was holding the blood-smeared sword.

He punched my shoulder lightly with a grin. "Not bad for a new kid."

I half-smiled, stunned, and watched the dragon burn.

"Beginner's luck." Chase folded his arms. "Don't forget which one of us was stupid enough to head straight into a dragon's lair."

Something about running for my life made me a lot testier than usual. "And who was stupid enough to follow me?" I shot back.

Chase didn't have an answer for that.

"Rory, this is my brother, George," Lena said.

George smiled and moved his sword from his right hand to his left before extending one for me to shake. "Nice to meet you."

"Sorry to break up the celebration!" a voice yelled across the clearing.

We all turned to look.

Chase laughed. "I totally forgot about her."

Tangled in the pile of hot pink canvas, the girl who wasn't from EAS was still struggling to stand. "But could one of you dragon-slayer kids cut me out of this stupid tent?"

By the time I took a shower and Amy started dinner, I was convinced that either Amy wasn't very observant or I had completely lost my mind.

I had spent the ride home terrified that Amy would notice the dragon blood on my clothes or smell the smoke in my hair. I was sure that she would force an explanation out of me, but she chattered on about her day and turned on the TV to watch while she cooked—as if nothing out of the ordinary was going on.

Safe in our warm kitchen, I was leaning toward the insanity option. I didn't really *feel* crazy, but crazy people probably never felt crazy either.

Don't get me wrong. I remembered everything that had happened in Yellowstone.

The girl stuck in the tent was almost as old as Lena's brother, and she was pretty nice after George cut her free. Her name was Miriam. Of course, she refused to shake hands with George and me, saying, "Don't take this the wrong way, but you're covered in blood."

Then Lena told us that dragon's blood mimics a mild acid and that it would slowly eat away at our skin. So George and I cleaned up as much as we could in a nearby stream.

George sent up his flare, and we waited around together. Chase reexamined the dragon's head, muttering to himself. While George and Miriam talked, the girl peeked at him curiously through a curtain of hair.

Lena told me that she had run off to find help as soon as I went after the dragon. The first person she found was her brother. "It was *my* idea to position us on the rocks up there," she added proudly.

When the other kids from EAS arrived, I started to feel like I was dreaming again, and my legs began trembling. I'm pretty sure that's a symptom of shock.

The first guy to reach us was an older man with salt-and-pepper hair. He looked a lot like my science teacher from two schools back—except for the fact his shirt was made out of golden chain mail. He examined us and the blood on our clothes and then the dragon's head. Then he stepped into the dragon's lair and came out shaking his head. "Typical. The Fey report a dragon in their lands, they send *us* to do their dirty work, and then *they* get the hoard. We should at least get half."

When they arrived, the fifth graders swarmed around the head, and one of them shouted, "Look! It's as big as I am!"

On our way back, a bunch of people congratulated George, and a few complimented me too. "It would've sucked if you had died your first day," one of the triplets said, which made me feel even more shaky.

Then a girl rushed up and tackled Lena and George in a tight hug. As soon as she found out that they were okay, she started yelling at them for ruining their clothes with dragon blood. Lena bent toward me to whisper, "My sister, Jenny. She *always* knows best."

It was already dark in the courtyard by the time we returned. Ellie bustled me straight through the ruby door and down the dark hallway. Just before she pushed me outside, she handed over my backpack and plucked the sword out of my hand. I hadn't noticed that I was still carrying it. "We'll keep this for you here," she said kindly. "See you tomorrow!"

I definitely remembered all that.

But something about pulling out your math textbook and looking up all the problems your teacher assigned makes you doubt that dragons exist. Even if one chased you into its lair an hour before.

When the clock struck seven, the front door swung open, and a voice rang out, "Where's my favorite daughter?"

Mom was always home just in time for dinner. Some actors demand special kinds of mineral water in their trailers, but Mom makes sure that all her contracts have a clause about being home in time for dinner with me. (Well, not exactly. But they have to pay her triple overtime bonuses if she works past 6:45 p.m., which does pretty much the same thing.)

"We're in the kitchen, Maggie!" Amy called back.

Two seconds later, my mom strode in, her honey-colored hair a little flat from the wigs she had to wear on set, her skin flawless under an invisible layer of makeup. She smiled when she saw me.

"I'm your only daughter," I reminded her.

"Then it's a good thing you're my favorite," Mom told me, which is what she always replied. She took my head in her hands and covered my face with kisses, which also happens a lot. It made me feel a little more like myself. "Sorry I'm late, sweetie," she murmured, hugging me, and I hugged her back, pressing my face in her stomach.

"Hey." Concerned, Mom looked from me to Amy. "What happened?"

Amy shrugged, looking pointedly at me.

I hesitated. If I could tell anyone, it would be Mom. On the other hand, if I *were* going crazy, she would probably send me to see a child psychologist. The ones I visited after my parents' divorce were really annoying. If anyone else asked me what I saw in an inkblot, I really *would* go nuts.

"Nothing," I said firmly.

Mom didn't believe me. "How was school?"

"Fine." Ms. White's mirror flashed through my head, but I ignored it. "We played soccer during P.E. again. I scored two goals."

"Only two?" Mom teased. (I'd scored three yesterday.)

"You haven't been very chatty since I got you," Amy said, eyeing me as she tossed the salad. "Did you not like the after-school thing? When Ms. White talked to your mom and me, they made it sound great. A cool place for older kids to hang out and do homework and take classes and stuff."

The first thing that popped in my head was, *Well, a dragon in Yellowstone couldn't decide if it wanted to eat me raw or flame-broiled.* I didn't know what to say, but it couldn't be the truth.

Luckily, the phone rang, which saved me from having to answer.

Mom picked up. Her voice dropped an octave, like it always does when she's on a business call. "Hello?" She listened for a second. "Oh," she said, scowling, and I knew exactly who it was. She only used that flat, angry tone for one person.

"Oh, no! Your dad's shoot ended yesterday," Amy said. "We were supposed to call him. I completely forgot."

"Yeah, she's right here." Mom looked at me, and I reached eagerly for the phone.

"Hey, Dad!"

"How's my princess?" he said, and I winced.

I wished he wouldn't call me that. He didn't before the divorce. Three years ago, during the custody hearing, a photographer had snapped a picture of me coming out of the courthouse with Mom and Dad. *People* had printed it with the headline: AMERICA'S PRINCESS TORN BETWEEN TWO KINGDOMS.

It hadn't even been a *good* picture—at least, not of me. Mom looked cool and competent in a black designer suit she had bought especially for the occasion. Dad's dark hair stuck up in all directions—the only sign that he was stressed. Between them, I definitely looked like the Ugly Duckling. I was wiping my nose, my eyes red from crying. The kids in my class couldn't stop talking about my parents after that article.

Life started to suck even more when my best friend, Marta, moved away. At Christmas, her dad got transferred to Copenhagen— of all places. Then, a week or two later, the class bully pestered me one too many times, and I dumped a trash bin over his head. Which led to my first ever fistfight and a new round of headlines like WARRIOR PRINCESS: LANDON AND WRIGHT'S DAUGHTER BATTLES IN PLAY-GROUND.

Third grade, in general, wasn't the best year.

Mom immediately put me in counseling. Dad tried to make a joke out of the articles, saying "No press is bad press." And he started calling me "Princess" at every opportunity.

"Rory? Are you there?"

"I'm here. You sound tired."

Production was always really tough on him. He was usually

planning before everyone else got up, directing during the day, and reviewing takes after everyone went to bed.

"I am. Your old man is getting *old*."

I rolled my eyes, smiling a little. He was only thirty-six. "Are you at home?"

Across the kitchen, Mom and Amy exchanged glances. I kicked myself for choosing that word. They always felt guilty when I called L.A. "home," but I hadn't really thought of it that way for a while. It was where Dad lived, that's all.

I jumped off the chair and walked over to the couch to give myself a little privacy.

"Nah. Still in Thailand. I've got a shoot in New Zealand in eight days. Anyway, it didn't make sense to fly all the way home and all the way back and miss a few days of quality sleep. Hey, Rory. You're done with school in June, aren't you?"

"I think so. Why?"

"Well, I've got another shoot then. In Oxford. Did you want to come?"

"Um…" Dad got three weeks of custody every summer, and I always looked forward to seeing him. But visiting during a shoot was *never* a good idea.

"You *love* England! Remember? You were in second grade and I took you to Harrods. I said you could pick out one toy in the whole store, so you picked out the *biggest* teddy bear you could find. We had to ship it home because the airline wouldn't check it."

"That was kindergarten, not second grade." He was making me sound like a baby.

Dad went on like I hadn't said anything. That's how he gets when he's excited. And he actually thinks that I'll *love* everything. "Listen, this shoot—you'll love it! It's a modern take on Narnia. There will be a bunch of other kids around, and the actress attached to the project, Brianna Catcher. You've heard of her, right? Redhead, real sweet and spunky? You'll love her."

If I went to this shoot, it would be a disaster—just like the shoot I visited two spring breaks ago. I had spent most of it tucked in an empty corner of the studio, headphones in, a book in my lap.

"I'd have to think about it." That was what I usually said when I was really leaning toward *no* but didn't want to hurt anyone's feelings.

"Okay, honey. Think it over." Dad said, a little subdued. "Rory, really, you'll love Oxford in June. All the gardens are in bloom. I'll have my assistant schedule in a few days so we can explore together. We'll rent bikes. You love bikes—"

If Dad told me what I loved one more time, I would scream. I had to interrupt him before he got too carried away. "Dad, I haven't said yes."

"Well, not yet, but—"

Suddenly, Mom stood over me, thin-lipped. I knew what that look meant. "Let me talk to him."

"Uh, Dad. Mom wants to say something. I love you," I said quickly, just a half second before she snatched the phone from my hand.

As soon as I let go, I knew I had done the wrong thing.

I half-reached for the phone, trying to grab it back, but Mom had already turned away. Then the fight began, just like I knew it would.

"Don't *bully* her." Mom stalked down the hall toward her room, kicking off her shoes so violently that they thunked against the wall. "It's not about visitation rights. It's about whether or not she wants to go."

Wait. Let me talk to him again, I wanted to say, but the words were trapped in my mouth.

"Don't you dare call your lawyer, Eric. You're just pitching a fit, because you may not get your way." Then she closed the door behind her, and I couldn't hear her anymore.

"At least this house has thicker walls than the last place we rented." Amy pointed at my abandoned math textbook with a wooden spoon stained spaghetti-sauce red. "Don't you have homework?"

I slid off the couch and returned to the stool silently. What could I say? Amy already wasn't Dad's hugest fan. I wasn't going to give her another reason to not like him.

Besides, he didn't *mean* to bully. He just gets so excited some-times that he forgets to listen. "Don't take no for an answer," he often told me, back when we all still lived together. This was a great quality for a director to have, but not so much for a dad.

I imagined going to Mom's door. Demanding the phone back. Telling Dad no.

But I couldn't force myself off the stool. I just copied out the next math problem.

I knew how easily I could make it worse. What if I asked and Mom wouldn't even give me the phone? Even worse, what if she *did* give me the phone? And what if I lost my nerve the second Dad started talking? What if I *still* couldn't tell him no? Then the whole thing would happen all over again—an even bigger mess than before.

So, I just curled lower over my homework, trying to breathe normally around a dragon-size knot in my chest.

"Hey," Amy said softly.

I looked up from the flames I was doodling in the margin of my notebook. When I met her eyes, I knew she had guessed exactly what I was thinking.

"Read my mind."

"I know." I sighed. She always told me the same thing. "It's not my fault."

But even though I said it, I didn't actually believe it. My parents wouldn't argue half so much if I could just *speak up*.

"That's right," Amy said, "and also, sometimes, parents need to grow up even more than kids do."

I forced a smile and nodded.

Mom's door swung open, and she came running out in her monkey pajamas. She hadn't taken her makeup off, but her hair had weird lumps and tufts.

Next came the hardest part of the whole disaster—the part where we pretend it didn't happen.

"Okay, how was Ever After School?" Mom hopped on the stool beside me, and even the fake smile dropped off my face.

It was my cue to pick up right where I left off.

I wanted to *do* something. To rip my math notebook to shreds, or to burst into tears, or at least to ask Mom what Dad had said. Anything would be better than being trapped like this. It was like their hidden concern pinned me to my seat, but their fake cheer wouldn't let me talk about it.

Unfortunately, I knew from experience that my outbursts could upset Mom for days.

"It was fine," I said.

"Did you take any classes?" Mom asked. "Ms. White said there would be a fencing class! I thought you would like that."

Memories of the afternoon came rushing back: the dragon's yellow eyes, the heat of the flames, and the run up a slippery slope of gold coins. I missed the lair. At least *there*, I had something to fight. "There were swords."

But when I remembered swinging the sword and feeling it hit something, the pressure in my chest drained away.

At least I had done one thing right.

That is, if I hadn't gone crazy and imagined the whole thing.

"Were the other kids mean to you?"

Who wants to bet we have a screamer? Chase had said. "Not really."

"Did you make any friends?"

"Yeah, I think so." Lena *had* risked coming back to a dragon-infested valley to help me.

Amy sighed. She always got exasperated when Mom beat around the bush. "But the real question is, do you want to go back there tomorrow?"

She had no idea it was a life-or-death decision.

Well, I couldn't tell them *now*. That was the quickest way to get Mom to call Dad back and accuse him of upsetting me so much that I started making up crazy stories.

But should I go back?

It hadn't exactly been fun, but for a couple hours, I stopped wondering if I was doing the right thing or worrying about what people thought of Maggie Wright and Eric Landon's only child. If there was even a *chance* that I could take a break from being the daughter of my famous parents, nothing could keep me from going back.

"Absolutely," I said finally.

Mom and Amy smiled.

The first weird dream came that night. I mean, I've had night-mares before. They usually come after stressful situations or after eating Amy's spicy enchilada casserole, but this was different. This dream was very clear and very still—as if someone had paused a scene in a movie and placed me inside it.

I dreamed of a door in a dark corridor. It was made of ancient black wood, old and solid, cracked in the corners and bound with rusting iron bars. The only decoration was by the keyhole. A silver, scrolling *S* was welded into the iron. From the bottom hung a delicate snowflake so sharply pointed that it looked like it could cut you. In the dream, I knew I had to go through the door, and I was afraid of what was waiting on the other side.

The next day, after school, the bronze nameplate still read, *Ever After School*, which I took to be a *very* good sign for my sanity.

With a deep breath, I knocked.

No one answered.

I knocked again, three smart taps, as loud as I could make them.

Still no answer.

I wiped my hands on my jeans nervously. Maybe it was a one-day ticket deal. Maybe dragon-slaying filled the adventure quota for one student, and I wasn't allowed to come back. Maybe I *had* hit my head on something and hallucinated the whole thing.

After one last knock, I turned away from the door and stepped glumly down the short stairway, wondering if maybe they just didn't like me—if they were too busy to remember that I was coming.

I stopped. Maybe they *were* just busy. Ellie couldn't wait by the door for every student—she probably only did that on your first day.

When I went back and tried the door, the knob turned easily. I took a deep breath and hoped that I hadn't made it up, especially since that would make this breaking and entering. Then I stepped inside.

It was the same hallway, still too dark to see clearly. I ran to the other end with one hand on the wall, feeling ridges and shapes in the stone under my fingers, more excited with every step.

Outside, I got my first good look around.

Definitely real.

The grassy courtyard was even bigger than it had seemed the day before. It was about the size of a football field and lined with dozens of doors surrounding the perimeter—plain doors, carved doors, glass doors, windowed doors, doors with knockers, doors without, a couple metal doors like you see with elevators, and even one that looked like it was made out of marble. EAS's decorator must have really liked the rainbow theme, because each door was a different color.

Every once in a while, a door would open, and a kid or two would come out. Most of them made straight for the middle of the courtyard, where everyone was gathering.

The Tree of Hope looked exactly the same. Its low branches were covered with bookbags, jackets, and raincoats.

Under the Tree, someone had set up furniture. Not plastic patio chairs, but real furniture. Coffee tables carved with jousting scenes sat in the grass. Girls a few grades older than me had collapsed together on an overstuffed leather couch, giggling loudly.

As a practiced new kid, I knew that first-day awkward is nothing compared to second-day awkward. On the first day, you don't know anyone, and no one knows you. It's a clean slate all around.

The second day is different. You're expected to remember people's *names*. You want to find the quasi-friends you met the day before, but you have no way of knowing if they'll be as friendly on Day Two. You're expected to know the routine and follow it. It was *twice* as important to do that at EAS. I could only imagine the epic screw-ups that could happen at a magic after school program.

Lena could probably point me in the right direction *if* I found her.

Unfortunately, I didn't see Lena—or George, or Chase, or Adelaide, or the triplets, or anyone I recognized. Forget finding a familiar face— I would settle for a friendly one.

One girl wearing ripped jeans and heavy eyeliner fed handfuls of grass to a fawn with a spiked collar. When she caught me staring, she glared, and the fawn said with an angry boy's voice, "What are you looking at?"

Too shocked to even apologize, I hurried through the crowd—so fast that I accidentally bumped into a massive dining room table.

"Whoa," I said, realizing what was on it.

Pizzas covered the section closest to me—cheese and pepperoni and sausage and mushroom. A little farther down, cakes rose in tiers—five kinds of chocolate, two vanilla, one red velvet, one carrot, and a yellow-white cake that looked like lemon with raspberry jam icing. Beyond that, the other desserts were piled in mounds so big that they reminded me of the dragon's hoard yesterday: fudgy brownies, snickerdoodles, peanut butter cookies, ice-cream sandwiches studded with chocolate chips. In the middle of the table, there was even a soda fountain—like an *actual* fountain. A stone fairy statue stood on top with cola pouring out of the jug she held on her hip.

I leaned forward to see the snacks at the far end, but someone pushed me back.

"No cutting," said a scowling high school boy at least two feet taller than I was. I stumbled out of his way as fast as I could.

"Go easy on her. She's new," said the girl next to him. She handed me a metal plate. "Here. The line starts over there." She pointed at least twenty people back.

My face burned as I hurried to the end. I had only been at EAS for three minutes, and I was already making people mad. What a disaster.

I heaped my plate with goldfish crackers and brownies. At the end of the table, I felt like I should have something healthy. So I grabbed a fruit tart, the last one on the platter, covered in strawberries and blackberries. Unfortunately, another hand had reached for it at the same time.

The hand belonged to a teenage girl. For a second, I thought she was the same person I had seen in the mirror yesterday, but this girl's hair was *actually* silver. It was so long that the end of her heavy braid brushed the ground.

She didn't speak. She just smiled a little and pointed to the tart in my hand.

"Oh, sorry!" I said. "You can have it."

When I put it on her plate, she gave me another smile, this one wider, and she pointed to the table.

The round platter was magically full of fruit tarts again.

I turned to thank her, but the girl had disappeared.

Apparently, I was the only one who didn't know that these plates automatically refilled themselves. One chubby kid had even pulled up a seat by a plate of mini-cupcakes. He ate them one by one until they were all gone and waited until more appeared.

"No more for you, Evan. You'll eat yourself sick again. The Table of Never Ending Refills wasn't designed to help you gain thirty more pounds," said a tall woman with slate-gray hair and a stern expression. She picked up the whole dish of cupcakes and headed off with it.

She walked oddly when she rushed—kind of a shuffle-hop, shuffle-hop. When she kicked up her skirt, you could see her foot was made out of a weird dark metal. There was no way to know if it was a prosthetic or if she had accidentally dipped it into some enchanted pool.

The boy chased after her. "But it's my favorite."

At the end of the table, I worried where I should sit for about a minute before I noticed someone waving—at me, I realized with a relieved grin. It was Lena, sitting at a gilded table next to the Tree of Hope. Beside her sat the youngest person I had seen at EAS so far, a girl with blond curls. She couldn't be more than seven.

"Welcome back!" Lena said when I reached them. I had forgotten her glasses were so thick, and it took me a second to get used to how big her eyes looked. "This is Kelly," she added, pointing at the girl.

"Nice to meet you." Kelly smiled, stroking the white cat in her lap. The feline wore a dress embroidered with purple flowers, but being from a big city, I had seen people dress up their pets before. "Not everyone comes back the second day, you know."

The table was covered in books. I shoved a stack of them over to make space for my plate and settled into the chair next to Lena. "I can't imagine why. Where are we going today? Scotland? To battle the Loch Ness monster?"

I meant this as a joke, but Lena said sadly, "No, we don't get to go on field trips every day. That was a special treat. Besides, I really doubt the Loch Ness monster would make trouble. All the books say it's gentle."

Kelly nodded. "Mom says all it wants is a little attention. It's one of Oberon's pets, and he never goes to play with it."

"Oh." I decided not to make jokes until I knew more about this place.

"Guess what?" Lena said excitedly. "I figured out what kind of dragon George killed yesterday. A *draconus melodius.* The singing serpent."

"Should I know what that is?" I asked.

Kelly tapped the cover of the book in front of me. A golden dragon breathing flame was embossed on it. In fact, all the books on the table had dragons on the cover or in the title. "She's been researching since she got here."

"This one must've been a male, because the female's growl sounds like a harmony," Lena continued. "That's how they get their name."

"She talks a lot when she has a breakthrough," Kelly whispered to me.

Then Lena hummed a little. The growl of a female *draconus melodius* sounded a lot like the *Jaws* theme with one extra hissing note.

I shivered. "That's creepy."

"I second that." Chase slid into the last empty chair at the table. "Hey, Rory."

I frowned at him, not sure what he wanted. I mean, he hadn't exactly been nice the day before.

"*Incredibly* creepy," Lena said thoughtfully. "That's why Solange favored them in the war. During a siege, she would station them outside to terrorize her enemies."

"Gretel says she still has nightmares about the sound," added Kelly.

I opened my mouth to ask who Solange was and what war they were talking about, but Lena kept talking. "Nowadays, the singing serpents live mostly in Canada, in the tundra plains. This one must've been forced south by another bull. It was an adolescent male. It still had its baby teeth."

"*Those* were its *baby* teeth?" Chase said in disbelief at the same time I said, "The teeth get *bigger*?"

"Show them the picture," Kelly said to Lena.

Lena dug through her pile until she uncovered a sketchbook. The first drawing showed a dragon just like the one I remembered in tiny, precise pencil strokes—green and gold scales, yellow bulging eyes, and smoke streaming from its nostrils.

She pointed to the mouth with a red colored pencil. "See how the teeth look gray? If these were the adult set, they would look yellow. It's easier to see in the other sketch."

She turned the page, where the dragon chased two kids with its mouth open and all the teeth visible. The girl running with a sword wore the same blue shirt I had on yesterday.

Inspecting it, Kelly told Lena, "Looks like you got Chase just right."

"You drew this? It's really good," I told Lena. She smiled and ducked her head, embarrassed.

"I don't know," said Chase. "I don't think I looked that scared."

George appeared over Lena's shoulder, glancing at the drawing. "You looked plenty scared. Besides, Lena doesn't exaggerate. That's why they call it a photographic memory."

Chase didn't seem too thrilled, but Lena smiled gratefully at her brother.

"I'm supposed to give you this, Rory." George handed over a sheathed sword. I took it by the hilt, and as I lifted it, my shoulder hurt in places that hadn't felt sore before.

"Is that what you fought the dragon with?" Kelly asked, perking up. Even the cat in her lap stood up to look.

"'Fight' is probably the wrong word." I pulled the sheath off.

Someone had cleaned the sword. It was the first time we had

seen the blade without blood on it. Chase gasped beside me. Interlocking squiggles were etched onto the metal on both sides. They looked like really ornate Celtic knots.

"It's pretty," Lena said.

It was beautiful, and it was mine. I couldn't wait to try it out.

"It's too big for you," Chase told me quickly.

"I'll grow," I replied, a little more fiercely than I should've been on only my second day, and we scowled at each other.

"You would think that dragon-slaying together would make them friends," Lena commented, and we both scowled at her.

"There you are, Rory!" said another cheerful voice—one of the adults I recognized. Today she wore a red apron, wiping her hands on it as she walked. "I have been looking all over for you."

"Hi, Ellie," I said.

"Hi, Mom," said Kelly, which made me do a double take. You *could* see the resemblance, if you were looking—the same heart-shaped lips and wide-set eyes.

"I heard you did well your first day," she told me. "Kind of a trial by fire."

Then she laughed, shaking her head. The kids looked embarrassed. Especially Kelly, who said, *"Mom."*

In a clipped accent, the white cat explained, "Ellie is quite fond of her puns."

It would've surprised me much more if the fawn hadn't yelled at me earlier.

Ellie showed me through the amethyst door for orientation, waving good-bye cheerfully as I entered the building. The Director's office was covered in white marble, with roses inlaid in the walls over a pattern of thorny vines. Silver fountains ran in the corners, and the sound of trickling water bounced off the walls.

Two kids sat in puffy floral armchairs, next to a humongous marble-top desk carved all over with roses. One kid was Miriam, and next to her a boy about my age slumped in his seat. He had the same dark, glossy hair she did.

"When do I get a wand?" the boy asked.

"You don't. You have the wrong idea about magic. That's what I've been trying to tell you." The voice belonged to a woman, who sounded *a lot* like Amy, but I couldn't see where it came from.

"You don't *control* magic," said the voice. "We can't. Magic is a wild thing, a force of nature, like the wind, or the weather, ever shifting, ever changing. We might be able to observe its patterns and predict its path, but it is— Oh, you must be Rory! Welcome!"

"Rory!" Miriam jumped up and gave me a hug. "This is my little brother, Philip. Philip, Rory was one of the kids who saved my life."

I half-laughed. "Not really. Chase and I would've been dead meat if George hadn't shown up."

"How is that any different?" Miriam dropped back into her seat. "My life passed before my eyes right before you got there."

I started to shrug, and then I realized: She was right. I had kind of saved her life. How had I not noticed?

Oh, right. Worrying about my sanity had kept me occupied.

Philip waved a little without meeting my eyes. He seemed kind of uncomfortable.

Then something on the desk moved. It was a very tiny woman, waving to get my attention. She wasn't any bigger than my hand. After the talking fawn and cat, meeting her shouldn't have surprised me, but it did.

"Oh, oops," she said. "Not on the list, but introductions, of course. I'm—"

"You're Thumbelina!" the boy burst out.

"Thumbelina is my *Tale*, not my *name*." I was close enough now to see the irritated look on the woman's face, the tuft of auburn hair on her head, and the nylon jeans she wore—like something she had stolen from Barbie and altered to fit. She also wore a large needle on her belt, like it was a sword. "Honestly. Don't you think my parents had more imagination than that? If I were called Thumbelina, do you think I would have ever taken my husband's name? Tom and Thumbelina Thumb? How ridiculous. My name is Sarah, Sarah Thumb."

For such a little person, Sarah Thumb had a powerful voice when she was upset. Philip shrank back into his chair, obviously wishing he hadn't said anything.

This was why I tried to keep my mouth shut as much as possible, especially during the first couple days.

"Better apologize," Miriam whispered.

"Sorry," said Philip quickly.

"Yes, well, me too." Sarah Thumb sounded sheepish. "I get a little carried away sometimes."

She held out her hand and shook each of our index fingers briskly. Then she started leafing through pieces of paper on the desk. They were so big that she could've used them as picnic blankets. "The Director normally handles these orientations. She's gone out to meet with the MerKing, but she wrote down a list of things we should talk about. Here we go."

She wrestled a pink memo free and stood on top of it. The elegant cursive was as tall as her hand was long. "Fairy Tales do not equal make-believe," Sarah Thumb read aloud. "Well, duh. If you still think that magic isn't real after a dragon almost eats you, you have serious problems."

"*I* didn't see any dragons. And everybody at home says *she's* crazy." Philip jerked a thumb toward his sister. "It was even on the news."

"Really?" Suddenly, I was even *more* glad that I hadn't mentioned dragons to anyone the night before.

"Yep. They even called it something when they interviewed her about the dragon and the kids who killed it. What was it again?" he asked his sister.

Miriam glared daggers at him. "Shut up."

A grin stretched across my face and wouldn't go away, no matter how hard I tried. I covered my mouth so that Miriam wouldn't think I was laughing at *her*.

"Oh, yeah." Philip folded his arms smugly. "Post-Traumatic Stress. I shouldn't believe anything she says."

Sarah Thumb put a hand on her hip. "Yeah? So, it's pretty normal for you to meet women only four inches tall?"

Philip didn't reply, and it got harder not to giggle.

It wasn't them. It was just . . . Something I did *made the news*. Well, technically, George had done it, but I helped. After all those tabloid articles, this was the first time the press covered something I had done that made a *difference*. I had saved Miriam's life.

And honestly, it was nice to be the one in the family making headlines for a change.

"I have a question." Miriam raised her hand.

Sarah Thumb obviously enjoyed this sign of respect. She nodded once, very pleased.

"*Why* do they think I'm crazy?" Miriam said. "I mean, the dragon's body was right there. They called it a *buffalo*. I guess it was on fire, but you could still see the scales."

Sarah Thumb nodded again sagely. "A century and a half ago,

most people would believe you, but nowadays, logic has a pretty strong hold. Logic says there are no dragons, and logic says that the person who believes in dragons must be bonkers."

That kind of made sense.

"But even my *friends* didn't believe me," Miriam said. "The same friends who were *there* when the dragon showed up."

"The human mind is very strange," Sarah Thumb said. "When it comes into contact with something it doesn't understand, self-defense mechanisms are often unleashed. I'm sure you've noticed. Didn't you wonder if maybe you *were* crazy? Or if you were dreaming?"

Yesterday *still* felt like a dream.

I nodded. So did Miriam. Philip looked bored.

"Now we can practically conduct whole battles under most people's noses, and they'll just take themselves off to see a shrink," Sarah Thumb said. "Right. 'Item number 2: Children here are Characters-in-training.' Okay, being Characters means that you're part of both worlds—this one and the one you woke up in this morning." She started to sound pretty dreamy. "Magic loves people like you. It clusters around you, and someday it'll snag you and pull you into its current."

Philip looked a little alarmed. "Is it dangerous? Is it like an infection?"

"No, it's like a Tale," Sarah Thumb said, irritated. "Like a *fairy* tale. Miriam, you've already been in one, but since it was George's, not yours, there's a pretty good chance that you're going to have your own. In fact, you might even have it soon. You and Rory. Tales tend to be catching—don't look at me like that, Philip. *Honestly*, it's not a *disease*—when a Tale starts, it's like a fire, throwing out sparks. Whoever's close to the Character having the Tale has the best chance of catching flame. Rory, Miriam, Lena, and Chase were with George while all the good stuff was happening. The probability that their Tale will start soon is pretty high. I'm sure the Director wanted me to mention that."

A Character, I thought to myself. It actually sounded impressive.

"So, uh—now that his Tale is over, what happens to George?" Miriam asked. "Does he graduate or something?"

I wondered what kind of Tale I would get. Hopefully something cool, where I got to fight something. Didn't Red Riding Hood beat the Big Bad Wolf?

"No. That was just his first Tale. It's not uncommon for a Character to have two of them," Sarah replied. "Or even three. In fact, he *should* get another one. That was the shortest version of 'George and the Dragon' we've ever had. It didn't even start until his sister ran to get him, and then it was over ten minutes later. George will probably stick around until he's eighteen. Ninety-seven percent of Characters will get their Tale or Tales between the ages of ten and eighteen."

With my luck, I would have to wait all seven years.

"And then what? What happens after we're eighteen?" Miriam sounded a little distressed, but I guess she was a few years closer to the cutoff age than Philip and me.

"Well, a few stay on to help train the next generation—like myself," Sarah Thumb said proudly. "But most Characters go back to the magic-less world. They're just more successful than most. Back in the day, a lot of *happily ever afters* included getting a kingdom, but those are in short supply now. So, we get a lot of mayors, CEOs, and PTA chairwomen at our EAS reunions." That didn't sound too appealing, and it must have shown on our faces. Then Sarah added, "A few presidents, too. Both the Roosevelts were ours."

That made Philip look slightly more cheerful. I wondered what you had to do to get an EAS job.

Sarah Thumb stepped back, reading the list under her feet. "'Item Number 4: Like begets like.' I never figured out why she insisted on telling kids that. It's not like anybody new to EAS knows what that means."

I could tell Miriam understood just about as much as I did, which was not much. "So, should we start watching out for dragons in our backyards?" I asked.

"Of course not," said Sarah Thumb, startled. "Fairy tales don't repeat themselves that often. *That* particular Tale won't occur again for months, or years. Maybe even decades. More common Tales with lots of variants—like 'Cinderella'—come up at least once a year."

"Then what will happen to *us*?" Miriam asked.

"We don't know. We can't. Don't you see?" Sarah Thumb had that far-off look again, her eyes glittering in her tiny face. "Magic is so unpredictable. You won't know what your Tale is until it starts, and maybe not even then. That's the beauty of it."

She sounded a little loopy, but I knew what she meant. Yeah, the dragon yesterday was scary. But after the shock and the adrenaline wore off, I felt—I don't know. Like I could do great things.

Getting a Tale of my own, where *I* was the main Character. . . . I gripped the sheath of my sword eagerly and glanced at Miriam, who started to grin.

Philip looked like he might puke. "What if I don't want to be a Character?"

"Then you're totally lame," Miriam snapped.

Sarah Thumb looked just as annoyed. "You might not have a choice. It tends to run in families. But there *is* one way to tell for sure."

The little woman walked over the desk to a small wooden chest. She took the metal latch in both hands and flipped it up, saying, "Ms. White, our scout, visits classrooms all across the country, handing out our registration forms. They're totally unnecessary, of course, but—" She grunted a little, struggling to lift the lid.

Miriam reached over the desk and flipped it open. Sarah Thumb glared at her.

"I could've gotten it," she said, a little out of breath. "I'm *small*, not helpless."

The corners of Miriam's mouth twitched suspiciously, but she didn't say a word. Neither did I. I *liked* Sarah Thumb and her fierce independence.

"Anyway, this is the *real* test." Sarah Thumb climbed up to sit on the edge of the box. "It's a shard from the mirror in 'Snow White'— you know, the mirror on the wall." This shard was shaped like a pear, different from the one Ms. White brought to my class yesterday. "Characters always see something. Rory had a go yesterday. That's how we knew to recruit her."

Sarah Thumb didn't pause to ask me what I saw. She just looked at us eagerly. "Well? Philip, you first. The suspense is killing me."

hilip peered nervously into the shard. "Nothing." Then he added glumly, "No, there's a guy. Wearing red."

"Bummer," said Sarah Thumb.

"He's playing an instrument," Philip went on. "Something like a flute, but made out of wood."

"Interesting." The little woman's eyes glittered again. "Characters see different things. A lot of people see the Tree of Hope outside, or the door that will bring them here, but some see a glimmer of their future Tale."

I remembered the chilly expression on the girl wearing the icicle crown with a stab of worry.

"Miriam?" said Sarah Thumb cheerfully.

Miriam looked and quickly glanced away, her cheeks red. "George. I see George."

Sarah Thumb grinned wickedly. "Romance also tends to be part of most happily-ever-afters. Riches, too."

"Miriam and George sitting in a tree," sang Philip, "K-I-S-S-I—*Ow!*"

Blushing even harder, Miriam had elbowed her brother in the ribs and hissed that he better shut up if he didn't want their mother to find out who broke her favorite vase. (Times like this make me wish I had a sibling too.)

"Looks like you're stuck with us, Philip. Okay, time for the tour." Sarah put two fingers in her mouth and whistled.

A bird chirped from a fountain in the corner. He flitted over, landed on the desk next to Sarah Thumb, and ruffled his feathers, looking guilty and defiant. I wondered if he would start talking too, but apparently not.

"*Stop* that, Mr. Swallow. No one's going to tell the Director that you're using her fountains as a birdbath again. Right, children?" Sarah added, eyeing Miriam, Philip, and me.

We all quickly shook our heads.

Mr. Swallow was a pretty bird with blue wings and a long tail that cleft into two sharp points. He didn't *need* to talk to show us how vain he was. He puffed up his scarlet chest and preened his wings for us as Sarah Thumb struggled to fold her list.

Then the tiny woman settled into the saddle on Mr. Swallow's back, and we followed the bird out the door.

As we hurried to keep up (I never noticed swallows were so fast), Sarah Thumb kept telling us how lucky we were to have a place like EAS. "I wish I had known about this place when I was a kid. I could've used the preparation. I didn't even know anything about 'Thumbelina' when I started."

"How could you not know?" Miriam said. "There are so many books, and movies—"

"Well, my childhood was a little sheltered," she said.

We returned to the courtyard so that Sarah Thumb could point out the doors to each place. She said that for training, we would need to find them on our own later.

The reference room was through double doors painted the color of grass. Oak bookshelves lined the walls, and students sat at long tables. Some kids were just doing homework, but a lot of them read from beautiful, leather-bound books with gilded pages. These definitely weren't for school.

"Aren't they a little *old* for that?" Philip pointed to two teenage boys bent over *The Complete Works of the Brothers Grimm.*

The swallow landed on the closest table, and Sarah Thumb gave Philip a stern look. "Not when you're a Character. Knowing what Tale you're in and how it's supposed to go can make the difference between a happy ending and getting killed."

"Killed?" Philip repeated, in a higher voice than usual. Apparently, he hadn't thought the Yellowstone dragon was that dangerous.

"Relax." Miriam squeezed her brother's shoulder. "I'm sure that when the red dude finds you with his deadly recorder, you'll be ready for him."

"Flute," Philip corrected automatically, but he did look less freaked out.

"But on the other hand, it's very dangerous to meddle with the Tales," Sarah Thumb added. "You usually kick it off yourself, but it *has* to be an accident. Don't try to jumpstart a Tale on your own. A few years ago, a Cinderella-wannabe bought some glass shoes and tried to dance in them at her prom. Her feet took months to heal."

Before we could get properly grossed out at that little story, Sarah Thumb also pointed out the volumes for researching the magical realm and the creatures that lived in it—and then the books that helped Characters interpret their dreams. "Sometimes they show our future. You know, hints like what you saw in the mirror shards," she told us.

Last night's dream popped back in my head. I had no idea what fairy tale had a door in it.

Miriam grimaced. "Don't tell me that. I had one of those go-to-school-naked dreams last night."

"Well, it probably won't come true unless you dream it three times, but—" Sarah Thumb shook the Director's list out and read, "'Item Number 5: It's best to be prepared.'"

Next, we visited the EAS workshop—or at least we tried. Bitter-smelling smoke billowed out as soon as Miriam opened the steel door. The hot air blew the swallow off course, and he and his passenger tumbled head over tail feathers. The rest of us coughed, choking on the smoke's chemicals.

"The Director's going to have to show you that one herself when she gets back." Sarah Thumb stroked Mr. Swallow's head soothingly as he chattered angrily at the workshop door. "Same thing goes for the dungeon—I mean, the menagerie. Last time I was there, one of the trolls tried to eat Mr. Swallow for breakfast."

Then she pointed out the yellow and blue door that led to the dormitory for the Characters who needed to stay overnight and then the orange-gold door that led to the instructors' quarters. "Which you will stay away from, if you want to keep all of your fingers and toes. Jack's pet wyrm doesn't like strangers," she added.

On the way to our last stop, Sarah Thumb showed us a heavy wooden door studded with iron. "The training courts. Hansel's the instructor."

"I get to learn how to use a sword?" Philip said. It was obviously a close second to the wand he wanted earlier.

"Or a spear. Or a bow." Sarah Thumb looked down at her list. "'Item Number 11: We require all our Characters to study weaponry for at least one year, and we encourage further study.'"

Winging her way around the courtyard, Sarah Thumb added that for most Tales, being kind to strangers and being tricky with bad guys was all that you needed for a happy ending, that violence should be the last resort, etc.

Finally Sarah and Mr. Swallow stopped at a violet door gilded with words I couldn't read. "Here we are! The library!"

Bookcases towered over us, almost as tall as the Tree of Hope outside. The bronze shelves were spaced at least three feet apart. Bronze ladders ran from the floor to the ceiling, welded to the bookcases. The rungs were placed very close together, like the ladders you see on playgrounds for really little kids.

Unlike the reference room, the library didn't have any desks, or even any chairs. Everything smelled like dust and paper.

But something about it gave me déjà vu. Each shelf was full of heavy-looking volumes in every color. Blue, red, gray, brown, violet, pink, and green leather spines glittered with gold embossing. Each book was at least two and a half feet tall, and I realized with a start why they seemed so familiar—they looked exactly like the one I had seen in the mirror.

Mr. Swallow perched on a bronze shelf just above our heads.

"'Item Number 14: Characters-in-training are not permitted into the library, but it is of the utmost importance that new Ever After School students see it once and understand its significance,'" Sarah Thumb read. "So, kiddies, this is where we store the collections. Every fairy tale since the founding—failed or finished—is stored here, all eleven centuries."

"Eleven *centuries*?" Miriam stared up at the bookcases, awed.

Honestly, my grasp of history has never been the best. I couldn't remember anything that happened in the ninth century. King Arthur found Excalibur, maybe?

"Well, we really only have the books since the North American Chapter was founded. The fairies have the earlier ones," said Sarah Thumb sadly. "Our librarian keeps bugging the Fey monarchs to let him complete the library. Speaking of our librarian, he's supposed to be here. I hope he didn't fall asleep in the stacks again. Hold on." She let out another sharp whistle.

"Coming!" said a voice high above us. Near the ceiling, a man in a purple tweed suit hurried nimbly down one of the bronze ladders, carrying over his shoulder a book as big as he was. At first I thought the book was bigger than the others, but when he reached the floor, I realized that the *man* was smaller. He barely came up to my shoulder.

"This is my dear friend and our librarian, Rumpelstiltskin," said Sarah Thumb.

I looked carefully at his wrinkled face—the huge, hooked nose and the round spectacles resting on top of them. "I know you!"

The man was so surprised that he nearly dropped the dark green book he was carrying. "Indeed?"

"I saw you in the shard yesterday!" I said. "Are you part of my Tale, then? What happens in 'Rumpelstiltskin'?"

"A miller tells a king that his daughter can spin straw into gold," Sarah Thumb explained, amused. "The king orders her to do it. A dwarf shows up and spins the straw into gold for the miller's daughter, but only because she promises him her firstborn child. She saves the baby by guessing the dwarf's name—Rumpelstiltskin."

The words "firstborn child" sent a jolt through me, because having kids wasn't something I thought about much, being eleven and all.

"But I'm not a miller's daughter," I said uncertainly.

"And you can't have her firstborn child," Miriam added. "She already knows your name."

Sarah Thumb covered her mouth with her tiny hands, but we could still hear her laughing.

Rumpelstiltskin took off his spectacles and rubbed them with a long-suffering sigh. "Honestly, you have a troubled youth, and no one ever lets you forget it."

"You tried to steal a *baby*," Miriam reminded him.

"I wasn't going to steal it. I'm not a *fairy*. We had a bargain, the queen and I," he said, shaking his head.

"You weren't going to *eat* it, were you?" Philip said worriedly.

Rumpelstiltskin looked appalled. "Certainly not. I was lonely. That's all. I would've given him back after he grew up. I thought a human boy would make a good pet."

Philip's eyes widened. Miriam and I stepped in front of him protectively.

"No, no, no," Rumpelstiltskin said, "I'm quite reformed, thank you. Come along, children."

Sarah Thumb waved us forward, still laughing, and we followed the short man to the only piece of furniture in the room, a large bronze table with a small staircase on the side. Rumpelstiltskin ran up these steps and meticulously opened the book he was carrying.

We gathered around warily.

"This is the current collection. As soon as your Tale starts, this volume lists it in the front of the book, as you see here." He flipped straight to the end of the table of contents and showed us the only Tale listed on that page:

46. George and the Dragon..........349

"The Tales in this volume are still ongoing, so the book continues to write and revise the stories within," the librarian said. "Note the page numbers."

He paused for a moment so we could see the number change from 349 to 376 to 360. Then he stuck a bookmark between the pages. He flipped through the rest of the book so quickly that the text blurred to gray and the illustrations slid by with a splash of color. The page he stopped on had a dragon every bit as realistic as Lena's, right down to the yellow eyes and the long gray teeth.

Underneath the illustration, the Tale started.

Rumpelstiltskin read aloud, "'George and the Dragon: Once upon a time, a dragon set up residence in Yellowstone. He was still too young to terrorize villagers, as he wanted to, so he made do by eating pet dogs and blowing fire at unsuspecting campers.' You'll find the whole adventure here," he added, turning pages much more slowly.

On the next page, an illustration showed Miriam trapped in the hot pink tent as the dragon blew fire over her head, and two pages after that, there was one of Chase and me trapped at the back of the dragon's lair. (To be honest, he *did* look more scared than I did.)

"As the Tale progresses, the happenings are chronicled here," the librarian explained. "It will continue to change a great deal in the coming weeks, but it will settle soon enough. Meanwhile, this volume will continue adding Tales as they occur—fairly straight-forward, but difficult to grasp if it is not right in front of you. Any questions?"

What I really wanted to ask him was why he and Snow White had locked themselves in the library to talk about me the day before, but I didn't want Miriam to think I was full of myself. Besides, he probably wouldn't answer honestly with three other people and one opinionated swallow around.

"Can we read it?" I asked. "George's Tale, I mean?"

"Yeah, I want to see that dragon again," said Philip.

"Yes, yes, of course." Flipping to the Tale's beginning, Rumpel-stiltskin told Sarah Thumb, "The children *always* want to read the

Tales they take part in. Self-centered little creatures."

We ignored this insult and eagerly gathered around the first page.

"The beginning's changed!" Miriam said.

"And the illustration," said Philip, disappointed, pointing at the new picture—an elegant woman with silvery-blond hair and a glittering crown, staring out a window. Her back was to us, her face hidden.

"I did mention that it would happen," said Rumpelstiltskin. He and Sarah Thumb exchanged amused, tolerant smiles, as if they had gone through this routine many times before. "Even now, the book may be writing a new passage about the afternoon when George's lady love read of his actions and swooned again over his valor—"

"I am not *swooning*," Miriam said, annoyed.

"'The queen grew restless in her glass prison,'" I read aloud, wanting to back Miriam up before Philip teased her again. "'She had waited patiently for many years, and she grew tired of pretending that she was not dangerous. She sent one of her dragons to a park much favored by the human world—'"

Rumpelstiltskin slammed the book shut so quickly he almost smashed my fingers.

He and Sarah Thumb stared at each other.

"We must tell the Director," he said, horrified.

"She's with the mermaids."

"We must call her back."

"Is it that important?" Sarah Thumb asked.

"My dear Sarah, this is *Solange* we're talking about. She—"

"Hush!" the little woman said fiercely, with a pointed glance in our direction.

We knew a secret when we heard one. "So, who's Queen Solange?" Miriam asked brightly.

"Is she part of EAS too?" Philip said.

"Will we meet her?" I added.

"No, child," Rumpelstiltskin said distractedly. "Hope you *never* meet her."

"Now look what you've done," Sarah said, hands on her hips. "It'll be all over EAS before the sun sets. Ignore him," she added, turning to us. "He always overreacts."

Rumpelstiltskin didn't seem like the kind of guy who over-reacted. He *looked* insulted at the thought.

"If—" Miriam started, but a deep ringing gong interrupted her, like the kind you hear in old churches.

"Oh, good. Saved by the bell." Sarah climbed back into Mr. Swallow's saddle.

Rumpelstiltskin opened the volume again. In the table of contents, a new entry had appeared under George's Tale:

47. The White Snake........372

"This is unprecedented," he murmured to himself. "Three Tales in two days. Interesting times, indeed."

"Who had the third Tale?" I asked.

The librarian only ran his fingers down the cover's edge, avoiding my eyes.

"Rumpel's already told you more than you need to know," Sarah Thumb said as Mr. Swallow started winging down the hall. "Come on, kiddies. Tour's over now. A new Tale has started."

In the courtyard, Sarah Thumb and Mr. Swallow sailed over the crowd around the Tree of Hope, telling us to keep up. "You've never seen this. Let's get you some front row seats," she added. The other students moved aside so that we could get to the trunk.

A boy stood next to the podium—the same boy who had stationed himself beside the cupcake platter at the Table of Never Ending Refills. He fidgeted uncomfortably, but that might have only been because the same woman who had taken away that platter was glowering at him.

"That's Gretel," Miriam whispered. "I met her earlier."

Mr. Swallow landed on the podium and chattered angrily as Sarah Thumb slid off his back.

"The bird says that you don't have time to deal with a Tale right now. You have to tell the Director," the boy said. "What do you have to tell the Director?"

"Well, he's got animal speech all right," Sarah Thumb said to Gretel. "How did he find the snake? I thought we kept it locked up in a silver Tupperware or something."

Gretel narrowed her eyes, her mouth in a very thin line. "Evan followed me back to the kitchens and went through the fridge."

"I was *hungry*," Evan said. "I thought it was sausage."

Mr. Swallow eyed Evan's biggish belly with one beady eye and chirped something else.

"I am *not* overfed," Evan said outraged. "Mom says I'm a grow-ing boy, and I need to keep up my strength."

While Miriam, Philip, and I tried not to laugh, Gretel gave him a stern look that clearly said she'd heard *that* before. "You better get started," she told Sarah.

The little woman nodded and climbed to the top of the podium. "Evan Garrison," Sarah Thumb said in a formal voice, nothing like how she talked during the orientation. The crowd grew quiet, expectant. "Congratulations. Your Tale has begun. Since it is a questing Tale, you may choose two Companions for your journey. Do you accept this privilege?"

Sarah Thumb had never explained what a questing Tale was or even mentioned them.

Evan just nodded. He looked like he couldn't speak.

"Which Companions do you name?" Sarah Thumb asked in the same serious tone.

Evan swallowed and surveyed the crowd. Everyone held their breath, hoping it would be them. The air seemed to buzz with anticipation, and even though I knew that there was no way he would ever pick me, my stomach churned with butterflies.

Plenty of kids also looked a little jealous, but I wasn't. Well, not yet. As much as I wanted to go on an adventure, it would probably be a good idea to study the Tales before living one. I mean, I didn't even know what a White Snake was.

"Come *on*, Evan," Sarah said in her normal voice. "I *do* have things to do, you know."

"Russell Hale and Mary Garrison," Evan said quickly. Two figures made their way forward—a very small boy wearing a school uniform and an older girl who had the same freckles and red curls that Evan did, probably his sister.

When they reached the front, Sarah Thumb asked them, loud enough for the whole crowd to hear, "Russell Hale and Mary Garrison, do you consent to undertake this journey with Evan? To advise and protect him to the best of your ability?"

"We do," they chorused.

"Very well. We wish you the best of luck in this Tale." Mr. Swallow fluttered to the top of the podium, and Sarah Thumb clambered back into the saddle. "Please follow me to the library. Rumpelstiltskin has some research to share with you."

She and Mr. Swallow flew off, and the three followed her solemnly. Evan waited about two seconds before biting his fingernails.

I wondered if everyone looked that nervous when their Tale started, or if it was just Evan. He had seemed a lot more excited about the mini-cupcakes earlier.

Once the violet door with gold lettering closed behind them, everyone started talking.

"Who would've thought that Evan would be the first in our year to have his Tale?" one of the seventh graders said.

"Except for Bryan and Darcy, of course," said one of his friends, and both the girl with the eyeliner and the fawn with the spiked collar looked up.

"Yeah, but who would want 'Brother and Sister'?" said the first seventh grader. He didn't seem to notice when Bryan and Darcy glared at him—probably because an angry fawn isn't all that scary.

"I wonder what Evan's Tale is."

"It can't be a very good one. This is *Evan* we're talking about."

Over at Lena and Kelly's table, the sixth graders were talking about the same thing.

"What does Evan have in his family tree?" Adelaide said scornfully. "Just the Enchanted Pig and the Three Snake Leaves?"

"He probably doesn't have one of the better-known Tales, then," Lena said. "It's a questing Tale, though—" I must have looked confused, because seeing me, she started to explain, "*Like begets like.* Your Tale is similar to ones your family has."

"But what's a questing Tale?" I asked.

"The Tales where you travel. Usually to retrieve an object or to pass some test," Lena said. "They're longer and more difficult, so you're allowed to pick two Companions to help you."

"But only for the questing Tales. 'Cause it'd be dumb to recruit help if you were a Cinderella and all you had to do was go to some dance," Chase added.

I definitely wanted a questing Tale.

The cat in Kelly's lap looked up, flicking her tail. "You were in Rumpel's library, weren't you? Do you know what his Tale is?"

All the heads at the table turned to me. I knew peer pressure when I saw it. I hesitated, wondering if I was going to get detention or something my second day.

"You might as well tell us," Kelly said. "I'll find out from Mom at dinner."

"It'll be all over EAS tomorrow," Lena said eagerly.

If Lena was okay with it, there was no chance it could get me in trouble.

"It's the White Snake," I said.

Obviously, everybody but me knew what that meant.

"*Oh,*" Adelaide said, scornful again.

Chase grinned with relief. "Is that all?"

"I thought for a second he had gotten Aladdin or something," said one of the triplets.

"The White Snake is a pretty good Tale." But Kelly sounded a little unsure.

Adelaide smiled in her not-nice way. "You're right. He could've been a Town Musician of Bremen. That wouldn't have been embarrassing at all."

Chase and the triplets laughed, and Adelaide smiled wider.

I made a mental note to search online for "The Town Musicians of Bremen" and figure out what was so funny. "What's wrong with The White Snake?"

"There's nothing *wrong* with it," Lena said slowly, "but—"

"Have you heard of it?" Chase asked me.

"No," I said defensively, sure that he was going to make fun of me.

"Then it can't be the most impressive Tale in the world, can it?" Chase said.

"Somebody eats a little bit of a white snake when he's not supposed to," Lena explained, "and then he can understand animals. He helps some of them out, and in return, they help him with some impossible tasks. Then he wins the princess or riches, depending."

"Oh," I said, wondering what a seventh grader would do with a princess. "That doesn't sound so bad."

"It's *boring*. It's too easy. He's going to let some ants do all the work," Chase said. "When my Tale starts, you'll know it. It's going to be the best one in decades."

"Me too." Adelaide shook her long blond hair back. "Snow White hasn't happened for a while, and we haven't had a new Sleeping Beauty in over a century."

"How do you know?" I asked. "Sarah Thumb said that we don't find out what our Tale is until it starts."

"Don't let them confuse you, Rory," Lena said. "They're just guessing. Wishful thinking."

"Chase and I have a better chance of getting a good Tale than *you* do, Lena," Adelaide said scowling. "What do you have in *your* family tree? You're descended from Madame Benne. Big whoop."

"Madame Benne was a great sorceress, an inventor—" Lena started, insulted. She pronounced "Benne" with a long "e."

"And who's ever heard of her? How about you, Rory?"

I hadn't heard of her, but I glared at Adelaide rather than say so.

"That's not fair, Adelaide. Everyone *used* to know about her. When she was alive," said the shortest triplet, the one with darker hair. "She died a long time ago, that's all."

"Besides, Lena's brother had his Tale just yesterday," Kelly said loyally.

"Yeah, but let's be honest," said Chase. "'George and the Dragon' is about a saint. It's not even a real fairy tale."

Lena jutted out her chin stubbornly, but she didn't say anything, which meant that she probably couldn't think of a comeback. So, I told Chase, "Yeah, but you still wish *you* got to slay the dragon."

"I don't *need* to slay any dragons," Chase said, and I knew I'd struck a nerve. "I already told you. I'm going to have the best Tale this place has seen for centuries. Maybe even *two* awesome Tales. I could be one of the Brave Little Tailors or the Boy Who Went Out to Learn What Fear Was—"

"You definitely aren't the second one," I said. "It looked like you had fear all figured out when the dragon cornered us."

From the way Chase's face turned red, I was one more insult away from turning the playground into a battlefield again, or whatever. I hoped none of the other sixth graders knew any reporters.

But Lena, who had looked like she was about to cry a few

seconds before, tried not to giggle. I guessed it was worth it.

"Well, Chase may be climbing beanstalks and killing giants like his father soon," Adelaide said. "We haven't had a new Jack in years."

"That's right," Chase said, calming down a little. "Do you even know anything about the Tales in your family?"

I had no idea, and I was beginning to worry that I was supposed to figure that out by myself. The phone calls would be so awkward: *Hey, Aunt Lucy. Was Uncle Billy a frog before you kissed him?*

Adelaide stared down her nose at me, which took skill, because I was a couple inches taller than she was. "Are your parents even Characters?"

I glanced at the other sixth graders, bracing myself for those faraway glazed expression that people get when they think about those famous people, Maggie Wright and Eric Landon.

But nobody had that look—not even one. They were all interested more in the argument than what I would say about my parents.

They didn't know.

Well, except for maybe Lena. She glanced at me uncertainly, but she wasn't the type to make a big deal over celebrities.

My mouth fell open.

Of course, Chase and Adelaide thought I was speechless for a completely different reason. They both looked smug.

"So, keep in mind who you're talking to," Chase said. "My dad's Jack, and Adelaide's mom was a Cinderella."

I looked at Kelly, surprised. She and Adelaide didn't act anything like sisters.

"Not *that* Cinderella," Adelaide said with a sniff, and both Kelly and Puss-in-Dress glared at her.

"I think they're coming back," the shortest triplet said, looking at the violet door with gold lettering.

Sure enough, Sarah Thumb and Mr. Swallow came flying out. The crowd parted under her, and Evan Garrison and his two Companions hurried through. Each of them carried a green pack, all looking very pale. Evan was still biting his nails.

"That was way faster than normal," Chase said.

"Maybe they'll at least send them someplace cool," said the shortest triplet. "Maybe Atlantis."

"Atlantis?" I said, so loudly that a dozen people turned away from Evan to stare at me. My face burned.

"That's right," Lena said softly. "It's a Fey realm, like Avalon and the others, hidden from humans. Sarah Thumb showed you a map, right?"

She definitely *hadn't*. Apparently, my orientation hadn't covered everything.

"But how will they get there?" I whispered, as Evan and his Companions passed us.

"The Door Trek system," said the tallest triplet. "Of course."

"Don't tell me," Adelaide said sarcastically. "Sarah Thumb didn't tell you that either."

I frowned, not sure if she was mocking Sarah Thumb or me.

"It's a transportation system, faster than the Fey railway. It's simple if you have a door and something to tie you to your destination," Lena explained quickly.

"You know, like how we got to Yellowstone," said the triplet with darker hair.

"I wonder," said Lena thoughtfully. "Where was the last White Snake Tale? And when?"

"Muirland. Ten years ago," said Puss-in-Dress. "But only one of the Companions came back. There weren't enough animals to complete the tasks."

Sarah Thumb landed on the Director's podium, and the soon-to-be questers assembled themselves in front of her. As the crowd started to quiet down, Lena whispered, "And when was the last successful White Snake quest?"

No one answered, and butterflies in my stomach morphed into a tight, anxious knot.

"Evan, Russell, and Mary," Sarah Thumb said in the same formal tone she had used before. "The time has come for you to venture into the Fey realm to complete Evan's Tale. We wish you luck, courage, and cunning on your journey, and we bestow upon you these three rings." The rings glowed electric blue, dangling from a silver ribbon in Mr. Swallow's beak. They looked a lot like party favors from a laser tag birthday party. "If at any time during your travels you find yourself in a fatal situation, twist your ring around your finger three times and think of this courtyard. You'll find yourself here."

As Evan reached up and took the rings from Mr. Swallow's mouth, the whispers started up again.

"When was the last time EAS gave out the rings of return?" Lena asked Kelly and Puss-in-Dress.

"Not since The Yellow Dwarf," the cat replied. "That one is always supposed to end badly."

"Two years ago," Kelly added. "They must be worried about this one too."

"It's long for a quest, right?" said the triplet with darker hair.

"The standard time period for a White Snake Tale is five to six weeks," Lena replied in her tinny, reciting voice. "The third longest quest of all, which only increases the Character's peril."

Since so many people were talking, I couldn't hear what else

Sarah Thumb told the three travelers, but pretty soon she and Mr. Swallow led them out. Some of the students patted Evan on the back and waved good-bye mournfully, as if they never expected to see the questers again.

Even Chase sounded sympathetic. "Who knew such a dumb Tale could be so dangerous?"

"But *why*?" I asked. "These are fairy tales we're talking about. Don't they all end with *happily ever after*?"

The tallest triplet shuffled his feet. Lena and Kelly looked at each other and didn't answer. Chase shoved his hands in his pockets, and even Adelaide looked uncomfortable.

"They didn't take her," said one triplet.

"They don't take *everyone*," Puss-in-Dress reminded them. "Usually, no one younger than twelve."

"Too scary," said the other two triplets together.

"But Rory faced a dragon. That shows guts," said Lena, and if I had felt less nervous, I would have smiled.

"Must've been the other new kid. The boy. He looked freaked out the second he got here," Chase said, and everyone nodded.

"Are you going to keep me in suspense?" I asked, half-joking, mainly because I didn't want anyone to guess I was starting to freak out myself.

"No." Puss-in-Dress leaped out of the girl's lap, her white tail lashing. "Your orientation isn't over quite yet."

"I'll take her," Chase said quickly.

"Me too." Adelaide's smile looked way too sympathetic to be real. I wondered if there was any way I could request the feline tour guide instead.

"You guys go tell Miriam," Chase added, and Lena watched us go anxiously.

Adelaide led the way across the courtyard in the setting sun.

We came to an old-fashioned door made out of dark wood, black ribbons hanging off its frame and rippling in a wind I couldn't feel. With Adelaide on the lookout, Chase pulled out a skinny metal tool and picked the lock.

My heart banged in my chest, and I gripped the hilt of my sword tightly in my sweating hands.

Finally, the door swung open. "You're not scared, are you?" Chase whistled a loud cheerful note, and torches flared from bronze fixtures hanging from the ceiling. "It's just a wall."

The wall was made out of marble, five times as tall as I was and as long as the dragon George had killed the day before. It was covered in names, columns of them etched into the stone and gilded, like the markers you see sometimes in national monuments.

"This is the memorial to the Failed Tales," said Adelaide gravely.

Chase scanned the last column. "It looks like seven Characters have died on 'White Snake' quests in the past century."

A lump clogged my throat.

"Stop it, Chase. You're scaring her," Adelaide said. "Rory, it's not that bad."

But there were so many names—thousands.

"Most of the deaths in the last few centuries happened in the war," Adelaide added. "It's really been so much better since the Director started implementing all of her new policies. She's the reason why we take Companions on our Tales now. Safety in numbers, she says. Instead of being executed if you Fail a Tale, your Companions help you escape. That kind of thing."

"And we rehabilitate a lot of the villains nowadays," Chase added. "That helps too."

That wasn't comforting. It just made me worry that Rumpelstiltskin could still be a problem.

"Yes, before the Director started, we lost three out of five Characters. Now, the death rate is . . ."—Chase examined the wall thoughtfully—"less. I'm pretty sure."

Then they left me.

I stared up at the wall, counting names. My gaze stopped at the last column, only half-full, and even though I didn't want to, it was easy to imagine "Rory Landon" in the same curly letters.

I was still stunned when the bell rang again. Time to go home. I walked back out to the courtyard on leaden legs.

I didn't want to know that over half of all Characters Failed their Tales. I didn't want to think about how many of us might die. But I couldn't stop a little voice in the back of my head from screaming, *And you still want to go back for Day Three? Are you nuts?*

Right before I reached the red door, Ellie caught up with me and pushed an envelope into my hand. "With all the excitement, we almost forgot to give you this. The Director wanted to make sure you had it before you went home."

"Thanks," I said automatically and headed through the dark hallway.

But I definitely wasn't crazy. Which meant that I needed to figure out how to explain all this to Mom and Amy.

I trudged out to the driveway.

Behind the windshield, Amy scanned the whole place—from the shingles on the roof to the bushes in the front garden—with a skeptical frown. She clearly didn't think it looked like much.

Amy wasn't alone in the car. Mom sat in the passenger seat. She never came to pick me up.

Suddenly, it clicked: Maybe Mom *was* a Character. Maybe she had come to get me, because she knew that I would be *really* freaking out after orientation.

I dashed across the yard, over the sidewalk, to the car, and threw open the back door. "Mom, I—"

"Shh," Amy said quietly.

Mom pointed to the cell phone on her ear with an apologetic grimace.

"Interview," Amy mouthed. *"EW."*

Or maybe not.

"I can't tell you how much I enjoy working with Mike," Mom said into the phone. That meant she was promoting the film from three moves ago, which would be released in a week.

Sighing, I threw my backpack on the seat and climbed in, closing the door as quietly as I could. It figured. Mom couldn't get out of work early unless she had some sort of PR excuse. Her world didn't revolve around me.

Of *course* I was going back. I couldn't remember the last time people saw *me* and not just my parents' daughter whenever they looked at me.

If I didn't go back to EAS, where would I find any real friends? School? Yeah, right.

So, I just turned the envelope over. It was addressed to "Aurora" in gold calligraphy. I made a face (no one ever called me by my full name) and opened the letter.

Dear Ms. Aurora Landon,

Welcome to Ever After School. We are so pleased that you have joined our fine establishment, and we hope that your time here with us will be both memorable and nonfatal.

Looking through our records, we can report finding the following Tales in the last five generations of your family:

- *The Boy Who Went Forth to Learn What Fear Was (paternal grandfather)*
- *Cinderella (mother of your maternal grandmother)*
- *The Garden of Paradise (great uncle of your paternal grandfather)*
- *The Goose Girl (great aunt of your paternal grandfather)*

The first one had to be a good Tale, if Chase wanted it, *but* I would never recover from my disappointment if the most exciting thing I ever did in my Tale was lose a stupid shoe. Even if it was made of glass.

> *If you have not already done so, please take a little time this evening to read these Tales in Anderson, Grimm, and/or Lang, as there is an increased likelihood that you will have a similar Tale.*

> *After a minor divination spell, we have discovered your mother and father have no knowledge of Ever After School's magic and associated issues.*

So Mom wasn't a Character. She didn't know. Which meant trying to explain would suck.

> *Should you choose to enlighten them, please ask Ellie for our helpful Dos and Don'ts brochure.*

> *Best Wishes, and Best of Luck,*

> *The Director*

As Amy drove through the streets, I was suddenly glad Mom was on the phone.

It was a good thing I couldn't tell her now. If I did, she would want a tour, and we would end up at the Wall. Then she'd pull me out of there—and that would be the last time I ever saw Lena.

The handwriting on the back of the letter was a lot messier, like it had been scribbled hastily. Sarah Thumb had certainly gotten in touch with the Director fast.

P.S. It has come to my attention that you were present when our administration learned of the Snow Queen's involvement in the most recent occurrence of "George & the Dragon." Please refrain from sharing this information with anyone else—here at EAS or at home. If I hear of any difficulty following these instructions, you will join me here in my office.

It occurs to me now that being new to our program, you cannot know who the Snow Queen is. She was, in her day, a significant threat, and her fame has given her name the same effect as the boogeyman. Such a fearful figure looms large in our imaginations, and we can invoke her to get our children to behave. However, she has now been imprisoned for many years. It is safe to say that she has been defanged. You should consider this incident as something rather like Napoleon sending his hounds from Elba to the coast of France to strike terror into the hearts of those who still feared him. Though she is no longer capable of any real damage, the fear that the Snow Queen inspires would be very problematic.

I hadn't even known that the Snow Queen was supposed to be scary. The Wall of Failed Tales freaked me out much more.

I sighed. There was *so much* I didn't know. When I told my parents and Amy, I knew they would have a million questions. Maybe it would be better if I waited to tell them—just until I knew enough about EAS to survive the interrogation.

One month, I promised myself. *Or whenever Dad called next. Whichever comes first.*

I just hoped that it would be enough time. I was ready to stop feeling so scared.

When I threw my stuff down the next day, my backpack was so heavy that it shook Lena's table. She looked up from the inventor's encyclopedia she was reading.

"What's in there?" Lena smiled. "Enchanted Stones from the Garden of Immortality?"

"Just books," I said and stuffed my mouth with a forkful of chocolate cake from the Table of Never Ending Instant Refills (I had made one detour on the way). I started flipping through the closest volume.

Lena peeked into my backpack, reading the books' spines. "Grimm. Andersen. Lang. Are those all the fairy tale collections in your school's library?"

"As many as they would let me borrow," I said, skimming "The Wild Swans." The fear that started fluttering in my chest when Chase and Adelaide had shown me the Wall of Failed Tales hadn't gone away when I went to sleep, or when I woke up, or ate breakfast, or went to school. I had to do *something*, and freak-out study mode was the best I could come up with. "I want to be as prepared as possible."

"That's dedicated . . . ," Lena said uncertainly.

"Incredibly dedicated." Chase slid into the only empty seat. I didn't like the way he was looking at me, already grinning—as if he had done something and couldn't wait for everyone else to find out.

"Monumentally so." Adelaide stood directly behind Chase and glanced over my books gleefully. That couldn't be a good sign either.

"Well, don't get *too* dedicated," Lena said. "All the sixth graders are supposed to report to Hansel's training courts in five minutes."

"Plenty of time." Chase rested his chin in his hands. "So, Rory. Why so dedicated?"

"*I'm* not going to end up on the Wall," I said stubbornly.

Adelaide laughed, little ladylike giggles, but Chase *roared*, wiping tears from his eyes.

"I *knew* I shouldn't have let them finish the tour yesterday," Lena said.

I glanced from Chase to Adelaide, not sure what was going on, but absolutely positive they were making fun of me.

"Rory, what did they tell you?" Kelly asked.

"We just showed her the names on the Wall," Adelaide said.

"*All* the names." Chase smiled so widely his dimples showed.

Lena turned to me. "First of all, a Failed Tale doesn't always mean dead. I bet they didn't tell you that. Sometimes, a Character just gets enchanted or imprisoned during their tale, and we have to go rescue them."

"Right, so of all the names up there, only maybe two-thirds died in their Tale," Chase said smugly.

I gulped. That was still *thousands* of dead Characters. "So, what happens if you Fail your Tale and *don't* die?"

"Nothing," Lena said, which was very reassuring. "You can still hang out and wait to see if you get another Tale."

"Sure, but only if you can stand the public humiliation," Chase added with a smirk. "Remember the ninth grader who Failed 'The Flying Trunk' in December? He dropped out by Christmas."

"And five years back," called Adelaide, "an 'Aladdin' Failed his Tale, because he *lost his genie*. He couldn't let it go."

"I heard he's still looking for it," Chase said.

"But there really haven't been many Failed Tales *recently*," Lena added quickly. "I think only eight in the past decade. The Director has been so careful. You know, since the war. She has all these extra rules and precautions. Like the rings of return yesterday."

Now I started to realize how well I'd been duped. "If there have only been eight Failed Tales in the past ten years, where did the *rest* of the names come from?"

"I guess we did forget to mention that," Adelaide said innocently.

"The Wall actually shows all the names of Failed Tales since the founding of EAS's North American Chapter," said Chase.

"And how long ago was that?" I asked Lena evenly, knowing that *she* would tell me the truth.

"Same day as the founding of the United States," she replied, watching me worriedly. "A Revolutionary Character decided it was her patriotic duty."

So, I had seen two and a half *centuries* of Failed Tales.

I didn't know how to react. Horror and fury both seemed like good options.

"It's just a little fun between friends," Chase said, and suddenly anger gained the upper hand.

"We're *not* friends," I said sharply.

"So, tell us about it, Rory. Could you sleep last night? Did you have nightmares? Did you—"

Something about the way he didn't listen—the way he just kept talking like I hadn't said *anything*—sent me over the edge. It happened enough with my dad. I was *not* going to put up with it from a stupid bully my own age.

Before I really thought about it, I grabbed a handful of chocolate cake and shoved it in Chase's face.

I regretted it the instant the cake smushed. I could practically see the headline now: LANDON & WRIGHT'S DAUGHTER GIVES CLASSMATE A CHOCOLATE CAKE FACIAL. It would be third grade all over again.

But then I remembered: They didn't know. *Nobody* here knew. There was no way that this would make it to the press. It wouldn't even get back to my parents.

Then Adelaide gasped a little, and with a surge of triumph, I let myself do exactly what I wanted to do—exactly what Adelaide deserved. I scooped up the rest of the cake and smeared it over her hair.

Adelaide shrieked in a very satisfying way, but Chase only scowled, drawing a fingertip over his cheek and licking off the icing.

Lena and Kelly stared at me, and I didn't blame them. I would've stared at me too.

Adelaide ran off, still wailing, to the girl's bathroom, and Kelly handed me a napkin to wipe my hands. Lena giggled a little.

After a second, I smiled back, my anger draining away. I *liked* it, almost as much as the Yellowstone adventure.

Maybe I had to watch myself at Ridgefield, and all the other schools I had been to in the past few years, but here at EAS, things were going to be different. *I* was going to be different.

"We are *not* friends," I told Chase again, and he glared at me through a mask of crumbs and icing.

"Time for sword practice," Lena said brightly.

• • •

The walls of the training courts were covered with mirrors, the floors with slate. Lena led me to the corner where the triplets waited, their swords in hand.

I couldn't help but notice that we were the youngest Characters in the room. I wasn't used to being so much shorter than everyone else. A kid just beside us either had giant blood, or he'd repeated a grade ten times.

"I kind of feel outnumbered," I said, as more and more older students filed into the room. "Why are there so many high schoolers?"

"Well, there *are* twice as many EASers in high school than in middle school," Lena said slowly. "Each grade gains a few more students every year. By the time we're George's age, we'll have, like, thirty kids." She leaned in close and added, "But just so you know, the longer you've been here, the better your Tale is. Nine times out of ten."

So, maybe waiting on my Tale wouldn't be *such* a bad thing.

Adelaide came in late, refusing to look at me. A long streak of chocolate matted the back of her hair, which made me smile.

Right behind her was a man with salt and pepper hair—the same guy who inspected the dragon's hoard in Yellowstone. He had to be Hansel, because everyone straightened up as soon as he entered the room.

"What are you looking at *me* for?" he bellowed when he saw us assembled in front of him. "Someone get out the practice dummies." He pointed to one of the triplets. "You, Kevin."

I bounced a little on the balls of my feet.

If I blinded a dragon the first time I ever touched a sword, obviously I would be able to slay whole *packs* of them with just a little training. Well, maybe not packs, but at least I could graduate from the *slash-and-escape* trick to the actual slaying.

Kevin ran over and threw open an iron-studded door on the other side of the room. Metal clanged, and a second later, dozens of black figures filed into the training court: small dragons, ugly trolls, wolves lashing their black iron tails, miniature giants with clubs, and evil-looking fairies whose iron wings fluttered with excitement.

"Your mouth is open, Rory," said someone behind me.

I closed it abruptly. Chase had just entered the courts with a crowd of tardy high schoolers. I noticed with relish that he had needed to change his shirt.

"Don't worry, Rory. I was pretty shocked too, the first time I saw them," Lena said.

"They're alive?"

"No, but they do move on their own. One of Madame Benne's inventions," Lena added with pride. "Hansel says that they're the only thing that keeps beginners from hacking each other to pieces."

"That's stupid," I said. "What about practice swords?"

Then I realized my mistake. The dummies had stopped moving. The practice courts were silent. Everyone was looking at me, including Hansel.

I gulped. As fast as someone flipping a light switch, my face burned red. I watched it in the practice mirrors. It was twice as embarrassing when I could actually see it.

Across the room, Chase snickered.

"If it isn't the famous Rory Landon," said Hansel, "who took it upon herself to slay dragons on her very first day."

Obviously, Hansel was as much of a bully as Chase and Adelaide, but the grown-up kind.

I glanced at Lena beside me. She was sending me a warning with her eyes, but I didn't know what she was trying to warn me *about*.

"You seem very sure of your skills," Hansel continued. "So you won't mind helping me with today's demonstration."

I stepped forward nervously, not seeing any way out of it, but Lena said, "She hasn't got her sword, sir."

"Conner, do you know which one is hers?" Hansel said, without turning away from me.

I smiled at Lena and shrugged helplessly. She had tried.

When Conner darted into a closet, Hansel began his lesson. I stood at his side, avoiding everyone's eyes.

"We have been practicing the disarming technique for a week and a half now. Those of you who are still terrible at it will probably be terrible your entire lives," Hansel said.

A bunch of people winced, including Lena, and I scowled at Hansel. That was *not* how you were supposed to teach.

He didn't notice. "There's nothing we can do about it, so we might as well move on. Today I'll teach you how to counter the disarm."

Conner ran out of the closet and held out both sword and sheath to me, a little awkwardly, with both hands. I didn't realize why until I reached for it.

The unexpected weight almost made me drop it. A few people laughed, including Conner.

In my reflection, my neck turned as red as my face.

"You're a beginner, but surely you know you're supposed to hold on to your sword." Hansel eyed the blade in my hand very skeptically, as if he had his doubts whether or not I could handle a toothpick, much less a sword.

"It's a lot heavier than it was before," I mumbled, not daring to look at Chase. I knew he was laughing at me too.

"Well, you can't rely on adrenaline in practice," Hansel said. "Sword tip up."

Slowly, muscles straining, I raised the sword.

"You, over here." Hansel pointed to one of the evil fairy dummies. It came closer and stood right across from me, and I willed myself not to take a step back. Metal wings included, it was four feet taller than I was.

I had felt a lot more confident before Conner handed me the sword.

The weight made me clumsy. One palm cramped around the hilt, and the other one sweated like crazy.

"To review, the trick to most disarming techniques lies in locking your hilt guard with your opponent's and twisting quickly so you wretch it from their hand," Hansel told his class. "To counter this, you let go of your sword, predict the arc of its movement, and snatch the hilt out of the air. Simple."

I hoped everyone else didn't think it was as simple as Hansel did.

But a lot of students nodded. Chase looked impatient, like he had heard all of it before.

I shook myself a little and tried to concentrate despite my burning face. I was already up in front of everyone. I had to do my best.

"Now for our demonstration." Hansel turned to me with a smile I didn't like. I held my sword a little tighter and reviewed the instructions. I was still thinking about the arc of the blade when the evil fairy dummy lunged forward, hooked his black hilt guard around mine, and sent my sword spinning through the air.

It landed ten feet away. A few of the older kids laughed as I scrambled after my sword.

"I wanted you to demonstrate the *counter* to the disarming technique, not the technique itself," Hansel said, as I returned to the evil fairy dummy. "Again."

The dummy came at me before I even got a decent grip. I raised the blade hurriedly and felt the sword leave my hand.

"Don't forget to catch it!" Hansel shouted.

I watched it spin and reached toward the hilt. Pain opened across the back of my hand. I snatched it away as my sword clattered to the floor. A neat slice marked three of my knuckles, just a little wider than a papercut.

"Class, Rory has just demonstrated how *not* to counter being disarmed. I'm sure most of you will realize what kind of problems you'll create if you injure *yourself*," Hansel said dryly.

I stomped over to where my sword had fallen and grabbed it, half furious with myself and half mad at Hansel. It was like he was *trying* to humiliate me.

"Do you need to visit the infirmary?" Lena whispered.

I shook my head and turned to face the evil fairy dummy again. "It isn't deep."

"Beginners," said Hansel scornfully, arms crossed over his chest. "Full of bravado. You have no idea what you might be up against. You would all be dead in two moves if the war hadn't ended. Especially you girls."

I stared at him, not believing I heard him right. The older students fidgeted uncomfortably. Even Adelaide looked annoyed.

I don't know what made me speak out. Maybe the chocolate cake incident started something, or maybe I was too mad to think clearly.

"You shouldn't say that. Someday, we might even be better than you," I told Hansel hotly. The evil fairy dummy shifted, and I braced myself for the attack that I knew was coming.

"Pretty words. You won't be the first Character to die saying something like that," Hansel said. "But not today. I'll set you up with an easy dummy to practice blocking, but first we have a demonstration to get through—Rory, out. Chase, in."

I let my sword dangle at my side and stepped into the crowd, still fuming.

Lena must've noticed. "Hansel always picks on the new Characters," she said in an apologetic tone.

Chase shouldered through the other students, and he paused in front of Lena and me, just to smirk. I clenched the fist that wasn't holding my sword.

"He's just trying to get back at you for the cake," Lena whispered.

I should've known that he would be good, the way he had walked in with the older students. With an easy grace, he twirled his sword around in an elaborate flourish, and he turned to the evil fairy dummy. This time, since I wasn't the one in the hot seat, I saw Hansel signal to the dummy by flicking three fingers. The dummy attacked, and Chase let it.

With a sound like a knife getting sharpened, Chase's sword spun up, rising directly above his head. Chase jumped up after it, kicking the dummy squarely in the chest. The dummy tumbled feet over wings over feet and crashed into the mirrored wall behind them. The glass shattered.

"Chase," said Hansel, exasperated. "What have I told you about breaking the training mirrors?"

"Sorry," said Chase, landing lightly. He didn't sound sorry. His sword was in his hand.

"He jumped five feet in the air," Adelaide said in a dreamy tone.

One of the older students shook his head, impressed. "At least six."

I didn't want to, especially since Chase was smirking around the room like he expected everyone to applaud, but I had to admit the move had been cool.

"Well, that's one variation," Hansel said, yawning a little. "Of course, if you let your sword get away from you like that, there's a good chance you'll have to defend yourself. Which is why Chase kicked the dummy across the room."

"You know, besides showing off," I muttered.

Lena snorted, and Chase shot me an evil look.

"Chase, try it again. This time, keep your feet on the ground." Hansel gestured to the fairy dummy. Glass tinkled to the floor as it stood up. It ran at Chase. I blinked when their blades struck, and when I looked again, Chase had his sword and the dummy's in his hands.

"*Definitely* a show-off," I said, and beside me, Lena nodded with a rueful shrug.

When the older kids and Chase paired off to practice, Hansel assigned each of the sixth graders to a specific dummy, according to their skill. He took me to a little dummy in the back. It was wizened and hunchbacked like an old witch, and the sword it swung looked a lot like a long wand. I felt a little insulted.

Hansel showed me how to block in four positions: high, low, left, and right. Then he left me to practice and walked around, correcting people's stances and giving tips. Every once in a while, Hansel would announce that every single one of us would be dead if the war was still underway, but he didn't bother to come back and check on me.

So, I didn't have anything to distract me from the pain.

First, my arms started to burn. Then I started to feel it in my stomach. Soon after my legs began to tremble, the witch dummy started to get past my guard. She poked so many holes in my shirt that it started to look like lace.

It didn't help to find out that I was the only one having trouble with the drill. Adelaide performed hers like a ballerina, rapping her dummy—an evil fairy—on the neck, chest, and leg in time with Hansel's count. The triplets were solid fighters, able to fight with either sword or staff, and even Lena could punch holes in her troll dummy with a spear. And the *other* new girl in the class, Miriam, hit her practice dummy with so much force that every stroke rang out like a bell across the room.

"How did you *do* that?" I asked her finally.

"Tennis. I'm on the team at home." She pushed her hair out of her face and raised her sword above her head, mimicking an overhand serve. "Some of the movements are the same."

So, I didn't even have being new as an excuse.

I was *terrible*. I couldn't believe it. Usually, I picked up new sports so easily.

"Pathetic attempts—the lot of you. None of you would stand a chance if war came upon us again," Hansel bellowed. "Villains aren't going to be nice enough to let you pick your sword up after they've knocked it from your hands. Do you expect mercy from the likes of General Searcaster?"

I rolled my eyes. It didn't work if you *tried* to scare people.

"They say she plucked out her *own* eye—sacrificed it for her mistress's magic." Hansel corrected the stance of a tenth-grade boy and moved on. "Do you think a fierce giantess like that would hesitate to slay you if you made it easy?"

Gulping, I blocked another strike from the witch dummy. Maybe it did work a little. The eye comment, especially.

"And you've heard of Iron Hans, I'm sure," Hansel lowered his voice to a rasping whisper. "He's a Character, maybe even the oldest still alive—ten centuries or so. A huge wild man, covered in hair, with skin the blackish-gray of iron. No blade can pierce it. They say he escaped from a Fey prison, just a few months ago. If you ever meet this villain, you should turn around and run the other way. None of you are good enough to face him."

If possible, my palms got even sweatier.

"He always carries the same weapon, an enormous double-headed ax, almost as old as he is," said Hansel. "With one blow, he can behead a man in full armor. With two, he can fell a castle wall. In the final battle alone, defending the rooms where his queen hid, he cut down sixty-seven Characters, one by one."

"Uh, Lena," I whispered around my witch dummy. "Are villains what I think they are?"

"Of course," said an unwelcome voice. "Bad guys."

I was instantly annoyed. I didn't know if this would happen *every* time I saw Chase, or only on days when I was already mad at him.

He stood with his arms crossed, holding his chin in one hand, on the back of a small dragon dummy that Hansel hadn't assigned to anyone. It was at least seven feet off the ground, and I wondered exactly how high he could jump.

I turned back to the witch dummy—to show him exactly how much attention he deserved.

"Wow, you really suck," he said. "You *should* be scared."

I gave him a dirty look. He didn't *have* to rub it in.

I raised my sword again. When the witch dummy repeated the drill, I blocked all four hits, pretending like it was easy. The muscles in my arm were *not* happy.

Chase leaned over the dragon dummy's head and told me in a low voice, "You know, it was my dad who finally took Iron Hans down. So, if you ever want any pointers—"

That was really too much. I couldn't let him get away with that. "You two, switch," I told the dragon and the witch dummies, hoping that they were spelled to follow everyone's orders, not just Hansel's. "I'll practice with the dragon now."

The dragon dummy moved so quickly that Chase didn't have a chance to brace himself. He tumbled to the floor, just like I hoped he would.

I smiled. He scrambled to his feet, glaring at me, and then he glanced around the room to see if anyone had noticed.

"I won't always suck," I told Chase cheerfully. "And I can defend myself with a few other skills until then."

Chase opened his mouth to say something, but a heavy hand fell on my shoulder.

I jumped the height of a troll.

Hansel stood over me, scowling. "I didn't tell you that you could switch dummies. You'll stay after class today and straighten up the weapons closet."

"But—" I protested, as Hansel steered me back toward the witch dummy.

"I hope you're not planning to tell me that you weren't actually going to practice with the dragon dummy, that you were simply trying to make a point," Hansel said, glowering at me. "Because that's not what the dummies are for."

I bit my tongue to stop myself from getting into more trouble.

Chase grinned at me and headed off.

Twenty minutes later, just as I started to feel like I couldn't lift my arm even one more time, Ellie arrived and announced that it was time for everyone in Eastern Standard Time zone to go home.

Sighing, I watched a dozen students file in and out of the weapons closet.

"Don't feel bad. Hansel really *does* always pick on the new Characters," Lena said, standing next to me. "I'll help you straighten up. It'll go fast."

"No, you won't," Hansel called from across the room, nodding pointedly at the doorway.

"Thanks anyway, Lena," I whispered.

She reluctantly jogged outside under Hansel's stern gaze. With one final scowl in my direction, Hansel stepped out too and closed the door after him.

I headed for the closet. Every step echoed in the big empty room.

Almost sure that I was the worst swordswoman that EAS had ever seen, I started on the messy piles of weapons.

I turned one spear over and over in my hands, wondering if maybe I was training with the wrong weapon, but my arms were so weak that I kept losing control and knocking over the row of staffs I had just put away. I gave up, settling the spear back where I found it.

Maybe I was just bad at everything.

Then the torches snuffed out abruptly.

I squinted, looking back at the open door, now the only source of light in the closet.

"Hello?" I called uncertainly.

No one and *nothing* answered, but metal clattered behind me. I winced, wondering what *else* I had knocked over.

Then I heard the clanking sound again, this time behind the door, and peered closer into the shadows. I wasn't alone. A large figure rose to his feet in the back of the room. "No way," I murmured and nervously stepped back.

The figure lurched forward clumsily, hair standing in tufts on his hands and shoulders. The dim light reflected dully on his dark gray skin. It looked like metal.

Iron Hans? Here? My mind flew to the story that afternoon, but I couldn't believe that even Hansel would be mean enough to send a villain after a kid.

One gray hand fell on a shelf of unused swords, clanking again like metal on metal, and in his other hand, he held the double-headed ax. It was as tall as I was. It could cut me in half with one chop.

I froze, terrified. I knew I needed to run. I tried to move, but my body wouldn't obey. My mind went blank.

Iron Hans stumbled forward another step, raising the ax above his head.

I squeezed my eyes shut, shoulders hunched forward, waiting for the blow to fall. From the back of my throat came a very small, very embarrassing squeak.

Then someone laughed in a very familiar way. Two someones.

I opened my eyes a crack. The torches burned again, and I saw Chase letting Adelaide down from his shoulders. They were both laughing so hard that he almost dropped her.

I stared at them, filled with a completely different kind of horror. I would never live this down, not in a million years. Chase wouldn't *let* me.

Once Adelaide's feet were on the ground, Chase straightened up with a clink. Both of them wore chain mail, their hands and faces covered with pewter paint. "I knew Yellowstone was a fluke," Chase said, grinning. "You're no braver than the rest of us."

"I never said I was," I murmured. Adelaide carried a small hatchet, and I couldn't understand how I thought I'd seen a double-headed ax.

"A room full of weapons and she didn't even reach for one," Chase said gleefully, as if I hadn't said anything, and my fists curled at my sides.

"She didn't even *move*." Adelaide slid the hatchet back into a row of axes.

"Not a Companion I would want on *my* Tale," Chase said.

"Basically, a Failed Tale waiting to happen," Adelaide said.

It was true. It was so true that I felt sick to my stomach. I couldn't even argue, and that upset me more than anything.

Without even looking at the rows of weapons I was supposed to be straightening, I turned on my heel and ran out of the closet.

In my head, a voice a lot like Hansel's said, *Class, Rory has just demonstrated how* not *to handle an ambush. I'm sure most of you will realize what kinds of problems you'll create if you don't move when someone attacks.*

What if I froze up this badly during a real Tale?

ory Landon, what are you hiding under your desk?" Mrs.
Coleman asked.

I froze, caught, as the whole class turned in my direction. I'd
been reading "The Sleeping Beauty in the Wood." I was so far
back in the classroom I thought the teacher would never notice.
Oops.

"Nothing." I shoved the library book deep within the desk.

"Give it to me." Mrs. Coleman crossed the room briskly. My face
burning, I surrendered the book. *The Complete Works of Charles
Perrault*?" The students laughed, but Mrs. Coleman seemed more
puzzled than angry. "See me after class."

For a second, I wished she had just sent me out of the room,
where I could have sneaked to my locker to grab another collection
of fairy tales.

I had been reading since I'd got home the night before. After
Mom had turned off my light around ten, I'd read under the covers with a flashlight. When I woke up hours later with drool on the
page, I read over breakfast.

Reading was better than thinking.

And I really wished I didn't have to think. I'd just found out that
the original Sleeping Beauty was called Aurora. I'd never hated my

name so much. I spent the rest of the period miserable, ashamed that I was such a useless coward. I was only fit for the kind of Tale where I pricked my finger and slept for a hundred years.

The bell rang, sounding about a million miles away. After my classmates filed out, Mrs. Coleman sat me down for "the Talk." I had heard six different versions of it.

"Rory, your behavior is absolutely unacceptable. I don't know what teachers at your previous schools overlooked because of your . . . circumstances."

The word she wanted to use was "parents."

"But," she continued, "if *I* catch you reading in class again, you'll face some very serious consequences."

Most of my teachers treated me differently from the other kids. Half tried to make me a teacher's pet so they could cozy up to Mom during the parent-teacher conference. The other half tried so hard *not* to play favorites that I ended up getting in trouble.

"Sorry, Mrs. Coleman," I said dully, just hoping she would let me go soon. "It won't happen again."

I got off relatively easy. She had me alphabetize all the documentary videos in the supply closet. Next time, she promised, she would send a note home to Mom.

A week ago, Mrs. Coleman's speech would have really bothered me, but now I had bigger things to worry about.

In fairy tales, all Characters were special. Some sort of trait set them apart.

Rapunzel had her hair. Red Riding Hood had her outfit. Thumbelina and Tom Thumb were both amazingly small. Even an ordinary Character usually got some sort of magical item to help them through their Tale, like Aladdin getting his lamp.

The more I thought about it, the more it made sense. Didn't

Kelly have Puss-in-Dress? Hadn't Evan's appetite made him eat the White Snake?

I wasn't special, not like that.

Chase and Adelaide were probably right. Maybe Yellowstone *had* been a fluke.

If I wanted a cool Tale, I would have to hope for some sort of magical item. Then again, what use would it be if I froze the second I needed to use it?

I felt a little more hopeful by the time I finished with the videos and Mrs. Coleman let me go. Names and Tales were separate, right? That was why Sarah Thumb had gotten so mad when Philip called her Thumbelina. Maybe the name Aurora was just a coincidence.

Bursting back into the courtyard only a half hour late, I spotted Lena at her usual table under the Tree and jogged over. An odd wooden crate-thing took up most of the table space. I couldn't see what was in it, but lavender smoke spilled over the top and unfurled down the sides, dribbling over the rim of the table and into the grass. Except for the color, it was like a dry-ice experiment.

It had to be weird even for EAS, because most kids gave Lena and the smoke a wide berth.

It couldn't be too dangerous, though—not if Lena was sitting in the middle of it, staring into the smoke with a fixed maniacal gleam in her eyes.

Besides, anything was safer than the Table of Never-Ending Instant Refills. Chase was there, with the rest of the sixth graders.

So, I kicked through the weird smoke. It was warm and kind of sticky, like steam from a very hot shower, and it smelled like applesauce.

"I'm kind of afraid to ask," I told Lena. I dropped into a seat next to her and tried not to freak out when the herd of sixth graders headed our way.

"No. *Ask*," Lena said without looking up from the smoking box. All of her fingers were crossed. "Ask me *anything*. I need a distraction."

The other sixth graders were ridiculously close now. I avoided looking at Chase. "Okay. What's the Director's name?" If the newest Sleeping Beauty was named Aurora too, I was done for.

"Mildred Grubb," Lena said automatically.

I was too surprised for a second to even be relieved, and I wasn't the only one. Adelaide snickered, and the triplets looked stunned.

Lena's head snapped toward all the other sixth graders. "I overheard Rumpel talking to her. We aren't supposed to know."

"Don't use it," said Chase. I could see him watching me out of the corner of my eye, but I couldn't make myself look back, even to glare. I didn't want to find out what he'd say if I did.

"Everyone just calls her 'the Director,'" Lena added hastily, obviously wishing she hadn't said anything. "Even the rest of the Can—"

Glass shattered inside the box, loud and startling as a gunshot.

"Oh, no!" Lena buried her face in her hands.

"What was that?" Kevin asked. At least I wasn't the only one who didn't have a clue what was going on.

I waved the last of the smoke away and peered inside warily. Mirror shards sat in the bottom, reflecting my face in each piece. "Seven years of bad luck?"

"No, that only happens if the mirror is cursed." Lena dropped her hands and sighed dramatically. "Those are the remains of my special project. I got here early to work on it."

"That sucks." Kyle patted her shoulder sympathetically, and Lena stiffened like she'd been electrocuted. Her eyes were so wide behind her glasses that you would've thought that she had spotted an ogre climbing the Tree of Hope.

"What's the big deal?" Chase rolled his eyes. "You *always* have a special project."

Lena's face fell, and the words shot out of my mouth before I could stop them. "Was she talking to you, Chase? . . . I didn't think so."

Chase looked mad for only about a second and a half, just long enough for me to regret it. Then an evil look crossed his face. Slowly, he squeezed his eyes shut, hunched his shoulders, and squeaked. I knew exactly who he was imitating.

My face burned. The squeak was the worst part.

Adelaide laughed a little. Lena and the triplets just looked confused.

"Uh, what?" said Kevin.

Adelaide and Chase exchanged a smirk. "You tell them," Adelaide said graciously, and Chase opened his mouth.

The knot in my stomach got so tight that I knew I was either going to cry or throw up, and I didn't know which one would be worse.

"Chase!" Gretel started across the courtyard, obviously irritated. "Didn't the Director assign you to help me with the spring cleaning in the menagerie?"

Gretel suddenly became my favorite grown-up at EAS.

"You get to muck out the aviary," she said. "Tough job, though, with all the phoenixes. Perhaps some of your friends would like to help."

Adelaide and the triplets scattered. Chase tried to get away too, but Gretel grabbed the collar of his shirt and dragged him back across the courtyard. I couldn't even enjoy it properly. I could tell by the way Chase was glaring at me—he'd get revenge by spreading the weapons-closet story around even faster.

I couldn't think about that right then. Changing the subject was the best I could do

"I'm sorry it broke," I told Lena, pointing into the box. "What was it?"

Lena shrugged. "Well, I was *trying* to make magic mirror walkie-talkies. In theory, it'll work great. All I have to do is divide one mirror into several pieces in easily transportable sizes with a limited communicative scrying spell, but they keep *exploding* in the middle of cooling down. The Shoemaker says that I should really rinse them with water steeped in foxgloves—he says he's saved more magic mirrors that way, but I'm not sure that's it." She sat back, shoulders slouched, still scowling.

She really did talk a lot when she got worked up. I was trying really hard not to find it funny.

"I bet this never happened to Madame Benne," she said sourly. "Of course if Madame Benne had published her notes rather than writing it all in that one book, I wouldn't *have* this trouble. Maybe if I use regular silver rather than Fey-tempered silver . . ."

Then she looked at me, blinking, obviously just then remembering I was there, and that there was absolutely no way I could follow along.

"I wouldn't know," I said apologetically.

"Apparently, neither would I," Lena said, and we grinned at each other.

"But it's okay." She sucked in a very deep breath, staring into the box with so much concentration that she must have been searching her photographic memory. "It doesn't matter how many times I mess up. I only need it to work *one* time, and then I'll have the formula for a new invention."

She was so determined—and probably ten times smarter than the rest of us. She would get an amazing Tale.

All the sixth graders probably had a good chance of getting decent ones.

The triplets came in a set of three, which even *I* knew was kind of a fairy tale must-have. Even though it kind of hurt to admit it, Adelaide *was* beautiful—which is *also* a fairy tale necessity. And Chase—well, he could really fight.

I was still just me. And there was nothing I could do to change it.

"The rest is just practice," Lena said, trying to convince herself.

Wait—yes, there *was*.

Chase couldn't have started *out* that good. He just had a lot more practice than everyone else. A year of mandatory weapons classes wasn't enough. If I wanted to catch up, I knew what I had to do.

I stood up so fast I nearly knocked my chair over. "I need to go to the training courts."

"Good. I'm headed back to the workshop." Lena pushed away from the table and picked up the box. Broken glass tinkled inside. "I need to tell Stu—I mean, the Shoemaker—what happened to the mirrors, but I think, maybe, I can use two salamanders at half heat rather than one at top speed."

"See you," I said, and I dashed toward the dark door studded with iron before Lena even said *Bye*. I didn't have any time to lose. I needed to learn how *not* to suck.

So, from that day on, I practiced. It was a lot easier to channel my energy into beating up a dummy than memorizing fairy tales and obsessing over what kind of Tale I would get.

In all of Hansel's classes, I ran through drills doggedly and stayed late to practice an extra half hour. On days we had off, I found a smaller training court where I wouldn't bother anyone. I guess it was allowed. Once, Hansel came in. I waited to be yelled at, sword in hand, but he just grabbed a stack of shields and walked by without even looking at me, as if I wasn't there.

But by the end of the first week of extra practices, I could block everything the little witch dummy could throw at me. Maybe it wouldn't have been a big deal to anyone else, especially stupid good-at-everything Chase, but it was definitely an improvement.

My sword was always heavier than I remembered, and I got used to being sore. Actually, I got used to a lot of things.

That's EAS for you. It's amazing what starts to feel normal. One day, you're screaming at dragons or gaping at talking fawns, and a few weeks later, you have trouble remembering a time when you didn't know magic was real. I kept my head down at school and rushed down the street to the red door as soon as the bell rang.

Chase and Adelaide still played tricks on me. Apparently, they viewed me decorating them with food as a declaration of war.

Once, I opened the ruby door to go home and discovered a closet full of ball gowns in floral patterns. Most of them had so many ruffles that they could double as Little Bo Peep costumes. Confused, I closed the door and discovered that it was actually pink with yellow trim, a couple doors to the left of the one I wanted. Out of the corner of my eye, I could see Chase beside the Tree of Hope, watching me, but I didn't give him the satisfaction of seeing me glare. Ignoring him was the easiest way to annoy him. "He must have some way of casting illusions," Lena said when I told her later. "A rowan branch would do it, if you found a Fey or a Sorcerer to enchant it for you."

During one class in the training arena, I raised my sword to the old witch dummy and found a golf club in my hand instead. I looked at Lena, who pointed to Chase, who started laughing so hard that he doubled over, arms wrapped around his waist. Hansel pretended not to notice.

But he did interfere later when the bell rang and class ended. I was so worn out that I didn't notice Chase stick his foot out as I passed. I tripped and nearly skewered myself on my own sword.

"What's your *problem*?" I snapped.

"Chase Turnleaf!" Hansel bellowed, and Chase looked uneasy— like he knew he had gone too far. "We're visiting the Director right now."

I felt I had won that round until I glanced at Chase. He just squeezed his eyes shut, hunching his shoulders. With all the noise of students bustling in and out of the weapons closet, I couldn't hear him squeak, but I had heard it enough recently so that it echoed in my mind. I stopped smiling.

Chase had performed his *Rory-in-the-weapons-closet* impression for half of EAS. I didn't even try to protest. Depending on how many people were around, I had two reactions: flushing the color of Red Riding Hood's outfit or seeing "Rory Landon" in the curly lettering of the Wall.

Then, I usually went back to the training courts to vent some frustration.

No new Tales started, but at the end of the month, on the same Tuesday I promised myself I would talk to my parents, I did see my first Fey.

I noticed his hair before I noticed the wings. It was bronze-colored—not just a brassy shade of yellow-brown, but actually metallic, glinting in the sun like burnished metal. Since I was distracted with figuring out how to explain EAS, I thought he was just wearing an exotic helmet until his hair rippled in the breeze. Then I noticed the cobalt wings, as long as he was tall, threaded with red spirals like flames.

He stalked forward in a way that reminded me of the dragon when it cornered me and Chase—smug and expectant, like he already knew he would get what he wanted. I shrank nervously backward in my chair.

"Torlauth di Morgian," Lena said, following my gaze. We both watched as he crossed the courtyard.

EASers rushed out of his way. One high school boy didn't notice quick enough and bumped into the Fey. He stumbled back when Torlauth scowled at him.

"You know him?" I said.

"Well, not personally, but I know *of* him," Lena said. "Three years ago, he held a jousting tournament in San Francisco's Golden Gate Park. He even kidnapped an award-winning cheerleading team to cheer for the competitors. Caused a real stir."

"Is that *allowed*?" I asked, horrified.

Lena shook her head. "No, a bunch of other EASers went to go rescue them. It was George's first mission." I nodded. A mission was a dangerous assignment the Director sometimes sent EASers on—like the field trip to Yellowstone my first day.

Torlauth di Morgian walked past the rest of the EASers and disappeared through an ebony door with silver hinges, the one that opened into Atlantis.

"Why do you think he came?" I asked Lena, suddenly more

worried about meeting that Fey in a dark fairy-tale alley than talking to my parents that afternoon.

"Has to be the Fairie Market next week," Lena said.

"What Fairie Market?" I asked.

"You don't know about the Fairie Market? Geez, you *have* been in the training courts too much," Lena said. "It's not just a festival. Wait until you see it—the Characters that show up there, and the things they bring with them." She sounded a bit like Sarah Thumb did when she talked about magic.

Chase slid abruptly into a chair at our table, for no reason *I* could figure out. He looked pale. Maybe he had decided teasing us was the best way to cheer himself up after seeing the scary Fey.

"My dad'll be there," he said. I rolled my eyes, because this was the fifth time in three days Chase mentioned that his dad was coming home. He'd told us all about his dad's recent trips at least eight times. If Jack really was gone that much, I felt sorry for Chase's mom. *She* was the one who had to handle Chase for weeks on end. "Usually, he's too busy, but he just defeated E'Kennild the Destroyer in the New Mexico desert and he said he needs a break."

Lena acted like she hadn't heard him. "Potion ingredients and magic books and Fey trinkets—singing harps and carryall bags. We're going to buy a Table of Plenty, the self-setting kind."

I knew from experience that she would go on for ten minutes if I didn't interrupt her. "So your grandmother's coming on Friday to find one?"

"No, she doesn't get around that well anymore, and she hates crowds." Then Lena added proudly, "But she's going to let *me* pick it out. I've been researching Tables of Plenty for months now."

"Dad stole a Table of Plenty once," Chase said. "From Gholsend the Giant."

Sometimes, Chase had a one-track mind. One of his many annoying qualities.

"Is he selling it at the Market?" Lena asked.

"No, he gave it away," Chase said. "To an orphanage for changelings."

The look on Lena's face clearly told Chase how unhelpful he was. Adelaide and the triplets wandered toward our table. They'd probably spotted Chase. They usually followed him everywhere.

"But why are the Fey coming?" I asked Lena. "Do the fairies run it?"

"No, we do," said Kyle. "It's a fundraiser. The Director uses it to pay for EAS-related costs. That's why everyone can attend free."

"Be glad we have it," Kevin added. "EAS has to pay the instructors somehow. They used to just take a quarter of whatever riches you got in your *happily ever after*."

"But the Fey come," Chase said. "Nearly everyone comes."

"There aren't that many neutral places left after the war," Lena said. "That's why the Director can charge so much. She rents out every stand."

"I doubt Torlauth came to negotiate the price of a stand, though," Chase said. "He has minions for that."

He was right. Two minutes later, the Director stepped up to the podium, like she always does for new Tales or important announcements. Her dress that day was a sky-blue ball gown with golden thread that sparkled even in the Tree's shade.

"As most of you are aware, Torlauth di Morgian came to visit me this afternoon," she said, "and he convinced me to hold an impromptu tournament at the Fairie Market. He has offered a grand prize of a thousand gold coins."

I had no idea what that meant, but obviously other EASers did.

Almost every Character started talking. The triplets whooped and did a celebration dance, which made Lena giggle behind her hand.

The Director waited a moment for the crowd to become quiet again. "Unfortunately, only those of you in high school will be allowed to compete."

The triplets immediately booed, but when she looked at them sternly over the podium, all three shut up. "Due to time constraints, only one event will be held: the traditional duel. Good luck!"

She left the podium, and then everyone really *did* start talking. George announced he was competing. Kevin and Conner cursed fate and the Director for the age limit. Kyle asked Lena if she thought he could pass as a tenth grader if he glued on a moustache, and Lena stammered back that he'd be better off wearing a full suit of armor, including a helmet to cover his face.

In fact, in all of EAS, only Chase looked more sick to his stomach than excited, but I chalked that up to him finding out he couldn't enter.

Then the bell rang. It was time to go home, and suddenly, all my worries about telling my parents came rushing back.

I called Dad in the kitchen, where Amy and Mom stared at an open cookbook and argued over what to make for dinner.

"Beef Wellington doesn't look *that* hard," Mom said.

"It's hard, Maggie. Definitely too ambitious for a Wednesday night." What Amy really meant was that it was too ambitious for *Mom*, but saying so would crush her.

My hands were so shaky that my fingers fumbled over the keypad. I had to redial Dad's familiar number at least three times.

The call went to voice mail. I was disappointed. No, relieved. Well, kind of both. I was glad I didn't have to figure out how to nego-tiate a four-person-conversation on speakerphone. Unfortunately, having this conversation hang over my head didn't really appeal either.

But two seconds later, he called *back*.

"Dad!" I said, so happily that Mom and Amy both looked my way, surprised.

I didn't know what time zone he was in, but he sounded wide-awake. "Rory. What is it? Are you okay?"

"Yeah, fine. I just—" I swallowed hard around the lump in my throat. "I need to tell you something."

Amy nudged Mom with a questioning look, and Mom shrugged. Which meant that they recognized that by "something," I meant "something important," and they were trying to figure out if the other one knew. My thumb shifted to the speakerphone button, and I took a deep breath, about to launch into an explanation that started with dragons in Yellowstone.

But Dad wasn't exactly clued in. He sighed. "I really don't have time for this right now, princess."

"This won't take long," I said quickly, even though I privately worried that it might take a while.

"Rory." Now he sounded a little stern. "I told you that I can't help you now. I'm supposed to be in a really important meeting."

Great. That made me guilty for disturbing him and annoyed that he couldn't make time the *one* day I needed to tell him something.

"If it was so important, why did you call me back?" I said, more sharply than I meant. Apparently I felt more annoyed than guilty.

"Well, you never call. I thought it was an emergency. Look, I really have to—"

"I can't even call my own father without you thinking something's *wrong*?" I said. "It's been over a *month* since we talked."

Mom stepped closer worriedly. I wouldn't meet her eyes.

Even Dad seemed to realize he hadn't said the right thing. "I'm sorry, Rory. You know you're my princess. I always miss you, every day. Hey," he added in a completely different tone. "Did you decide about that shoot in Oxford? I was talking with Bree yesterday—you know, Briana Catcher—and she said she really wanted to meet you."

I couldn't believe he was asking me *again*. Right after scolding me. Like *that* made me want to hang out with him on his stupid shoot. "I'm sorry I bothered you. Good luck with your meeting," I said and hung up.

I hadn't hung up on him since the first few weeks of Mom and Dad's separation. I did feel a little guilty, but only a little. After all, he had made time to talk to some random actress the day before, but not to call me.

"Our little baby, all grown up and telling people off," Amy said with a little applause.

"Here, let me talk to him." Mom reached for the phone.

I snatched it up and hid it behind my back stubbornly. She didn't even know what was wrong. She just wanted an excuse to yell at him, and I refused to give it to her. They should at least *try* to get along—for *my* sake.

Amy cleared her throat. I looked up. She glared at me in the thin-lipped steely way that she only used when someone bothered Mom. Then I saw Mom's face, looking a little hurt, and I really *did* feel guilty.

This was why I tried never to make a scene at home. When I did, Mom usually got more upset than I did. Sometimes, it bummed her out for weeks.

I couldn't tell her now. The whole EAS conversation would have to wait.

"Please don't call him," I said quietly. "It's better if I talk to him myself."

Mom smiled a tiny bit. "Who's my favorite daughter?"

"Me. But I'm your only daughter," I replied.

"Then it's a good thing that you're my favorite." Mom's smile widened, and I knew I was forgiven. "Don't you have homework?"

I did. I headed back to the stool, dragging my feet dramatically until Mom laughed.

"Hey, Rory," Amy said. I scrambled to come up with an answer to the *what-important-thing-were-you-going-to-tell-him?* question, but it never came. "Do you want to invite a friend to sleep over this weekend?"

You might think that she was just being nice, but I wasn't fooled. Whenever Mom or Amy asked if I wanted to have a sleepover, it meant that they were worried about the kind of friends I had made during this move. Me being less-than-nice to Mom had set off little warning bells. They thought I might be hanging out with the wrong kind of sixth graders.

"Sure," I said, trying to sound enthusiastic. I couldn't say no.

I worried about the sleepover all the next day.

I wasn't worried about who I should ask. Of course I would ask Lena. She was my first pick—the same way she would be my first pick for a Companion if I got a questing Tale. I *wanted* to ask Lena, but sleepovers had become unsafe territory. In fourth grade, it's still a coveted honor—a friendship milestone—to ask someone to sleepover. By sixth grade though, if you ask the wrong girl, she might accuse you of acting like you were still in elementary school. Somebody like Adelaide would be mean enough to *say* so to your face—rather than wait until she could talk about you behind your back, like a normal bully.

If I had been at school, or any other place where people knew about my famous parents, I wouldn't have been concerned. No matter how old they were, my classmates usually got pretty excited to meet my mom. Even more excited about that than hanging out with me.

But this was Lena. She wouldn't act like Adelaide or the kids at school. I was almost sure.

Still, when I sat down at our regular table under the Tree, I glanced around to make sure Chase or Adelaide weren't in earshot.

"You okay?" Lena put down her book, *Magic Mirrors 101*, and pushed her glasses farther up on her nose.

The worst she could do was say no, I told myself and half-believed it. "Lena, do you wanna sleep over on Friday?"

"Oh," Lena said, clearly not expecting that. My heart sank, and I tried to figure out a way to give her an easy out. Then her eyes widened eagerly behind her glasses, and I knew she was one of the diehard sleepover-lovers. "Yeah! I mean, I'll have to ask my grandmother first, but if she says yes, then absolutely! Did you want me to bring anything? My movies? A candy stash?"

Lena's grandmother said yes, so that wasn't the problem. The problem was the *other* consequences of Wednesday's almost fight.

The night before the sleepover, I dreamed of the door again—the black wood cracked with age, the scrolling silver *S*, and the snowflake with sharp points. I needed to open it. There wasn't much time, but I was frozen, too scared even to reach for the handle.

I woke up with a jerk that almost toppled me out of bed. Then I remembered that it was true—or that it could *become* true if I dreamed it just one more time. I tossed and turned for ten minutes, but it was no use. I kept hearing Adelaide's words in my head, *a Failed Tale waiting to happen.* Sleep definitely wasn't coming back.

So, I tiptoed down the hall to keep from waking anyone up and went downstairs for a cup of tea or something.

The light was still on in the kitchen, and when I reached the last few steps, I realized that someone was still *in* there. Mom sat on the same bar stool where I had done my homework earlier.

I almost blabbed out the whole thing—the truth of EAS, the dream, and what it might mean. Picking the right moment or seeming crazy didn't matter anymore. I just wanted her to make me feel better.

But I hesitated—just long enough to look closer.

A glass of white wine stood on the counter beside her. It had been out so long that the condensation had turned into big fat drops. Screenplays were stacked beside it. Without looking at anything in particular, Mom ran her finger around the glass's rim, making it sing.

She looked so sad, and I knew it was my fault.

This was what always happened when she saw me upset. She acted cheerful during the day, but alone at night, she blamed herself.

It wasn't always this way. We were all happy once. It was hard to remember sometimes, but I kept the proof upstairs, hidden away in the drawer of my nightstand, just in case. A photograph of us at the beach—me and Mom laughing in the foreground, and Dad behind, hugging us both. Our noses are all peeling.

I'm about eight in the picture—before Amy, before the divorce, before even *Never Leave Home*—the box-office success that made Dad famous and earned Mom an Oscar. I usually only take out that photo when I'm packing or unpacking—or when I feel as sad as Mom looked right then.

Suddenly, I wanted to run across the room, throw my arms around her, and tell her that everything was going to be okay, but

I stopped myself. I had done that once, the night I had found her staring at that same picture and crying. I had held her very tight and promised that we were going to be fine, but when she pulled away, I'd realized I had made it worse.

The next day, Mom had dragged Amy and me on a surprise weekend getaway to the mountains, which she spent being aggressively cheerful, *annoyingly* cheerful, trying to prove how okay she was. When I tried to get her to talk to me, she would just pat my head, saying, "Oh, Rory. *I'm* the mother, you know." The third time she did that, it made me so mad that I ran off. I guess that wasn't the most helpful thing the world, especially since Mom was already upset, but I *hated* feeling helpless.

When Amy found me, I asked her what Mom's problem was. For a moment, she had looked away, which made me afraid that she wouldn't answer me either. But then she'd said, "It's easier for her to just pretend that everything's okay."

Well, I could do something. I could pretend too. My mom was an actress. I knew how it was done.

I went down the rest of the stairs with firm, loud steps.

Mom straightened up and spun around on the barstool, a wide smile on her face. She had already taken her makeup off, which always made her seem younger and more vulnerable. "What are you doing up?"

I didn't need to tell Mom my troubles. She had enough of her own. I forced a smile. "I must be excited about Lena coming over tomorrow night. I couldn't fall back asleep."

Mom pointed to the screenplays beside her. "I'm just finishing up some work. Did you want me to make you some chamomile tea? That always helps."

"Sure." I let her make me tea, and cheerfully complain about how much she had to read, and then walk me up to bed. At the time, I thought I'd done the right thing.

On Friday afternoon, as I walked through the dark hallway behind the red door, I was still worrying about Mom. Maybe I had just taken the easy way out. I felt like such a coward.

If I really *was* brave, I told myself, I would have made Mom talk about what was really wrong. I would have forced her to be honest with me.

With a shaky breath, I opened the back door and stepped into the courtyard.

Golden coins rained over my head in big stripes of red, yellow, green, and violet light. The coins were almost as big as my palm, heavy enough to sting wherever they hit.

I spotted the bucket rigged over the door, and then glanced across the courtyard, past the tennis court–size platform where high schoolers practiced dueling for the tournament, to the Tree of Hope. Chase leaned against the trunk, arms crossed with a hand on his chin. He grinned at me with a welcoming wave, and beside him, Adelaide sent me a smile, as triumphant as she would've been if it were *her* idea.

At my feet, the gold coins disappeared, one by one, each with a distinct pop. The evidence was gone.

I kind of lost it.

"Don't you have anything better to do?" I shouted, marching across the courtyard. My nose prickled, but when my eyes began to tear, I blinked rapidly before I reached him.

Gulping, Chase stared at me. I couldn't tell if he had seen, but if he started to tease me about crying, I would have really let him have it. "Rory, you're taking this a bit hard—"

"No, I'm asking you. Do you think you're impressing anyone?" I said.

"*I'm* impressed," Adelaide said haughtily while Chase eyed the bucket in my hand like he expected me to hit him with it.

"You don't count," I said.

"Why not?"

"Because it doesn't take much to impress you. You would probably be impressed if he sneezed," Lena said, coming up to stand beside me.

I couldn't tell who was more insulted at this statement—Chase or Adelaide. It was nice to have an ally. "So, what's it going to take to get you to stop bugging me all the time?" I asked.

Adelaide just screamed at the top of her lungs.

8

My first thought was that Adelaide had serious problems if she would throw a temper tantrum like that for Chase, but then she pointed.

I looked over my shoulder and froze.

Twenty feet away, slumped on the ground between us and the Tree of Hope, a ragged figure lay very still. Then two more figures appeared, one carrying the other, so suddenly that dust swirled around them. The one standing staggered and fell to his knees, choking on the dust. All three were covered in brown and red muck, so it took me a few seconds to recognize them.

On the fourth finger of the coughing boy's right hand, a ring shone neon blue.

"Evan?" I said hesitantly.

He glared at us. For a second, I thought I was wrong. He didn't seem like the same kid who had left here weeks ago biting his nails. The look in his eyes was completely different. "Are you just going to *stand* there?" he said, and his voice broke, ragged with coughing.

Then George was beside him. He knelt on the ground and gripped Evan's shoulders. "What happened?"

Seeing George there made the scene seem more real. I could move again.

I ran. I reached the girl first—Evan's sister, I couldn't remember her name. She was slumped over on her stomach, her leg twisted underneath her. I flipped her over without thinking, wanting to see her face, to check if she was okay, but she screamed, even louder than Adelaide.

"Mary." Evan sounded like he was only a few seconds away from fainting himself. "Her shoulder."

Then I noticed too late the puncture wound just above her collarbone and the blood seeping from it.

I knew suddenly what all the red muck was. She had lost a lot of blood.

What happened next was weird. My hand reached out and pressed hard against the wound, but I felt like I was watching it from very far away. Under my palm, her right shoulder felt feverish and wet. I knew I should say something comforting, but my mind couldn't find the words.

"Evan, what *happened*?" George said again.

Shaking his head hard, Evan held George's forearms, like he couldn't stay upright on his own. Blood dripped off the cuff of his left sleeve.

"Evan, you *have* to tell me," George told Evan. "If you pass out before Gretel gets here, someone has to tell her what happened to you three."

He blinked at George, like he just now realized who was talking to him. "Trolls. Captured us. Took the rings. Not sure how long. Days? Hard to tell. They held us in a cave. They couldn't decide if they wanted to sell us as livestock or slaves. Kept asking questions about EAS."

Chase ran up next and tossed a handful of leaves in my lap. "From the Tree of Hope. They'll slow the bleeding and dull some of the pain."

I stared at him, remembering dimly that we had been fighting about something a few moments before. It all seemed very stupid and far away with Evan and Mary and Russell here.

Chase completely misunderstood the look. "Gretel taught me, all right? And isn't *anything* better than your bare hands?" he said, exasperated, dashing around George and Evan to Russell.

My palm was very red when I took my hand away, and the leaves looked shockingly green against it. When I pressed the leaf to Mary's shoulder, she whimpered again, but nowhere near as loud as before.

"How did you get out?" George asked Evan.

"They kept us in cages. On the ground," Evan said in the same halting monotone. "I asked a squirrel to help me dig under the bars one night. I crawled out and broke the locks on Mary's and Russell's cages, but it woke the trolls up. We ran. We hid, but we couldn't come back—we had to steal the rings . . ."

"But why is Russell unconscious?" Chase asked impatiently.

"Mary was h-hurt," Evan said. "A troll threw a dagger when we left. So Russell and I went back alone. I found the rings, but one of the trolls caught Russell. I stabbed his foot, the troll let go, but he dropped Russell on his head. I slipped a ring on his hand to send him here, and I ran for Mary."

"You did a good job," George said, trying to sound encouraging. "You got everyone back."

Tears ran down Evan's cheeks, clearing tracks through the smeared mud, and he covered his face. I saw what was wrong with his left hand, and my stomach lurched. He had two stumps where his ring finger and his pinky should have been.

"*My* fault," Evan said, his voice thick and muffled. "Russell and Mary. It's all my fault. What if they never wake up?"

"Hush," said someone else. "Let's not give up hope before we reach the infirmary and I get a good look at you all."

It was Gretel, right behind us. Lena stood next to her, panting, obviously the only one smart enough to run for help. I had never been so glad to see a grown-up in my life. Gretel took charge immediately, directing two-foot-tall men with their names stitched on their work suits—the Shoemaker's elves. My knees weak and rubbery, I stepped away from Mary to make room for the stretcher carried by two named Bob and Rufus.

The whole courtyard fell silent while the elves loaded up the questers and carried them off. Gretel led the way. I didn't see what door they entered, because Miriam dragged me to the bathroom to get cleaned up.

I scrubbed and scrubbed my hands under the faucet with almost a cup of soap, watching the bubbles turn from pink to white, and still, I couldn't forget the way Mary's shoulder felt under my palm—slick with blood and unnaturally hot.

"You're okay, right?" Miriam handed me a paper towel, and I realized she was worried.

I nodded and dried my hands, and I *was* okay. I walked out of the bathroom without stumbling, and I made my way over to Lena's table under the Tree, where all the sixth graders had gathered. Kelly sat with her feet propped up on the seat, her arms wrapped around her knees, her eyes very wide. Kyle, Lena, and Chase occupied the other chairs, so I sat on the ground.

I *was* fine, but seeing Evan and his Companions come back like that . . . well, Failing a Tale felt a lot more real than just seeing a name on a wall.

The whole courtyard waited for news. You could practically taste the worry in the air. All the seventh graders were a mess, which surprised me in a numb, distant way. They hadn't seemed all that fond of Evan and Russell *before* they went on a Tale.

"What could possibly be taking so long?" Kevin's voice shook a little, but we all pretended not to notice.

"They should be fine," Chase said from the chair beside Lena. "I've seen worse. Well, as far as the Garrisons go, anyway. Head wounds are a different story."

"You're really doing a great job of cheering everybody up," Kyle said, and Chase shrugged.

We fell silent again.

I spread my hands in my lap, palm up, and tried to imagine what they would look like if I lost the same fingers Evan had.

Both hands trembled. Not a lot, but enough to notice if you were looking.

Great—not only did I freeze (again) at the first sign of trouble, but my hands shook afterward. If I got this freaked out over a Tale I wasn't part of, my own Tale would be a disaster.

"Whoa," said Chase, staring down from the chair above me.

I sat on my hands and glared at him, waiting for the teasing to start. I almost wanted an excuse to fight back. It was easier to be mad at him than to be scared.

He didn't get the chance.

"Look." Lena pointed across the courtyard. I scrambled to my feet to see.

Ellie stood at the Director's podium, looking more serious than I had ever seen her. "The Director asked me to make a brief announcement. I'm sure you're all worried. But Evan, Mary, and Russell will be fine."

I let out a deep breath I hadn't known I was holding, and Lena echoed it beside me. Chase propped his chin on his hand, sharing a relieved grin with Kyle, who slumped in his seat. Kevin thumped Conner's back, Conner's eyes looking a little teary.

"None of the injuries are life-threatening," Ellie continued, "and under Gretel's care, they're expected to make a full recovery. Barring only a few scars." Evan's missing fingers flashed in my mind.

"Now, Gretel's infirmary is a bit full at the moment with Evan, his Companions, and a few particularly concerned friends. 'The White Snake' isn't for the *faint* of heart," Ellie added with a small smile. Nervous giggles rang out across the courtyard, but I didn't get the joke. "So, if anyone else is feeling lightheaded or shaky, please come see me right away. I've got a special restorative tea you'll need before you go home."

Chase looked pointedly at me, but I stuffed my hands in my pockets. I didn't want anyone else to see them trembling.

"Who fainted?" Kevin asked.

All across the courtyard, kids started gathering their things and talking. Every once in a while, someone laughed, too loudly, and shook his head with relief. Darcy had cried all her eyeliner off, while her brother, the fawn with the spiked collar, nuzzled her hands, trying to comfort her.

"One of Jenny's friends," said Lena.

"And Adelaide," said Chase.

"Do you think it counts as a Failed Tale?" Kyle asked in a hushed voice, and everyone fell quiet again. I'm pretty sure we were all imagining "Evan Garrison" carved on the Wall.

"No. They never ran across any of the trials," said Puss, jumping up onto our table. "Rumpel says that they should have survived at least two. Evan's Tale is still ongoing."

"But the last White Snake Tales always concluded in six weeks tops," Lena said hesitantly. "I mean, Rumpel told me—"

"This one is different. I've just seen the current Book myself." The cat's accent sounded even more clipped than usual. "New lines have appeared: 'Evan came to the sinking realization that this Tale would take much longer than anyone expected. He was years away from his *happily ever after*.'" She looked me up and down with her piercing green gaze.

"What?" Uncomfortable, I checked my clothes, thinking maybe I was a bloody mess, but the only spot I saw was a grass stain on my knee.

"It seems the Tales are changing." Puss turned and licked her white shoulder, as the bell sounded to dismiss us. "Now, if you'll excuse us, Kelly's mother wants her." The cat leaped into Kelly's open arms.

Without a word, Kelly ran all the way across the courtyard, past a group of girls, and straight into Ellie's arms. When she buried her face in her mother's stomach, her shoulders shook a little, and I felt terrible that I hadn't noticed she was upset. She knew so much more than I did. Sometimes I forgot she was younger than the rest of us.

Then Ellie murmured something and smoothed her daughter's hair. Suddenly, I wished my mother was around too. I wished that I had already told Mom the truth about EAS.

Lena turned my way, looking about fifty times more cheerful than me. "Ready?" Over her shoulder, she carried a weathered canvas duffel, the straps a little frayed.

I had completely forgotten about the sleepover. I grinned at her, relieved. More than anything, I didn't want to face a whole weekend worrying over Failed Tales by myself. If Lena wasn't coming home with me, I probably would have cracked and told Mom and Amy the truth—whether it was *actually* a good time or not.

"So," Lena said, waiting while I shrugged on my backpack. "Is there anything I should know about your family?"

One of Mom's movie posters came to mind, but Lena probably knew about that already. I led the way to the ruby door. "Um, yeah, actually. They don't know about EAS. I mean, about the magic side of it."

"Really?" Lena's eyes widened behind her glasses. "I was thinking bad temper, or a weird mole someplace, but that's definitely good to know."

Lena had a talent for grown-ups. She was probably the best person to bring to my house for a sleepover when my family was worried about my friends.

Amy was charmed. Lena even shook her hand and said, "Nice to meet you, Ms. Stevens." In the privacy of the backseat, I gave Lena a thumbs-up. Amy loved it when people called her Ms. Stevens. She took it as a sign of respect. She doesn't get a lot of that from work.

Mom was even easier to please than Amy. She *wanted* to like Lena, and she wanted Lena to like her. So, from the moment we walked in the door, Mom was her most friendly.

"We're home!" I called from the doorway.

"In the kitchen!" Mom called back.

"Uh-oh," I said. Amy and I exchanged a worried glance.

My mother *loved* to cook. She mentioned it in all of her interviews. Publishers had approached her to see if she would consider doing a cookbook. She was really flattered. It only encouraged her. But since she worked so much, she never got a lot of practice. On a good day, Mom's meals were edible. On a bad day, I hid most of it in a paper napkin.

Lena would eat anything, I was pretty sure, but I didn't want to have to apologize profusely later for Mom's Chicken Florentine or Provimi Veal disasters.

"Be brave," Amy told me. "If it's awful, I'll accidentally-on-purpose spill soda on it and order us pizza."

Sometimes, I didn't know how we ever managed without Amy.

"What's wrong? Is there something else I should know?" Lena said, as we dumped our bags at the bottom of the staircase and headed into the kitchen.

"Yeah—Mom can't cook," I whispered back. "Don't tell her fans, though."

"Her fans?" Lena repeated, frowning.

Mom stood in front of the oven. Seeing us, she waved both hands at Lena, two hands that happened to be covered in oven mitts—one shaped like a pig and the other shaped like a cow. Her hair fizzed out in wayward tufts. She was definitely at her least intimidating.

"Hi, Lena!" she said. "I've heard so much about you! All good things, don't worry."

"Hi," Lena's voice dropped off to a whisper. She looked startled and embarrassed—like she'd accidentally just swallowed her gum.

She'd just recognized Mom. Lena hadn't known who Mom was. She hadn't even suspected. She had come to hang out with me, and only me. Wanting to meet the famous Maggie Wright hadn't even entered into the equation.

I felt like laughing. I felt *happy*.

Then Lena shot me a look, which clearly said, *Why the hiccups didn't you tell me?* I couldn't keep myself from grinning.

"Nice to meet you, Ms. L—" Then Lena stopped herself. Obviously she had just remembered that my parents were divorced.

But Mom rescued her before I could. She shook Lena's hand wearing the cow oven mitt. "Call me Maggie."

Lena still looked stunned, like she didn't know what else to say, so I changed the subject. "Mom, you're not cooking, are you?"

"No . . . why?" she asked.

I pointed at the oven mitts. "I thought we were having pizza."

"Oh!" Mom said. "Just brownies. The pizza is on its way."

Behind Mom's back, Amy lifted up an empty box of brownie mix, giving me and Lena the A-OK sign.

Lena covered her mouth, trying not to laugh. When Mom turned around suspiciously, Amy strolled forward, dropping her car keys and opening the freezer.

Then the oven timer beeped, which did a really good job of keeping Mom from catching on. "Ooh, brownies. While I dish these up, why don't you two change into your pj's and make this a real pajama party?"

It was the best sleepover I ever had. The brownies had baked into a hard, solid sheet in the pan (Mom swore up and down that she had followed the directions exactly), but they still tasted good after Amy crumbled them over ice-cream sundaes. Since we ate them before the pizza came, Mom said, "It's just the kind of day when you need to eat dessert first." We hadn't rented any movies, so we flipped through the channels until we found one of Mom's old films—something she had made near the beginning of her career, a teen movie that started with a cafeteria foodfight and ended with prom. With the TV's volume turned on low, Mom entertained us with anecdotes about the filming—here, the director and the lead actor had an hour-long fight over whether the actor's collar should be flipped up or folded down.

During the intense confrontation scene, the male lead had

apparently farted loudly after declaring his love for Mom's character. When he looked into the camera with wide earnest eyes and said, "I love you, Carrie. I always have," she cracked up again, so hard that she dropped a spoonful of ice cream down her front. Which made Lena laugh so hard that Sprite poured out of her nose.

When the teen movie ended, *The Last Shoe Standing* came on.

Amy made a face, her hand poised over the remote. "Do we have to watch this? I hate these movies."

"What's wrong with it?" Mom asked. This was one of her favorites.

"It's just another Cinderella-type, rags-to-riches story. It's so unrealistic," Amy said, and I wondered what Ellie might think of that.

Then Lena asked a question that made me choke on my pizza. "What's your favorite fairy tale?"

Amy patted my back as I coughed and sputtered. "Are you okay?"

I was *not* okay. I was kind of concerned that my friend was going to rat me out.

"Oooh, that's a good question," Mom said. "'East of the Sun, West of the Moon.' Do you remember it, Rory? I used to read it to you when you were little."

"No," I said hoarsely.

"Pizza probably went down the wrong way." Amy passed me my Sprite. "Drink some of this."

"It's about a girl who marries a bear," Mom told me eagerly. "When she finds out that he's really a prince in disguise, a troll princess *kidnaps* him, and the girl has to go find the four winds to figure out where he is and rescue him. I'm sure you remember."

A vague memory stirred. "Wasn't that one of my picture books?"

Mom nodded excitedly. Lena looked at me with a questioning look. She wanted to know whether or not I wanted her help explaining.

I shook my head just a tiny bit. Not yet.

If Mom found out I spent the afternoon trying to stop a girl from bleeding to death, she would never let me go back on Monday.

"That's creepy," Amy said.

"It's romantic and exciting and an inspiration to young adventurous girls everywhere," Mom said, offended. (She meant me, by the way. And maybe Lena.)

"She marries a *bear*," Amy pointed out icily. "I don't believe in fairy tales."

But Lena and I exchanged another glance, and a smile grew on our faces. It was a lot more fun to keep secrets from my family when there was someone to help me keep them. Someday, I would totally burst Amy's bubble.

"I do," Mom said, "but I think they're a lot more messy and complicated than people give them credit for."

"Does that mean we're watching the movie?" Amy asked, making a face.

"Well, it's not like there's anything else on," Mom said stubbornly.

So we watched the movie. Mom fell asleep halfway through, the pig and cow oven mitts stuffed under her head like a pillow. When the end credits rolled, Amy sent me and Lena to my room and then concentrated on Mom.

"Wake up, Sleeping Beauty," Amy told Mom softly, shaking her shoulder.

"She works too hard," I told Lena as we ran up the stairs. "She probably *could* sleep for a hundred years."

Lena grinned. "If you run down and kiss her, she might be a Character yet."

"Yeah, right—I don't think Mom thinks of me as her ideal Prince Charming."

We laughed, really hard. Amy frowned and made shooing motions. Still giggling, we ran the rest of the way.

"It was nice of you to go back for second helpings on the brownies." I flopped on the bed and burrowed under the covers. I wasn't sure I could sleep after all that sugar. "Mom *is* a terrible cook. Someday, we'll break it to her."

"I like your family." Lena sat on her bed—a twin I never used except sometimes to throw my book bag and dirty clothes on.

"Thanks." With an embarrassed sort of grin, I beat my pillow into a more comfortable shape. "I like them too."

"I didn't realize that you were one of *those* Landons, the Hollywood kind," she said, half-accusing. "You never said."

"I kind of thought you knew." I didn't know what else to say. It would've been too awkward to thank her for not making a big deal out of Mom.

Lena tugged the blankets free from under the mattress. "They would be proud of you, you know. If you told them."

That was why she brought up fairy tales. She wanted to feel it out—warm them up to the idea. Maybe I *could* tell Mom—someday.

"Even Amy," Lena added with a small smile, "after she got over the shock."

Lena wanted me to tell them. Her grandmother had been telling Lena, Jenny, and George stories about Madame Benne since they were born. Keeping secrets was probably weird for her.

"I'll tell them. Eventually. After I have my Tale." It wouldn't matter as much then if Mom pulled me from EAS.

"What Tale do you want?" Lena rolled over onto her stomach and hugged her pillow. "You never talk about it."

"Nothing where I sleep for years, waiting around for some random guy to come and kiss me," I said, hating my name with a passion. When Lena started laughing, I was surprised and kind of hurt. "What? If I'm going to all the trouble of suffering through Hansel's class, I want to *use* my sword." Not to mention all my extra practices.

"It's not . . . that." Lena gasped for breath between fits of laughter. "But when . . . we asked Adelaide"—here, Lena laughed twice as hard—"she said, 'Anything where I get kissed.' . . . No wonder you two don't get along," she added, and I laughed too.

I guess we were too loud, because the door opened. Amy poked her head in. "What is going on in here? Did you two sneak in some laughing gas or something?"

"No," I said, trying to stop giggling. "We're just talking."

Amy looked from me to Lena and smiled, glad that I was having fun. "Well, just don't wake up your mom. Good night, girls."

"'Night, Amy!"

"Good night!"

She closed the door, and Lena and I listened to her footsteps on the stairs, waiting until she reached the first floor before we started talking again.

"What Tale do *you* want?" I asked in a whisper. "You never talk about it either."

"Well," Lena said slowly, "I do want a Tale. It doesn't need to be a famous one, though. What I *really* want is to be an inventor like Madame Benne."

"Really?" *That* was impressive. I didn't think much about what I wanted to be when I grew up. The only thing I knew for sure was that I didn't want to make movies, but Lena was already making magic mirror walkie-talkies. "How long ago was she alive?"

"Here. I'll show you." Lena climbed to the end of the bed, where she had left all her stuff, and she dug to the bottom of her backpack and pulled out a book—a fancy one bound with leather. *Madame Benne: Genius Inventor or Fey Traitor?* was gilded on the spine. It was very worn. She flipped to a dog-eared page near the end and passed it to me. "It's there in the appendix."

It was a genealogy chart, starting with Madame Benne's birth in 927 AD and ending with Tobias Freeman in 1919. At the bottom, several more generations had been penciled in, with George, Jenny, and Lena LaMarelle squeezed in at the very edge of the page. I recognized Lena's tiny, precise handwriting.

"You wrote in here?" I tried counting how many generations there were between Madame Benne and Lena, but I lost count at twenty-one. Then I flipped to the front. The bookplate said, very clearly, PROPERTY OF EVER AFTER SCHOOL, NORTH AMERICAN CHAPTER, REFERENCE ROOM. DO NOT REMOVE. "You stole a book and *then* you wrote in it?"

"She's *my* ancestor," Lena said. "And Gran wouldn't let *me* pick out the Table of Plenty next week if I didn't know so much about her and her inventions."

I had hurt her feelings. So it probably wouldn't be a good idea to point out that since she had a photographic memory, she didn't *need* to keep the book. "I'm impressed you can trace your family tree back that far. I can't even remember my great-grandparents' names." I closed the biography and passed it back to her.

Lena returned it to her bookbag, smiling a little. "It did take some doing."

She took off her glasses. It was the first time I had seen her without them. She was very pretty, just as pretty as Adelaide. She had the smooth dark skin, high cheekbones, and full lips that all the LaMarelle siblings shared, but her eyes seemed much more gentle than Jenny's. Or maybe that was just a sign that Lena couldn't focus on me without her glasses on.

She set her glasses on the nightstand and slid deep under the covers. "Rory, who do you have a crush on?"

That was definitely a change in subject. "Nobody. Why?"

Lena didn't answer, but no one brought up the subject of crushes at a sleepover completely out of the blue—not unless you secretly wanted to talk about the boy *you* liked.

"Lena, do *you* have a crush on someone?" I asked.

"No," Lena said, too quickly.

"You do! Tell me who it is!"

"I said that I don't," Lena said firmly, sounding a lot like Jenny. "Besides, you aren't telling either."

"But I really *don't* have a crush on anyone," I protested.

Lena ran her hands over the covers and didn't say anything.

She would probably tell me if I guessed. I ran through the possible candidates. Not Chase. Too mean. But the triplets were a possibility. In fact, when *one* of them touched her, the day her mirrors exploded, she had acted suspiciously weird.

"Kyle. It's Kyle," I said decisively.

"Oh, no! Is it that obvious?" Lena moaned and pressed her face into her pillow.

She *had* wanted to talk about it. I did what I could, since I was failing in friend duties by not gushing about a crush of my own. "No, that was just a guess. But really, I think he's the best of the triplets—of the whole sixth grade, actually."

Wrinkling her nose in embarrassment, Lena groped at the

lamp, but without her glasses, she couldn't find the light switch. I turned it off for her and did my best not to laugh.

She didn't say anything for so long I was pretty sure she had fallen asleep. I didn't mind. Some girls change crushes almost as often as they change clothes, without really caring who knows about it, but Lena wasn't that way. Me finding out was a big deal.

Then she whispered, "You won't tell, will you?"

"Of course not," I said, aghast. "I promise I won't tell."

Lena sighed. "Good night, Rory."

"'Night, Lena."

Then she really did fall asleep. I could tell, because she started to snore. Not loudly. Gently, like a cat purring. It was a comforting sound.

It took me a while to do the same. It wasn't the afternoon's events that kept me awake. Even though I'm kind of ashamed to admit it, I didn't think of Evan or his sister or his friend once. I relived the sleepover, thinking about how nice it was when someone stayed the night. It had been so normal, so *girly*, to stay up late, watching movies and gossiping over boys, even if I didn't have much to say. It had been a long time since I had gotten a chance to do that. Since third grade. Since Marta, who had known me from kindergarten.

I had missed it while we were traveling, and I hadn't even known I had missed it. I had forgotten what it was like to have a best friend.

That was the night I dreamed I saw "Lena LaMarelle" on the Wall of Failed Tales.

It started out completely different. A humongous flat-screen TV played *The Wizard of Oz*. Adelaide was a munchkin, which she didn't like. Chase was Glinda the Good Witch, which he *hated*.

Lena was Dorothy, apron and all, and I ran around as Toto.

Then the giant TV morphed into the Wall, and I saw Lena's name, carved into the stone with bubble letters, like you find doodled in binders and notebooks, with hearts all over them. Even though I knew I was dreaming, I sat crying at the base of the memorial and said, "It's all my fault. What if she never wakes up?" The bouquet of yellow roses in my hand grew vines and crept up the Wall, sending tendrils into the stone, and I heard the crunch and crack as it broke above me.

I woke just before the pieces rained down over my head, sitting up in bed with a gasp so loud that Lena opened her eyes.

"What?" she murmured sleepily.

"Nothing." My heart hammered so wildly that I felt vibrations in the mattress.

"Well, I don't want to go to school," she grumbled and turned over on her side, which made me think that she wasn't as awake as she'd seemed.

I had to stifle a giggle, and then I was twice as worried, remembering her name in bubble letters.

The dream wasn't telling the future. It couldn't be.

Lying back down, I pulled the covers up to my chin with a burning stab of shame. I had been such an idiot, worrying over whether or not I would Fail my own Tale. It would be so much worse to lose my friend and know I was to blame.

It wouldn't happen to Lena, I promised myself. No matter what Tale we had, or what villains we faced, I would make sure Lena came home in one piece.

The only problem was that if we were in danger, I didn't know what *I* could do to save her.

t EAS next week, everyone couldn't stop talking about the Fairie Market. Even Evan and his Companions.

On Monday, I saw him talking to the other seventh graders. I was sure he was filling them in on what happened in Atlantis, but when I passed him, he was just telling everyone how much Fey fudge he was going to buy during the Market. Nobody mentioned the bandage on Evan's hand, or the bruises on Russell's face, or the sling Mary wore over her left arm. Friday's scare seemed to fade from everyone's mind in all the excitement.

Jenny stopped by Lena's study spot once every afternoon to nag.

"Remember—Gran wants a *pine* Table of Plenty to match the other furniture," she told Lena at first. "And it can't be any longer than six feet. We need it to fit in the kitchen."

On Tuesday, she added, "The Table should specialize in blueberry pancakes and upside-down cake. We're going to save a ton of money on groceries, but it's not worth it if the food's inedible. Ask the dealer for a taste test before you start talking prices. I don't want you to be afraid to demand it if you have to. If you get nervous about bargaining, come find me. I'll help you."

By Wednesday, I was almost as annoyed as Lena was. "Make

sure you check it for dings and scratches," Jenny said. "Just because it's magic doesn't mean that Gran will let us put it in *her* home if it looks like junk. I'm sure there are plenty of gently used antique pine Tables of Plenty out there, if you know where to look."

Lena nodded obediently, but as soon as Jenny walked off to join her friends, she scowled fiercely. "She is stressing me *out*. It would be one thing if Gran let me skip school to get here when it opens, but noooo, my education is more important, blah, blah, blah. How many good Tables do they think will be left just a few hours before closing?"

But her eyes glittered behind her glasses, as impatient for Friday as the rest of us.

On the day of the Fairie Market, I rushed to the red door, and the hallway behind it was lit. That was the first time it had happened. I was so used to barreling through a dark corridor that I stopped short. At first, I thought that someone might have gotten lost, but it was only a girl—the same girl who I'd met beside the fruit tarts on my second day. I'd almost forgotten about her.

She knelt in front of the wall, where a bright lamp hung from a silver chain. It was either magical or battery-operated, because it didn't have a plug. The girl's silvery braid fell in a coil at the floor. All of a sudden, the purple material under her knees sprang up and started dusting stone chips off the carving with its tassels.

I jumped—I had never seen a magic carpet before—and the girl turned to stare at me. It was kind of creepy. With such dark eyes and very light hair, she looked a little more than human—like a Fey who had lost her wings.

I pointed to the metal tool in her hand. "I didn't know this hall was still under construction."

"I started it long before you came." Her voice was quiet, musical, and lonely.

Her carving was only half-finished, but with the tiny precise marks already chiseled, I could make out a woman in profile and her towering crown. "She looks like a queen," I said, and the girl nodded.

The carved queen looked familiar—a little like the silver-haired girl but with a longer face and much shorter hair.

The girl pulled her braid over her shoulder and brushed bits of stone from it. She had a scar, one that I hadn't noticed before—a grayish-pink line that wrapped around the nape of her neck. I wondered what Tale had given her that.

She caught me staring. Her smile was slow but warm. "I like children your age. You have no idea who you will become."

I scowled. She didn't look *that* much older than me, but several EASers had made it very clear that they think the difference between being eleven and being sixteen is a big deal.

The girl pointed at the door to the courtyard. "Lena is standing beside the Tree of Hope. You'll need to bury the ashes when she's gone."

I hesitated, almost positive that the last bit didn't make any sense, but there wasn't anybody else around to agree with me. Lena had told me that some Characters had a hard time after their Tale. Whatever had given her that scar around her neck had to be pretty intense.

"Go on, Rory," she said softly, turning back to her carving. So I went through the door.

My mouth immediately fell open.

The courtyard was transformed. It was four times bigger than I had ever seen it, and a new mountain range loomed over one side.

Red, orange, and yellow banners were tied to the Tree of Hope's branches, all proclaiming welcome in all different languages. Some of the writing wasn't even human. Stalls and tables lined a cobblestone avenue that stretched on as far as I could see. A thousand voices were talking, laughing, or shouting at the same time.

Every few seconds, one called out louder than the rest.

"Dragon scales! Fresh dragon scales! You can still smell the sulfur on them!"

"Portable carriages here, disguised to look like a pumpkin! Demonstration in ten minutes!"

"Carryall backpacks, guaranteed to hold three medium-size cars."

Black birds the size of dogs roosted in a branch above the nearest stall. It looked like it sold feathers. Robin feathers; eagle feathers; tiny bluebird feathers; fancy peacock plumes; furry, lion-colored feathers; feathers crafted out of silver or maybe plucked from metal birds. I didn't think anyone was watching the stall, but when I leaned forward to get a better look at a long scarlet plume that seemed to be on fire, one of the giant black birds fluttered down. When it reached the ground, a man with long black hair and a proud arch in his nose stood in its place.

"That's a phoenix feather, miss," he told me. "Genuine. I can produce the certification. Would you like to touch it?"

I was tempted, but Lena appeared, grabbing my arm just in time.

"No, thank you!" She pulled me away, whispering, "Ravens! Indigenous to North America. Not to be trusted."

"He seemed nice," I said, but Lena shook her head.

"Tricksters, all of them." She led me out of the busy traffic, behind a silver truck parked next to the Tree of Hope.

Dozens of glittering lights darted and buzzed over the windshield, like a swarm of gnats in summer. Then one light zipped away and landed on one of the Tree's lower branches, and I saw her tiny lean body, even smaller than Sarah Thumb's, her dress made from lily petals, her long silver hair, and her sky-blue wings threaded with black, like a monarch butterfly.

Then she spit at the truck and gnashed her teeth, which kind of spoiled the image of loveliness.

Lena grinned. "Guess what I have in my backpack."

It looked normal enough—green with pink zippers, but plenty of other things hadn't struck me as very magical either. "Three medium-sized cars?"

"What? No."

"A gently used pine Table of Plenty with a talent for blueberry pancakes and upside-down cake?"

"No, this is even better." Lena unzipped her backpack and pulled out a book even older than the volumes in Rumpel's library. The wooden covers were painted gold, and the leather spine was cracked and peeling. She handed it to me.

"It's a book." It was heavier than it looked.

"Look at the first page."

I lifted the cover. The page was blank except for the bottom left-hand corner:

"It's Madame Benne's symbol," Lena said in a little singsong. I braced myself. She really did talk a lot when she got excited. "See the three lines here. It's supposed to represent her first invention—

the singing harp. She kept it with her until her death. This symbol is on everything we inherited from her."

"You inherited stuff from her? I thought she lived a thousand years ago."

A group of one-foot-tall men passed in front of us. Brownies. I recognized them from a picture in Lena's sketchbook. They were the color of mud, from the skin on their hands to the caps on their heads and the jackets they wore. All of them gave the truck a wide berth, and one even threw a rock at it, so hard that it scratched the paint.

"Well, we have a spoon of hers. And a mitten Grandma swears Madame Benne knitted herself. And now," Lena said with that faraway smile she got whenever she talked about her ancestress, "her spell book. Everything she invented—all the Tables of Plenty, rings of invisibility, magic mirrors, singing harps, seven-league boots, even the Glass Mountain—her notes on how to make them are in this book."

I examined the old, beat-up book with more respect. "And you bought this here?"

Lena nodded eagerly. "I don't know if the dwarf who sold it to me knew how valuable it is. I could never afford it otherwise. It was just sitting in this box of books. I started looking in it, because I was trying not to look too interested in the Table of Plenty he had—Jenny said that's the most important thing in bargaining—but once I saw the spellbook, the table really was no comparison—"

"Wait," I interrupted. "You didn't buy the table?"

"No, I just said that," she said impatiently. "I only had enough money for one."

With a prickle of nervousness, I asked, "Does Jenny know that you didn't get a Table of Plenty?"

"Not yet." Lena's chin was jutting out, the way it gets when she feels stubborn. "But, Rory, you aren't *listening*. With Madame Benne's spellbook, I don't *need* to buy one. I can *make* as many Tables of Plenty as I want. The instructions are in there."

Jenny would definitely be upset if she found out that Lena didn't follow her plan. "Is it easy? Maybe we can make one before Jenny finds out."

"Well . . . ," Lena said uncomfortably.

I flipped to the middle of the book. The pages were covered in elaborate symbols that looked a lot like Celtic knots, and I hoped that they were just some sort of weird decoration, not the actual text.

"It's written in Fey," Lena told me slowly. "I've been meaning to learn the language for years, and now I'll actually do it."

"You mean, you can't read this?"

"Some of it." Lena pointed to a symbol with a long squiggle hanging off of it, like a tail. "That word means 'mushroom.'"

"Lena . . . ," I said slowly with that sinking sensation that usually happens right before I get in trouble.

"Jenny will be glad. I know she will," Lena said in her most cheerful voice. But a shadow passed over her face, and I knew she was feeling the same thing I was. I started to say that we could find the stall and see what their exchange policy was, but then Lena added quickly, "Please, Rory. I don't want to think about what could happen right now. Let's just enjoy the Market. Okay?"

So, I put the book into Lena's backpack and zipped it up.

Lena smiled gratefully, and slung her backpack on.

"Quick question," I said, as the tiny winged figures buzzed around the truck. Someone had produced a basket of eggs so big it took five of them to lift it. One by one, they each picked up an egg, hugging it in both arms, and zoomed six feet above the vehicle. Then, with a gleeful sound like Christmas bells, one dropped her egg. It splattered across the windshield in a yolky mess. "Why are the little fair—"

Lena gasped. "Don't say it!"

"Say what?"

"They're pixies, not fairies." Lena had lowered her voice so much that I had to lean in to hear her. "Fairies are always much bigger and more powerful. Don't let anyone catch you calling them fairies. If the Fey take offense, they might turn you into a pig for a century. They've done it before."

"Oh." I made a mental note *not* to talk about fairies at all, if I could help it. I was pretty sure that Mom and Amy would still force me to go to school if I got turned into a piglet. "But why are they egging that truck?"

Lena glanced over at the gunk on the windshield, and then the cluster of pixies armed with eggs hovering above it. "Oh, my gumdrops." She yanked me out of the splash zone.

"Shouldn't we do something?" I asked Lena, but it was too late. All the pixies dropped their eggs at once, with a huge crunch. The splatter hit passersby, including a dwarf dressed in a double-breasted suit. Seeing eggshells in his beard, he shook his fist at the pixies.

"It's Jack's truck. He calls it the Axe. I'm sure he knew what he was doing," Lena said, as we walked away.

"Is it magic?" I asked.

Lena snorted. "Only a minor glamour. To make it look shiny."

The truck was so polished that it shone as brightly as real silver, even under a layer of egg slime. This *was* Chase's dad we were talking about.

"Usually, before a Market, the Director clears the courtyard of all iron and steel, as a courtesy to our guests," Lena explained.

"Why?"

"Because the Fey and most nonhumans can't touch iron. If you pressed it against their skin, then they get these big welts, like jellyfish stings. That's why the elves have to work with Fey-tempered silver. Didn't Sarah Thumb cover that in orientation?"

She tugged me down the cobblestone path, lined with stalls and stands. It stretched on and on and ended in a lake, maybe a mile away, but the whole aisle was filled with figures. The only humans I saw were two fifth graders goggling a stall with mini-demonstrations of fireworks. "Parking the truck here is like a slap in the face to the Fey. Jack *had* to do it on purpose. He hardly ever uses that truck. He even leaves the keys inside."

Half-listening, I stared at a pottery stall where twenty centaur figurines battled each other so fiercely that ceramic bits flew everywhere.

The fairy in charge of the stand wore a T-shirt that said I ♥ HUMANS, so I thought at first he might be friendly. But then he saw me looking and turned around with a tiny smirk. The back of the T-shirt read EACH ONE IS GOOD FOR AT LEAST SEVEN YEARS OF TORTURE. I immediately hurried on, hoping he wouldn't get any ideas.

Up ahead, near the Tree of Hope, the Shoemaker's elves noticed Lena and waved her over. Some of them had green veins showing behind their pale skin, but besides that, it always surprised me how human they looked—no wings, no pointed ears. They had dressed up for the occasion. The one Lena introduced as Kefmin wore a tuxedo with tails—a foxtail, a raccoon tail, and a dog tail. (The last one wagged so hard it kept hitting people.)

The one named Bob showed off the carnival rides the elves had set up, and Lena asked questions full of magical jargon I couldn't follow. The Ferris wheel looked like an enormous circular vine. The mechanical horses on the carousel came to life and galloped straight off the ride. A scarlet roller coaster threaded through the branches of the giant tree. When it paused on the grass for new passengers, you could see each metal sleigh, shaped like a maple leaf curling elegantly.

"George's duel doesn't start for a while. Do you want to try one?" Lena said, as the roller coaster entered a corkscrew loop, half its passengers screaming. A fairy rider panicked and flew out of her seat, gliding away on silver wings fifty feet above us.

I suppressed a shudder, my mouth very dry. Just the *idea* of being up that high made me feel sick to my stomach. "Maybe the carousel later." That was the only ride that stayed relatively close to the ground. Lena and the elves looked a little disappointed, but nobody pushed it.

After we said good-bye to the elves, we passed a carnival stand, and Lena whispered, "That's a goblin."

The stallkeeper tossed and caught a golden ball with a long-fingered hand that had too many joints to be human. A wig of thick brown curls sat a little askew over batlike ears, and when he licked his lips, his tongue was bright red and forked, like a snake's.

"They feed on your fears and dreams," Lena explained as we hurried past. "The strongest among them can sense yours, just by looking at you, but they all use them to manipulate people. It's how their magic works."

A dwarf mechanically threw a golden ball at a tower of goblets. Every throw would knock a couple over, but never more than that. The dwarf swore and yanked whole chunks of his beard out, but when the goblin stallkeeper extended a hand palm up with a smile, the dwarf drew a silver coin out of his pocket and paid for another turn.

"He probably can't leave," Lena said, a little pityingly. "The stallkeeper must've cast a spell to make the customer think that he'll win if—"

"Lena, what are you doing here?" asked someone beside us, low to the ground. Puss had changed into a new silk dress. "George's match is about to start."

"But—" Lena checked her watch. "He's not supposed to go on for another half an hour."

The cat shook her head. "The competitor ahead of him saw who he was matched with and dropped out. George is up next."

"Where are they?" Lena asked.

"Over there." Puss flicked her white tail to our right. "Dueling on top of the Ivory Tower."

When I looked up, Lena had disappeared. She may not be the most athletic Character in the world, but that girl can really move when she feels like it.

I followed as quickly as I could, dodging scowling Fey, big groups of tipsy dwarves, and a herd of short, red-bearded, green-clad men that had to be leprechauns.

Finally, a few hundred meters beyond the Tree of Hope, I saw the Ivory Tower—a white marble structure that I was *sure* hadn't been there when I arrived. It was about the size of a tennis court and two or three stories tall. The walls were perfectly smooth—without a door or a window or even a seam to show where the slabs joined together. I ran around it, searching for Lena and the rest of the audience.

Then I turned the corner and froze. At least a hundred Fey milled around, more than I had ever seen in one place. A Fey with yellow wings and a dark suit shook his dark gold hair like it was a mane, blinking tawny eyes. A row of Fey knights waited for their turn in a line, fidgeting in armor that gleamed with jewels, twisting long hair under their helmets, checking their swords and maces. Another—with green hair and the kind of ballgown that I would've expected to see on a fairy godmother—saw someone she knew across the clearing and flew up over everyone's heads to land beside her friend.

I wished I could do that. Somehow, it didn't seem like a good idea to push through the cranky Fey just to see if there were EASers on the other side.

"Rory, over here!" Lena stood on top of a convenient boulder, waving both arms. She was so loud that half of the Fey looked at her and then at me. Face burning, I hugged the Ivory Tower wall and rushed past.

"Rory, he won!" Lena cried. Miriam grinned just behind her. "It took less than thirty seconds. George disarmed Torlauth and had his sword at the Fey's throat. He won!"

"What? The whole thing?" I asked, thinking of the waiting Fey knights.

"No, just this round," Miriam explained. "There are three matches."

"Why did they stop then?" I asked.

"They're taking a break," Miriam said. "Standard duel procedure."

"In honor or political duels, an unbiased third party shall deliver one undiluted spoonful of the Water of Life to each contestant prior to each match so that they may be restored to full health," Lena said in her tinny, reciting way. Then she sighed and added in her regular voice, "But this really isn't that serious."

"Here, they just get five minutes," Miriam said.

"But why are there so many *Fey* here?" I whispered. Two of them—a male and a female wearing matching red tunics with golden embroidery—watched us dispassionately, probably wondering who to torment first.

Lena shrugged. "Well, I don't think the rivalry will ever go away *completely*. The Fey and human Characters haven't been allies for all that long, just since the last war."

"Really?" Miriam said, which made me feel better about being confused.

"Yeah, Maerwynne of Lorraine got tired of the Fey manipulating humans all the time and founded Ever After School to help educate people," Lena said. "She started just walking around the countryside, telling stories about Characters besting magical creatures. Most of them were about the Fey. People started calling them 'fairy tales,' and the name stuck."

Miriam and I stared at Lena blankly.

"Sarah Thumb didn't tell you that, either?" Lena said.

"Rory, do you ever feel like maybe we should have another orientation?" Miriam muttered, and I laughed.

Before I could ask more about the rivalry, a bell sounded.

Lena and Miriam immediately stared straight up. Two figures fought on top of the structure, and above them, two larger images battled across the sky—a lot like a hologram or a light-show projection—kind of see-through, but larger than life. At first, they moved too fast for me to recognize them, but then one stepped back for a breather. The smaller one was George, and the big, bronze blur was Torlauth di Morgian.

I shuddered. He wouldn't be a Fey *I* wanted to fight.

George pressed forward, leaping and jabbing at once, and

Torlauth fell another step back. George was making the Fey retreat! He was winning! George hooked his hilt around his opponent's and twisted. He disarmed Torlauth. The Fey's blade flew in the air.

Then Torlauth planted a kick on George's chest, and George tumbled head over heels across the platform. It was a move I had seen before, between Chase and a dummy in Hansel's training courts, so I wasn't surprised when Torlauth caught his sword.

High above our heads, a smile curled slowly across the fairy's face, and I knew Torlauth wanted to kill George.

I scanned the crowd desperately for a grown-up to stop the fight—Gretel, Stu, even Hansel. The Director hadn't mentioned anything about a duel to the death. All I saw were students and Fey. My blood ran cold. Every single fairy leaned forward, licking their lips, eager for blood.

Then Torlauth launched forward, drawing his sword back for a slash at George's throat.

Lena gasped. "George!"

A third figure appeared—a smaller Fey with very pale green wings—and blocked Torlauth's sword with a small dagger, just inches from George's skin. Then they retreated out of sight.

I breathed again. Lena stared at the ground, blinking hard.

"It's okay." Miriam patted Lena's shoulder. "The Director knows that fairies can get a little carried away. The ref is up there with them. George is safe."

"He lost the match, though," Lena said in a very small voice.

Miriam smiled. "Still one more."

But that wasn't how the Fey saw it. Most of them smirked and glanced slyly at each other, like Torlauth had already won. Many also looked a little disappointed that no one had gotten hurt. If these people were our allies, I wondered what the bad guys were like.

"Hey! He's going to finish his story!" Conner called from around the corner of the Ivory Tower, and Kevin came running.

"Who?" I asked.

"The self-appointed halftime entertainment." Miriam shrugged, annoyed. "Go see if you want."

Lena led the way. My first guess was Chase, but when we rounded the corner, we found a college-aged guy in jeans and a ripped T-shirt leaning against a tree in a grove of birches. His arms were crossed, but he kept running a hand through his dark curly hair as he talked. Half of Ever After School had gathered around him, listening. The triplets had front-row seats, eyes wide, mouths gaping a little—even Kyle, the most sensible of the three.

"Wow," Lena whispered. "He actually made it."

"Who?" I asked again, because I was pretty sure she didn't mean Kyle.

"Jack." Lena pointed to the college-aged guy. "Chase's father."

"He's too young to be Chase's dad," I said.

"He's older than he looks," Lena said. "He was only twenty when he became part of the Canon."

"Cannon? Is that some sort of secret warrior society?" I asked.

Lena gave me a weird look, clearly stunned at how much I didn't know. "No. *Canon*. As in a body of literature. It's the council of Characters who are kind of in charge. Every Tale has a repre-sentative. Ellie, Hansel, Gretel, Sarah Thumb—they're all in it. You stop aging when you join."

"Really?" I had a sudden vision of Jack in a powdered wig like George Washington. "How old *is* he?"

"Not sure. Pretty young in comparison to some of them. The Director is over two hundred years old—come on." Lena threaded her way through the crowd. "Let's listen."

I could think of a lot of things I would rather do at a Fairie Mar-ket, but I didn't argue. Lena probably needed something to keep her mind off her brother.

"He picks me up," Jack said, "this twenty-five-foot monster, and he says, 'Fee, fie, fo, fum, I smell the blood of an Englishman.' I don't even have my sword out, so I say, 'You need to get your nose checked. *I'm* from Idaho.'"

His audience chuckled like a laugh track on TV sitcoms—automatic and way too enthusiastic for the joke.

It reminded me of the time right before my parents' divorce when Mom starred in a really big movie that my dad directed. Every time she came to pick me up from school, my classmates, and their parents, and sometimes our teachers, would crowd around her, laughing at her jokes. That was when Mom had started to send Amy to pick me up.

"Don't trust it. Everybody's looking for their fifteen minutes of fame," she had told me.

Apparently, no one had told Jack that. He smiled widely, probably thinking he was actually funny.

"It didn't look good," Jack continued. "I was hanging upside down from a giant's hand. But we got to talking about Idaho. He had never been there. I told them that everybody raised in Idaho tastes a lot like potatoes." A lot of people laughed again. "And that we're really bland unless you cook us right."

Chase lurked a few feet behind him. They didn't really look alike. Jack was much stockier and his hair was too dark, but when they smiled, all their dimples were in the same places.

This was the widest grin I had ever seen on Chase's face. Obviously, he enjoyed all the attention his dad was getting. He was also standing exactly like his father—arms crossed over his chest, leaning against the building at exactly the same angle, a hand on his chin.

"So, I give him this recipe—lots of vegetables, lots of spices," Jack said, "and while he's down the street at Jolly Green Giant's Grocery Store, I work one of his knives out of the cupboard and cut myself free."

Suddenly, I thought of something a lot more fun than listening to Chase's dad brag about himself—payback.

I crept up behind Chase, and I leaned against a tree too, folding my arms and holding my chin, trying to imitate Jack's cocky expression. "Aren't you taking 'like father, like son' a little far?" I whispered.

Chase noticed the way I was standing. He dropped his arms and stood up straight, glaring at me.

Jack didn't see or hear any of this, which made him even dumber than his son. "He gets back, carrying in two plastic bags. He doesn't see me standing just inside the door. So, I stab him first in one ankle and then in the other, and he falls, in slow motion, like a tree, his groceries flying everywhere, horrible packaged goods like dead man's toes and brain of baby rabbits. And I—"

"Jack, *there* you are!" Sarah Thumb and Mr. Swallow landed on a branch above his head. "The Director sent me to get you. The meeting was supposed to start ten minutes ago, and you're the only one who didn't show up."

For a second, Jack the Giant-Killer got a panicked look in his eyes, exactly like Chase did when the dragon came after us. Then he smiled at his audience. "Looks like we need to take a mandatory intermission here, folks. Duty calls."

The little Thumbelina Character rolled her eyes, and Mr. Swallow took off, not bothering to wait. Jack had to run to catch up.

As soon as his dad was out of sight, Chase shoved me hard in the shoulder. "That wasn't funny, Rory."

I smiled. So far, the score that night was one point to me, and none to Chase. "When you get a little taller, are you going to wear his clothes, too?"

"You should show him more respect." His face got red like it does when he's really mad. "He's a Jack with two Tales, both Beanstalk and Giant-Killer. That only happens once every three centuries."

I shrugged. "I thought he was a little full of himself."

"He has a right to be." Adelaide stepped up behind Chase. The triplets were right behind her. "Since he joined the Canon, he's killed twenty-five giants."

"That's the most in the history of Jack the Giant-Killers," Kyle said.

"Yeah, what do your parents do?" Chase added. "Sit at a desk all day?"

I just laughed. Moviemaking was pretty impressive, but I wasn't going to tell them about it.

"Rory, you're as bad as he is," Lena said in her best *children-play-nice* voice, as she glanced toward the Ivory Tower to see if the match had started again.

Maybe it was a little mean of me, but I didn't care. "I wouldn't rely on Jack's fame if I were you," I told Chase. "Without your dad, you're just a kid waiting for your Tale to start. Just like the rest of us."

Chase opened his mouth to say something else, but nothing came out.

"Lena!" someone shouted. We all looked.

Jenny pushed her way through the crowd. Her friends followed her, looking tall and scary and distant—like most eighth graders.

The sinking feeling came back. Lena's eyes widened. She obviously hadn't remembered that *both* of George's sisters would be watching the tournament. Then she raised her chin, determined to look cheerful.

"Did you get the Table yet?" Jenny clearly planned to show it off to her friends. "We thought we'd try it out. Get some snacks to eat during the match."

"I got something even better," Lena said, but she didn't sound as confident as she had when she told me. She pulled the book out of her backpack and handed it to her sister, who stared at the faded gold cover. "It's Madame Benne's spellbook."

There was a beat of silence. The other sixth graders glanced first at Lena and then at the grubby old book. I would never admit it out loud, but it did sound pretty unbelievable.

"*You* found Madame Benne's spellbook?" Adelaide obviously didn't believe a word of it.

Lena's gaze slid toward Kyle, and I knew she wished that she were anywhere but in a crowd that included the triplets. "Now we can make as many Tables of Plenty as we want."

Unfortunately, Jenny seemed skeptical too. "Did the vendor *tell* you that this was Madame Benne's spellbook?"

Lena shook her head slowly, her eyes large and solemn behind her glasses.

Jenny leafed through the pages with a frown. "I can't even read this."

Unasked, Chase pointed to the page on the right. "It's a recipe. 'Mushroom and Chive Scones,'" he read. He looked my way with a tiny smirk, and I knew he was saying it to get back at me. "It's just a Fey cookbook," he told Jenny.

I could've hit him. I almost did just to wipe that smirk off his face, but it wouldn't help Lena.

"But it has her symbol in it," Lena said.

"Forgers must've added that," Jenny said, exasperated.

Damage done, Chase smiled at me again and waved good-bye. Adelaide followed him, looking equally smug. The triplets slipped awkwardly into the crowd.

"All the sources say that she bound her notes in a golden book," Lena said hesitantly.

"Don't you think the forgers know that, too? Lena, how much did you spend on this?"

Lena looked at her feet and mumbled something. I watched helplessly, insides churning.

"All of it?" Jenny repeated, horrified.

I had to do something—at least *try* to get Lena out of it. "Look, you really shouldn't listen to everything Chase says. He's always full of it, and—"

"Rory," Jenny said sharply. "Can you give us a minute?" She turned to her friends. "You guys, too. I need to talk to Lena alone."

Lena didn't look at me, twisting the straps of her backpack, probably only a few seconds away from crying. I really didn't want to leave her, but I didn't have much choice.

"I'll see you later, Lena," I said and walked away.

I felt sick to my stomach and almost as guilty as if it had been *my* idea to buy the book. After all, Chase had been trying to get back at *me* when he called it a Fey cookbook and sealed Lena's fate.

Chase, I thought again, suddenly so angry that my hands automatically curled into fists. Pulling pranks on me was one thing, but getting Lena in trouble to get to me turned him from a regular bully to a true slimebucket. I was going to tell him so.

I had to find him first.

I ran in the direction he'd gone. He wasn't anywhere in the tournament's audience, but around the side of the Ivory Tower farthest from the Tree, I glimpsed him running along the wall of a weird building. If I hadn't been so angry, I might have stopped to stare at it. The circular outer wall was made out of tree trunks, kind of like a log cabin, but the trunks rose vertically from the ground. The bark was still on them.

Chase dashed through a small door, cut from a trunk, designed to blend in.

I rushed in right before the door closed and stomped up the staircase just inside the door. Planning what I was going to say, I dimly noticed that the stairs wound in a very tight circle, the grain's pattern identical on every step, as if the whole stairway was carved from the same trunk. At the top, branches spread out in every direction, as if the builder had preserved the tree exactly how it grew.

Chase knelt in the center of the attic, where light shone from below. He hadn't noticed me yet.

Seeing him, I darted across the uneven surface and shoved Chase with every ounce of my fury. He caught himself on a couple of nearby branches, narrowly avoiding falling through one of the holes in the floor.

"What do you think you're doing?" he whispered, staring up at me as if I was the last person he expected to see.

"What do you think *you're* doing? You can bug me as much as you want, but Lena isn't—"

"Keep your voice down!" Chase pointed at the hole beside him. "Do you want to get *caught*?"

I looked automatically, not through the hole, but at the floor. It had leaves on it—not the silk and plastic kind, but the real kind, the plant kind. The leaves were attached to a branch—no, a whole bunch of branches. The roof above us rustled too, like leaves in a slight breeze.

I'm not proud of it, but seeing how easily I could fall through, I completely forgot about Lena's problems.

Dropping fast, I clung to as many branches as I could get my arms and legs around, my heart hammering. That's how much I don't like heights.

"We're up a tree." My voice cracked in the middle. Not just one tree, but it looked like all the trunks that made up the outer wall still had their branches attached. The branches, woven together, made up the floor. There were bigger holes in the middle near me and Chase. I was at least fifty feet from the stairs. The attic started to spin around me.

"Well, duh," Chase whispered.

Only one thought filled my head. "I have to get down."

Chase glared at me. "You won't fall unless I push you. I will if you don't shut up. I can't hear what they're saying."

He wasn't bluffing. I became very still and very quiet.

Then I heard the voices coming from the first floor, directly underneath us.

"Then we are unanimous. We won't tell the young Characters about this particular Tale," said a familiarly formal voice.

I looked through the branches to the ground below. Forty or fifty Characters sat in a small auditorium, most of them grown-ups. They sat in elaborately carved chairs arranged in a circle. If the chairs were a little taller and made out of gold or jewels, they would have looked like thrones.

"The Canon," I murmured.

Chase fiercely motioned for me to be quiet. I bit my tongue.

"We agree that there is no need to frighten them needlessly," the Director continued in the same formal tone. She sat in a chair close to the center, carved all over with climbing roses and vines, a lot like the ones in her office.

"If it is true, if we are reading the beginning of the Tale correctly, we will have plenty of time to prepare," said Gretel. Her chair and Hansel's rose up side-by-side, decorated like a gingerbread house. "Four years make a big difference in a child's development."

"And her hands are full enough already," said Ellie at the other side of the room (her chair looked like a miniature pumpkin carriage, with a seat carved out of it). Several other Characters chuckled grimly, like she had made some sort of a morbid joke.

I looked at Chase for an explanation, but he only shrugged. He didn't know either.

"There are no secrets where children are concerned. Not true ones," said another quiet voice. It was the girl who had been carving earlier. Dust still covered her clothes. Her chair was a little taller than the others, like a tower, and her silver braid hung over the side.

"Who's that?" But I guessed as soon as the question was out of my mouth.

"Rapunzel," Chase said.

"I thought she was a student," I said.

"She's pretty old," Chase said. "She's probably the oldest person in that room. Only the Director's older, but I don't know if it counts since she was asleep for half of it."

"They hear our whispers." Rapunzel looked up, straight through the hole where Chase and I were watching.

"She knows we're here," I said dryly, waiting to be caught.

Chase looked worried for a second, but he shook it off. "Doesn't matter. Everybody knows she has a few screws loose."

"Are you always such a jerk?"

"I'm not trying to be mean," Chase snapped back. "It was her Tale that did it. She was left alone in her tower too long. She's supposed to have the gift of prophecy, but mostly she just freaks people out."

A lot of the Characters sitting below did seem uncomfortable, shifting in their wooden chairs, but the Director said, "Thank you, Rapunzel. We'll keep that in mind. We should all take care not to speak of it outside these walls."

Chase gave me a look that proudly said *I told you so*.

I pointed right below us. An old man sat in his chair, looking straight at me and Chase, his enormous gray eyebrows raised very high. Then he winked slowly and turned back to the meeting.

I enjoyed watching Chase gulp. "Looks like he isn't going to do anything though."

"On to other business." The Director looked over a sheet of paper. I was beginning to think that she was the type of person who had a list for everything. "Rumpelstiltskin, you had something to report?"

"We must do something about Solange," said Rumpel. "She's already started to move."

Several people below gasped at the name. Apparently, the younger Characters weren't the only ones who freaked out over the Snow Queen.

"Has she escaped?" asked someone I hadn't met. She wore an old-fashioned red hat (it was pretty easy to guess which Tale was hers).

"Not yet," the Director said and motioned to Rumpel to continue.

He flipped through the enormous book to a different page and read, "'The queen grew restless in her glass prison. She had waited patiently for many years, and she grew tired of pretending that she was not dangerous. She sent one of her dragons to a park much favored by the human world and waited to hear of the havoc it wreaked.'"

A sigh of relief escaped from half the audience.

From a chair carved with huge leaves and giant faces, Jack said, "If all she has done in twenty-some years of imprisonment is let loose one dragon, then we should count ourselves lucky."

Most people laughed, but not the Director, or Rumpel, or Rapunzel—or even Chase.

· "The point is that Solange shouldn't be able to do anything at all." The Director sounded so stern that all the Characters in the room became quiet again. I wondered what happened to the Snow Queen being like Napoleon—all defanged and everything. "Someone needs to go out there and make certain that her glass prison is secure."

A glass prison didn't sound very secure to me, but several members of the Canon grumbled that this was unnecessary.

The Director shook her head. "If it were anyone else, I would agree, but Solange is too dangerous."

That sneaky, self-important grown-up—she had *lied* to me. She'd hid the truth like I was a little kid that needed protecting. I *hated* it when grown-ups did that.

"Now, who will go?" asked the Director. "Jack?"

Jack shifted in his seat uncomfortably as everyone turned to look at him. I liked him even less. "Don't you have any more giants that need slaying?"

"You are the Canon's champion," the Director said firmly. "It is your duty."

Jack glanced around at all the faces watching him. "Fine, but not until after the weekend. I need to spend some time with my son."

"Your son!" said Sarah Thumb, outraged, and her husband tried to hush her. "You only remember you're a father when it's convenient for you."

I felt Chase move before I saw it. I reached forward to stop him, to keep him from giving us away, but he was already halfway through the branches before I grabbed him. His weight dragged me down with him, and I hung there in the middle of the meeting, an attic branch in one hand and Chase dangling from the other.

"Chase!" said Jack, surprised.

His weight wasn't helping me keep my grip. My heart thumped hard, and I knew I really would fall. "I'm slipping!"

"Nobody can talk about my dad like that," Chase said.

"She's, like, four inches tall, you idiot," I snapped, but I shouldn't have looked at him. The drop made me feel sick. "What are you going to do?"

"Let him go, girl," said the old man who had been sitting below us. "He's close enough to jump."

I dropped Chase. He landed lightly on both feet, glaring at everyone around him. The old man reached up and plucked me from the branch too. He was *really* bald. The only hair on his head grew on his ears. He had a wide mouth, thin lips, and eyes that bugged out a little. But he seemed friendly.

The old man set me on the floor and picked up his walking stick, which had a warty animal carved on top.

I was so grateful to be back on solid ground that I felt a little light-headed. "Oh, you're the Frog Prince."

He snorted. He also had hair in his nose. "These old bones don't feel princely anymore. The name's Henry. And who might you be?"

"Rory. I'm new."

You know when all of a sudden, a whole room gets quiet, and everyone's trying not to look at you in a weird way, and you realize that people have just been talking about you?

That happened.

It's a lot more disturbing when it happens with a bunch of important grown-ups.

My face grew hot, like always, but I found myself wondering why they would talk about a random sixth-grade Character. And why Chase was staring at me like that, eyes narrowed, arms crossed, looking kind of jealous.

For the first time in my life, I didn't think it had anything to do with my parents.

"Exactly how long have you two been up there?" the Director asked, and I knew we were in trouble.

"Chase came in right about the time we were voting on whether to tell them," said Henry, "and Rory came in when you said the vote was unanimous."

"If you knew they were up there," the Director said, exasperated, "why didn't you tell us?"

"I *did* tell you," Rapunzel said, equally exasperated. "I said, 'They hear our whispers.' Is that unclear?"

Several members of the Canon groaned. I couldn't keep myself from giggling. It looked like understanding what Rapunzel said was a common problem.

"They didn't hear much," Henry told the Director, patting my shoulder.

"We heard enough," Chase said. "What's the Tale that you don't want to tell us?"

"Shut up. Let him get us *out* of trouble," I whispered, and the Frog Prince chuckled.

The Director stared at us for a long moment until we both started to squirm uncomfortably under her gaze. Even Chase had the sense to look like he felt guilty. Visions of punishments danced in my head.

"You can't blame the children for trying to find out what concerns them as much as us," said the Frog Prince.

The Director sighed. "I suppose so. It is up to their parents to find fitting punishments."

I grinned and then tried to hide it. That didn't seem likely. There was no way I would tell my mom, and Jack gave Chase a thumbs-up. Chase grinned like he had won some sort of prize.

"I trust that you won't want to leave the same way you came in," the Director said. "The door is there."

She pointed. Chase and I ran that way before she could change her mind. The Canon began whispering before we had even left the room.

Outside, the Ivory Tower was gone, and so was the crowd. The tournament was over. I wondered who had won, and where Lena was, and what Jenny might have said to her.

The doors closed behind us with an audible click, like we were being locked out, and Chase scowled at me. "Now look what you've done. Do you have any idea how long it took me to find a good place to eavesdrop?"

"What *I've* done? *You* were the one who lost your temper." Thinking about Lena and Jenny made me mad all over again. "I wouldn't have come at all if you hadn't said that about the book."

"What book?"

"*Lena's* book," I said, furious that he could forget so quickly. "That was a dirty trick, hurting Lena to get to me. She never did anything to you."

Chase looked at me sharply. "I'll leave Lena alone if you leave my dad alone."

"I never did anything to your dad. I never even saw him before tonight."

"You made fun of him."

"I made fun of *you*," I said. "Your dad never even noticed.

You got Lena in a lot of trouble. There's a huge difference." Chase glared at me without answering, and it made me even angrier that he didn't look even a *little* sorry. "I don't care how good you are with a sword, or what Tales your dad has. You're just a dumb bully—"

Chase looked smug again. "You think I'm good with a sword?"

"You—" I stopped myself and took a deep breath. "I don't have time for you right now. Jenny's probably done talking to Lena." Before I could accidentally compliment him again, I took off running.

"Rory!" Chase called. He was really loud. A man so ugly he must have had troll blood turned to look, and three fairies with dark green wings stared as I rushed past.

The courtyard was half-deserted. The dwarf was still at the game stall, tossing the golden ball to knock down a stack of goblets. He swayed on his feet, exhausted, eyelids drooping, while the goblin counted a huge pile of the dwarf's silver.

Most of the vendors were either packing up or already gone. The elves in their tuxedos stood at the base of the roller coaster, deconstructing it with wrenches. A tall old woman with a hunchback raised a wand. Her goods—bags of herbs, bottles of potion—flew into a trunk so small that looked like it belonged in Sarah and Tom Thumb's house.

I found Lena by the lake. Torches blazed atop bronze posts along the shore. Stars were coming out over the water, and half a moon glittered in the lake's ripples. I knew we didn't have much time before we were sent home.

Lena sat on a low, flat boulder, her feet on the ground. The book was in her lap, angled toward the torch just above her head. She inspected each page carefully, her back to me, her head bent very low. Part of me got mad at Chase all over again, but mainly, I felt a lot like I did when I found my mom sitting alone in the middle of the night—helpless.

My chest tight, I touched her shoulder to let her know that I was there. There wasn't anything else I could do.

She didn't look up. Her voice was hoarse, and I knew she had been crying for a while. "He was gone by the time I came back."

"Who?" I asked.

"The dwarf who sold me this book," Lena said. "I couldn't return it."

"Oh." I wanted to do something—*anything*—to cheer her up. "Did George win the tournament?"

Lena half-laughed, and her voice had a bitter note to it. "No. Not a great day for the LaMarelles all around. George will have to find some other way to pay for college."

I cringed and bit my tongue.

"This cost a whole month's grocery money." Lena slowly turned page after page. "Jenny says she has some savings, so we won't starve. But I've never seen her so mad. It's just our grandmother at home, you know—raising us three. There isn't much money."

Lena had never talked about her family like this before. Rather than say anything else idiotic, I just sat down beside her awkwardly. I didn't know where to put my hands.

"It was a big deal. Jenny letting me pick out the Table of Plenty." The pages crackled faintly and smelled like dust. Even if it was fake, the book had to be a very *old* fake. "It was my idea to get one, and I did most of the research. But still, George said it means Jenny thinks I'm growing up."

Lena came to the last page. It had more Fey writing I couldn't understand and an illustration of a golden harp. She stared at it for a moment. "And now Jenny says that this is the most irresponsible thing I've ever done."

"It's not *that* irresponsible," I pointed out. "I mean, you bought a book. A really old book that looks like it belonged to your great-great-times-whatever grandmother. Most kids our age would buy, I don't know—video games or a lot of candy or something selfish like that."

Shaking her head slowly, Lena closed the book and stared at the faded gold cover. "Ever since I heard about Madame Benne, I've wanted to be an inventor, the same way she was. We wouldn't even *have* Tables of Plenty, if it weren't for her. Or singing harps. Or seven-league boots. Who knows what we could get if someone continued her work? When I saw this book, I thought—"

She sighed. "Well, I wanted that someone to be *me*. I thought it was destiny." A small, sad smile flickered across her face. "But really, I was being selfish. Very selfish and very stupid. And Gran, Jenny, and George all know it."

Her voice cracked on the last word. I put an arm around her shoulders.

"I should just destroy it right now." She thrust the book toward the torch, miming like she would burn it. "I can't look at it ever again."

Her gaze was on the ground, and I was looking at her face. So neither of us was paying any attention to how close the book was to the flame.

Then I heard a hiss and a crackle at the end of Lena's arm and turned.

"Lena!" I cried.

Lena glanced up. "Oh, my gumdrops."

For a second, we were too stunned to move.

The flames spread quickly. After all, it was only made of wood and paper. Before we could react, the only uncharred corner of the book was the one Lena held, her fingers just an inch from the flames.

"Don't burn yourself." I knocked the book out of her hand. It fell to the sandy ground at our feet.

The wood cover turned to glowing embers. The burning pages curled and flaked into black ash.

"I'm going to be in so much trouble," Lena murmured. "So much *more* trouble."

"It was an *accident*. I can tell them—" But I was worried too. It had to be worth *something* if it had been so expensive.

Lena took a deep shaking breath. "No, I think I need to just take my lumps at this point." She stood up and wiped her face. "I should go. No sense in letting Gran scold me for being late on top of everything else."

"Good luck," I said with as much sympathy as I could muster. Lena's grandmother was even tougher than her big sister.

She smiled. "Thanks, Rory. See you Monday."

I stood too and almost went with her. If Lena's grandmother were looking for her, Amy would probably be looking for me, too.

The charred remains of the book were at my feet.

You'll have to bury the ashes when she's gone, Rapunzel had said, hours ago. I had almost forgotten, but now goose bumps rose up on my arms.

Chase was right. It *was* kind of creepy. But, I thought, as I started kicking wet silt from the lake's edge over the last of the embers, it had to be *much* creepier for Rapunzel. There was no telling how much stuff she knew about beforehand without having any way to stop it.

omething terrible happened that weekend.

Friday night, I dreamed that I fell out of something very tall and very leafy, and I woke up with a scream still stuck in my throat. At first, I figured it was just a side effect of Chase and me falling through the attic floor, but the night after that, I dreamed the same dream again, except longer. I had time to notice that it wasn't a tree I fell from. It didn't have bark on the trunk. It was green and bumpy and covered with thin flexible spikes, like the stem of a sunflower.

The next morning, my heart still beat too fast all through breakfast. I didn't want to believe that the falling dream could become a Tale. It seemed like a nightmare, the kind where you hope to wake up before you hit the ground.

But it could still be nothing. Sarah Thumb had said that you couldn't be sure it was part of the future unless you dreamed it three times.

"Where's my favorite daughter?" Mom called from the next room.

"Here!" I flipped through the phone book. I couldn't find the LaMarelles, and I wondered if they were unlisted, or if I just wasn't spelling their last name right. I wanted to call Lena—to find out how grounded she was. I didn't look up when Mom and Amy walked into the kitchen. "And I'm your *only* daughter."

"Well, I'm glad you're here," Mom said. "I have two offers on the table, and I need your help. Where would you rather go next— Colorado or New Mexico?"

I let the pages of the phone book settle, jolted back to reality. If she was talking about leaving, then we probably only had three weeks left, just until the end of the school year.

Mom didn't notice. "I was kind of thinking Colorado, because it's going to be summer soon. But then there's the altitude, which creates a whole bunch of problems."

"I need to think about it." It was out of my mouth before I could stop it.

Mom and Amy knew what that meant, and they both turned to me—Amy, sad but sympathetic, and Mom, with horrified guilt.

I looked at the floor so I wouldn't have to look at their faces. I didn't need to think about it. I didn't want to go at all. I didn't want to leave EAS, and I *really* didn't want to leave Lena.

Mom and Amy both knew it, but we would have to move anyway.

"I'm going to do my homework," I mumbled, heading for the staircase. Even though I wanted to, I couldn't let myself do something as obvious as cry in front of them.

Halfway up the stairs, I heard Mom run after me. "Rory." She stood on the bottom step, and I couldn't miss the pleading note in her voice. "It's a chance to make a fresh start. Right?"

She wanted me to agree with her. Even a little desperately.

The thing is, you only want a chance to make a fresh start when you don't like the start you're currently working on. This wasn't *like* the other places we had moved. Wherever we went next, I would just be Maggie Wright and Eric Landon's daughter again.

I smiled at Mom a little, until she smiled back, relieved. It was easier for her when I was optimistic. It was easier for *her* to keep pretending.

But I stumbled into my room clumsily, my feet feeling unnaturally heavy. I wasn't sure how much longer I could keep up this act. I was afraid to find out what that would do to Mom.

When the dream came on Sunday night, I looked around. Above me, the clouds were close. Far below, I could see the tops of trees and people running around, looking like little squares of color moving across the grass. In the dream, I knew that we were in a hurry, but I couldn't tell if we were climbing up or down. I also knew that Lena was climbing too and that she was way ahead. I moved faster. The leaves were wet. My hand slipped. I started to fall.

I woke up that last night with my sheets drenched in sweat, and I couldn't go back to sleep. It was the only dream that I had dreamed three times.

If the dreams were trying to tell me my future, I definitely wasn't looking forward to it.

Then I remembered: It didn't matter what dreams I had anymore, or what happened in them. We were moving soon. I wouldn't be around long enough for them to come true.

I lay back down, mouth twisting strangely. I couldn't figure out if that thought made me feel better or worse.

I know I probably should have told Lena as soon as I found out, but it didn't seem like a great idea. I mean, she had enough to deal with after the Fairie Market. I didn't want to distract her with *my* problems. At least that was what I told myself when I walked to the red door on Monday. But really, I was nervous. Plenty of kids wouldn't want to hang out anymore after discovering we would only have a few more weeks together.

It was bad enough finding out that my Tale probably wouldn't start before I had to leave. I couldn't imagine losing Lena early too.

But something else was happening at EAS that day—something so big that I even forgot my moving troubles and bad dreams for a while.

The courtyard was deserted. I found everybody beside the lake. Some students had brought snacks from the Table of Never Ending Refills. They munched and looked around eagerly, like you do with popcorn at the movie theater.

It was obvious what the excitement was. A beanstalk grew by the shore.

"Whoa." I went to stand by Lena and bent my head back, straining my neck to see the top.

The beanstalk's base was about as big around as a small car. Leaves curled off the trunk every couple feet, higher and higher until it disappeared into the clouds.

"I know," Lena said. I had expected her to start talking my ear off about the approximate height of the stalk, and what species of bean, and how many leaves it had, but she just sounded tired. It must have been a really long weekend for her, too.

"How are you?" I asked.

Lena shrugged. "I got off easy. I'm only grounded for two weeks. George and I were sure that it would be a whole month." She pointed at the beanstalk, obviously changing the subject on purpose. "We don't even have to guess which Tale this is. There hasn't been a Beanstalk in thirteen years. It's kind of a big deal."

I had a sudden, horrifying thought. "Please don't tell me it's Chase's. I don't think I can handle that."

Lena looked pointedly over my right shoulder. When I turned around, there Chase was, glaring at me. Adelaide and the triplets watched him too, waiting for an answer.

"No, it's not mine," he said, irritated. "I haven't had contact with any beans. I told my dad the same thing when we found it here this morning."

"Then whose is it?" asked Adelaide.

"Nobody knows," said Lena. "We're waiting for the Director to come out and tell us."

It could be anyone's. It could even be mine. *That* would be a miracle—my Tale starting the day after I found out I had to move.

But probably not, I thought with a sigh. The beanstalk only grew after the Jacks' "fake" magic beans had been thrown away. I hadn't bought anything all weekend, not even at the Fairie Market. I didn't get a chance between the tournament and Lena's—

Lena, I thought. Lena had definitely bought something.

I examined the beanstalk's base more carefully. It grew just a few feet from the water's edge, and a small, familiar-looking boulder leaned against it.

"Hey, isn't that the same rock we were sitting on the other day?" I asked Lena, just to be sure.

She looked at me suspiciously, as if I were trying to change the subject *back*. "I think so, but the beanstalk moved it a little."

"And isn't that the spot where you burned that cookbook?"

"Coincidence," she said dismissively.

I shook my head, beginning to smile. If I couldn't have *my* Tale, at least Lena could have hers. That would definitely cheer her up. "I don't think so."

"Wait, you burned it?" Chase said, alarmed.

"So?" Lena said. "There are more Fey cookbooks."

That shut Chase up, which served him right.

"But, Lena," I said, waiting for her to connect the dots. "Magic Beans. Madame Benne's book."

Lena thought it over for a moment. Trying not to look hopeful, she said, "That's a stretch. . . ."

"Weirder Tales have happened." I grinned. "I buried the ashes. Rapunzel told me to, even before I knew you had the book."

"So, it's *your* Tale?" Kyle said. "Way to go, Lena!"

Lena ducked her head, half-grinning, and I knew she was especially glad that Kyle had been the first one to congratulate her.

Kevin sighed in satisfaction. "Our grade's first Tale, and it's the Beanstalk."

Kelly hugged Lena, and Puss-in-Dress twined around their ankles, purring. "Mom always said the sixth graders would do well," said Kelly, smiling at Lena. I laughed a little, proud of her.

Lena pressed her lips in a tight line to keep herself from smiling too much, but then Chase said, "*Lena's* the next Jack? But she's such a nerd."

Lena's face fell.

I scowled. Wasn't it enough that Chase got her in trouble on Friday? Did he really have to ruin Lena's Tale for her *too*? "Way to rain on someone's parade."

"I didn't mean it like that," Chase said impatiently. "Usually the Tales match the Character better. The Beanstalk is a really physical Tale. She could get hurt."

My hand curled into fists. "That doesn't explain why you're calling her names."

"She's smart," Chase said. "She's good at books and stuff. She would be better at a Tale that needs someone clever—Hansel and Gretel, or Puss-in-Boots, or even the Brave Little—"

"Stop arguing, you two." Puss-in-Dress licked her paw lazily. "The Director's coming out."

The Director left the violet door with gold lettering—the one that led to the library—and lifted her skirts off the grass as she crossed the courtyard.

The crowd got quiet. Lena clasped her hands together and then unclasped them to wipe her palms on her jeans. But I'm pretty sure I was even more nervous than she was. If I'd guessed wrong, I could officially be named "Worst Friend Ever" for getting Lena's hopes up.

The Director climbed on top of the boulder next to the beanstalk, and Sarah Thumb and Mr. Swallow landed on her shoulder.

"Lena LaMarelle," said the Director. I breathed a sigh of relief, glad I hadn't guessed wrong. "Congratulations. Your Tale has begun."

Lena stepped toward the podium in a daze, like she was sleep-walking.

I clapped happily, louder than all the other sixth graders put together, and when I looked around for Lena's family, I saw George whistling ten feet behind us. His left eye was a little swollen, but that was the only sign that he'd been beaten in the tournament three days before.

"I don't care if she *is* grounded." Jenny clapped too. "I'll take the blame if Gran gets mad at us for letting her go."

"I can't imagine Gran getting mad," George replied. "Aren't riches part of the Jacks' *happily ever afters*?"

Lena cleaned her glasses on her shirt self-consciously with a huge grin. No wonder she looked so happy. This was her chance to earn back all the money that she spent on the counterfeit book.

The Director waited until all the noise died down. "Since it is a questing Tale, you may choose two Companions for your journey. Do you accept this privilege?"

I had completely forgotten about Companions. George popped into my head, a perfect choice for this tale, but then Lena said, "Rory Landon."

A silly smile just like Lena's grew on my face, and I couldn't make it go away. Someone patted me on the back. The crowd parted in front of me. I hurried to go stand beside Lena, trying to remember everything I had ever read about giants.

Since everyone's attention was on Lena, I didn't even blush. Standing up there with her felt right. Maybe I wasn't going to get to have my own Tale before I had to move, but helping Lena with hers was the next best thing. It would be—

It would be selfish. My stomach twisted, the same way it did when I lied to Mom. It *was* kind of like lying. Lena didn't know I was moving. She hadn't seen the way I froze up when I was scared. She wouldn't have asked me if she knew. Seeing Kevin and Conner watching jealously and George giving me a thumbs-up, I squirmed, but I tried to shake it off.

I won't freeze, I told myself. I had been training. And if Lena and I couldn't spend much more time together, I just had to make sure that I didn't mess up. I could do that.

I could definitely be the best Companion EAS had ever seen.

"You can choose one more," the Director told Lena.

It would be nice, though, if Lena could find a second Companion who actually knew what they were doing.

Slowly Lena looked over the crowd. From this angle, you could see everyone draw in their breath and hold it. Even Adelaide, who was the *last* person I could imagine confronting a giant.

Lena might still pick George. Or possibly Kyle, which might be awkward, since I would probably be demoted to Third Wheel status. But maybe she would pick Jenny. Then the Tale would almost be like a sleepover every night, except with man-eating giants and a really big house.

"Chase Turnleaf," said Lena firmly.

I stared, not sure I had heard her right. It didn't register on Chase's face at first. Then one of the triplets congratulated him, and a surprised, delighted smile began.

"No, not Chase!" I said before I could stop myself.

"Thanks," Chase said sarcastically, coming to stand on Lena's other side.

"Rory, you really don't get a say," Sarah Thumb hissed. "It's *Lena's* Tale."

"He just called you a nerd," I reminded Lena and shot a glare over her shoulder at Chase.

"He had a point." Lena pushed her thick glasses farther up on her nose with a small shrug. "This is a dangerous Tale, and he's one of the best swordsmen in all of EAS. And because of his dad, he knows more about fighting giants than anybody. We need him."

"Thanks," Chase said again, very softly, and this time, it sounded like he actually meant it.

I bit my tongue. Lena was too nice for her own good, but I didn't *trust* Chase. He might try to take over Lena's Tale. I would have to keep an eye on him for her.

The Director gave all three of us a stern look. Obviously, she wasn't used to the students having conversations in the middle of her ceremonies. Lena gave her an apologetic smile, and the Director said, "Rory Landon and Chase Turnleaf, do you consent to undertake this journey with Lena? To advise and protect her to the best of your ability?"

"We do," Chase and I said.

"Very well," said the Director. "Please proceed to the library. Rumpelstiltskin has some research to share with you."

The crowd stepped back, clearing a path to the library door. I noticed many disappointed faces, especially among the older students, way more disappointed than people had been when Evan Garrison left on *his* quest. A new Jack was a *much* bigger deal than the White Snake. Following Lena and Chase past the violet door, I felt even more grateful to be going.

In the hallway leading to the library, the other two stopped so abruptly that I nearly ran into Lena. Then I saw why. Rapunzel stood in front of the library door, clearly waiting for us. From the looks on Lena's and Chase's faces, I guessed her visit wasn't normally part of the New Tale routine.

"There is before, and there is afterward," Rapunzel explained, pulling her long silver braid over her shoulder. Her face was blank and unreadable, which made her seem a little more creepy than usual. "This is before. Everything will change."

Chase had a look on his face that plainly said, *How long until the crazy lady lets us go?* Lena glanced past Rapunzel at the library door, way more interested in what Rumpel had to say.

But Rapunzel *was* the one who had told me to bury the ashes. She probably knew something we didn't.

Like she was reading my mind, Rapunzel looked straight at me and said, "Fear is inevitable."

I looked back at her guiltily, sure that she knew that I froze up at the first sign of danger. I thought that she would suggest that Lena pick someone besides me, but she only smiled. "But for every fear that makes you weak, there is a fear that can make you brave. If you are to succeed, you must discover what you fear more than what you fear the most."

That last part obviously didn't make any sense, but I nodded politely.

To Lena, Rapunzel added, "You are too young to know regret. Take the time you need, and do not leave anything undone that you wish to do. It will haunt you for many years."

Then Rapunzel looked at Chase. "Disappointment is terrible, but you shall see more clearly afterward. Do not be too hard on your father. He can't help that he foolishly values all the wrong things."

Chase scowled, but besides that, he behaved himself. Even he knew better than to talk back to the oldest Character in the Canon.

When she realized that Rapunzel wasn't going to say anything else, Lena thanked her and hurried to open the library door.

At the far end of the room, Rumpelstiltskin waited for us at the library's table. The stack of books next to him was nearly as tall as he was.

Chase and Lena rushed in. I was the only one who saw Rapunzel's worried frown. It made her look even younger, a bit like she was pouting. She watched me as I passed, which made me feel so awkward that I dropped my eyes to the floor and scurried into the library as quickly as I could.

"You'll have to remember, Rory," she said softly as she closed the door behind me. "They will not."

This was obviously weird even among the weird, but since Rumpel started talking, I didn't have time to dwell.

"Lena, my dear, congratulations!" Rumpel's smile made all the wrinkles on his face more visible. I wondered how old he actually was. "I really am quite happy for you."

"Rumpy hates kids," Chase whispered to me, "but he likes her. That means she has to be *really* good at books."

I didn't dignify this with an answer. He was just trying to justify calling Lena a nerd.

"Now, the Beanstalk has a long, impressive history," Rumpel continued. "Rather than bore you with all of it, since you children have terrible attention spans,"—Chase looked at me smugly, as if this proved his point—"I've pulled out every occurrence of Jack and the Beanstalk in the last three decades. There are some situations that you should be aware of. Oh, Lena. You're always so prepared, bless you."

Lena, who had produced a small notepad and pencil from somewhere, smiled.

"All of them occurred in a span of only four days, from the instant the Jack went up the beanstalk to the instant the beanstalk came down. Your father set a precedent," Rumpel told Chase, who smiled. Lena took notes. "We have no way of knowing where this beanstalk will take you to up in Catanage, but as you know, time can become . . ."—he searched for a word—"strange up there. You'll need to take that with you." The dwarf pointed to a small hourglass on the corner of the table. "Turn it right before climbing, and refer to it often. Each line etched on the glass represents the passage of one day. When all the sand runs out, four days have gone by."

Lena picked up the hourglass reverentially.

"I trust you know what will happen if you exceed the time limit and thus deviate from the Tales before you," Rumpel said, and Lena nodded, her mouth set in a determined line.

I started to ask what would happen, especially since the Tale already seemed different from the traditional one, but Rumpel obviously wasn't ready for questions.

"The Tale itself is pretty straightforward," said the dwarf. "You'll need to gain entry to the giant's home and convince his wife to hide you. I would recommend not using your real names when you introduce yourself. Then find a means to enter and exit the house undetected. You will have to enter the house at least three times to gather all the items. After supper, the giant will count his coins before he falls asleep. To make sure the giant stays asleep, many Jacks have used slumberwort. You must steal the coins before retreating to a safe distance to make camp for the night. Each of you will have a carryall pack, so transporting these objects should be no trouble. Did you get all that?"

Lena scribbled furiously. Over her shoulder, I read, "Carryall x 3." Then she flipped the page and looked up, pencil poised.

The dwarf smiled proudly. "On the second day, you'll repeat the process in order to steal the hen who lays golden eggs. You'll need to figure out a way to make sure it stays quiet. A word of advice: if you decide to duct-tape the beak closed, make sure you don't cover its nostrils. We've lost more hens that way."

Chase snickered.

Rumpel ignored him. "On the third day, go back to steal the singing harp. Then you'll need to climb down as quick as you can and chop down the beanstalk. Simple enough. Any questions?"

Lena dotted an *i* with relish and flipped another page. "Yes. How many pounds of slumberwort would we need to knock out a giant?"

"Very good, Lena," said the dwarf. "At least three pounds. Possibly five. Giants vary in size as much as any species. Ellie will give you some if you ask her."

"What about the beanstalk?" I asked. "I thought it was supposed to grow overnight. Why did it take a whole weekend?"

"That doesn't matter. The beanstalk has never grown out of a book before either. A carton of ice cream once, and a crashed car another time." Rumpel sounded so impatient that I kind of wished that I hadn't asked. "You're getting caught up in the details. The previous versions are more like guidelines. Be prepared for the unexpected. In the last Beanstalk Tale, the Jack found a golden Walkman instead of a harp."

"So we should be looking for a golden iPod?" I said incredulously.

"Would that be human- or giant-size?" Lena said, pencil hovering.

"My dear, if I knew what you would find, I would have told you," the dwarf said. "There is only so much the book tells us at the beginning of a Tale."

That made me wish that Rapunzel had come into the library. She seemed to know more than she could tell us.

"I have a question," Chase said. "Have there been any Failed Tales in the history of Jack and the Beanstalk?"

I saw "Lena LaMarelle" carved in bubble letters on the Wall again, but I pushed the image to the very back of my mind. I wouldn't let that happen. That was my first responsibility as her Companion.

"None recently," said the dwarf dismissively, "but there was one casualty. About fifteen years ago, when the Jack took four and a half days, the giant caught one of the Companions. Cooked the boy in a . . . let me see . . ." Rumpel put on his glasses and skimmed the orange book open beside him. "Human pot pie."

I gulped.

Lena took a few more notes, and Chase peered over her shoulder. "'Don't let giants eat anyone,'" he read. "I don't think you actually need to write that down." It might have been the very first time in my life that I agreed with Chase.

"Ah," said the dwarf, "here's Ellie with the packs. Now you can all leave my library. Good luck to you, Lena."

The carryalls that Ellie had brought looked just like normal backpacks, maybe a little small and old-fashioned, and all the same shade of faded green. When Ellie helped us into them, it didn't feel any heavier than mine did when I packed all my math and social studies textbooks.

"You've got sleeping bags in here, plenty of food for five days. Water, toothpaste, and toothbrushes—the usual," Ellie said as she led us back to the courtyard. "You have the hourglass, Lena?"

Lena nodded, showing it to her. "Slumberwort?"

Ellie smiled. "Come this way." She knocked on the wall seven times, and a white door appeared under her fist. "Every Tale is allowed to pick one item from the storeroom, but the Director won't let us give it to you unless you ask for it. Doesn't want us to be accused of playing favorites," she said as she and Lena disappeared inside.

Chase reached into a steel-studded trunk against the wall and pulled out his sword belt, slinging it around his waist easily.

I saw mine in there too. It was even heavier than I remembered, and when I buckled it on, my sore muscles protested. Chase watched me, looking like he was going to say something.

"What?" I said defensively.

"Nothing," Chase said, too quickly.

"No, really—what were you going to say?" If he was going to remind me how much I sucked, I was going to remind him what a bad idea it would be to go without any weapon at all.

"Rory, please." Lena emerged from the storeroom, rezipping her pack, and I bit my tongue. "This is going to be a long trip," Lena told Ellie, digging through the chest for her own sword.

"Chase, I'm sure your dad will be disappointed that he left so early this morning," Ellie said with a knowing look in her eye. "He wouldn't want to miss this."

"Will you tell him for me?" Chase asked eagerly.

"My mom. Amy." I'd completely forgotten about them. "They'll worry—"

Ellie smiled kindly. "We *have* handled parents before."

Privately, I wondered if she had met a parent as overprotective as Mom. Ellie was completely underestimating the level of freak-out that would happen if I didn't show when Amy came to pick me up. I tried to estimate how much trouble I would be in when I got home, but the more rebellious side of me—the same side of me that had hung up on Dad the week before—didn't care much. I didn't even care that I would have to explain everything as soon as I got back. Mom would make me move anyway. *She* was the reason I wouldn't be able to stick around long enough to have my own Tale. *Let Mom worry,* I thought stubbornly as we followed Ellie down the hall. I would face the consequences later—*after* I had my adventure.

"Have a *big* time, kids." Ellie opened the door, laughing a little. "This is one small step for Lena, and one *giant* leap for sixth grade–kind."

Lena and I winced, but Chase said, "That was nothing. She was holding herself back."

Once we stepped outside, every head in the courtyard turned our way, and it grew so still that you could hear the waves lapping the lakeshore and the leaves rustling in the Tree of Hope. Suddenly, it felt very formal and very serious. I looked at the grass, feeling my face heat up, and placed my steps carefully. I promised myself that I wouldn't trip and embarrass Lena before we even left EAS.

Someone had moved the podium across the courtyard to a spot just beside the beanstalk. The Director stood behind it, Mr. Swallow and Sarah Thumb still perched on her shoulder. Rapunzel and the

Frog Prince had joined them. I wondered if Rapunzel had forgotten to tell us something.

When we stopped in front of the podium, the Director looked at us for a long moment. I'm pretty sure she did this for dramatic effect.

"Lena, Rory, and Chase," she said finally, "the time has come for you to venture out into the Fey realm to complete Lena's Tale. We wish you luck, courage, and cunning on your journey." She gestured at the beanstalk. "Lena, you may proceed."

Lena stepped hesitantly up to the base of the beanstalk. She took a second to turn the hourglass attached to her backpack, and then she started to climb.

Climb, I realized with a sick jolt. How could I have forgotten that part of the Tale?

"Go, Lena! We love you!" Jenny called, and when Lena looked down to wave, George whistled.

She climbed ten feet, twenty feet, fifty. Nausea made me sway woozily, and my palms started to sweat. I was going to have to climb soon too.

"I was wondering when you were going to realize how high up we were going," Chase told me. "Don't think about the height. Think about the next branch, and *don't* look down," he added with a cocky little smile.

I glared at him as he ran to the beanstalk and started to climb, faster than Lena was going, like it was a race. "Show-off," I muttered.

"So little." The Frog Prince patted my head, and knowing that my turn was next, I just looked up, numb with dread. "So determined."

I didn't *feel* determined. I felt like backing out. All my plans for being the best Companion ever wouldn't mean anything if I was too scared to even climb the beanstalk.

"Henry, *please*," said the Director, exasperated like she'd expected something like this. "I'll make you go stand with the students."

There were too many reasons for me *not* to go: Lena wouldn't have invited me if she knew I was moving. Mom would worry like crazy. I was afraid of heights.

"But don't you think they get younger every year?" The Frog Prince leaned on his cane until he blocked me from the Director's sight, and Rapunzel stepped closer to me. With one eye on the beanstalk, I distantly suspected that I was watching a diversion. "I do. She's such a wee one, that Rory—has so much responsibility already."

In fact, I only had one reason for going: I wanted to get to do something before I had to leave all this behind. That wasn't good enough.

I glanced toward Lena's brother, a second away from slinging off my backpack and sending him in my place.

"*You* must go," whispered Rapunzel, emphasizing the first word so much that she must've known what I was planning.

I stopped looking for George. To be completely honest, I was really relieved she said something. I wanted to go too much to be that noble.

"That's it," the Director said impatiently. "Henry, I must ask you to leave the podium."

Scowling and muttering to himself about how Mildred Grubb had no respect for the elderly, the Frog Prince hobbled pathetically away, making a big show of it. He also moved *very slowly*, his patched and frayed purple bunny slippers shuffling along the ground.

"Be kinder to Chase," Rapunzel said so quietly that only I could hear. "His heart is good, but his upbringing was not the best. In truth, he needs your friendship even more than Lena."

I didn't *want* to be friends with Chase. If that was the future Rapunzel saw, she was losing her touch.

"You'll need to follow him through the letter," Rapunzel added.

"You mean, *to* the letter?" I was definitely not going to do that.

Rapunzel shook her head. "*Through* the letter."

That didn't make any more sense than what she had said before.

Sighing, I started toward the beanstalk. If I was going, I needed to hurry. I didn't want to find out what Chase would say if he got too much of a head start and I arrived hours behind the others.

As I walked past, Rapunzel grabbed my pack and stuffed something inside. "You'll need this. The young will lie in the dark. Hold this to your mouth and whistle softly, and it will give you light."

The Director had noticed. From the suspicious look on her face, I guessed that Rapunzel was definitely acting out of character for this Tale. "Okay," I said uncertainly as Rapunzel zipped my pack closed and let me go. "Thanks."

The leaves on the beanstalk were as long as I was tall, and the stems at the bottom were rubbery but sturdy. I took a deep breath and grabbed one right above my head.

"Rory!"

I looked back.

"Falling is the fastest way down," Rapunzel said earnestly, like this was helpful information.

I gulped. I didn't need to hear that.

Apparently, the Director thought so too. Alarmed, she added

quickly, "However, we would much prefer you to return with all your bones intact. Good luck, Rory."

I was only one foot off the ground. I stared up at the spot where the beanstalk disappeared into the clouds, guessing I had at least a mile to go.

I tried not to think about it and began to climb.

I thought I did pretty well—for the first part of the climb anyway.

After a few minutes, I found a rhythm: I reached up for a leaf above me, stepped on the next stem, and stood up straight before I reached up again.

It was manageable, as long as I only let my mind focus on certain things—like where the next leaf was, for example, or how helpful all the tiny spikes on the stems were. They made getting a good grip much easier despite my sweaty palms.

Then, just over halfway up, my foot slipped. Both hands grabbed the next leaf, and I caught myself easily. So, that part wasn't so bad.

But then I automatically looked down to reposition my foot and saw how far we had come.

The Tree of Hope was just a small green circle, barely bigger than my thumbnail. The square EAS building looked a lot like a grass-colored napkin with a gray border. Speckles of color moved across the lawn. *People*, I realized with a start.

I had seen this view before. I had dreamed this. *Three* times. I really *would* slip. My stomach turned over inside me, weightless suddenly, as if I were already falling.

I didn't *exactly* freeze.

I leaped at the beanstalk's stem and wrapped both arms and both legs around it.

Fear is inevitable. I hadn't known Rapunzel meant my thing with heights.

It wasn't like that time in the weapons closet. I couldn't make myself move, but instead of going blank, my mind buzzed.

I tried to tell myself that there were plenty of things that scared me more than falling. Looking like an idiot in front of everybody in EAS, for instance. Or giving Chase the opportunity to make fun of me later. Or letting Lena down, because I was too afraid to climb a measly Beanstalk.

Unfortunately, none of this made me start climbing again.

I shouldn't have listened to Rapunzel. I should have sent George up the beanstalk in my place.

For a while, the only thing I heard was the blood pounding in my ears. I refused to fall. I wasn't going to die here, not on Lena's first Tale, not before we had even gotten to the giant's house.

I clutched the stem so tightly that my fingernails dug through the surface, and I tried not to remember what it felt like, falling in my dream, with the wind ripping my breath away and my scream trapped in my throat and my hands groping at empty—

"You're not going to fall, Rory."

It was Chase. His voice was only a few feet away. I breathed again. I hadn't noticed until right that second that I had been holding my breath.

"Look at me," Chase said. Slowly, I raised my head. He squatted on the leaf a little above and beside me, his limbs sprawled out carelessly. He leaned closer, just one hand holding the stem above him. "You're not going to fall, but we have to keep moving. Lena's got someplace to be."

I nodded stubbornly. I knew *that*.

"Come on, then." Chase started to climb again, and in two seconds, he was out of sight.

I tried to follow. I stared at my arm, telling it to move. It didn't want to let go. The most it did was twitch a little.

"Rory." Chase was back. He stepped on the same leaf I was sitting on. It dipped wildly. I clawed at the stem, scraping some of the bristles away. A little whimper escaped, and I hated myself for it. I waited for Chase to tease me.

"Rory, you're not going to fall. I promise. You know how I know? 'Cause I'm going to climb right under you. If you slip again, I'll catch you."

I wasn't so sure that would help. Chase wasn't much bigger than I was. I would probably just drag him down with me.

"But you know what? It wouldn't matter if we both fell. I overheard the Director and Ellie talking. They sent the magic carpet out. It's scouting around the stalk, just out of sight. The Director wouldn't let us be in any *real* danger."

Chase leaned forward so that his face was right beside mine. The leaf wobbled under us again, but I forced myself to turn, to look at him.

"Do you believe me?"

I did. He sounded so confident. He always did. Most of the time, it annoyed me, but at that moment, when I was twenty times higher off the ground than I had ever been in my life, his cockiness reassured me.

"Yeah." My voice came out like a croak.

"Good. Now we're going to start climbing." My breath came in noisy gasps, but Chase ignored it. "I know you can do it. I'm going to do it with you. Ready? See the leaf a foot above your left hand?

On the count of three, you're going to reach up and grab the stem. One . . . two . . . three!"

I was still numb with terror, but my hand moved. It held the stem so tightly that I watched my knuckles turn white.

"Perfect." Chase patted my shoulder. "Now you're going to stand up. That's it."

My legs had straightened of their own accord. Standing, I could feel how much I was shaking. The leaf shivered under my feet.

"Right hand now. To the stem at two o'clock. See it? Good . . ."

That was how we got up the beanstalk. Chase never stopped talking. We climbed slowly, but we went up.

When we were almost to the clouds, so high that dew collected on the leaves, making the stems wet, I slipped one more time.

The weightless feeling entered my stomach again, but Chase's hands were on my back, shoving me upward.

"It's fine. Don't worry. I got you." He grunted a little. Realizing how heavy I must be, I yanked myself upright before he could drop us both. "All right. We're almost there. Three more minutes. You can handle three more minutes. Look, you can already see Lena. She's waiting at the top."

I *could* see Lena. Her dark face peered down at us through a hole in the clouds. Her lips were pressed flat, like they only do when she's really worried.

I hated making her worry. I grabbed the next stem, stepped, and stood slowly, trying not to meet her eyes.

It felt like a lot longer than three minutes, but we made it. As soon as I was close enough, Lena grabbed both my arms and hauled me up.

We tumbled together on a lawn even greener than the court-yard we had just left. I collapsed, so relieved, I could cry.

"Why didn't you tell me that you were afraid of heights?" she asked.

I couldn't answer. I was still breathing too hard. The blades of grass around me were as tall as I was and as wide as my hand.

"Oh, Rory—you're *shaking*," Lena said, still worried, which made me feel even worse. It hadn't taken long for my plan to be the best Companion ever to completely fall apart. Maybe it was a good thing that I wouldn't be around long enough to have my own Tale.

Chase jumped through the hole in the clouds. His hair was a little windblown, but otherwise, he looked just like he always did. Cocky. But he had been so cool on the beanstalk.

"I'm okay." I stood up, my legs feeling rubbery after the strain. My clothes were sticky with sweat, which was so far from being ladylike that it was gross.

Chase brushed a few of the stalk's bristles off his jeans. "Let's go. We've lost a lot of time."

"Maybe we should take a break," Lena said doubtfully, glancing at me.

"We're on a time crunch, Lena," Chase said impatiently. "We can't afford to let *her* slow us down anymore."

I scowled, hot with shame. I still couldn't really feel my legs, but I walked forward anyway, pushing stalks out of my way, determined not to hold the other two back any more than I already had. I was also determined not to let them see how close I was to crying. Or that my hands were still trembling.

I knew what Chase was like, or at least, I thought I did. But on the beanstalk, he had been like a different person, the kind of person I might want to be friends with. Seeing him revert to his old self—well, I was the teeniest, *tiniest* bit hurt. And there was no way I would ever admit that to him.

"Rory buried the ashes," Lena reminded him icily. "Without her, we might not even *have* a beanstalk."

That *did* make me feel a little better. After all, climbing the beanstalk was only *part* of the Tale. I could help out plenty of other ways.

"Just don't freeze up again on the way down," Chase replied. "I won't wait around for the giant to catch us both."

He was right. We had to go down. My dream could still come true after all.

I pushed the thought away. That was days from now. We had to concentrate on the other stuff first.

"You know, I *was* thinking about thanking you, Chase." I shoved my hands in my pockets and tramped off farther ahead. My voice was still a little shaky, so I cleared my throat. "But you just ruined it."

"Well, if you're already mad at me . . ." Chase snatched my sword from its sheath at my waist.

"Hey!" I tried to grab it back, but he scampered just out of reach. "What are you doing?"

"Making sure it's battle-ready." He turned the sword over, hilt over blade, three times, and murmured a few words I couldn't quite catch.

"What?" Lena said.

"Nothing." Chase handed the sword back to me.

For the first time since Yellowstone, I didn't struggle to raise the sword. "What did you do? Why is it so much lighter?"

Chase shrugged, but he wouldn't meet my eyes. "I just took the training wheels off."

"Oh, my gumdrops. It's one of *those* swords?" Lena said.

Chase just wove his way through the grass stalks ahead of us.

"What swords?" I asked, sheathing mine.

"Some of the oldest Fey blades have spells built into them," Lena explained. "Even most humans can activate them as easily as flipping a switch on a flashlight. One of the more popular spells triples the weight of the blade. It's supposed to build up the wielder's strength."

"Couldn't you have taken the spell off *before* the climb?" I asked Chase. "It was hard enough."

"Not without the Director finding out what he'd done," Lena pointed out.

"You should be thanking me," Chase said. "I bet your right arm's a lot stronger than it was a few weeks ago."

I glared at him, jaw clenched, but honestly, I was secretly grateful to have something to be mad about. I didn't really owe him anything. Apparently, I'd needed a reminder why Chase and I could never be friends.

"Found something." Chase held back a blade of grass so that Lena and I could pass.

Beyond him, the lawn ended, and the ground ahead was paved with slabs of slate the size of Ping-Pong tables. And beyond that, water glittered in the afternoon light.

"A lake?" I said.

"Doubtful," Chase said. "See the tiles on the opposite side?"

Lena nodded. "And it smells like chlorine."

Once she pointed it out, the chemicals in the air smelled so strong that I started to feel a little woozy. "A swimming pool? Just how big are these guys anyway?"

"It varies from Tale to Tale." Lena shrugged, but she sounded a little nervous.

"I'm guessing they're about four stories tall. There's their house," Chase said.

It looked surprisingly normal—brick with light blue shutters in every window. There was only one weird thing about it, actually.

"I've seen smaller mountains," I muttered. I also spotted a green house-shaped blur very far away, and a smaller yellow blob beyond that, sitting like lone peaks in the distance. "Are you sure this is the right place?" I really hoped that the answer was yes. It would take us *hours* to walk to the next house.

"It's always the building closest to the beanstalk." Lena squared her shoulders and strode forward, so determined to be the fearless leader that I had to hide a smile. "We're going to need to find a place to stash our packs."

"Those geraniums should work." I pointed to the bushes on either side of the front door, hoping I could be helpful.

"Yeah." Chase rolled his eyes like this was completely obvious. "They're big enough to hide my dad's truck."

We hid the backpacks and started for the door. There was only one step, but it was taller than me.

Chase leaped up and offered a hand to Lena.

Lena let him pull her up. "We need to get inside, keep the giant's wife from getting suspicious, and find a way in and out of the house."

"Got it." Chase extended a hand to me.

I ignored it coldly and scrambled up by myself. I scraped my knee on the brick, but at least I didn't accept any more help from Chase.

"Now we just need to knock," I said, dusting off my hands.

Chase took a long length of climbing rope off his shoulder. A three-pronged hook swung off one end.

"What's that?" I asked suspiciously.

"Dad calls it Jack Attack," Chase said.

"Your dad named a grappling hook after himself?" This was perilously close to making fun of Jack, but even Chase had to realize how ridiculous that was.

Chase didn't answer, which made me suspect he knew. He swung the rope in slow circles, like it was a lasso.

"What are you doing?" Now even Lena seemed a little suspicious.

"Earning my keep." Chase released the rope, and the metal clunked against the wood about halfway up. He whirled the rope and released it again.

"Well, that's one way to knock," Lena said, impressed in spite of herself.

"That's how Dad always does it." Chase coiled the rope carefully. "You know, seeing as I'm the only one here who has any experience in this Tale, maybe I should do all the talking."

I gave him a dirty look. I knew he would pull something like this. He was trying to steal Lena's Tale. Good thing Lena was way too smart to fall for—

"Fine," Lena said.

"What?" I said sharply.

"And you two might want to step back a little." Chase slung the coiled rope over his shoulder. "We wouldn't want the giant's wife to think that we were trying to ambush her."

"We're less than a tenth of her size. It would be like three mice coming at us," I said, but Lena just dragged me to the side, a little behind a pot as big as my classroom, with Amy-size pansies. "Lena, it's *your* Tale."

"*Shhhhh!*" Lena hissed. "Someone's coming."

Someone *was* coming. Huge steps thumped closer and louder from inside. Then the door swung open with a squeal like a car with bad brakes.

"Yes?" boomed a voice. Lena's fingernails dug into my forearm, and my heart banged around behind my ribs.

With the huge clay pot in the way, the only part of the giant's wife I could see was the bottom of her white apron and the leather sandals on her feet. Her toenails were painted red.

"Mistress Giant, I have heard that you are kind to travelers, but I had not heard of your radiant beauty," Chase said loudly.

I rolled my eyes. He was certainly laying it on a little thick.

He gave the giant's wife a sad smile, barely big enough to show his dimples. "My Companions and I are on a quest. We no longer have our packs, and I'm afraid that we'll run out of food. We would gladly trade a crust of bread for a day's work around the house."

"No," the giant's wife said, a little uncertainly. "No, I don't think so. Thank you anyway."

"Just a few crumbs?" Chase looked astounded that his flattery hadn't worked.

"Try up the road. The yellow house," said the giant's wife. The door began to close. Lena looked about as panicked as she had when she realized the Fey cookbook caught on fire.

We couldn't Fail *now*, not before we even got *inside*.

I ran out. Lena flailed a little, trying to catch me before I got far.

"Wait!!" I waved my arms to get the giantess's attention.

"Oh, little girls!" said the giant's wife in an entirely different tone, spotting me and Lena. She knelt so quickly that the calico fabric of her dress blurred. Her face was as big as a set of French doors, but except for the fact that her teeth were too big and pointed, her smile seemed kind. "I've never had little girls come to the door before. Just little boys, and I've had *such* trouble with *them*."

I smiled back. Maybe I wasn't such a terrible Companion after all. At least when climbing wasn't involved.

"Nice to meet you, Mistress Giant," I said and held out my hand.

The giant's wife laughed a little and gave me her index finger to shake. It was covered in flour, which rose in a cloud around my head. I coughed a little.

"My name is Lily. This is my friend, Rachel. And that's Chip," Lena added in an apologetic tone, pointing at Chase. "He likes to talk a lot. I'm sorry if he insulted you."

Chase gave an angry little snort, but other than that, he kept his mouth shut.

"Wonderful to meet you, Lily, Rachel, and Chip," said the giant's wife warmly. "I suppose I *have* to let you help now. My mother-in-law is coming this evening, and I'm terribly behind on dinner." She laid her hand, palm up, on the ground. Lena stepped on it in her fearless leader mode. I tried not to think about heights and followed, grabbing on to a finger to keep my balance. "Besides, I've always wanted little girls in the house. But Jimmy—that's my husband—just keeps eating them. He says they taste like sugar. And sometimes cinnamon."

Lena and I exchanged a nervous look. Then the giant's wife stood up about five times faster than elevators move. Making a break for it was no longer an option.

"I'm told that I taste like brussels sprouts," I said shakily, clinging to the giantess's ring finger.

"Earwax," Lena said, pointing to herself.

The giant's wife laughed again. This close, it sounded a little like thunder. "Don't worry. *I* don't eat humans." Lena and I let out tiny relieved sighs, but then the giantess added, "They give me *terrible* indigestion."

The giantess headed down a hall about as long as an airport runway. Car-size frames hung on the walls, and each photo showed

Shelby Bach

the giantess smiling with a man with dark green skin.

"Hey!" Chase said from the front step. "What about me?"

"I guess you better come in too," the giantess said without turning around. "Close the door behind you."

Chase stepped slowly over the threshold and looked up at the door in horror. It was at least fifteen times as big as he was. Served him right for trying to take over Lena's Tale.

The giant's wife told us to call her Matilda, and she put us to work.

"You, boy," she said when Chase came in after closing the front door. I had the feeling that she didn't like Chase much and wanted him out of the way. I warmed to her a little. "Sweep out under the fridge."

Chase looked shocked. This was obviously the first time a giant had actually taken him up on working for a meal.

"I'm sure there's dust and crumbs and who knows what else under there," Matilda told me and Lena conversationally, "and I've been meaning to do it for years."

I could see why she hadn't gotten around to it. "The fridge is as big as a hotel," I whispered to Lena. Even a giant would have a hard time moving it.

Matilda gave Chase a small black-bristled brush.

"Terrier," Lena said, pointing at the brush, and when Chase took it, it seemed about that size.

"Yes, ma'am." With a sigh, Chase scurried toward the crack between the fridge and the floor.

Chores seemed easy compared to getting up the beanstalk and inside the house. It almost felt like the hardest part of the Tale was over. Finding the gold, hen, and harp would be a cinch.

Lena and I helped Matilda cook. Our first task was to stand in the sink and pull the silk off the oversize corncobs. We discovered pretty quickly that Matilda liked to talk.

"It's just *so* lucky that you girls showed up. I don't normally need the help, but—" Matilda bit her lip.

"Her front teeth are the size of cookie sheets," Lena whispered to me. It wasn't exactly a cheery observation.

"Well, I don't like to criticize," Matilda said, "but my mother-in-law is so *particular*. I've been dreading this visit for months now. Last time she stayed with us, I fixed whale for dinner, and she complained because she had to pick the bones out of her teeth."

I yanked a bunch of silk strands off the corn. "Jump rope," I said, holding them out to Lena, and she nodded. I tried to imagine it getting stuck in my teeth. Then I tried to imagine being big enough to get it stuck in my teeth. This was probably how Sarah Thumb felt all the time.

"What will you serve tonight?" Lena asked Matilda.

"Do we *really* want to know?" I whispered, alarmed.

"It's important to be friendly," Lena whispered back.

"Condors," Matilda said, chopping a potato the size of my mom's Jeep. "I had to get such a lot of them, but she said she prefers white meat. They're already in the oven so I don't need to worry about them."

"Where's your husband now?" I asked, determined to steer the conversation away from dinner. "She's his mother. He should be helping you."

"Help cook? Jimmy?" Matilda laughed thunderously again. "You humans have such silly ideas. No, he's at work."

"What does he do?" I said, relieved. Work was a much safer subject than dinner.

"Oh, transport," Matilda said airily. "He owes a fairy fifty years of labor. Only thirty-one years to go—nearly thirty. Rachel—"

Lena nudged me, and I remembered that Rachel was supposed to be me. "Yes, ma'am?"

"Would you mind getting the rosemary from the spice cabinet? I want to put some in the potatoes."

"Lena, do I need to look for the wine?" I whispered. When she gave me a strange look, I added, "For the slumberwort."

"I decided against the slumberwort," Lena whispered back.

"Oh." I wondered if she had another plan. Or if we would end up tiptoeing past a snoring giant, only to see an enormous eye crack open. . . .

Oh, well. It was Lena's Tale.

"Sure!" I told Matilda, and the giant's wife put her hand in the sink and offered her palm to me. I clung to her thumb and pretended I was only two feet away from the ground until she deposited me gently in the open cabinet above her.

"Thank you, dear. When I look, I always end up pulling half the spices out."

I walked among the bottles, skimming labels. With a shudder, I sidestepped a barbeque rub that claimed to be good for condor, turkey, human, and eggplant.

"I'm just glad that I only have to fix *two* meals for her—dinner tonight and breakfast tomorrow morning," said Matilda. "The hotel will take care of the rest."

"Oh?" Lena said innocently. "You're going out of town?"

I spotted the rosemary on the back of the shelf. This Tale would be a piece of cake.

"Just for a couple days. We're taking my mother-in-law skiing in the Arctic Circle—for her 650th birthday."

The spice bottle was almost as tall as I was, and I had to shove my shoulder against the glass to shift it.

Matilda noticed. "Oh, you found it! Wonderful!" She reached into the cabinet and grabbed me and the rosemary at the same time, pinning my back against the bottle. My feet dangled over empty space, and overcome with dizziness, I wondered if Matilda would still use the rosemary if I threw up on it.

"Maybe I should go help Cha-Chip," I said, correcting myself just in time. "It's kind of a big job for one person. One person *our* size anyway."

Lena shot me a pained look that clearly said she resented being abandoned, but I couldn't help it. If I was going to be any help, I needed to spend some quality time on solid ground.

"Suit yourself." Matilda set me down on the floor gently.

I took a second to steady myself on wobbly knees. "I'll let you know when we've finished."

The fridge sat just low enough that I had to duck my head as I went, so I almost ran into Chase before I saw him. He leaned on the brush, arms crossed. I was annoyed before he even said anything.

"You haven't done any work at all!" My hands were still sticky with the residue from the corn silk.

Chase scowled. "Wow, you're really determined not to like me." I wanted to say that this wasn't true, that *he* was the difficult one, but then he continued, "I already finished. I'll prove it."

He hopped off the brush and walked to the back wall. "She didn't give me a dustpan, so I just pushed it through this mousehole."

The mousehole was a small round opening in the paneling that edged the floor. I touched a black streak that covered one side of the arch. Soot came off on my hand. "Why are there scorch marks?"

"I don't know. Maybe the giants tried to smoke out the mice." Chase strode through the arch confidently, even though it was even darker past the hole than it was under the giants' fridge. "Come on. It goes all the way outside."

Half a minute later, a slight breeze cooled my face. Chase stopped in another opening, a dim light behind him.

He pointed out a dust bunny that came all the way up to my chest, just a few feet away from the mousehole. Beside it stood a mound of dust, some crumbs, and a few assorted items, which included a shark's tooth.

Beyond the mound, the sun was setting. It turned the pool orange.

"You found it!" I cried, delighted.

"Of course I did. I put it there, didn't I?" Now that we were outside, I noticed the sweat at his temples. He *had* been working hard.

"Not *that*. An easy way in and out of the house." This Tale was looking easier and easier all the time.

"Oh, right. I knew that."

I rolled my eyes. "We better get back. If the sun's setting, then I bet the giant will be back soon."

"And his mom," Chase said as we turned around. "Trust me. It's usually the moms you have to worry about. If she's old enough to survive her first six centuries, she's definitely a threat."

If *that* was true, I didn't want to leave Lena alone inside the giant's house any longer. I hurried through the dark space and then under the fridge with my head bent.

"We're done!" I shouted up to Matilda.

The giant's wife wiped her hands on a dishtowel. "Wonderful! You can help Lily dice."

"You mean, *I'm* done." Chase shoved the brush in front of him. "I'm still waiting for your apology, you know. You accused me of slacking off."

"You'll get it right after you tell me you're sorry for spelling my sword and making me look like an idiot," I said as Matilda stooped and offered us her palm.

"No way. That was really funny."

I stepped onto Matilda's hand, too busy glaring at Chase to remember to brace myself against a thumb or a finger. Matilda stood without warning, and I started to topple.

Chase lunged and caught my arm just in time. "You know, for someone afraid of falling, your balance really sucks."

Only *Chase* would insult me while he was saving my life. So, why the heck did Rapunzel want me to be his friend?

"I always have the hardest time getting pieces small enough. I've never had enough patience." Matilda deposited us on the counter. "But Lily is doing a superb job."

Lena's cheeks were wet, which made Chase look a little freaked out.

"Is something wrong?" I asked.

"Onions." Lena pointed to the pile of white smelly bits in front of her with her sword, and Chase let out such a relieved sigh that I almost laughed. "They're a lot more potent when they're this big."

"I can't believe the first time we get to use our swords is to do battle with a vegetable." Chase looked pained at the thought.

Lena wiped tears away with the back of her hand. "Would you rather fight Matilda?"

Chase glanced over at Matilda, who opened her oven, checking on the roasted condors. "No," he admitted. "She's pretty big, even for a giant."

Lena gestured to the next onion sternly, and Chase raised his sword with a grimace.

A key scraped the lock down the hallway, and a few seconds later, a man's voice boomed, "We're here! Do I smell Englishmen cooking?"

I froze. He sounded a *lot* meaner than his wife, and I couldn't imagine them *both* being allergic to humans. The barbeque rub came to mind, and I gulped, wondering if Matilda was planning a second course.

"No, darling, it's a surprise!" Matilda shouted back, so loudly that the counter shook a little. To my relief, she whispered to us, "They're early. You'll have to hide. Quickly! Into the bread box."

It was at the far end of the counter—a painted wooden box, labeled in curling blue letters. We ran, our sneakers squeaking on the marble. Chase reached it first and waited outside.

"Matilda?" The giant was halfway down the hall. I ran faster. I didn't want to find out what would happen if we didn't make it in time.

When Lena reached Chase, he helped her over the rim, and then he helped me too before jumping in after us.

"In the kitchen, dear!" Once she saw we were all inside, Matilda slid the door closed, telling us, "Try to be as quiet as possible."

It clicked shut, and we were left in the dark. Our heavy breathing sounded way too loud in the enclosed space, and every noise echoed off the walls. The only light came from a small crack between the door and its frame. An odd smell crept into my nose—a little bit like chalk, but less earthy and more animal-like.

Even hidden, I still didn't feel very safe. If Jimmy decided he wanted a roll or something with dinner, we wouldn't have anywhere to run. "We need an escape route. Just in case."

"Did anyone think to bring a flashlight?" Chase whispered back.

"I did." I heard Lena fumble in her jacket pocket, and she flicked it on.

Chase breathed in sharply, and I had barely enough time to clap a hand over his mouth to keep him from shouting.

Then my eyes adjusted, and I could see what was worth screaming about.

"Skeletons," Lena said breathlessly.

ozens of skeletons sat in the bread box behind us, stretching all the way to the end, tumbled carelessly on top of each other. It was hard not to imagine the faces that went with the skulls.

"'Be he alive or be he dead, I'll grind his bones to make my bread,'" I whispered, realizing why the skeletons were there with a horrified shudder. Chase's breath came in panicked bursts over the back of my hand.

The thought of what kind of dust was entering our lungs made me gag, so I tugged up my shirt and breathed through the fabric.

Lena nodded and pressed a hand over her mouth like she was fighting the urge to throw up too.

Maybe Matilda was way sneakier than she pretended to be. The thought of Jimmy finding us and swallowing us whole had been bad enough. The idea of Matilda systematically smashing up our bones and kneading us into bread was so horrible that I had to push it out of my head before I panicked, bolted out of there, and got us all caught. "Do you think she'll ever let us out?" I asked Lena.

"Yeah. One way or another." Her voice shook. "All these skeletons are dry, and there are easier ways to get the meat off our bones than letting us rot."

The thought brought me an image of Matilda and a deboning knife.

I gagged again, so hard I tasted bile, and Chase made a strangled sound. Shoving my hand away from his mouth, he stomped to the corner, as far away from the skeletons as he could possibly get, and he sat down with his head between his knees and his sword dangling from his hand.

Then Lena squeezed her eyes shut. "It's only an experiment. Only an experiment. Only an experiment." The mantra must have worked. When she opened her eyes, she had the curious distant gaze of a scientist rather than a freaked-out eleven-year-old.

"I'm guessing she's just putting us in here to hide our smell." Lena shined her flashlight on the rib cage at her feet. There were two spikes on the shoulder blades. "Not all of these are human. I've never seen a nonhuman skeleton before."

"Your academic interest astounds me," I said, but watching her act so detached did calm me down a little.

Chase moaned. "Can we *not* talk about them, please?"

"Shh!" Lena and I said together. I glanced outside the bread box. He had spoken way too loud to be safe, and through the crack, I could see Matilda's husband and mother-in-law enter the room.

Luckily, they hadn't heard him.

"Jimmy! Genevieve!" Matilda raised her arms to hug them. "I wasn't expecting you so soon."

The giant looked like his picture: green-skinned with warts on his nose and coarse black hair thinning at the forehead. But when Jimmy smiled, his teeth shone, and I could see how Matilda could like him. "Mother's train got in early."

His mother had the same green skin and even the same warts, but her short hair was gray and stuck up in bristles over her head.

When she looked up to glare at Matilda, I saw she wore an eye-patch. "You may call me Mrs. Searcaster."

Matilda's face fell. I felt a little sorry for her.

"Genevieve Searcaster," Lena said thoughtfully. "Why does that name sound familiar?"

"She was rumored to be the Snow Queen's general," said Chase without lifting his head.

Lena's eyes bugged out. Hansel *had* mentioned a giantess named Searcaster, but he had been trying to scare us.

"No . . . ," I said slowly, watching Matilda bustle around her mother-in-law, settling her in a seat. It looked so normal, except for the size. Evil generals just didn't sit around and harass their son's wives at the dinner table.

"Sounds like her. Green skin, missing eye, and carries a cane with the cast-iron corpse of a basilisk?" Chase said.

Genevieve Searcaster leaned her cane against her chair, and I got a good look at it. "There *is* some sort of snake thing on it."

"Let me see," Lena said. I moved out of the way, and she took my place at the crack. I kept my back to the skeletons. It was easier not to panic if I didn't have to look at them. "It *is* her. I thought she was captured and tried for war crimes."

"She *was*," said Chase. "She got off, because she said that the Snow Queen had her son."

I snorted. "Jimmy? Isn't he a little big for kidnapping?"

"They did it a lot during the war," Lena said gently. "The Snow Queen would imprison loved ones of her allies. If they turned, the prisoners would be tortured to death."

I gulped, glad that the war was long over. I would probably give in too, if the Snow Queen had Mom, Dad, or Amy. "That's horrible."

"That's war," said Chase, like we should expect such horrible things. "Or war with the Snow Queen, at least."

Lena didn't sound so indifferent. "It made it really hard for the Canon to tell afterward who was actually guilty and who wasn't."

"Well, Searcaster's supposed to be under house arrest until the end of the next millennium," Chase said. "I don't know why she's going on a ski vacation."

"I think she's guilty," I said.

"My dad always thought so too," Chase said, which actually made me feel a little less certain.

Through the bread box's thin sides, we could still hear the murmur of the giants' voices. Genevieve Searcaster's cut through everyone else's like the screech of a chainsaw. "When I said I liked white meat, I meant *human*, not *poultry*."

Apparently, Matilda had just served the main course.

"I didn't know we were considered white meat," Lena whispered dryly, and I smothered a giggle behind my hand, wondering if I was hysterical.

"I just hope you don't pass this embarrassing allergy to my *grandchildren*," said Searcaster. "I've already had to accept that they might not come out a proper *green*."

"What's going on now?" I asked Lena.

"Jimmy and Genevieve are sitting at the table, and Matilda is pouring everyone some wine." Lena bit her lip. "Hopefully, this won't be a long dinner. We have a lot to do."

To reassure her, I told her about the mousehole that Chase found—how it led from the kitchen straight to the backyard. I expected Chase to interrupt me and start bragging at any time, but when I turned back to look, Chase's head was still between his knees, bent almost to the floor.

"Chase, what's your problem?" I said.

He didn't answer. He just slid his hands through his hair.

I moved a little closer, despite myself. It annoyed me to be so concerned about someone I didn't like. "Hey? Are you okay?"

"Fine," he said hoarsely, but he had sweated so much that his curls looked wet. Each breath made his entire chest shudder.

No matter what Rapunzel had said, being nice to Chase didn't exactly sound appealing, but if I was honest with myself, only one part of me wanted to hate him forever—the same stubborn side that Mom always said reminded her of my dad. That's never a compliment.

I sighed deeply and sat down next to him, moving my sword so it didn't poke either of us.

"I'm *fine*." Chase lifted his head to glare at me. "I just don't like skeletons."

"Uh-oh. I forgot about that," Lena said. "He's afraid of bones."

Then Chase scowled at *her*. "Bones and confined spaces. I got locked in a tomb for three days. You'd be scarred too."

"Oh," I said thoughtfully.

Rapunzel had known. I'd thought she had been talking just to me when she mentioned fear, but maybe not. Maybe she'd been talking to all of us.

Lena rubbed her face, murmuring, "Way to go, Lena. All of EAS to choose from, and you pick the sixth graders with phobias."

Guilt churned in my stomach. She was right. I should've told her to pick a better Companion before we climbed the beanstalk.

"It hasn't stopped us, has it? We've helped," Chase said fiercely. "I found an easy entrance, and if it hadn't been for Rory, we would never have gotten inside."

Wide-eyed and stiff, Lena jerked back to the crack as if he'd struck her, and I knew she didn't mean it the way it sounded. That didn't stop it from hurting.

"Is it specific types of bones?" I asked. Chase shot a glare in my direction, but he didn't say anything. "Like skulls? Or femurs?"

Chase flinched. He didn't even like their names.

It would've been so easy to tease him. All I had to do was ask if funnybones counted. But somehow, seeing him struggle like this made me lose my appetite for payback. It reminded me too much of when I got stuck on the beanstalk. No matter what else he'd done before this trip, he hadn't teased me then.

"Look at it this way," I told Chase. "The worst that could happen is that they could find us. Then you would get to fight them."

Lena stared at me like I'd eaten some enchanted cabbage and grown donkey ears.

"Right," Chase said sarcastically. "Then there would be two Jacks on one Tale—a Beanstalk one and a Giant-Killer."

"Chase the Giant-Killer." I tried to smile encouragingly. "Actually, it does have a nice ring to it."

Chase eyed me carefully. He couldn't tell if I was joking or not. "Are you trying to cheer me up?"

"To distract you," I replied, a little defensively. "Fair's fair."

He knew what I was talking about. He shrugged. "It's not my first time up a beanstalk. Whenever my dad would rescue a group of people, somebody would get stuck. I was more patient than my dad when we had to help them down."

"I'm glad you were." It was as close to thanking him as I could make myself go.

Chase smirked a bit—not meanly, but more like he knew exactly what I was thinking. I grinned back.

"You guys." The light from the crack illuminated Lena's face.

She looked frightened, and for a second, I thought maybe Jimmy was heading toward us. "I think we need to listen to this."

Genevieve Searcaster's voice was much louder now, and her words ran together a little. "The Arctic Circle. Pah. In my day, we went skiing in the Himalayas, like *normal* folk. I still remember racing my older brother down Mount Everest—"

Her day had to have been a *long* while back. Two giants skiing on Everest would've made headlines even in 1850.

"Matilda's been pouring a lot of wine," Lena whispered. "I think she's trying to make sure her mother-in-law goes to bed early."

"Sorry, Mother. The Himalayas have a lot of humans running around." Jimmy was even louder than his mom.

"If you're seen—" Matilda began.

"Humans," Searcaster scoffed. "We never worried about what the humans saw before Her Majesty was imprisoned."

Chase stiffened, and Lena sent us a look that clearly said, *How the hiccups will we get out of this?*

"The giants have a queen?" I asked hopefully. They shook their heads darkly, and I knew Searcaster meant the Snow Queen. A chill ran down my spine, but I couldn't understand it—hadn't the war ended a long, *long* time ago?

"*There* was a woman who understood the *dignity* of our people," said the old general. "She knew that the world belonged to *us*, not the pitiful little humans." Searcaster's devotion rang out in every word, and hearing it scared me more than anything. The general would never stop until the Snow Queen was out of prison. "She didn't expect us to crowd in the forgotten corners of the world. Overpopulation did pose a problem, but there's an easy solution to that when you're on the top of the food chain—even if a few of us have *allergies*."

The whole deboning knife scene returned to haunt me, but it was in Searcaster's hand instead of Matilda's. I shuddered.

"No matter. Our day will come again. We won't have much longer to wait." Genevieve Searcaster let out a cackle like thunder shattering old windows.

I didn't want to know what she meant. I couldn't imagine a world where green-skinned giants like Searcaster walked city streets and plucked humans out of a house to munch on the same way we ate potato chips. The Canon would never allow it. Searcaster would need an army—

An army. That last thought grabbed me and wouldn't let me go. "She's not talking about what I think she's talking about, is she?"

Dumbstruck, Lena pressed against the bread box sides like she couldn't stand without them.

"Sure it does." Chase's eyes were squeezed shut, but when he gulped hard and opened them, he just looked resigned. "It means war."

"What do you mean?" Matilda asked. "Has Her Majesty—"

"I'm not at liberty to discuss the details," Searcaster said, as if her son and daughter-in-law were too stupid to grasp those details. "But the Canon has long ceased their careful watch, and my queen grows restless. Tell me, Jimmy, have you made a decision about what Her Majesty asked?"

I didn't like the way she said that—like she already knew she would get her way.

"Well, Mother, you *know* what will happen if the Canon finds out I helped her," Jimmy said uncomfortably. "I mean, it's bad enough that we'll be near her old hideout—"

If Jimmy's ability to stand up to his mom was all that stood between EAS and war, then we were doomed.

"Nonsense, son. You have no *faith* in Her Majesty," said his mother. "You have no faith in *me*. Last time, I admit, we underestimated those children of Mildred Grubb's—"

How many Characters would we lose in this round? How many of them would I know? My imagination carved not just Lena's name on the Wall, but George's name too, and all three triplets', Gretel's, and Evan Garrison's. Goose bumps sprouted on my arms.

"How do we stop it?" I whispered. "How do we stop the war?"

Chase and Lena didn't answer me.

"That won't happen a second time," Searcaster continued. "My queen has a plan for that Ever After School."

"They *did* have some fierce warriors," Matilda agreed reluctantly.

Standing at the crack, Lena flinched and took a nervous step back. "Matilda just looked this way."

"Do you think she recognizes us?" Chase said in a low voice.

"Where else would kids on a quest come from?" Lena asked.

Suddenly, the bread box felt much more like a trap than a hiding place. Where could we run? Where could we hide? If we buried ourselves in skeletons, they could still see us.

"You *have* heard what they've been saying, haven't you?" Searcaster said slowly. "About the new Character everyone can't stop talking about?"

I wasn't EAS's only new Character, but somehow, as Jimmy and Matilda murmured that yes, they had heard, I knew that they were talking about me. My face even flushed hotly, like it knew I was the center of attention.

This was it. I knew it. This was when I would finally find out why everyone kept talking about—

"They haven't seen anyone like her since Solange's first arrival," continued the general. "Years before she became the Snow Queen, of course."

No, it couldn't be me.

I'd been wrong. I wasn't special, not at all.

"The arrival of this new Character has forced Her Majesty's hand," said Searcaster. "War is returning, Jimmy. You must decide what side you will fight for."

I certainly wasn't this special—not special enough to make anyone start a war. I couldn't be.

The room was silent for a long moment. Standing at the crack, Lena began to tremble, and I wondered what she saw. Out of the corner of my eye, I saw Chase put his hand on his sword.

Matilda laughed. It was high-pitched and obviously fake, but some of the tension in the room disappeared. Lena's trembling stopped, and I could breathe again.

"Of course we *know* what side we'll be on," Matilda said. "It's just that Jimmy has gotten a little attached to it."

"Is that true?" the old general asked. Jimmy didn't reply, and it seemed like answer enough for his mother. "When I gave you the object before my trial, it was only for safekeeping. I'm sure that she will compensate you handsomely. I don't care about any of the others, but you must return that—"

"Oh, I know what we can do!" cried Matilda. "We can get out that old harp. Its music always cheers us up. You *are* supposed to be on vacation, Mrs. Searcaster."

"Ugh." Lena wrinkled her nose like she smelled something a lot more foul than bone dust. "Matilda just looked this way again. She's definitely on to us. She interrupted her mother-in-law so that we wouldn't find out what the Snow Queen was after."

Privately, I thought this was a good sign. Matilda wouldn't have risked interrupting someone as scary as General Searcaster if she just planned on killing us afterward.

"Watch her. See where they keep the harp," Chase told Lena.

"Get all three of them out of the desk, Matilda," Jimmy said. "I want to show Mother."

"Second door on the right," Lena said. "She's coming back."

"Here we are!" Matilda cried. Something rattled the table as she set it down.

"That's a nice safe," said Searcaster. It was impossible to tell if she was being sarcastic or not.

"Elf-made," Jimmy said proudly.

"Turns you to stone if you don't get the combination right," added Matilda.

I gulped, imagining Lena-, Chase-, and me-shaped statues, but Lena just watched the giants through the crack calmly.

"I bet she said that for our benefit," said Chase. "She might be lying."

Lena shook her head. "It's true. Jimmy is being really careful."

The safe's door squeaked open, and the next thing we heard was a chicken clucking.

"The hen that lays golden eggs?" said Searcaster. "I had no idea it was still alive."

"Isn't it immortal?" said Matilda, surprised.

"It's getting on in years. Only lays an egg every other day now," said Jimmy with real regret.

"It might be depressed," Matilda pointed out. "It might lay more if we let it run around a little."

"We can't let it out!" said Jimmy. "It's too valuable. There are thieves everywhere!"

Like us, I thought, feeling slightly guilty.

"Matilda just looked this way again," Lena said.

"Never mind the hen. Let me see that harp," said the old general greedily.

When he took it out, both of the giantesses gasped in surprised delight.

Matilda sniffed, like she was tearing up. "She gets more beautiful every time I look at her."

"Oh, crackers," Lena said, irritated. "Matilda just moved and blocked my view. I can't see it."

"Sing, my lovely," Jimmy cooed.

Music came. It was the kind of song you feel in your chest. In the notes, I heard harps and flutes, and the kind of high clear singing they use for angels' voices in Christmas movies. I felt my nose prickle, right under the bridge, and blinked rapidly before Chase could notice.

"I don't think it's a golden iPod," I whispered.

Chase shook his head, and all the tension left his shoulders. My heartbeat slowed down too, but as soon as the music faded, it started hammering again.

"They've fallen asleep," Lena said.

"All of them?" I asked, surprised.

Lena shook her head. "Jimmy and Searcaster. Maybe Matilda put slumberwort in the wine herself."

"It was the harp's lullaby," Chase said. "My mom used to sing it to me."

I wondered if maybe the music sounded different to each person. I hadn't even heard any words in the song.

Matilda's deep sigh sounded like wind whistling past the bread box. "And before I've even served dessert. How rude."

We heard two thumps. "Matilda's carrying *both* of them," Lena said, amazed. "She's helping them to bed."

"Great. Now we can get out of here," Chase said, jumping to his feet, and I agreed wholeheartedly.

"Matilda said she would let us out," Lena reminded him.

"Who *knows* when that'll be?" I said. "And I, for one, am not spending the night with a bunch of skeletons."

Chase gave us both a scathing look. "Do you really think she's going to let us go? After everything we've heard?"

"I see your point." Lena laid both hands on the door of the bread box. "Do you think it's true? Do you really think that the Snow Queen is starting to move?"

"Probably. Even the Canon's worried about it, remember?" I asked Chase.

"They sent Dad to the Glass Mountain," Chase said softly. "If I could get a message to him . . ." He was concerned, and I couldn't blame him. I worried about my dad whenever he had a shoot. I would freak out if he went off to visit a master villain.

Lena pushed so hard that her voice sounded strained. "He's probably halfway across Atlantis by now. There's no way anyone could reach him."

"I know *that*," Chase snapped.

"Well, don't bite my head off. Right now, we need to worry about our own problems," Lena said. "Like this door. It's stuck." She pushed harder. "No, it's *locked*," she said, looking at us with horror.

"That's okay." Chase pulled something out of his pocket and picked the lock. The door unlocked with a click. He started to slide the door open, but I heard a thump.

"Wait!" I said.

Lena and Chase both looked at me like I'd lost my mind, but then they heard it too—the unmistakable thuds of a giant's approaching footsteps.

"What do we do?" Lena whispered to Chase.

"Hope they're just coming back for warm milk before bedtime," Chase whispered back, but he put his hand on his sword.

I wrapped a hand around my hilt too. I didn't know how I could possibly fight someone over ten times my size, but Chase and I could probably distract Matilda long enough for Lena to get away. That was what Companions were for, right?

The footsteps stopped at the counter, directly in front of the bread box. The door slid open.

We looked up at Matilda's humongous, frowning face.

"orry about that," said Matilda. "I meant to get you three outside well before they got here, and it took *forever* to get them to fall asleep."

None of us moved. We all expected a trick. The giantess glanced behind us.

"I know this wasn't the most cheerful place to put you, but don't worry," she said. "Most of those bones aren't even human. Jimmy has a special liking for Fey-bone bread."

Chase retched and slapped a hand over his mouth.

"Come on out," said Matilda. I looked at Lena. I would do whatever she did. Back in fearless leader mode, she climbed stiffly over the ledge and hopped onto the counter. Chase and I followed apprehensively.

Once we were close enough, Matilda grabbed all of us at once, pinning us together, and walked briskly down the hall. I grabbed frantically at whatever was nearest.

"Ow." Chase looked pointedly at my hands gripping his arm. I scowled back, but I wasn't embarrassed enough to let go.

"Don't fight," Lena hissed, too low for the giantess to hear. "We're not out of this yet. We might have to run."

But Matilda went straight to the front door and opened it. Even the moon looked bigger than normal. Its reflection filled the whole swimming pool. When my feet hit the front step, I stumbled and fell, hard enough to bruise my knees.

"Great getaway," Chase said, but he offered a hand to help me up.

"Oh, I almost forgot." Matilda pulled something out of her pocket—a roll as big as an armchair. She set it down between Lena and Chase. "Your payment. This should be big enough to feed the three of you."

"Thank you," Lena said quickly, and Chase and I echoed her.

"No, thank *you*," Matilda said. "I would've never finished in time without you three. Even if no one ate dessert." She turned back inside.

Lena, Chase, and I glanced at each other. There was no way we could get off so easy.

When the door was halfway closed, Matilda spoke again. "You know, I like humans."

Chase and I grabbed our sword hilts again, and Lena fell back a startled step.

"Not to eat! I didn't have Jimmy's upbringing," Matilda said hastily. "I think humans are adorable. So cute and small, especially little girls." She smiled at me and Lena so warmly that I started to return it hesitantly. Then she added in a completely different tone, "But I don't think anyone can be blamed for defending her own."

She did suspect us. She wasn't an idiot.

On the balls of my feet, ready to dash away if we needed to, I nodded once, slowly, to show that I understood.

Another smile—a sadder one—filled Matilda's face. "Good night, children. Good luck on your quest." Then, slowly, she shut the door behind her, and we listened to Matilda's footsteps fade down the hall.

Sometimes, the bad guys didn't seem so bad. The stories always skimmed over that part.

"That was incredibly decent of her," I said quietly.

"Almost stupid, actually," Chase said. "Especially if there really *is* a war coming."

"She seems very nice," said Lena uncertainly, and I knew she felt guilty too.

Chase stared at her hard. "So nice that we shouldn't go back in there and grab the gold?"

I could go either way. I didn't want to Fail the first Tale I'd ever been a Companion on, but stealing from Matilda didn't seem like much fun.

"No," said Lena stoutly. "That part's too easy. They left the safe open on the kitchen table. And now we'll also need to learn what the Snow Queen wants. That'll help the Canon stop her. If we have any luck, we'll also figure out what they're saying about Rory."

I started to feel defensive before Lena even finished saying my name. "Who's talking about me?"

"Searcaster, the Snow Queen, everyone," Lena said.

"My name wasn't mentioned anywhere in that conversation," I said icily.

"Of course they mean you, Rory." Lena bent down to pick up the bottom of the roll. "Help me carry this."

Chase crossed his arms. "There's no way we're eating that."

"Waste not, want not," Lena said lightly.

"You *do* remember what they use to make the bread here, right?" Chase said. "Matilda's trying to tell us what she'll do if she catches us stealing."

Lena dropped the roll. "Oh."

"It can't be *me* they're talking about." I knew that I was trying to convince myself even more than Chase and Lena, but that didn't make me any less desperate. "Miriam is newer than I am. And Philip. And that fifth grader I haven't met yet."

"Nobody talks about Miriam, though," Chase said. "They talk about you."

It got harder to keep denying it at that point. Chase wouldn't agree with Lena if he didn't believe it. The problem was that I didn't *want* to believe it.

Lena inspected the roll thoughtfully. "Well, we can't leave it here. That would be rude. Help me push it into the bushes."

"Rude. They want to eat us, and we're worried about *rude*." Chase snorted, but he put his shoulder to the roll and shoved with me and Lena. The roll bounced off the front step, behind the bushes, and then out of sight.

"Where's this mousehole?" Lena asked, a little out of breath.

I had no idea, but Chase pointed left.

I lowered myself carefully from the front step to the ground and changed tactics. "Besides, how the heck could Searcaster have heard of me?"

"The Canon meeting during the Fairie Market. They were talking about you right before you came," Chase said, and I remembered how everyone in the Canon had stared at me after I'd introduced myself.

Lena looked up at me, wide-eyed. "You never told me you went to the Canon meeting."

"Me and Rory eavesdropped," said Chase proudly. "A pair of troublemakers."

Lena looked between me and Chase, raising her eyebrows as if to suggest that I *did* have a crush I hadn't told her about.

"I went to *yell* at him. We also got caught." Things were already complicated enough. Lena didn't need to make weird assumptions on top of everything else.

"What did they say about Rory?" Lena said.

"If I had known that, I would've already told you," Chase said impatiently.

Who else was out there, talking about me? And were they saying the same thing as Searcaster? That they hadn't seen any Character like me since the Snow Queen herself, the worst villain the world had ever seen? Were they *all* saying that my arrival meant another war?

I didn't want people to think of me like that. What a terrible reason to be famous—even worse than having celebrities for parents.

Could I really be like the Snow Queen? Could I really be evil without knowing it?

I raised a hand to rub my eyes. It was shaking. I stuffed both hands into my pockets, glancing at Lena and Chase to see if they had noticed.

They hadn't.

Chase's stomach rumbled, and then he moaned, just for extra emphasis. "Whose pack has the food? I'm so hungry my stomach hurts. I must be starving."

"You don't starve after missing one meal," I told him, glad for the distraction, but Chase just wrapped his arms around his middle and whimpered dramatically.

Maybe it was just the moonlight playing tricks on my eyes, but he did look a lot paler than normal. The bread box incident had really freaked him out—even if he *was* covering it up by acting as idiotic as he normally did.

"Maybe we should eat. It's been a really long time since lunch," I said.

Chase gasped. "Did you just agree with me?"

I ignored him. "The packs are over here, right, Lena? I'll get them."

I ran under the bush, without waiting for an answer. I wanted a few minutes to calm down without being watched.

"We just need mine," Lena called after me.

"No, it's not possible," Chase said. "Rory would never agree with me of her own free will."

"Shh," Lena said sternly.

"Excuse me. I'm savoring the moment. I don't know if this will ever happen again."

"*Nothing* will ever happen to you again if Jimmy or his mom hears you and wake up," Lena pointed out. Chase stopped.

I breathed in and out slowly and curled my hands into tight fists, clenching them until they stopped shaking.

"You know, you could be a Destined One, Rory," Lena said.

"What's that?" It was a struggle to keep my voice from cracking. Being a Destined One sounded a lot easier to swallow than a villain-to-be.

"One with a Great Destiny," Lena said. "There's probably a prophecy about you doing something the Snow Queen doesn't want."

"Would it be in Rumpel's book?" In Snow White's mirror shard, I'd seen him say my name.

"In *a* book, maybe," Lena said doubtfully. "Prophecies can turn up anywhere—on walls, in ancient ruins, in Fey nursery rhymes, on engraved crowns. There was even one, fifteen years ago, inscribed on a paper clip."

"Rory, aren't you supposed to be getting the food?" Chase said.

"I can't see anything under here!" I searched hurriedly before

Chase lost patience and came to find me. Then my foot found something squishy. "Wait. I think I stepped on it."

"Two years ago," Lena continued, "Tim Oakley fulfilled a prophecy to destroy the Glacier Amulet. That was a big deal. They said the Amulet caused the Ice Age. The Snow Queen looked everywhere for it, before and during the war. She broke things for days after she found out it was destroyed."

Halfway out of the bushes, I stopped in my tracks. I didn't want to know that there were amulets in the world powerful enough to bring on an Ice Age—that some people would want that kind of power.

"I never met a Tim Oakley. What happened to him?" I said slowly, not totally sure I wanted the answer.

"Nothing too terrible," Chase said. "He went to college."

I started to let out a relieved sigh, but then Lena spoke up again. "Or maybe you're going to vanquish the Snow Queen. There's a precedent for that."

Vanquish the lady who wanted another Ice Age? *Me?*

Chase snorted. "That'll be hard. She's real scary stuck in prison."

"Isn't it a *glass* prison?" I pointed out, emerging from the bushes.

Lena had to be wrong about this. There had to be other Characters, *better* ones, who were more qualified than I was.

"Madame Benne made it with ancient magic." Lena took the pack from me. "The structure was designed to temper and contain a sorcerer's essence, and two decades ago, the Canon rigged it to imprison the Snow Queen." I never understood Lena when she got technical like this, so I gave her a look until she added, "There's no way for her to walk, blast, or magic her way out."

"Let's just eat, okay?" It had to be a big misunderstanding. We would clear it up after we finished Lena's Tale.

"Sure," Lena said, so softly that I knew she was worried about me. "We need to wait awhile anyway. Until Matilda falls asleep."

I just needed to focus on getting us and the three items all down the beanstalk in one piece. The rest could wait.

We took a seat in a circle, and Lena handed me and Chase each a paper lunch bag.

Chase peered inside his with distaste. "Sandwiches? What about trail mix? Ellie always packs trail mix when I go on a Tale."

Lena zipped up her pack firmly and began to unwrap her sandwich. "No way. George told me that you always eat all the M&M's and leave the rest."

Chase scowled, but instead of denying it, he chomped off a third of his sandwich in one bite.

"How many Tales have you been on?" I asked Chase.

Grinning, he held out a hand, fingers spread wide, and then an extra thumb.

"Six?" I said in disbelief.

"Counting this one," said Chase happily through a mouthful of ham and bread.

"Is that even allowed?" I asked Lena. It certainly didn't seem fair.

Lena shrugged. "Between his dad and those Tales, he's got more experience than the rest of EAS put together."

"And I'm the best with a sword," Chase added.

Lena stuck out her chin stubbornly. "It's a toss-up between you and George."

"But you haven't had your own Tale yet?" I asked Chase.

His expression turned sour. "I'm still special."

I ate too quickly, finishing even before Chase. So, rather than waiting around and thinking, I cleared a campsite. I dragged away a dozen twigs as big as broom handles with so much gusto that I almost knocked Chase out.

"Watch it." He'd gathered a pile of fallen geranium petals, all about the size of dinner plates, and he was trying to shove them into my nicely cleared site.

I stepped in his path. "What are you doing?"

"Trust me. We need these. If we spread them out under us, sleeping on the ground will suck a lot less." I must have looked stunned, because he added, "I do have some good ideas every once in a while, you know."

But that wasn't it. It surprised me that Chase was helping—that he was trying to earn his keep as much as I was.

We finished spreading them out about the same time Lena finished her sandwich. "Okay, Matilda should be asleep by now."

Chase led the way. When we reached the mousehole, Lena said breathlessly, "Oh, my gumdrops."

I couldn't blame her. It was twice as tall as we were. It looked a lot creepier now that the sun had set.

"It's so big." Lena drew her sword.

"What's that for?" Chase asked.

"Do you see the size of this hole? The mice have to be *huge*."

"I haven't seen any." But Chase pulled his sword out too. So did I. My palms started to sweat somewhere between the mousehole and the low space under the fridge, making my grip slippery.

Matilda had turned off the lights. The kitchen was dark except for the digital clock on the oven, blinking *11:41* in green numbers.

Lena shined her flashlight over the top of the table. "They're still there."

"Let's hope they didn't lock the safe," Chase said.

"We just need a way up there." The tabletop was at least thirty-five feet high, and even the chairs were too tall to climb.

Chase pulled Jack Attack off his shoulder. He twirled it, and when he let it go, the hook fell against the edge of the table and held.

I wasn't sure if either Lena or I could climb a rope, but then Chase yanked on it. I blinked, and there was a second rope hanging a foot from the first. He shook them both. When Lena shone her flashlight up, the two ropes had transformed into a rope ladder.

"Cool," said Lena, and even though I didn't admit it, I was impressed too.

"After you," Chase said with a grin and an elaborate bow. Lena stuck her flashlight in her mouth and climbed.

"I thought humans couldn't do magic," I said suspiciously.

Chase just started up after Lena. "The ropes are enchanted to do that. A built-in spell. Like your sword."

It was a mistake to remind me about my sword. It made my mood about a million times worse. "That doesn't explain why you knew how to make it heavy."

I put my hands on the nearest rung of the rope ladder. I had to remind myself that this wasn't nearly as high as the beanstalk before I could make myself move.

The rope ladder swung a little bit, especially every time I stepped up a rung. The nausea came back, but not dizziness. Definitely easier than the beanstalk.

"I told you I'm special." Chase looked over his shoulder to smile at me in a way I didn't like. "Just like you, apparently—if no one's seen anything like you since Solange first showed up."

I scowled. I did not appreciate him bringing that back up when

I was twenty feet off the ground. "I'm not anything like the Snow Queen."

"Can you two *not* bicker?" Lena said. "There are giants sleeping down the hall."

"He just called me evil."

"I didn't say *that*." Reaching the tabletop, Chase pulled himself over the edge with his elbows.

"It can't be *me*." I rolled onto the table and stood up, brushing off my jeans. "What could I have possibly done like the Snow Queen? Freeze when I'm scared? Suck royally in Hansel's class? Throw rocks at her dragon?" A soft clattering noise came from the floor below, and I stepped away from the table's edge nervously. "Did you hear that?"

Chase grinned. "Are you trying to change the subject?"

"*No*. I really heard something. Clicking against the floor." I glanced over the edge, but there wasn't much point in looking without Lena's flashlight. "I bet there's something down there. Maybe the mice."

"Right." Chase rolled his eyes. "Or the giant's guard dog."

"It's okay, Rory. We don't have to worry about any prophecies now." Lena shined the flashlight across the table. "It's not like we don't have enough to do— Oh, look! They left the safe unlocked."

Neither of them believed me. I tried not to get annoyed. After all, I *had* wanted to change the subject.

Lena headed toward the safe, but Chase paused, scowling. "Why are you fighting this so much? Having a Destiny means you'll go down in history. You're not excited at all."

I wasn't.

I felt about the same as I had on my first day in Mrs. Coleman's class. There was a math test before lunch, and Mrs. Coleman made me take it even though I hadn't even been there for the lesson, much less studied. Panic was the best word. I didn't want to mess up before I even got a chance to start.

"I think I'm still trying to get used to the fact that giants are at the top of the food chain," I said softly, walking beside him. "Having them talk about me is way too much to handle."

"Yeah, but since when is it a bad thing to find out you're special?" Chase said, and I knew we both wished that he were the one with the Destiny, not me.

The safe was a little smaller than my bedroom closet and made of a hard gray stone like granite, even the door. The combination lock looked like silver, and the dial was tarnished. On the top shelf, the hen slept, its head under its wing. I don't have a lot of experience with chickens, but it looked pretty normal to me. The harp stood on the other side, head bent, her golden hair hanging down. It covered her face and waved a little while she snored harmoniously.

"The safe must keep them asleep," Lena said quietly. "It's pretty simple magic."

"She made a lot of noise for something so little," I whispered. The harp was only about a foot tall, a lot smaller than I thought.

Chase whistled very softly and pointed to the bottom shelf. It was covered in coins, several inches deep. "That's a lot of gold."

Lena knelt and pulled a sack out of her backpack. She loaded the coins inside slowly, careful to make sure none of them clinked.

I knelt beside Lena to help. The coins were heavier than they looked. "I know I'm new to this," I said slowly, "but wouldn't it be more efficient to take all three at once? I mean, they're all here."

Chase's eyebrows disappeared under his bangs, and he looked at Lena eagerly. Maybe we *could* go home early. Then we could clear up the whole Snow Queen misunderstanding so much faster.

Lena glanced up at the sleeping hen and harp, clearly tempted. Then she sighed. "We can't."

"Well, the safe *is* open," I pointed out. "And we—"

"No, we can't deviate from the other Beanstalk Tales," Lena said fiercely. "If we do, it'll decrease our chances of survival by eighty-seven percent."

Disappointed, I dropped two more handfuls of coins into her backpack and reached for the last of it, stuck far into the corner.

"Besides, I really don't want to take any chances with Genevieve Searcaster here," Lena said. "I'm pretty sure we'll wake the hen and the harp if we grab them. They might raise the alarm."

"Good call," Chase said. When Lena finished zipping up her backpack, he slung it over his shoulder. I looked at him suspiciously. He wasn't usually so helpful. "They're leaving on vacation tomorrow, so getting the other two should be easy. Shall we?" He gestured to his rope ladder.

"One second." Lena pulled another bag out of her pack and dumped it out, scattering gold coins across the bottom shelf, almost covering it.

"Is that what you picked from the storeroom?" I asked.

"Leprechaun's gold," said Chase with approval.

"The giants shouldn't notice anything's missing until after they get back." Lena dusted off her hands and smiled, proud of herself.

On the climb down, I got stuck just once for about a second, but I got myself going again before Lena reached me. A big improvement, if I do say so myself.

As soon as we were hidden under the fridge, Chase started humming the same lullaby that the harp had sung earlier, but it wasn't until we emerged in the cold night air that we realized Chase was eating.

"Lena *told* you not to touch the trail mix." I tried to snatch it back.

"What?" Chase just raised the bag above his head. He was way too tall for me to reach it. "I'm hungry."

"I *knew* you wouldn't carry Lena's backpack just to be nice."

"Lena's not complaining." Chase looked over my shoulder.

Lena didn't even look at him, but she stumbled over one of the twigs I had pulled out of the campsite earlier. "I don't like it, but I need to save my energy for more important things. Like finding my sleeping bag." She yawned hugely.

I glared at Chase. He looked slightly ashamed, but he still stuck his hand into the trail mix bag. "How 'bout we make a deal? You let me snack, and I'll take the first watch."

"Fine. With the caffeine in all that chocolate, I bet you're the only one who can stay awake." Lena fell heavily to the ground between the other two backpacks. "Which one has the sleeping bags?"

"Don't eat all the M&M's," I told Chase fiercely and went to help Lena.

Digging through the packs, I found what Rapunzel had stuffed in my bag—a glass vial on a silver chain. It was the same light she'd used while she was carving the night of the Fairie Market.

The young will lie in the dark, she had said.

Well, of *course* we would. It was time to sleep. Did she think we needed a night-light?

I shoved it in the front pocket and searched deeper in the back-pack.

The sleeping bags were midnight blue with silver beads stitched on them. If you squinted, they looked a little like puddles reflect-ing the night sky, which was probably supposed to be some sort of camouflage. Lena was asleep even before I finished rolling out the other two. I could hear her soft purring snores.

I wriggled into my own sleeping bag. I expected to feel every bump and groove on the hard ground beneath me, but it was as soft and yielding as my mattress at home. Either Ellie had given us magic sleeping bags, or the petals helped a lot.

I glanced at Chase. *Since when is it a bad thing to find out you're special?* he'd said.

Chase dropped M&M's into his mouth one by one. "Go to sleep. I'm waking you up for the next watch, Destined One or not."

I gave him one last dirty look and then closed my eyes.

It took me a while to fall asleep. It wasn't just the Great Destiny.

It was knowing that people were talking about me. I had dealt with my celebrity parents all my life. I had even hated it sometimes, but if I was really honest with myself, hadn't I wanted to be famous too—not as my parents' daughter, but just as Rory? Hadn't I wanted to do the kind of great things that people talked about?

But it's one thing to be famous for something you've already done rather than something you're supposed to accomplish someday.

I didn't want to be the one destined to destroy an amulet or whatever, only to let it accidentally slip through my fingers at the last moment.

I was still just me.

It might not be enough, I realized, drifting off, as Chase started to sing that lullaby again.

I dreamed of the beanstalk. This time, Chase was there, climbing down right beside me. The top of his T-shirt was red with blood, and he moved clumsily. He fumbled, and I reached a hand up anxiously, ready to catch him.

When we fell, he started to scream.

It didn't surprise me to have Chase there. It shocked me that I was more worried about him than about the fall.

Way *too* concerned, actually. Someone shook me awake about a hundred feet above the ground, and I opened my eyes to see Chase scowling at me, his hand on my shoulder, which didn't help me figure out what was dream and what wasn't. "You okay?" I asked him sleepily and squinted at his shirt in the dark, looking for signs of blood.

"Yeah." Chase gave me a weird look (one that I completely deserved, for once). "You need to wake up, though. It's your turn to keep watch."

"Oh." I sat up and blinked hard, trying to force myself awake. As Chase crawled into his sleeping bag, still giving me funny looks, I ignored him. I stared out at the Searcasters' pool and wondered what could happen in the next few days that would make me worry about Chase Turnleaf.

As Chase had put it over breakfast, "Even giants aren't stupid enough to leave an open safe on their kitchen table when they go on vacation." So, that morning, we went looking for the desk.

We found it easily. After coming through the mousehole under the fridge, we scurried down the hallway and slipped past the second doorway on the right. Chase used Jack Attack to turn on the lights. The desk looked antique, but fairly normal—wooden with flowering vines carved up the side.

I hadn't woken Lena for her turn to keep watch. I'd wanted to give her an extra hour of sleep. She needed the rest. As her Companion, it was the least I could do.

It was also a mistake. By the time we found it, exhaustion made everything a little fuzzy.

So I just stood there staring at the desk while Lena and Chase talked about it. It was as big as my school.

"It's a roll-top. My grandmother has one like it," Lena said. "Are you sure this is a good idea?"

"I *told* you," Chase said, irritated. "The giants left *hours* ago. I watched them leave myself. They took a magic carpet the size of this room. Matilda worried that the wind would mess up her hair, and her mother-in-law told her to be quiet or she would accidentally knock her off the carpet somewhere over Canada."

Lena glared at him. "I believe they're *gone*. I'm just not sure we should be doing this *now*. All the Tales say that retrieval of the items occurs in the *evening*. Late afternoon at the earliest."

"You're going to waste a perfect opportunity just because it's still *morning*?" Chase said.

"It does seem way too convenient." Being that tired made me even crankier than usual. "I thought that Tales were supposed to be harder than this."

"And *you're* complaining because it's too *easy*?" Chase rolled his eyes. "Look, in my family, we don't question getting lucky. We just work fast." He started climbing up the carving on the side of the desk. "If anybody else wants to get it over with, this is the best way up—petal, leaf, vine, petal, petal, leaf, and so on." He grabbed a new handhold with every word, demonstrating.

"I do want to get this over with," Lena said, more to herself than me. She grabbed a handhold and pulled herself up a few feet. She didn't climb as fast as Chase, but she was more careful, testing out each carving before she trusted her weight on it. Her carryall backpack swung across her shoulders, throwing her a little off balance. She had insisted on bringing it with us. She said it was so we could have the food nearby at all times, but I was pretty sure that the real reason had more to do with her gold coins. She wanted to make sure nothing happened to her new treasure, not when it was her ticket to making up for the Fey cookbook incident.

When Chase was halfway up, I forced myself to approach to the desk and reached tentatively for a wooden leaf. Lena screamed. I don't know if it would've freaked me out more or less if I had more sleep, but I jumped away from the desk, with my hand on my sword.

Chase landed lightly next to me and scowled up at Lena. "What?"

"You scared the hiccups out of me," Lena said. "You were almost there—over thirty feet up. I thought you *fell*."

"I'm fine. You won't have to carry an injured Companion down the beanstalk." He herded me toward the desk with a shooing motion. "Go on. I'll catch you if you slip."

It felt like he was babysitting me. Sighing, I reminded myself again that it wasn't nearly as bad as the beanstalk, and I began to climb. I was only a little bit nauseous.

Chase scaled the desk just a couple feet below me, saying, "Petal, leaf, vine, petal, petal—"

Annoyed, I almost looked down to glare at him, but I thought better of it. "I don't *need* you to tell me where to put my hands and feet."

"How was I supposed to know? You did yesterday."

"Can you two *not* bicker while we're in enemy territory?" Lena said.

"*You* just screamed a little while ago," Chase pointed out. "That was a lot louder than me and Rory."

"No bickering," Lena said firmly, sounding like Jenny. "I don't want to keep telling you."

Then Chase grumbled about the burden of overcautious Characters and how the giants were on vacation and how this was turning out to be the easiest Tale he'd ever been on. But he grumbled quietly.

It *was* much easier than the beanstalk. It was even easier than Chase's rope ladder the night before, which swung a little with everyone's movement. Maybe I was getting better with the heights thing. It only took me a couple minutes to reach the flat workspace where Lena was standing. She held a hand out anxiously, ready to help me.

I slowly eased my foot off the carving and toward Lena. Then came a sound none of us were expecting.

I froze, but so did Chase and Lena.

"Was that . . . ?" Lena said.

"A door slamming?" I finished, horrified.

Footsteps thudded down the hall—heavy ones that rattled the pictures on the walls and the paper on the desk shelves. They could only belong to a giant.

Chase leaped up to the workspace and grabbed my arm in the same motion, dragging me with him. We ran over the top of the desk with Lena, back toward the shelves, where enormous loose papers and checkbooks and folders spilled out of every cubbyhole.

"Feed them? Did I remember to feed them?" It was Jimmy, muttering angrily to himself. "Of course not, woman. If *you* remembered, why didn't you tell me before we left?"

"The door's open," I whispered, trying not to panic. "He'll see us when he walks by."

"Hide." Lena looked around frantically. "We need somewhere to hide."

"Here." Chase pointed out a rope hanging from the wood above us. To Matilda, it was probably a thread. It was attached to a handle at the top of the desk.

Chase launched himself at the rope, grabbing it as high up as he could reach.

"Don't!" Lena cried.

But it was too late. Chase had already tugged it with all his body weight.

With a faint rumbling, slat after slat slid down, curving over the workspace we stood on. The cover stopped at the edge of the desk, closing us in. Then it was completely dark, except for a small sliver to the far left, where the wood above didn't quite meet the wood below.

Of course Chase *would* pick the most dramatic way to hide us all.

"What?" he said. You could hear the grin in his voice.

"No more talking," Lena whispered fiercely. "Not until the giant leaves."

Jimmy's footsteps thudded closer. "But *no*, she reminds me hours later, so I have to waste good gold on using the hotel's Door Trek system. Come on, then." At first, I thought Jimmy was still muttering to himself, but then I heard some light tapping, like the sound a dog's claws make against a hard floor.

"A guard dog?" Lena said as quietly as she could.

"I *knew* I heard something last night," I whispered back smugly.

Something hit the floor in the room across the hall with loud wet slaps. "Steaks," said Chase. "Sounds like."

None of us mentioned how big a giant's dog would be. We would be lucky if it only had one head.

Meat ripped across the hall with disgusting squelching sounds. "There's plenty of food here for a couple days," Jimmy said. "Don't eat it all at once or you'll go hungry tomorrow."

We heard him stomp out of the room and slam the door. "I wouldn't even bother if they belonged to me, but no . . . Mother says, 'You must care for what is entrusted to you.'"

He did such an awesome impression of Genevieve Searcaster's rasping accent that Chase and I snickered. Lena hushed us. We heard him curse his luck, his wife, and his mother all the way down the hall, and he was still grumbling when he slammed the front door. Then the lock slid into place with an audible click.

"Lena?" I whispered.

"Shh. Wait a few minutes," Lena said.

"Yeah, he might come back for his keys or his teddy bear," Chase said in a normal tone.

"Shh," Lena hissed angrily. "You've gotten us in enough trouble, thank you."

Chase made a scoffing noise like he disagreed, but he was silent after that.

We waited. Something rustled in Lena's direction. A second later, sudden light blazed, and I could see Lena's flashlight swinging from a cord in her hand. She zipped up her backpack and glared at Chase.

Chase scowled back. "What have I done *now*?"

"What have you *done*?" Lena repeated.

"It looked like he made a wooden curtain," I said helpfully.

"I didn't make it," Chase said. "It was already there."

"It's the cover. My grandmother has one too," Lena said. "It locks automatically as soon as you close it."

Chase gulped. "Locks automatically?"

Lena nodded. "I know, because one time I was playing hide-and-go-seek with Jenny and George. I was the only one who could fit in the desk, but when I pulled the cover down, I locked myself in. No one found me for *hours*."

"Maybe this one doesn't lock." Chase wedged his fingers under the cover and tried to lift it. It didn't budge. I went to help, but it was like trying to pick up the side of a house—nothing moved. We just got tired.

Lena crossed her arms over her chest, unsurprised. "Even if it isn't locked, do you really think the three of us are strong enough to lift it?"

I examined the cover—all forty feet of wood. "There's enough wood for maybe three trees."

"Or more," Lena said shortly. Chase slumped against the cover, defeated. "We're stuck here until the giants come back."

"Longer than that," I said, which got both Chase and Lena's attention. "Until the giants need something from the desk."

"Well, we had to hide, didn't we?" Chase said softly.

"I meant in the papers!" Lena snapped. "Jimmy would've never seen us in there."

Chase didn't answer. He sank to the floor, his back against the desk, his head bent and both hands in his hair. He looked so much like he had when we were stuck in the bone-filled bread box that I couldn't get mad at him. Besides, I couldn't muster the energy.

"At least we don't have to deal with that guard dog for a little while," I said.

Lena stared at me. Her nostrils flared so much she kind of reminded me of the dragon.

"We brought the food, right?" I said. "We won't starve. Worst case scenario, we'll just hide until Matilda needs to write a letter or something. We could hide over there." I pointed to a row of dusty binders labeled *Fey Tithe*—one each for the last sixteen years.

Lena sighed. "They don't look like they've been touched in a while."

Chase let his hands fall from his head. He looked almost grateful.

I smiled at him, just a little, and hoped it looked sympathetic, not mocking. "While we're stuck here, why don't we look for the safe?"

It wasn't too hard. About five foot square, it was too wide to fit in any of the cubbyholes.

We found it under a stack of mail on the other side of the workspace. When we pushed the bills off, the weight of the envelopes knocked Lena over.

"They certainly didn't do much to hide it," I said and helped her up.

Lena dusted herself off. "They were probably busy. Last-minute packing."

"They *did* lock it." Chase examined the grate at the back of the safe. The hen's white feathers rustled behind the bars, and the harp's gold strings gleamed.

"So the hen can breathe," Lena guessed.

"Can you fit your hand through?" I asked.

Chase shook his head. He reached toward one of the holes, but when it got close to the grate, gray lightning crackled across the safe and up Chase's arm.

Lena and I jumped back, but Chase grinned, looking more like his usual self. "It didn't hurt."

"I guess we have to open it the old-fashioned way," Lena said.

"You know the combination?" I asked.

Lena nodded. "I watched Jimmy last night."

"You memorized it?" Chase said incredulously. "From a distance of two hundred feet through a crack barely an inch wide while surrounded by bones?" His voice dropped a little on the last word, and it was really hard not to smirk.

"Photographic memory," Lena reminded him, and she reached for the lock.

Chase and I looked at each other as the dial spun and clicked. We were thinking the same thing. One mistake, and we would have to escape the giants' desk with a life-size Lena statue.

I shrugged. "It's her Tale."

"Absolutely." Then she swung the safe's door open smugly.

I cheered. Tapping her fingers on the back side of the door, Lena smiled at me over her shoulder.

The leprechaun gold was already gone, and the hen and the harp were still asleep. The bird clucked a little in the middle of each snore. It didn't make any sense to wake them up before we had a way out.

So we walked to the back of every shelf and cubbyhole, searching for gaps in the wood big enough to crawl out of. Chase took the top levels, and I took the rest. The handle of Lena's flashlight pulled out to make a lantern that sat up by itself, but the light only reached fifteen feet or so. It was so dark we had to feel across the wooden wall with our fingertips.

"Okay, I've got good news and bad news." Chase wandered out of the last cubbyhole. "The good news: I found a hole."

"What's the bad news?" Lena said, without looking up from the papers she was pushing through. Each one was as big as a bedsheet.

"Well, the hole's only big enough to stick my head through. But more good news: there's another mousehole behind the desk, so once we get out of here, we'll have a direct escape route."

"Maybe we can make it bigger," I suggested.

"I think I saw a letter opener around here somewhere." Chase leaped up to a higher shelf. "It would make a good battering ram."

"What an ingenious way to get hurt. Maybe in a little while." Lena pulled a notebook from her backpack and began to take notes. "For now, we still need to figure out what the Snow Queen is after."

"Oh, no," Chase murmured to me. "She's gone into geek mode. We'll never get out now." I gave him a sharp look, and he added hastily, "I mean that in the nicest, most complimentary way possible."

"What did you find?" I asked Lena. Over her shoulder, I read, *Engorgement Spell.*

"The reason Matilda can make her garlic as big as a mixing bowl," Lena said.

Chase came to look too. "And how is this important to our survival?"

"Rumpel would like to see it," Lena told him, her chin jutting out stubbornly. "Since we'll be stuck in here for a while, it doesn't really matter."

Chase ducked his head guiltily.

I wandered to another stack of papers. It was too dark to read in the cubbyhole, so I had to drag each piece toward Lena's lamp one by one. It wasn't easy.

"Nobody get a paper cut," Chase said, starting to search too. "You might need stitches."

The first one I grabbed was a bill for a pair of leather work boots, size 216. The second paper looked like a pretty normal recipe for Ladyfingers until I read: *Ingredients: Two sets of noblewoman's fingers—or any maiden or human female not used to physical labor (*do not use toes as substitute*).* There was a scary-looking brown stain in the corner, so I rushed that one back where I found it.

"Hey, the giant's wife writes poetry," Chase said. "'My heart awakens in sight of your green skin, as clean and warty as a toad's has ever been—'"

"Don't!" Lena and I shouted at the same time.

"I don't want to hear any love poems written by a giant," I said, already a little freaked over Matilda's gruesome recipes.

"Besides, it's not very nice," Lena added. "Those are private."

Chase tossed the paper aside and reached for another one. "Girls."

"Oh, my gumdrops," Lena said.

"What? Did you find it?" I asked.

"No, it's Jimmy and Matilda's tithe statement," Lena said. "They make almost nothing. My gumdrops, it's practically slave labor."

"Lena, I say this with respect," Chase said with a nervous glance in my direction, "but that's just embarrassing. Come on—say it with me: 'Oh, my God.'"

"My grandmother's very strict," Lena said defensively.

"Then say Crud," Chase replied. "I'm sure you can say that."

But Lena shook her head. "She'd make me bite a bar of soap."

"Seriously?" I said, starting to think that Amy was really easy on me.

"That's rough." Chase actually sounded sympathetic. "The Director makes me write when I piss her off, but you win."

I found another recipe (this time for biscuits); a butcher's bill for three whales, four condors, and twelve heifers; and a letter from Matilda's mother telling her not to give up, that every giants' marriage has giant-size problems. I found some regular-size lettering and was incredibly relieved until I realized that it was the fine print for a Bank-Friendly Giant credit card.

Chase found some love letters from Jimmy and Matilda's courtship, wrapped in yards of faded red ribbon. He read one in Lena's light and started gagging loudly.

"Don't want to know," Lena told him firmly.

"Can't repeat." Chase pretended to gasp for air. "Too vile."

Then I found another letter, the envelope strangely cool to the touch. I manhandled it into the light. It was addressed to Jimmy in old-fashioned handwriting, the kind that I hadn't seen since studying the Declaration of Independence in fifth grade. I froze when I saw the symbol in the corner—something I had seen only a couple times before, in dreams.

"What's this symbol stand for?" I asked. "An *S* with a snowflake in the bottom curve."

Chase dropped the receipt he was reading. "That's the Snow Queen's seal."

It couldn't be.

"You found it!" Lena grabbed her flashlight lantern and ran toward me.

It didn't connect right away. For the first time, I was *glad* to be so sleep-deprived. Part of me felt like I was dreaming again. I looked closer at the snowflake, hoping that I had made a mistake, that it wasn't the same symbol. But it looked exactly like the one that had been in my dream, just clearer. Each point was long, as if wickedly sharp, with barbs on the end.

If I hadn't been so tired, I might have had a meltdown right there. But a detached part of me pointed out that we would have plenty of time to analyze dreams *after* we weren't locked in a giant desk anymore.

"I was starting to think that we'd never find it," Chase said, helping Lena wrestle the letter free from the envelope. They propped the paper up so that we could all read at the same time. It was studded with the same wicked-looking snowflakes and covered with the same old-fashioned handwriting as the envelope.

Lena raised the flashlight-lantern.

> *Jimmy Searcaster,*
>
> *I wanted to write you personally to tell you how much the harp would comfort me in my imprisonment. Your mother tells me that she has already applied to you on my behalf, and still, you hesitate. This glass prison won't hold me forever, and I have always known where to find my friends—and my enemies.*
>
> *—S*
>
> *P.S. Do take care of my darlings. They will take care of you.*

"Oh, my gumdrops," Lena breathed.

"The *harp*?" I wondered if my sleepy eyes had misread. "She wants the *harp*?"

"Matilda was *brilliant*," Lena said. "Last night, General Searcaster was just about to demand to see it. The Snow Queen probably gave her orders to make sure it was intact. But Matilda interrupted and brought the harp up first—to throw us off the scent. She knew we'd think she was just changing the subject."

"Well, it worked," I muttered. The harp was the last thing I expected her to want. A giant, glass-mountain-shattering hammer, maybe. A Glacier Amulet, yeah. But a musical instrument?

"I don't believe for a second that she just wants to hear pretty music," Chase said. "So this can't be any old harp. There's bound to be something special about it."

"Maybe it doubles as a key," Lena said. "I've read that some of the new elf-made locks use music instead of number or symbol combinations."

"Well, look at it this way. Now we don't need to waste time searching for a fourth item. We can hit two birds with one stone," I said.

"But we were going to let the Canon handle it," Lena said, hesitantly. "I hope it won't interfere with the Tale too much."

"It shouldn't," Chase said, "but it might be why this particular Tale came up at this particular time. Magic is weird like that."

Lena smiled slightly. "You've been listening to Sarah Thumb."

"'My darlings,'" I read, pointing at the postscript. "Do you think that she sent the guard dogs?"

"'Take care of you,'" Chase said. "A very polite way of saying 'eat you'?"

"Jimmy did say that they didn't belong to him," I said.

"But the Snow Queen isn't known for using dogs," Lena said.

"She uses wolves," Chase said. "She used to break whole wards out of prison and enchant convicts the way fairies used to enchant princes—turning them into animals."

"I thought that was a rumor," Lena said, looking horrified.

Chase shook his head. "They're true. My dad still has the teeth marks to prove it."

"What's the big deal about the Snow Queen anyway?" I didn't want to be bothered, but if this Destiny thing turned out to be true, I should probably find out more about her. "The way I remember it, all she did was take some kid back to her castle, and he *wanted* to go. Personally, the Big Bad Wolf scared me more."

Chase and Lena exchanged a look. "She's not a problem because she kidnaps boys," Chase said. "That was just how she got started."

"I guess you haven't been around long enough to know much about the war," Lena said. "None of the other sixth graders learned anything. The triplets don't know much, and Adelaide doesn't care. I only found out because I read a lot."

It was clearly going to be a long story, so I sat down on a pink eraser, my back to the letter. I didn't want to look at it any more than I had to.

"She's a problem because she can get the villains to work together," Chase explained. "Doing pretty much exactly what she wants."

"Before Solange showed up, villains weren't too bad," Lena said. "I mean, they were evil, of course. Wanting to eat people and everything, but they weren't much of a threat. They never teamed up."

"They knew better than to trust each other," Chase added. "The witch from Hansel and Gretel allied herself with some giants once, but they ended up eating her house. And her, actually."

"Characters only had to deal with them one at a time, which was manageable." Lena's voice started to sound distant and tinny, like she was reading aloud from a page in her photographic memory. "Then, by the end of World War II, the Snow Queen became more prominent. She attempted to rally others for decades, but on March fourteenth, Nineteen forty-five, she developed a new tactic."

"Nineteen forty-five!" I scowled, remembering the Director's Napoleon comment. She'd *wanted* me to believe that the Snow Queen hadn't caused any trouble in hundreds of years, but *why?* If Solange was so bad, what was the point in pretending she wasn't?

"Lena, no offense, but you're starting to sound like the History Channel," Chase complained.

I raised my eyebrows, but since it was true, I couldn't say anything.

Lena *did* look offended. "Well, *you* tell her, if you can do better."

"Look—can we just eat first?" Chase said, and I grinned. We were never going to miss a meal with Chase around. "*Please?* I haven't been this hungry since the Table of Never Ending Refills broke, and we had to eat Rumpy's cooking for a week."

Lena shrugged and slung her backpack off her shoulders. She handed a wrapped parcel to me, but when she tried to pass one to Chase, he took a step back.

"No, thanks," he said. "Those sandwiches suck."

"We would offer you some trail mix, but you ate most of it." Lena unwrapped her sandwich so roughly she ripped the paper.

"I left some chocolate," Chase said defensively.

Lena tugged the bag of trail mix from her pack and showed it to me. It was a third the size it had been when I had last seen it.

"Two M&M's!" I shouted, staring at the bag in Lena's hand. "That doesn't count as not eating them all!"

Chase disappeared into one of the cubbyholes and called back to us, "I thought I saw Matilda's secret stash in here earlier. If you're nice, I'll share."

I snorted. "If the table at EAS was broken, why wouldn't he just bring snacks from home?" I said, lowering my voice so he wouldn't hear.

"Chase lives at EAS," Lena whispered back, obviously still not happy with him. "He didn't have that option."

I wondered if EAS had a boarding school I didn't know about— bunk beds with blankets covered in silver beads like the sleeping bags. But no, Jack was the Canon's champion. His whole family probably lived in an apartment near the instructors' quarters. "Is Chase's mom a terrible cook too?"

Lena shrugged. "I don't know. I don't think she lives with them."

I unwrapped my sandwich slowly, quiet for a moment. From what Chase had said, it sounded like Jack was always on a mission. Mom traveled for work too, but at least she took me with her. If his mom wasn't around, that meant most of the time Chase was by himself.

"But," I asked slowly, "wouldn't it be lonely?"

Lena didn't answer. She took one look behind me and screamed.

hat woke me up.

I jumped to my feet and unsheathed my sword, ready to battle whatever oversize mouse, cockroach, or centipede had wandered into the desk.

"What?" Chase shouted from deep within a cubbyhole on the other side of the desk, where Matilda's stash must have been hidden. He sounded more amused than worried. "Did you find cat food in your sandwich? That happened to me once."

It was a man. He was short and wiry, his red hair braided down his back. His goatee made his face seem very pointed, like a fox. My first thought was that the Director had sent reinforcements, but I couldn't figure out which Character he was.

"He—he came out of the *letter*," Lena whispered.

"Kids? Not EASers." The man sighed. "And here I thought this was going to be so easy." He drew two swords strapped to his back. They were slender and glinted silver in the light of Lena's flashlight. Seeing their sharp points, I froze. He was *not* on our side. "I guess I'll have to kill you. She *did* say leave no witnesses."

I felt it. The fear was familiar at this point. All my muscles clenched, and I stopped breathing, my sneakers stuck to the wood desk like they were superglued there.

But then he went for Lena—Lena who was still sitting, who didn't have time to draw her weapon, who was my friend, my *best* friend. My dream about the Wall flashed through my mind again—her name carved in bubble letters. I couldn't let that happen.

I ran across the desk and knocked both of his blades to the side before he reached her.

From the way his eyes widened, I could tell that he hadn't realized I was there.

I stepped in front of Lena, trying to look as fierce as possible. And also like I knew what I was doing.

"Fine. You first, then." The man smiled and twirled both blades into a defensive position I vaguely remembered seeing in Hansel's class. "I'm not picky."

"Chase!" Lena shouted. "A little help!"

The man attacked. I dodged one slash and turned the other one aside, careful to keep Lena behind me. He sliced at me again, both blades at the same time, and my sword caught them, just a few inches from my face. He leaned on the three crossed blades, pressing them down farther, closer to my nose. I kicked him in the shin.

He hopped away, cursing and rubbing his leg. "That hurt!"

"Run, Lena," I hissed.

Lena sprinted out of the way so fast that I heard her knock into the safe door and slam it shut.

Then he leaped in the air, both blades high above his head. I dodged and repositioned myself carefully so that I was in front of Lena again.

The man grunted, frustrated, and the blows fell faster.

I still sucked. I couldn't do more than block whatever he threw at me, but somehow it was enough.

He did this flourish-y thing and stabbed at my torso eight times in a row. I blocked the first seven and sidestepped the eighth. Then he brought each sword to a different leg. I knocked one out of the way with my sword, and I kicked the hand holding the other one.

It was like a weird runner's high. I was only vaguely aware of my body, blocking and dodging. I couldn't let him reach Lena, and that was the only thought in my head.

He shouted again and spun so quickly that his swords turned in one circular blur like a chainsaw. I stepped out of the way easily. "Rory! Your sword's longer than his," Lena told me eagerly and made a jabbing motion.

Chase was only halfway across the desk, too far to reach me in time. "No!" he shouted, too late.

I shouldn't have tried. As soon as I moved, the man stopped spinning, and he locked my sword up with his left one.

"Fell for it!" The man hooked his hilt guard with mine and twisted the way I remembered so well from Hansel's class. "Finally, I get to kill one of you."

My sword left my hand, and I didn't even *try* to catch it. I lifted one knee and then kicked up the other leg as fast as I could. My sneaker connected with his chin.

His head snapped up with a loud crack, and he stumbled back, his sword falling from his left hand.

"Whoa," Chase said, close by.

I slid over the wood on my knees, snatched my sword from the floor, and stood up slowly, right in front of Lena.

"You little brat!" the man said, holding his jaw. He spit little white bits to the floor. "Those teeth have lasted me well over a hundred years. Now you're *really* going to die."

I braced myself, but then I felt a hand on my shoulder.

"Fall back, Rory," Chase said. "I got this."

I would never admit it to Chase, but I was incredibly glad one of Lena's Companions actually *did* know what he was doing.

"Another one?" The man picked up the sword he'd dropped. "How many of you *are* there?"

Expecting a surprise attack at any second, I slowly sidestepped over to Lena.

"You okay?" I whispered, and she nodded without looking away from the fight.

Chase raised his sword, smirking like he does before he pulls some sort of stunt. Then he did a front flip seven feet in the air and stabbed downward as he passed over the man's head.

The man blocked easily.

"He's just showing off," I said, annoyed with Chase all over again.

"Whatever you do, don't help him," Lena said. "You'll only get in his way."

I believed her. This guy was really good—good enough to keep up with Chase anyway. Chase did this cartwheel thing in midair— kick, blade, blade, kick—and the man blocked four blows, one after the other.

So, how had *I* fought him?

I remembered the runner's high feeling and examined the Fey lettering etched into my blade. Maybe it *was* magic after all.

When I looked up again, the man was down to a single sword. "Oh, Chase stole one."

"That's Ferdinand," Lena told me.

"The name of the move?"

"No, the name of the guy," Chase said, landing lightly, and he lunged in again. "Ferdinand the Unfaithful."

I snorted, wondering how they named these guys. "Is there a Ferdinand the *Faithful*?"

"Yep." Then Lena grabbed my arm and pulled a few cubby-holes away from the fight. "But Chase *is* showing off. Makes him less effective."

Ferdinand ducked under Chase's arm and dashed for the safe. He had stolen his second sword back. Chase muttered some curses and leaped into the air after Ferdinand.

"Let him go," Lena said unexpectedly.

"What?" Chase said, still a few feet above our heads, and privately, I agreed with him.

"The safe," Lena reminded him.

Chase made a face, but he dropped to the floor between me and Lena, breathing hard.

"Oh, you think the safe will finish me off?" Ferdinand panted too, but he was trying to hide it. He stepped backward, toward the safe, sheathing the sword in his right hand. "This is *too* good. I'll have to kill you *after* I open the safe, just to see the looks on your faces."

Chase sent Lena a pleading look, but she just shook her head, her eyes on Ferdinand.

He reached up for the dial and spun it confidently. Raising one eyebrow in our direction, he turned it clockwise, then counter-clockwise, and then clockwise again.

"Do you think that Searcaster gave him the combination?" I whispered to Lena.

"Yep." Then Lena began to smile.

Ferdinand looked at us and grasped the safe's handle firmly. The door swung open easily, but Lena's smile didn't falter.

Ferdinand waggled his fingers at us. "Not even a *hint* of stone."

"Can we attack him now?" Chase said.

Lena shook her head, and Chase sighed. I could relate. I wanted to put a sword through Ferdinand myself.

"Now, I'm in a generous mood," Ferdinand drew his second sword with a lazy flourish. "You three can choose who gets to die first. Now, my money's on—"

Still smiling, Lena pointed at Ferdinand's feet. We all looked down.

His boots were gray—the same smooth, granitelike gray of the safe.

"No!" Ferdinand fumbled in his pocket and pulled out a slip of paper. "I got the combination exactly right, I'm sure of it."

We watched as the fabric of his pants turned from green to gray. The stone color had reached his knees.

"You should've made sure that you had the *whole* combination," Lena said smugly.

With a cry of rage, Ferdinand threw a sword at her. I knocked it out of the way, and Chase caught it by the hilt.

My sword *had* to be magic. There was no way I knocked something out of the air *by myself*.

The stone color traveled past his waist, up his chest, toward his neck. He screamed and raised his other sword over his head.

"Too late," Chase murmured gleefully.

The stone had reached his shoulder and his upper arm, all the way up to his elbow. His muscles froze. He couldn't throw.

"You'll pay for this. You'll—" His mouth grayed and stopped moving. His eyebrows pinched together.

"I believe he's screaming insults with his eyes," Chase said, but then Ferdinand's nose turned gray, and his eyes, and brows, and hair. The last thing he did was curl his fingers toward us, crookedly, like he wanted to claw our eyes, but then those became granite too.

I did pity him, but only a little.

"Lena, that was awesome. How did you do it?" I said, sheathing my sword.

"There's a second combination." Lena pointed to the inside of the door. "I watched Jimmy tap out a pattern. He looked like he was concentrating. I was pretty sure General Searcaster didn't see it."

"You were pretty sure?" Chase stared at Lena. "*You* gambled?"

Lena shrugged, pleased. "I figured we could always fight him after he opened the safe. The harp would've slowed him down."

"He came out of the letter?" I asked.

"Yeah, it's a simple spell," Lena said. "It's a variant of the Door-Trek system. All you need is a doorway and something to tie you to your destination."

"Like a letter you sent there yourself?" I glanced back at Lena's lamp. The letter still leaned next to it, white and square in the dim light.

"It takes a lot of power, though," Chase said, walking toward the safe and Ferdinand.

Lena nodded. "Definitely the Queen's man."

"She must really want that harp," I said quietly. Lena looked at me, suddenly nervous again. "I bet that won't be the last one."

Chase whistled a low note, only a few inches from the Ferdinand statue's face. "Rory, that was some kick."

"Snap kick," I said absently, still thinking about the Snow Queen. "It's pretty much the only thing I remember from karate in first grade."

"Well, I think you broke his jaw." Chase stared at me over the statue's shoulder. "If you were a little taller, you would have knocked him out cold."

I shrugged, feeling pleased and foolish at the same time—and *really* grateful to have a magic sword. I didn't *want* to know what would've happened to Lena without it.

"Shh," Lena said. "Listen."

We strained our ears. Outside the desk, we heard the clicking of claws on the floor and an animal's rumbling growl.

"The guard dog," Chase said, shrugging.

"It must've heard all the commotion," I said.

Lena wrinkled her nose. "Do you guys smell rotten eggs?"

"Hey." Chase raised both hands in the air. "Whoever smelt it dealt it."

I rolled my eyes. Boys are boys, no matter how good their sword skills are.

"It's not *that*," Lena said shortly, but she did look kind of embarrassed. "I was thinking Ferdinand left something behind. Maybe something to attract the dog—"

"Yeah, blame the stone guy. He can't defend himself," Chase said, and he wandered over to the other side of the desk where he'd left a half-eaten, boulder-size bag of Matilda's potato chips.

Glancing at the letter, I tried to guess how long it would be before we had another visitor. The hair stood up on the back of my neck. "Somebody tell me about the Snow Queen."

"Bon appetit," Chase told us happily and then began to munch on an enormous potato chip. "Hey, Lena. Are we really going to sit around and eat and tell stories while we've got evildoers coming out from bits of paper?"

"I do need to *know* this, you know," I said.

"Do you have a better idea?" Lena asked, hands on her hips.

"As a matter of fact . . . ," Chase said. "Rory, come here and pull out your sword."

I did, expecting him to examine the blade and tell me everything he knew about its magical qualities, but instead he inspected my grip around the hilt and adjusted the position of my thumb. His fingers were oily with potato chip grease. "That's really the way you should hold it. Also, keep your elbow up a little more. When you keep it tucked in close to your body like that, it slows you down just a bit. It won't matter in practice, but it will when somebody big and bad tries to kill— What?" Chase asked, finally noticing the way that Lena and I were staring at him.

"You're being uncharacteristically helpful," Lena said slowly.

He shrugged. "I don't know if you noticed this, but Rory's going to kick butt." Chase met my eyes, smirking. "I have to get on her good side while I still can."

I couldn't tell if he was making fun of me. "I think the sword's magic."

"Well, you weren't holding the sword for the Mighty Snap Kick," he pointed out. "That was all you, Rory."

I had a sudden vision of Hansel's sword spinning out of his hand, my blade in the kill position, and the shocked look on the instructor's face. Grinning, I looked to Lena for permission.

Lena glanced from the statue to the letter. "Go ahead. If the Snow Queen wants the harp as much as we think she does, then we'll need all the help we can get."

I made a face at that cheery thought, and swallowing another mouthful, Chase showed me a drill to help keep my elbow away from my body.

Lena told war stories as I practiced.

By the end of the twentieth century, most magical creatures weren't happy. They had long gone into hiding, pushed into the forgotten corners and continents of the world. There were more humans than there had ever been, and it looked like they were leaving magic behind for good. They believed in antibiotics and vaccination shots, not in the Water of Life. Old-fashioned storytelling was replaced by radio, and then television. A lot of the old Tales were forgotten. If parents wanted to scare their children, they talked about bombs exploding, not big bad wolves.

"Watch where you're putting your feet, Rory," Chase said. When Lena gave him a dirty look, he added, "What? Did you want her to learn the wrong way?"

Then the Snow Queen began to advocate bringing back the world of yesteryear—where wolves could eat people's grandmothers in peace, and dragons could steal cattle and princesses, and giants could demand human sacrifices from villages to decrease their grocery bill.

You can see how it would sound appealing. Especially if you're, for example, a highland troll living hand-to-mouth so high in the Rockies that you always have icicles in your fur, and the only warm thing you can catch to eat is a mountain goat or two.

The Snow Queen had an army at her disposal—the trolls and ogres and giants and wolves. They followed the Snow Queen blindly. She also got a bunch of villains to swear allegiance to her—people like Ferdinand—usually for specific rewards. Ms. White's stepmother wanted all of Rhode Island.

"What did the Snow Queen want?" I asked, slashing and parrying and jabbing with my elbow up past my ear the way Chase had shown me.

"Oh, you know, the usual," Chase said.

"Power." Lena sighed. "World domination."

The Characters banded together to stop her. That was the easy part. Ever After School had been around for years, and they have a chapter on every continent except Antarctica. The Canon keeps meticulous records—so it was easy to recruit some of the older Characters.

The problem was that both sides were evenly matched. If you think about it, there's usually a villain for every hero. The stalemate lasted for decades. The threat tainted everything. Even the humans noticed and took precautions the best way they knew how.

"Then why is this the first time I've heard of it?"

"Oh, you've heard of it," Chase told me.

"Why do you think they called it the Cold War?" Lena said.

I blanched, and Chase grinned. "Left side."

Obediently, I started slashing, parrying, and jabbing to the left.

"No, left *arm*." When I scowled, Chase added, "Unless you want to be completely defenseless if someone injures your right arm."

"I don't know. Rory can always resort to the Mighty Snap Kick," Lena said with a small smile, but I passed the hilt from my right hand to my left with a grimace.

"Wow." Chase looked pleased with himself. "If I had known that teaching would get you to listen to me, I would've tried this much earlier."

"Well, you're a better teacher than Hansel," I said.

"Can you tell Hansel that?" Chase grinned. "Can I *be* there when you tell Hansel that?"

"Story," I said firmly.

> The Snow Queen knew she needed more allies to win the
> war. She turned to underhanded methods. She handpicked
> neutral parties and kidnapped family members as collateral.
> Her prisons must've been extensive, because she found
> thousands of new allies in this way. The tide began to turn.
> The Director says that for almost three years, the Characters
> could do little more than hide and defend their loved ones.
> The Snow Queen was a master at intimidation.

"For instance, look at her symbol again," Chase said, and Lena didn't look annoyed at all this time. "A snowflake isn't very scary, but look closely. See how sharp the points are?"

I squinted at it and realized what he meant. "Is it a throwing star?"

Lena nodded. "She gave them to her personal guards, the ones who kept an eye on her allies."

> She used it as her signature. If you crossed her, she left it with
> the bodies.
>
> For the first part of the war, the Fey stayed out of it. They
> didn't mind their anonymity from the human world. They
> enjoyed their privacy and their court games. Every once in
> a while, a fairy would join a side, but it was an individual
> decision. The King of the Unseelie Court's favorite daughter,
> for instance, joined our side—her and her betrothed.
>
> Then, one day, a couple of decades ago, their bodies
> showed up in her father's throne room, marked with the
> Snow Queen's flakes.

It backfired. The Fey were furious. The Unseelie princess
was the heir to the throne and very popular. Fairies joined us
en masse. They laid siege to the Snow Queen's palace. Her
army was defeated. She was captured.

"How?" I asked. "Aren't you skipping over the important bits?"
Basically everything that would help me if I ever *did* meet the Snow
Queen.

Lena and Chase looked at each other, waiting for the other one
to answer. "We don't know," Chase admitted.

"It was a Character," Lena said. "A Destined One. I know that
much."

"We could look it up," Chase said. "His name is on the Wall of
Failed Tales in big, golden letters."

"But *how* did he Fail?" I still wanted to find out something use-
ful. "The Snow Queen was captured."

"He died," Chase said. "That's pretty much an epic Fail."

I stopped practicing, feeling exactly like I'd been punched in
the stomach—breathless and slightly vomity.

"Chase," said Lena in a scolding tone.

"What?"

Lena pointed at me.

"Rory, *you're* not going to die," Chase said in a slow patient
voice, as if it were painfully obvious. "We're not even sure what the
Canon thinks about you. We'll just keep her from breaking out of
prison, and everything will be fine."

"If she's still such a threat, why wasn't she—" I didn't finish the
question, shocked that I could have such a ruthless thought.

"—killed?" Lena said, looking like she knew exactly what I was
thinking.

"They *tried*. They executed her no less than eighteen times," Chase said with a heavy sigh. "Burned her at the stake, stabbed her through the heart, then the usual: firing squad, beheading, lethal injections, and then, uh . . ." He stumbled a little, seeing the queasy looks we were giving him. "A bunch of tortures the Fey cooked up. For revenge."

"So, she can't be killed." My voice rose shrilly. I hated that I was panicking. I hated that Chase and Lena were *watching* me panic. I hated the pity on their faces. "And she can magic bad guys back and forth," I added, jabbing a finger at the letter.

I was shocked to see someone actually standing over there—a really old man.

"Evildoer!" Lena cried. "Evildoer alert!"

"You don't need to shout, Lena. I'm right here." Chase rushed over to intercept him.

The old man ran toward Chase, swinging a black ax. He had a hunchback, a very crooked nose, and warts on his hands.

"This is the most exciting story-time I've ever had," I told Lena. "Two villains in a little over an hour."

The old man turned to me and smiled. Most of his teeth were black. He took a tie-dyed sack off his shoulder, and when he opened it in front of me, the colors started to spin in a hypnotizing way. Suddenly, I felt dizzy, and even sleepier than I'd been all morning, and for some weird reason, I wanted to jump *in* the sack.

"Rory, don't look at it!" Lena cried. "It's enchanted."

"I noticed," I said, rubbing my eyes.

Chase crashed into the old man noisily. "Hey, Ugly—you're fighting *me*."

I looked back, just in time to see the end of the fight. Chase disarmed the guy neatly, stabbed him through the shoulder, and then kicked the old man backward. The villain fell through the letter, sack and all, and disappeared.

Looking a lot like his dad, Chase grinned with his arms crossed and one hand on his chin. "We don't really need to worry unless she sends Bluebeard," he told us, leaning back toward the wood that divided the cubbyholes, but he misjudged the distance and tumbled into the darkness.

"Smooth, Chase," I said, half-laughing. "Bluebeard will quake with fear."

But Chase didn't come out of the cubbyhole.

"Chase?" I called uncertainly, but no one answered.

"Oh, my gumdrops." Lena stared at the queen's letter. "He fell through."

"Through the desk?"

"Through the *letter*," Lena said, her voice a couple octaves higher than usual. "Of course the spell would allow for unexpected magics and persons to travel bilaterally. The Snow Queen wanted her villains to transport the harp back to her."

I had a hard time following Lena when she started talking technical, so I wasn't sure if I understood her right. "You mean, Chase went to the *Glass Mountain*?"

ena nodded, horrified. "This is bad. She'll capture him, hold him for ransom, maybe. Oh, maybe it would've been better for us to let her have the harp after all."

Something clenched in my chest when I imagined Chase, surrounded by villains, dozens and dozens of them, all staring at him with little smirks, more than he could ever fight by himself.

You'll have to follow him through the letter, Rapunzel had said. It *was* spooky how right she was, but I was on the verge of getting used to it.

"I have to go after him," I said.

"Why?"

"Rapunzel told me to."

Lena bit her lip, glancing between me and the letter. "Rory, it's hard for anyone to understand what Rapunzel means. I can't imagine she would want you to face the Snow Queen directly."

It was more than just what Rapunzel had said. I didn't *want* to leave Chase there alone. I didn't want to sit in the giants' desk helplessly, wondering if he was okay. I wanted to go after him.

I was *worried* about Chase. And kind of shocked to discover it.

"She said I would have to bring him back." In front of the letter, I drew my sword slowly and hoped that I hadn't used all the magic up in one go.

"Rory, please. She's bound to have allies in there with her, and if she catches you—if you both don't come back . . ." Lena faltered, wide-eyed.

If *she* were the one who had fallen into the Glass Mountain, I would have already jumped through the letter after her. I wouldn't have even stopped to explain myself first. I couldn't stay any longer, even to comfort Lena. "I'll bring him back, I promise."

Then I leaped through.

Cold radiated everywhere, starting as an ache in my bones, the same way it does when a winter wind blows through your clothes. Then my limbs stiffened, like a layer of ice covered my entire body. I couldn't move. I couldn't even breathe.

Just when I started to panic, I tumbled onto a thin blue-and-white rug patterned with snowflakes.

Chase was in the far corner, fighting with a pack of wolves bigger than he was. His sword was already bloody and a lump of gray fur lay motionless, so he had already beaten one of them.

At the other end of the room, the old man with the sack stood between a desk and a rack of spears. His shoulder was still bleeding heavily. He picked up the spear closest to him and began to smile in a way that meant trouble for Chase.

The man threw the spear, and I ran directly into his path. That weird runner's high returned, and my sword struck the shaft so hard that it fell to the rug with a muffled clatter.

Then the old man with the sack saw me and smiled so widely that I could see the gold caps on his molars.

"Ugh," I said, before I could stop myself. "As villains go, I think I liked Ferdinand better."

The old man didn't appreciate that. With a scowl, he grabbed a second spear from the rack next to him and advanced toward me.

I pushed all thoughts away and lifted my sword. He jabbed so fast the silver point sliced my left sleeve, nearly brushing the skin. He stabbed toward me again, and my sword knocked it out of the way a half instant before the point touched my face.

Then I heard Chase shout and the wolves growling behind me. He needed my help.

Without really paying attention to what I was doing, I grabbed a heavy book off a shelf beside me. When the old man tried to stab me a third time, I deflected the spear with my sword and threw the book like a Frisbee. It thunked him in the head, and the old man collapsed.

I whirled back to Chase, ready to charge the nearest wolf.

"*Genius*—using a book as a weapon," Chase said, impressed. "We should tell Lena. She always has one handy." He pulled his sword out of a dead black canine, and three other bodies lay still around him.

"You didn't need my help," I said accusingly.

"You came to help me?" Chase grinned. "Rory, I'm touched."

I rolled my eyes, distracted. Why would Rapunzel send me after him if he didn't need saving?

"As you can see, all the bad guys have been defeated," Chase continued. "In *this* room, anyway."

I glanced around, expecting to find evidence of an evildoer, maybe some torture devices tucked in a corner where normal people put their exercise equipment.

"It's an office," I said, surprised. It wasn't very big, but it seemed like a fairly normal home office besides all the spears, the dead wolves, and the unconscious villain. One wall was covered in maps, one with bookshelves, and another with filing cabinets that looked like they were made out of real silver.

I was distracted for a moment by the picture on the closest bookshelf. In a plain, wooden frame, a grainy black-and-white photograph showed a woman in an eighteenth-century dress. Her dark braid coiled at her feet like a rope. She looked familiar—something about the expression in her dark eyes.

I pointed it out to Chase. "Look."

"It's a Rapunzel," Chase said.

"But doesn't it look like *our* Rapunzel?" I asked Chase. He looked closer and shrugged. "Is this really the Glass Mountain?"

To answer, Chase pointed at the last wall.

It was made entirely of glass—a thick lumpy sort of glass with ripples in it, like you see in antique windows. Beyond it were great black and green bumps that looked a lot like mountains covered in forests. In the very middle of the glass wall yawned a dark empty doorway.

"Oh, good—I bet that's the way back." I took a few steps toward it.

"Just a minute. Now that we're here, we should look around," Chase said, sheathing his sword.

That was why Rapunzel said I would have to bring Chase back. He got distracted when he was by himself.

"Do you have any idea how worried Lena will be if we don't come back right away?" I said sharply.

Chase shot me an irritated look. "Lena is going to worry anyway. It's what she does. But do you think anyone else will be able to see this room?"

He had a point.

I sighed deeply. *Every second spent in the Glass Mountain dramatically increases the probability of a personal encounter with the Snow Queen,* said a voice in my head that sounded a lot like Lena.

But I couldn't leave Chase. If I didn't help him, it would only take longer to drag him back to the desk.

"If someone comes in, and we get caught, I'm totally blaming you," I said.

"If someone comes in, we'll dive through that doorway before Lena can say, 'Oh, my gumdrops.'" Chase went to the filing cabinet.

I tackled the desk, keeping my sword pointed at the old man and the sack, just in case he woke up. Each handle was shaped like a snowflake, but the drawers wouldn't open when I pulled on them. I had to content myself with the papers that covered the desk.

"Most of it looks like fan mail." I put aside one letter and picked up another signed by *Your Most Affectionate Troll, Lord Grumblot the DisGruntled.*

"This too." Chase slid another drawer closed, making a face. "She's *filed* them."

Your Illustrious Majesty, I read, *I sincerely hope that you can get the information you require in some other way. I deeply regret to inform you that the American EASers you recently offered to purchase have escaped with the help of the rings of return I'd meant to throw in as a bonus—*

I dropped the letter mid-sentence, heart thumping. I had the sneaking suspicion that the same hand that had written it had also cut off Evan's fingers a couple weeks ago.

"Torlauth sent her a letter. Just this weekend," Chase said, scowling at a file. "And he's included a detailed report on our fighting force. I *knew* the last-minute tournament was suspicious."

"Is he on her side?" I asked.

Chase shook his head and shoved the file back where he found it. "Torlauth is on *Torlauth's* side. He just likes blood. Do you know what he told George after the ref stopped them? 'I miss the war. They *wanted* us to kill people then.'"

My mouth went dry. No wonder George had lost the third match.

"Don't tell Lena," Chase said uncomfortably, realizing he'd said too much. "George made me promise not to mention it to anyone. He knew it would scare his family."

I nodded quickly and turned back to the desk. Lena definitely didn't need to know.

After reading the next letter, I checked and double-checked the signature. "Chase, look at this." I crossed the room, reading aloud. "'A Catalogue of Damages and Disrepairs incurred upon the Palace of the Indomitable Snow Queen, as reported by Her Majesty's Humble Servant Genevieve Searcaster.' It's dated yesterday. It's not a coincidence that Searcaster got Jimmy and Matilda out of the house and to the Arctic Circle. She was on a reconnaissance mission."

That worried Chase. "Keep looking. Maybe we can figure out why she wants the harp so badly."

"Did you see these?" On top of each file cabinet sat a stack of papers, held in place by a glass paperweight. When I moved it, it was cold to the touch, and I saw a face caught in the glass, frozen in agony. Goose bumps sprouted on my arms. Even though I couldn't explain why, I knew that it was a real person, trapped inside. I put it back as fast as I could.

Chase read the paper I held in my other hand. "'Confirmed Allies.' There must be tens of thousands of names here, way more than she had when she started out last time." He took the list and started flipping through. He stopped at the third page and stared at one of the names. "Crap. I *know* that guy. I used to fence with his son."

I picked up the other stacks of paper, making sure I didn't look closely at any of the paperweights again. "'Potential Allies—To Be Persuaded. Potential Allies—To Be Bribed. Potential Allies—To Be Blackmailed.' This is why she's keeping track of her fan mail. She's organizing the people who stay in touch with her."

Chase rubbed his face, still reading the list of confirmed allies. "She's a lot closer to getting her army back together than anyone guessed."

We couldn't let that happen. We couldn't let her get out of prison. We had to return to the giants' desk and figure out how to get the harp far, far away.

"Put that in your pocket," I told Chase and stuffed the other three lists in my jeans. "The Canon will want to see it." I strode across the room, toward the glass wall and the doorway waiting for us. "Let's go."

"Hold on. If Lena was *that* worried, she could've come after us." Chase hurried to the last file cabinet, half the size of the other three, and when he moved the paperweight to grab the stack on top, the whole file cabinet swung out of the way.

A door stood there, even though I knew it hadn't a moment before. My heart missed a beat. The doorknob had a graceful scrolling *S* under it, decorated with a snowflake, but this door—I realized with relief—wasn't wooden like the one I had seen in my dreams. It was made out of glass and swung slightly open, as if a breeze pushed it.

Chase hadn't noticed it yet. "'Known Enemies.' I wonder if I'm in this."

"Chase," I said, pointing.

Voices crept through the crack. The first was a high, musical voice that made me shudder harder than traveling through the letter. The second voice belonged to a young man, one that Chase and I both recognized.

"Dad," Chase whispered. He took a step toward the door.

I caught his arm. "He sounds fine. We have to go while she's occupied."

Chase knew I was right, but then we heard Jack's voice again.

"*Please*, Rory," he said, sounding a little desperate.

It was a terrible idea. So many things could go wrong. So many villains could get between us and the way back. So many doors could turn out to be the one I'd been dreaming about, and I wasn't ready for that yet.

Then I saw Chase's expression, and I knew that if it were *my* mother talking to the Snow Queen, nothing in the world would get me to leave before I made sure she was okay.

"Quickly," I said, remembering my promise to Lena. Besides, Chase was much more likely to get caught if I didn't help him.

When we stepped outside the door, I thought we were walking on air for one excruciating second.

I froze, hardly breathing.

Even the ledge we were standing on was clear. Outside the office, everything was made out of glass.

"Stand on the carpet." Chase pointed out the light blue rug that ran along the ledge. "That way you won't be able to see the drop."

I stepped onto it carefully and stood exactly in the middle.

We could still hear the voices but we couldn't see them—or even tell where they came from. The glass dome threw the sound around in a weird, echoing way.

"Why is it so hot in here?"

"Greenhouse effect," Chase whispered. He picked a direction and started walking. "It's a good thing. The heat makes it harder for the Snow Queen to gather magic."

It was also incredibly bright. Sunlight streamed in from every direction, and I could see the dust smeared on Chase's face and the gritty streaks on his shirt.

"You're filthy," I whispered.

"Look who's talking," Chase whispered back.

I glanced down. My dusty jeans were almost as gray as the Ferdinand statue. The light and the glass and the dirt on my clothes made me feel very young—and very conspicuous.

On one side of the ledge was a glass wall, just like the one in the office. On the other side was a maze of crisscrossing panes of glass, full of rooms and corridors and hallways. I sincerely hoped we wouldn't have to go down there. We might never find our way back.

Chase's eyes traced the maze too. "I wonder where all the people are."

"What people?"

"She's supposed to have, like, a hundred servants," Chase said.

Then with every step, I worried that someone was going to appear behind us.

Every fifteen feet, a portrait of the Snow Queen hung from the railing above the maze. I only examined the first one closely. The Queen was in profile, so pale that she looked like she was covered in frost. She looked a lot younger than I expected her to be, not much older than Rapunzel. She held her chin high, defiantly, as if she saw an army coming for her just beyond the frame. In each portrait, her crown changed—one with towering icicles, one covered in delicate filigree like airy snowflakes, another brilliant with diamonds, but her position and her expression didn't. She always looked beautiful and cruel.

She also looked like Rapunzel's carving.

The ledge curved, and the maze of glass panes gave way to one enormous room, bigger even than the giants' kitchen. It was bare, except for the long glass table that ran from one end to the other and the trolls and wolves standing like guards at the edge of the room.

"I guess we know why the maze was empty," Chase whispered.

He hadn't noticed the two figures at the end of the table closest to us, a hundred feet below.

The railing was glass too—we couldn't hide behind it—so I ducked behind the closest portrait and dragged Chase down with me. I pointed out the two figures—Jack seated at the head of the table and the young woman pouring something yellow and syrupy into his goblet. Her back was to us.

"Fey honey mead," Chase whispered in disgust. "How did she know?"

"Know what?"

"My dad's allergic to it or something. It affects him in a weird way," Chase said. "He doesn't always remember what happens when he has it."

"Then maybe he won't drink it," I said, but then Jack reached for the glass and threw his head back carelessly. It didn't seem like this was his first serving.

"He loves that stuff." Chase looked furious. "Don't ask me why. It tastes like dirt, honey, and grape juice gone sour."

"Delicious," we heard Jack say. "Can't get mead like this just anywhere."

"I can see how you might find my prison pleasant," said the

cold musical voice we had heard in the office. It came from the woman with the pitcher. "But it wouldn't feel so luxurious if you couldn't walk through those doors whenever you chose."

She turned, and I recognized her. She was the girl I had seen in Ms. White's mirror. She was the Snow Queen.

Her portrait didn't do her justice. She was very beautiful, but it was a dangerous kind of beauty, like ice glittering in the sun, dazzling you while you slowly froze to death.

Jack certainly seemed a little dazzled anyway.

Chase wrinkled his nose. "Thawed isn't a good look for her. See how yellow she is? And her hands are puffy."

"It does get terribly lonely here," the Snow Queen said. "Surrounded by guards and servants. I can't tell you how pleased I am that you came to visit. It's such a delight to have someone to talk to."

Jack didn't say anything, but he looked flattered. He held his empty glass up to her.

She refilled his glass with a smile, bending her head elegantly. Her shadow fell across him, and I knew something terrible was going to happen.

From the frozen look of horror on his face, I was pretty sure Chase felt the same way.

"I'm allowed so few comforts." The Snow Queen sighed. "Perhaps a nice bottle here and there. A vase of flowers from an old friend. But nothing the slightest bit magical. No magic mirrors. Not even a singing harp."

Chase and I looked at each other. "She *really* wants that harp," I whispered.

"I would be more than willing to pay for such an extravagance," the Snow Queen continued. "I do have a little of my own money left, but Mildred is so strict. Terribly unfair. I've heard that she's not always fair toward you, either."

"I can't say that," Jack said, so swiftly that I was proud of him. "She builds her reputation on being fair. I couldn't complain about that."

Chase winced.

"They say that she doesn't appreciate what you do." The Snow Queen began to smile, and it was awful. You could practically see her plotting. "Someone like you, a Giant-Killer. In centuries past, the Canon would have covered you in the glory you deserve."

"A little more appreciation would be nice," said Jack, and Chase looked furious again. "She has me sit in these meetings, and she sends me to the dwarves; to the mountain trolls, rock trolls, and ice trolls; to the valley elves—"

"Shut *up*," Chase whispered fiercely, but of course, his father couldn't hear.

"They do mention you, you know," the Snow Queen said. "Those *outside* the Canon. They know what kind of a warrior you are. They haven't stopped talking about the way you defeated Habbilar the Magnificent. Slew Cosid the Odd with his own sword."

This was why it was so easy for her to win allies. She found out exactly what you wanted, and she offered it to you but at a terrible price.

"Oh, you heard about that." Jack scratched the back of his head. "We didn't really mean to kill Cosid. The Director just sent me to check on him, to see where his loyalties were and all. He wasn't in a talking mood. More of a fighting mood. A *killing* mood, actually."

"Mildred has asked you to visit her allies?" the Snow Queen said politely.

"Don't tell her *that*," Chase whispered.

"Maybe if we sent him a message, threw something at him—"
I had a vision of writing a note and sailing a paper airplane over
to the table.

But even Jack wasn't *that* stupid. He only sipped from his glass
and stared at the Snow Queen, looking a little guilty.

Chase relaxed.

The Snow Queen set the pitcher down and pulled up the chair
next to Jack. "Don't mind me. I'm just making conversation. I
must be a little out of practice." She rested her elbows on the table
and dropped her chin to the palm of her hand. Looking through
her lashes innocently, she sent Jack a brilliant smile until he smiled
back crookedly.

"Tell me about the children," she said. "I'm always interested
in the children. I'm sure Mildred has some new ones by now. This
Rory Landon, for instance."

My stomach dropped a little bit. I thought I hadn't heard right,
but Chase looked at me, waiting for me to react. I peeked further
around the portrait we were hiding behind, trying to get a better
look.

"Chase talks about her all the time," Jack said. "Personally, I
don't see what the big deal is. They say that she half-blinded a
dragon in Yellowstone, but I'm not so sure that it wasn't *my* son.
Why would Chase bring his sword into the lair and not *use* it?
Ridiculous."

The Snow Queen didn't move, but her gaze slid sideways. She
looked up, straight at me. Her eyes were almost colorless, the pale
blue of glacier ice.

I knew suddenly how dangerous she was. She wouldn't just come
after me. She would come after Chase and Lena and Rapunzel. She
would enter the human world and charm Mom and Amy so easily.

They wouldn't recognize the danger until it was too late.

"She sees us," I told Chase, my mouth dry.

"But Sarah Thumb says she's going to change things, change the Tales," Jack continued, oblivious.

"Good." Chase stood up, where any minion could see him, and shouted, "Dad, if you say one more word about my friend Rory, I'll break every window in your truck!"

Jack's mouth fell open. *My* mouth fell open.

I don't know what surprised me more: the part where Chase completely gave us away, the part where he got mad at his dad, or the part where he called me his friend.

The Snow Queen lost no time. She gestured to one of her servants, and the guards at the edge of the room began to file out. They were coming.

"Run. Run now," I said, grabbing Chase's hand and sprinting back the way we came.

We rounded the corner at full speed. Bulky figures wove through the maze of glass panes, trolls with spears and huge wolves, and I pushed myself faster.

"There's the portrait with the icicle crown," I said hoarsely, pointing. "It's the next door on the right."

"Crap. The carpet," Chase panted. I looked down. It moved backward under our feet, so we made about as much headway as if we ran the wrong way on a conveyor belt.

It was like a cartoon. Or like one of those nightmares where you're running and running and not going anywhere, and the bad guys keep getting closer and closer. Chase pointed behind us. The Snow Queen walked up, only twenty feet away. The carpet didn't give *her* any trouble.

Up close, I realized what Chase meant about her being yellow.

Her hair looked as flat and dry as straw. Her skin was the same shade as half-melted slush with a little mud mixed in.

She smiled, the same terrible smile.

She was too close. She would catch us. She would catch Chase and blackmail Jack into doing something awful, something far worse than accidentally leaking information.

I had to get him out.

I snatched her portrait off the rail—the one with the icicle crown—and flung it at her.

Glass shattered, but I didn't turn around to look.

I grabbed Chase and pulled us off the moving carpet.

"Not me!" we heard the Snow Queen say. "After *them*!"

We slipped a little on the glass, almost sliding past the office. Chase snagged the door frame and swung us inside. The dark doorway in the glass wall was still open. Trolls in hockey masks clattered into the room behind us, shouting for us to stop.

Chase and I ran into the dark.

The cold wasn't so terrible this time, maybe because I was expecting it. I only had time for a few shivers before I tripped on wood.

Humongous papers loomed all around us. Lena hovered over me anxiously. We were back at the desk.

Chase moaned and slumped over.

"Chase? Chase!" I tapped his face gently.

His eyelids fluttered, but he didn't open his eyes.

"Don't go to sleep, Chase. Are you wounded? You have to tell me where." I squinted, but the light was too faint for me to see. "What happened to the flashlight? Why is everything so dark?"

"The battery's running out. You two were gone for a long time," Lena said softly. She was using that quiet, slow voice that she only used when she was trying to keep me from freaking out. She walked over to the Snow Queen's letter and touched it carefully. Her hand stopped at the paper. "As I thought, the spell is out of magic. It had to work hard for six transports so close together."

I didn't care much for the spell right then, not when it looked like Chase was unconscious. "But Chase—"

"That's why he was knocked out," Lena said calmly. "The spell had to take energy from you two to send you back. Aren't you tired?"

Now that she mentioned it, I was suddenly exhausted. My hands shook, my head spun, and my eyelids drooped.

Lena shoved one of Matilda's potato chips in my hands. "Eat this. Food will help. You and Chase will be fine after a little sleep."

It was hard to let go of the sense of impending doom. "The Snow Queen was after us. And her guards. If they come through the letter—"

"They can't," Lena said in the same quiet voice. "I told you. The magic's all used up. It'll be a while before she can gather enough power to send even one person. I would say we have at least twenty-four hours." Even in the dim light, I could see that she wasn't as calm as she sounded. Her face was strained. It must've been awful for her, waiting for me and Chase.

I hated to make her worry. I nibbled a little on the chip and tried to take longer breaths.

"You have to tell me what happened before you pass out too," Lena said. It was the same thing George had told Evan when he had returned from the White Snake Tale. For some reason, that calmed me the most. If we had come out of the Glass Mountain with all our fingers and toes, we couldn't be that bad off.

I told her.

Everything seemed much more serious watching Lena react to it. Fear crept into her eyes when I got to the lists. She seemed unsurprised when I described Jack's stupidity, but when I mentioned how I recognized the Snow Queen from Ms. White's mirror, when I said that the Queen asked about me, Lena sent me such a worried look that I knew I couldn't pretend anymore. It was definitely me, the newcomer everyone was talking about. I was like the Snow Queen somehow, and she was part of my stupid Destiny.

I was too tired to care. Sometime in the middle of describing our escape, still mumbling about the dark doorway and the guards in hockey masks, I slid to the floor beside Chase, fast asleep.

e have to go!"

Lena's fierce whisper nearly woke me up, but for an instant, I was still half-dreaming. I still saw the ancient door with the Snow Queen's symbol hanging from the doorknob. For the first time, I noticed the wood was covered in frost. My breath hung white in the air. I knew the fate of the world depended on what was on the other side, and I knew I had to go in alone.

It was also the third time I had dreamed of that door.

"Rory, get up! Chase!" Lena snapped. "They're back."

A door—the front door—swung open with a squeal, and there was Jimmy's voice. "I *hate* red-eye flights."

I sat up with a start.

"Five more minutes," Chase complained sleepily, and I clapped a hand over his mouth. He opened one eye and scowled at me, and I pointed outside.

"I'm sorry, dear. I was just so eager to get home." Matilda had come back too. "Besides, what's the point of having a magic carpet if you don't use it whenever you want?"

There was the thud of two humongous suitcases and the swish of very heavy feet wiping their shoes.

"Well, you better pay that bill if it was so important that we *had* to rush back," said Jimmy.

"Hide!" Lena whispered.

Each of us sprinted for a cubbyhole. The desk cover slid up with a rumble, and the light blinded me. I squeezed my eyes shut and walked farther into the desk, keeping one hand on the wall. I tripped over a forgotten pencil.

"It has to be around here somewhere," Matilda said. "I left it someplace where I could— Oh my goodness!"

I froze, sure that one of us had been discovered.

"Honey!" Matilda said, calling over her shoulder. "It looks like we had a visitor while we were gone."

"Do I need to get the flyswatter?"

"No, no, it looks like the safe already got him," said Matilda, and I breathed again. She had only found Ferdinand.

Claws clicked on the hard floors below, and then the sulfur smell that Lena had mentioned drifted toward me.

"Oh, no," Matilda said as a familiar eerie song filled the desk— like the *Jaws* theme with an extra hissing note. "Jimmy, can you come get Sparkia? Last time, she flew up on the desk and burned half of my poems."

Burned? I wondered, and my spine went cold. Opening my eyes, I edged toward the opening carefully.

"Good riddance," Jimmy muttered.

"What did you say?" Matilda asked in a sharp voice.

"Just grab her by the collar and pull her off the table," Jimmy called back.

I peered around the corner of the cubbyhole, just in time to watch Matilda curl her hand around Sparkia's collar. I also saw Sparkia's talons on the edge of the desk, her green-gold scales, and her yellow bulging eyes, staring at me.

A plume of fire unfurled in my direction.

"Stop it, Sparkia! Bad dragon!"

I stepped back quickly. A loose paper five feet from me caught on fire. It burnt to cinders in just a few seconds. The smoke seared my lungs, and I pressed both hands over my mouth. One cough would give me away.

"What's she doing, Matty?" Jimmy called.

"She just went crazy!" Matilda's voice sounded strained, and the dragon's claws scratched against the wood. They were struggling with each other. "Breathing fire and trying to get on the desk."

"She probably just wants the hen. She hasn't eaten in a while. Don't hurt her. We can't afford for Solange to be angry with us," Jimmy said.

"Rory," a human-size voice said softly.

I looked up, both hands still over my mouth. Chase stood in the opening of the cubbyhole and gestured for me to follow him.

We snuck to the other edge of the desk. Seeing us, Sparkia lunged again, nearly breaking Matilda's grip on her collar.

Matilda grunted a little and turned back to yell at her husband. "Can you come *help*?"

I stopped short when I noticed Jack Attack's hook stuck into the wood and the rope hanging down to the floor. All the old fear came rushing back—plus the nausea, and the dizziness.

Chase shot me a withering look. Jimmy's footsteps thudded closer. On the ground, Lena watched us anxiously. Chase leaped off the desk, dragging me with him. He grabbed the rope to slow our descent, and it almost yanked my shoulder from its socket. I had just a second to feel terrified, and then our feet connected safely with the floor.

I glared at him. "You *suck*."

"You really need to get over that heights thing," he said, watching the dragon. Jimmy had Sparkia by the muzzle, telling her what a bad dragon she was and promising her a fatted calf if she behaved. I tried to remember bone names from all the crime shows I'd ever watched.

"Femur," I whispered, and Chase flinched. "Humerus. Scapula."

"Not *now*," Lena said. "We need to get to the mousehole behind the desk."

Without another word, we ran along the wall, around the corner, and into the hole. Lena turned on her flashlight. It only had enough juice to show us four feet of the path ahead, so we had to walk slowly.

I snorted, shaking my head. "A guard *dragon*?"

"I know," Chase said, laughing a little. "But to a giant, it's about the same size."

"Don't talk." Lena sounded much more frantic than seemed normal, considering that we had just escaped safely. "Dragons can't smell much, with all the sulfur they breathe, but they can hear just fine."

Chase and I walked even quieter then. We came outside. The sunlight glittered on the pool so brightly that my eyes got a little teary. We were right beside the front door. It was morning.

"Hey, Rory," Chase said quietly. "Did we really go to the Glass Mountain yesterday? Or was that just a dream, and therefore something we can look forward to in the future?"

I looked at him, mouth twisting in a grimace, not answering. He looked at the ground, fingering his sword hilt with a dark expression. We both didn't want to think about it.

"Mmm, fresh air," Chase said with false cheer. "Fresh, non-sulfurous air."

I smiled, but Lena didn't even take a moment to appreciate our luck. She ran under the bushes toward where we left the other packs. Chase and I followed slowly, fighting about normal, non-evil things.

Yawning, I stretched. My arm muscles protested. "I'm so *sore*."

"Yeah, a wooden desk is no substitute for a good sleeping bag and some petals. My entire side feels bruised."

"It's not that. It was training. And now *both* my arms hurt instead of just one."

"I'm so sorry," Chase said innocently. "Want me to make your sword heavy again?"

"No."

"'Cause that kind of sore would blow this kind of sore way out of the water."

"I said *no*, Chase."

"Will you two stop bickering for just ONE MINUTE?" Lena shrieked.

Chase and I both froze. I wondered briefly if there was any possible way the Snow Queen could have taken our Lena and left a meaner, angrier one in her place.

She sat in the dirt under the bushes. Our sleeping bags, extra clothes, a first aid kit, the last of our food, and everything else that was supposed to be in our packs were strewn around her.

She clutched the hourglass that Rumpel had given her with shaking hands, and under her glasses, tears glinted on her cheeks.

"Don't you see what's happened?" she whispered.

There was no sand left. We had run out of time.

Horror washed over Chase's face.

"It's over." She hugged the hourglass to her chest. "We've failed. *I've* failed. I'm a Failed Tale."

I thought of the Wall, of her name carved there in bubble letters, and suddenly I felt like a Failed Companion.

"No," I said fiercely. After all that we'd been through, I refused to let it end this way. I knelt next to her and tried to work the hourglass out of her arms, worried that she could cut herself if she squeezed harder and broke it. "Lena, it's not possible."

"They'll put my name on the *Wall*."

"Lena, don't cry," Chase said in a small voice. "Crying really freaks me out."

I sent him a quick glare to let him know how unhelpful he was. I took off Lena's glasses and started to wipe her face with my sleeve until I realized how much dust and soot was on it. Then I used the closest sleeping bag.

She sniffled and hiccupped, but she stopped crying.

"Lena," Chase said. His voice was much gentler. "Dealing with the Snow Queen changes everything. No one's going to blame you, and they definitely won't put your name on the Wall. I mean, we should get points just for surviving."

Even though none of us mentioned it, I knew all three of us were thinking of the White Snake Tale. I touched my hand and remembered the fingers Evan had lost.

Lena looked at Chase with red-rimmed eyes, and she hiccupped again.

"Maybe you weren't *supposed* to get the hen and the harp," Chase said softly. "Maybe in this version of 'Jack and the Beanstalk,' we were just supposed to find out what the Snow Queen was up to. We'll just go down and tell the Director everything. If my dad's back, she'll send him and some others—"

I frowned. The idea of letting the grown-ups handle everything wasn't very comforting this time, and I couldn't figure out why.

"Easy for *you* to say," Lena said savagely. "You don't have to go back to my grandmother, who's still mad at me for getting conned out of a month's grocery money. You don't have to tell her you had a fortune of gold coins and then left them in a giant's desk. You don't have to explain how you Failed your Tale."

I looked around. We had only two packs. She had left hers behind—the one with all the food *and* all her new gold coins.

For Lena, coming home to her family without the riches of her happily-ever-after would be so much worse than the usual disgrace. Her Tale had been her chance to make everything right.

"Jenny will tell me how reckless I am," Lena mumbled, "and it'll be true."

"I'm sorry." Chase looked a little stunned. He was only trying to be nice. "I'm really sorry, Lena."

Lena covered her face in her hands and didn't answer. I knew I only had a few seconds before she started sobbing again.

"You haven't Failed," I said softly, and once it was out of my mouth, I believed it.

She made a scoffing sound. "Well, let's see—no gold, no hen, no—"

"Yeah, right *now*," I pointed out. "But it's only been a few days. The original Beanstalk Tales took *forever*. The Jacks used to let *months* go by before visiting the giants again."

Chase's eyes gleamed in a hopeful way, but he didn't say anything.

"But Rumpel said that we only had four days," she said slowly.

"The other Tales were just guidelines anyway," I replied. "He said that, too."

"The chances of survival decrease eighty-seven percent if you deviate from the previous Tale." Her voice was flat and emotionless, like she had already given up.

"The Tale's *already* different from the way it should be. You heard Puss—*all* the Tales are changing. This one deviated before we got here," I said. "As soon as the Snow Queen wanted the harp, the Tale started to change. There's a pretty good chance that all the other rules have gone out the window too."

Lena stared straight ahead, her hands curled in her lap.

"The only way we know we'll be safe is if we go down the beanstalk right now," Chase said in a rush. When I glared at him over my shoulder, wondering if he *wanted* the Snow Queen to get the harp, he added hastily, "I'm not saying I *want* to. It would suck to go home empty-handed, but *someone* has to say it. The only safe thing to do is to go home before the giants realize they had more than one visitor. And, Lena, I can guarantee that your family would rather have you alive than all the gold in the world."

I stared at Chase incredulously, and even Lena giggled in a half-hysterical kind of way. "That sounds ridiculous, coming from you," she said.

Chase smiled a little, but he didn't even look embarrassed.

"Okay, so we could pass this off to the grown-ups," I said. "Nobody would fault us. But do you think that the Snow Queen is going to stop sending villains? If we wait for the Director to send some people, it may be too late."

I could tell by the look on Chase's face, and Lena's, that they hadn't thought of this.

Lena sighed. "It would help if we knew why she wanted that harp."

I didn't answer. I thought of all the Snow Queen's lists—all the names of people who would join her army if she broke out of prison. She wanted it to free herself, I was almost sure.

Lena looked at her hands and didn't speak for a minute. She wasn't in any danger of crying again, but she had a blank deadened expression that worried me. I held my breath. Chase glanced between us nervously.

"Well, I can't go down the beanstalk right now," Lena said. Feeling triumphant, I started to stand, but then Lena added, "I'm too exhausted. I would fall off before we got a third of the way down."

I realized suddenly what she meant. "You didn't sleep at all while we were in the desk." She had been awake the whole time, waiting for us and worrying and then keeping watch after we passed out.

"Right." Lena looked at the hourglass in my hand. "And so, according to that, I've been awake for about two days straight."

I unrolled the sleeping bags. Lena slid into hers immediately and lay with her back to Chase and me. Then I shuffled around as quietly as I could, gathering everything Lena had thrown around while she hunted for the hourglass. My hand had just closed over the slender vial on a silver chain that Rapunzel had given me when Chase spoke up.

"Hey, Lena?" He sat on his sleeping bag, hugging his knees.

"Yeah?" She didn't turn around. She obviously resented still being awake.

"I'm sorry." He sounded miserable. "About the book. I didn't mean for you to burn it."

Lena didn't move. Chase's gaze slid toward me. I realized my mouth was open and shut it with a snap.

"That's okay." Lena sighed. "It was me who got too close to the torch. And me who spent the grocery money."

They didn't say anything else. I stuffed Rapunzel's glass thing in the front pocket of my backpack and finished gathering everything. In a few moments, the only sounds were Lena's purring snores and the wind whistling through the bush overhead. I lay down on my sleeping bag with my legs crossed and my hands behind my head. I looked over at Lena, worrying. I tried very hard not to think about the Snow Queen.

It didn't work. She knew my name. She had *asked* about me.

Apparently, everyone *was* talking about me. The reason why didn't really matter.

A tiny voice in my head reminded me, *You asked for this. You wanted to do stuff worth talking about. You wanted people to talk about you.*

That was true. If I was completely honest, I'd *wanted* the attention.

Well, I got my wish. I was so famous that the Snow Queen had heard of me, the villain who had a habit of kidnapping family members to make sure that she got her way.

Having celebrity parents was a pain sometimes—dealing with reporters who wanted a story and classmates who wanted their fifteen minutes of fame, but this was much much worse. Having a famous daughter could get Mom and Dad captured. Or even killed.

And I hadn't even told them about any of it. I'd had hundreds of chances to tell them, but I also came up with hundreds of excuses.

I knew now what the real reason was: I didn't *want* to tell them. I'd wanted to have this new whole world to myself—just for a little while.

They might have had some warning if I had explained things.

I would never forgive myself if anything happened to them.

"Rory?" Chase said softly.

I turned back to him.

"Do you think it's my fault?"

"No," I said flatly. "I was there. I noticed the book was on fire before Lena did."

"I meant about our time running out," Chase said. "If I hadn't gotten us trapped in the desk—"

I shook my head. "It was *my* fault, probably."

"Yours? Why?"

For being so famous that the Snow Queen noticed and made Lena's Tale harder. For being so scared. "For taking so long on the beanstalk."

"What?" Chase turned to me. His voice had a laugh in it. "No, that slowed us down an hour, tops."

"Oh." I paused for a second. "If we hadn't been in the desk, we wouldn't have found the letter. We wouldn't have been around to stop Ferdinand and the guy with the sack."

"Or gone to the Glass Mountain," Chase said darkly, and I knew he was thinking about his dad.

Why would Chase bring his sword into the lair and not use it? Jack had told the Snow Queen. I'd forgotten that Chase had brought a weapon to Yellowstone. He had been holding it then—the moment the dragon cornered us. Which meant that *he* had frozen, too scared to think straight.

It didn't make it okay, but suddenly it was a lot easier to understand why Chase had done his *Rory-in-the-weapons-closet* impression so often.

A couple of days ago, I would have happily pointed this out. I didn't want to anymore.

"Do you think she was putting some sort of enchantment on Jack?" I asked.

"No. The Glass Mountain limits her magic too much. That was *all* Dad," Chase said, sounding bitter.

He blinked a lot. I glanced away, recognizing the look on his face. I felt the same way when my parents had announced that they were getting a divorce and started to explain how holidays were going to work—Christmas with Mom and Spring Break with Dad and a set of clothes in each place, all very brisk and matter-of-fact, like they were planning a trip. That was when I first realized that my parents couldn't be who I wanted them to be.

I had been so angry at first. "Don't be too hard on him," I said.

Chase snorted. "'He can't help that he foolishly values all the wrong things.' Yeah, Rapunzel knew. It would have been easier if she had warned us."

"You wouldn't have listened," I said. He didn't answer, which meant I was right. "Me neither, actually."

"Hey, Rory?" Chase looked a little unsure, but he spoke fast. "We could go in right now, just you and me. We could get the gold and the—"

"It's Lena's Tale," I said furiously. Just when I started to think that Chase wasn't in it for the glory, he suggested taking over everything. "We can't just steal it from her."

"I didn't mean *that*," Chase said. "But the Snow Queen . . ."

I understood. We didn't have time to wait for the grown-ups to handle this.

"If Lena decides to go down the beanstalk," I said firmly, "then I'll go after it myself. Just the harp."

"So you'd rather die than let the Snow Queen have the harp?" Chase said incredulously.

I thought of my mother. I imagined what would happen if I never came back from this Tale—how she would have to call my dad and tell him, how they would fight over who was more irresponsible, how Amy would bring Mom a cup of tea and they would cry together.

I thought of the Snow Queen's slush-colored skin and of her

glacier-pale eyes. I remembered the feeling I had when she looked at me—like she would hunt down everything I loved.

It's not like I felt any braver, or any stronger, or more capable of stealing a harp from a giant four stories tall than the next Character. If Lena and Chase decided to go home, I was all we had. The one without the photographic memory, the one lacking in sword skills.

It didn't matter anymore that I wasn't special. There wasn't anyone else.

"Yeah, actually," I admitted. "If it'll keep her from getting what she wants. If it'll keep her in prison."

A long moment passed.

"Me too," he said softly, and I smiled in the dark, glad that I wouldn't be going in alone.

I didn't mean to fall asleep again, but I think my dream had something to tell me.

It was exactly the same as it had been before—the beanstalk in my hands and Ever After School far below and Chase next to me, half his shirt red with blood. In the dream, I knew Lena was climbing too, but she was way ahead, almost to the ground already.

I looked down. A flicker of color circled right above the Tree of Hope.

My hand slipped from the leaf, and Chase fell with me, screaming.

"I can't save us now!" he shouted over the wind.

I didn't answer, but I turned midair, bending my legs under me.

The strangest thing was that I felt no fear—only a grim sort of determination.

"We're going in."

Lena stood over me. Bags had formed under her eyes, but her hands were on her hips, her chin jutting out, the way she gets when she's ready for anything.

"We were hoping you'd say that," Chase said, already on his feet and rolling up his sleeping bag.

Very groggily, I stood too, tripped over a twig on the way to my backpack, and stuffed my sleeping bag inside.

"So, this is what I'm thinking." Lena shoved her sleeping bag into my pack with so much gusto that I sleepily stumbled back a step. "There's no way the others will get up here in time. First of all, the Canon takes *forever* to decide anything." Chase handed me his sleeping bag, much neater than mine and Lena's. "Second of all, the Snow Queen's bound to ramp up her attacks now that Jimmy and Matilda are back. I'm *sure* General Searcaster told her. Also, I don't believe for a minute that Matilda cut her vacation short just because she forgot a bill. She either didn't trust *us* or she didn't trust her mother-in-law, but it's too much of a coincidence that she headed straight for the desk."

Nodding, I zipped my backpack closed.

"Besides," said Lena, "Rapunzel said we should take all the time we need."

Chase stared at Lena. "You talk a lot in the morning."

"Afternoon," Lena corrected.

I smiled. "She's excited."

"Do we have everything? This way!" Lena started toward the front door. "There's no point in crossing the whole kitchen if we don't have to."

"There is if someone tied up their guard dragon in front of that mousehole," Chase said, pointing through the leaves. A tail with green and gold scales lashed on the front step.

Lena spun on her heel and marched off in the other direction. Chase and I hurried after her. "That's okay. We're more familiar with the kitchen anyway."

"If we're going to be in the kitchen, could we—"

"No, Chase. We're not stealing food." Lena ducked into the other mousehole. "We don't have time."

Chase made a face and followed her. "You're very determined."

"I had this dream," Lena said, as we came out under the fridge. "I think I figured out how I can get this to work."

"Are you going to share?" I asked, glad that *someone* on our trip had a helpful dream for once.

Lena grinned over her shoulder at me. "Get ready. We're running."

"I guess we don't have time to hide, either," Chase grumbled. "Crap."

We looked, and Lena had already run past the kitchen table. We took off too.

"Should we be concerned?" Chase asked.

"You tell me. You're the one who's been on ten Tales." Of course I was a *little* worried, but Lena's fearless leader mode was a major improvement over her zombie mode.

"Six. I've never seen Lena like this, though."

I shrugged. "When she decides to be reckless, she goes all out— Uh-oh."

Halfway down the hall, Lena swerved into Matilda's office without even turning back to check where we were.

"Matty!" Jimmy called from inside the office.

Lena shouldn't be in there all alone. I ran faster, but then Matilda came jogging down the hall, a can of bug spray dangling from her hands. It was as long as an SUV. I froze.

She hadn't seen us yet, but if she looked down, she couldn't avoid noticing me and Chase, pressed up against the door across from the office.

"There's nowhere to hide," I whispered. The hallway had no furniture, no convenient mouseholes. Matilda was almost close enough to trample us.

Chase pointed. The door we leaned against was open a tiny crack, just wide enough for a human kid to get through. I side-stepped inside, ready to run out again as soon as Matilda's back was turned. Unfortunately, Chase had other ideas. He shoved the giant door shut behind us.

"Hey!" The room was so dark that I couldn't see him, but I glared in his general direction. "We need to help Lena."

"We can't help her if we get caught," Chase reminded me. "Or stepped on. We can pick a good moment and roll under the door."

Still annoyed, I pressed my ear to the door.

Chase sniffed. "Sulfur?"

Matilda's footsteps turned sharply as she ran into the office.

"I asked for the flyswatter, not the spray," Jimmy said, exasperated.

"Do you hear that?" Chase asked.

On our side of the door, something—or several somethings—hummed in the dark. It sounded familiar—like the *Jaws* theme, but with one extra hissing note, a few octaves higher than Sparkia's version. I should have realized what they meant right away, but I was a little distracted by what was happening in the office.

I couldn't hear what Matilda said, but then Jimmy shouted, "He's too quick for the spray. I need the flyswatter. Or the ax. The ax would work on him."

"Him," I repeated, relieved. "The Snow Queen must've sent somebody else. Maybe they haven't seen Lena yet."

"Rory, this isn't the time to be worrying about other people," Chase said in a low voice.

Flame bloomed less than twenty feet from us. Green and gold scales glittered and faded into the darkness. Spots danced in front of my eyes, and the humming intensified.

"*Draconus melodius.* They don't usually move in a herd," Chase whispered. "I think we just walked into a litter of dragons."

"Don't tell me that Sparkia's a mom," I said, horrified.

Chase was ahead of me, closer to the danger. "We should have guessed there was more than one. Remember Solange's letter? *'My darlings'*? And I bet the mouseholes were dragonet holes."

"At least they're smaller." *We survived the Glass Mountain,* I reminded myself as my pulse thumped in my ears. *We could survive a bunch of overgrown lizards.* "And they stopped humming."

"So? The young ones are always hungry," Chase said. I heard scales slide on the ground, but I couldn't see anything. "This fight is going to suck in the dark."

That was the lightbulb moment—the *magical* lightbulb moment. *The young will lie in the dark.* I pulled my pack in front of me.

One baby dragon started to growl.

"That means they're about to attack," said Chase. As I dug frantically in my pack's front pocket, his sword rasped out of its scabbard. "Crap."

There was movement, and then the sound of a sword against scales, and then answering growls from the other dragons. "Go," Chase said. "Crawl under the door. I'll try to buy you some time."

Obviously, someone woke up in a self-sacrificing mood.

"Don't be so dramatic." My hand closed over the glass vial. I ripped it out, held it to my mouth, and whistled.

It flared to life, filling the room with white light. There were nine dragons, each only ten feet long from tail to snout.

"That's helpful." Chase slashed at a pair of jaws that nipped too close. He leaped into the air to give himself some distance, but he didn't see the dragon at his back rear up on its hind legs.

"Behind you!" I shouted, pointing.

It was too late. The closest dragon lunged forward and sank its long gray teeth into Chase's shoulder. He screamed.

"Chase!" I ran forward, Rapunzel's light in one hand and my sword in the other.

Suddenly, everything else was in slow motion, and the runner's high returned.

It was the exact same feeling I'd gotten when I realized that Ferdinand wanted to kill Lena—a fierce, clearheaded rage. By myself, I might have been baby dragon food, but I wasn't going to let Chase get killed.

If I had to fight off a bunch of baby dragons to make sure that happened, then bring the dragons on.

One dragon swiped at me, its claws extended. I slashed without slowing, and it howled.

Thank goodness for magic swords.

The dragon that had Chase shook its head, like a puppy playing with a chew toy. Chase yelled again, moving his sword from his right hand to his left. He tried to stab at its eye, but the angle was too awkward. Another dragon reached up to nip at his dangling legs.

I rolled to dodge the teeth of the baby dragon on my right, spinning until I knelt in front of the dragon trying to eat Chase's legs, and I shoved my sword into its chest. It gave a rattling sort of honk and started to topple over. I pulled my sword out as it fell and stepped on its shoulder, using it as leverage as I leaped toward the one biting Chase. As I fell back toward the floor, I pressed my sword down on its neck, the way I remembered George doing in Yellowstone. Its head thudded to the floor, and Chase fell with it.

"Ugh," Chase said breathlessly.

"We have to get out of the way." I shoved my sword between the teeth of the beheaded baby dragon, prying the jaws open. "The bodies are going to combust."

Chase cried out again as the teeth left his shoulder with a sucking sound. "No, they won't. Only one of them is old enough to breathe fire. Otherwise, we'd already be cooked— Crap, look out!"

Another dragon jumped toward us, its teeth open wide. I ducked and popped up on its other side to stab it through the eye. Something slimy covered the back of my hand, and I gagged, pulling back. It slid to the floor, its scales rasping across the tile.

"Three down," Chase said hoarsely, standing up. He held the teeth-marks with his good hand. The fabric at his shoulder was already soaked with blood. We had to get down the beanstalk fast. He needed medical attention.

The six remaining dragons stood between us and the door. They eyed their fallen siblings and growled. It definitely looked bleak.

"I guess this is the part where I go, 'Run. Save yourself,'" Chase said in a small voice.

"You already did that," I pointed out. "Besides, we've just started to get along. I can't let you get eaten now."

"Thanks, Rory," Chase said, and even though he was trying to be sarcastic, he did sound grateful.

I shoved Rapunzel's light toward him. "Hold this. How long do you think we have until Matilda and Jimmy come over to see why they're so noisy?"

"I'm sure the giants are preoccupied with the new intruder. If they hear anything, they'll probably think the litter is play-fighting. Dragonets do that, you know—same as puppies. And believe me— not even a giant wants to get in the middle of a dragonet scuffle."

The littermates started to move into a semicircle around us, their claws clicking on the hard floor. I didn't know any puppies that did that.

"Lucky us," I muttered.

"Don't even worry about killing them. We just need to make it to the exit alive." He sighed. "I'm not going to be much help."

"You can still run, right?"

"Yeah."

"That's helpful." Evan's sister hadn't even been able to do that much.

I stepped in front, wondering when I'd started liking Chase so much that I was willing to die for him.

The biggest dragon, the leader, warbled a long note. It was a signal. The two at the far ends galloped forward.

The faster dragon came straight at us, teeth extended. I dodged and smashed my hilt into its face, right between its eyes. It dropped.

"Knocked out," Chase said. "Point for Rory."

The other one ran in from an angle. I slashed at both eyes, and it retreated, howling. Chase and I sprinted forward.

Another two dove at us together, one biting high and one biting low. I kicked the snout of the one underneath ("Beware the Mighty Snap Kick," Chase muttered) as I stabbed the tongue of the one above.

"Rory!" Chase pointed to our right, where the biggest dragon leaped, claws out. I held my sword in both hands like a baseball bat, stepped between its forelegs, and swung. It fell on its back, wheezing, a huge gash across his chest.

We were only five feet from the door. I gestured to the crack, looking past Chase. Three dragons stared down at their fallen leader and started to regroup for another attack.

Chase nodded at the closest of the remaining dragons. It looked like it was about ready to burp. "Careful. That's the one that can breathe fire." He ran and skidded across the tile, sliding under the door.

I rolled after him, stumbling to my feet on the other side. Flames licked the bottom of the door, and I coughed. The smoke tasted like chemicals.

Chase leaned against the wall, breathing hard. He looked a little amazed. "Do you know what the chances of us making it out of there alive were?"

"The sword's magic," I reminded him, avoiding his eyes and wiping the sword clean on my jeans. The blood left a purple-black stain.

"Well, yeah, but you definitely figured out a way to turn the magic on."

I didn't know what to say. My hands started to shake, and I sheathed my sword before I dropped it.

Jimmy's voice boomed across the hall. "Trap him in a corner, Matty. Then I'll get him."

Now we had to figure out a way to help Lena.

In the office, Matilda held a wastebasket, trying to catch something human-size and blue that zipped across the room. Jimmy slapped the flyswatter around, always a second too late.

"I'm *trying*, dear." The giantess was obviously on the verge of losing her temper.

Something crashed to the floor in the office across the hall, and a bronze-colored lampshade as big as a Jacuzzi rolled through the doorway toward us.

"Lena!" She could be crushed in all the commotion.

"Here!" Lena jumped out of the lampshade. The right lens in her glasses was cracked, but she smiled widely.

The hen clucked a little, her head sticking out of Lena's backpack.

The golden harp was in her hands, gagged with what looked like half of Lena's sleeve, and she struggled against the shoelaces that Lena had tied around her arms.

"Ready?" Lena ran down the hall without waiting for an answer.

We followed. Chase lagged behind, muttering "Ow, ow, oww" with every step. So I ran back and slid his good arm over my shoulders to hurry him along.

Lena started talking as soon as we reached the fridge. "She sent Bluebeard—the Snow Queen, I mean. I saw that part in the dream. Jimmy was so busy fighting him that he didn't even notice me, not once," she said happily, "and I— Oooh, where did you get that light?" I opened my mouth to answer, but then Lena squinted at Chase, sounding alarmed for the first time. "What happened to *you*?"

Chase grimaced. "I was wondering when you would notice."

"Baby dragons," I said.

"Nine of them. I took one for the team, and now I'm bleeding to death," he said with a proud indifference, like he was practicing for when he'd tell the triplets later.

"At least none of us are afraid of blood," I said, but then I noticed Lena's queasy look. "Oh no, Lena."

"We better go," she said, averting her eyes from Chase's shoulder. "It's only a matter of time before the giants catch on."

We had to hurry—way too fast for Chase's comfort. Halfway around the giants' swimming pool, he even called a halt, sweating with pain and very pale. Blood soaked his collar and ran down his arm in red rivulets.

"I don't know if we have time for a break." I couldn't stop myself from glancing back at the giants' house.

But Chase just reached out and touched the harp's head with

one finger. She looked up at him, trying to say something through her gag, and golden tears ran down her face. One dropped to the concrete with a clink.

I didn't catch all the words, but Chase told her something like, "*Themora kish desrainth mereati cavolth* (mumble mumble)."

Whatever that meant, it worked. The harp blinked and stopped struggling. She even smiled up at Lena coyly.

"We can go," Chase said, and Lena jogged forward again.

"That wasn't English." I adjusted my grip on Chase's waist and followed her around the pool.

Chase winced and shook his head. "Fey. I'm going to die. If the dragon bite doesn't do me in, the chlorine fumes will."

Lena disappeared into the grass. It slowed me and Chase down a lot. He kept tripping over roots, and he was almost heavy enough to drag me down to the ground with him. I was very out of breath and very relieved when Lena stopped.

She bit her lip. "Um, does anyone remember where we left the beanstalk?"

"Doom," Chase moaned, holding a stalk of grass with a bloody hand. He started to slide dramatically to the ground.

"Not helpful, Chase." I yanked him back up with maybe more force than necessary. Then his breath hissed through his teeth, and I regretted being so rough.

"Ask the harp." When Lena looked skeptical, he added, "She won't scream."

Lena untied the gag very carefully, acting like she would clap a hand over the harp's mouth at the first unexpected noise.

The harp only nodded over to the left a little and spoke with an accent I didn't recognize. "That way, Mistress."

"Thanks!" Lena took off again.

"The light is growing dim," Chase said with another exaggerated sigh. "The pain is too great. My vision—"

"Cut it out, Chase," Lena called back. "You're scaring Rory. She doesn't have enough experience to know you're exaggerating."

"Is that true, Rory?" Chase asked, surprised. "You worried about me?"

"You're not looking your best." I didn't mention that he was leaning on me twice as much as he had when we left the house.

"Don't worry," Chase told me. "I'm as fit as a fiddle. I'm going to live to be an old man and die in my sleep. I—"

"Found it!" Lena cried happily.

The beanstalk had grown a couple feet taller since we'd left it, and through the hole in the clouds below, I could see the green square of the EAS courtyard and the darker green dot that had to be the Tree of Hope. Like clockwork, I started to feel sick to my stomach.

"He can't climb by himself," the harp said softly.

Lena and I exchanged glances. Whoever started climbing now would be the safest, and we had to figure out who that would be.

I pushed the nausea away so that I could think clearly. If they caught Chase, Jimmy would either give him to the dragonet litter or to the Snow Queen.

If they caught Lena, the same might happen, but the Snow Queen would get the harp, too. Lena had to go first, and as fast as she could.

"So, what are my choices?" Chase said. "Climb with the girl afraid of heights or with the girl afraid of blood? Tough call."

I promised myself that if we made it down alive, I would memorize all the bones of the wrist just for Chase's benefit. "Go on, Lena. I'll take him."

"Are you sure?" Apparently, leave-no-kid-behind was part of Lena's fearless leader mode.

"Yeah, are you *sure*?" Chase repeated nervously.

"I think you already have enough to carry," I told Lena, glancing pointedly at the harp.

Lena nodded and started to climb. "See you at the bottom."

I had to look down this time. I didn't have another option, but I tried to look close to the stalk, just as far as the next stem, ignoring all the blue sky around it. I held the sturdiest part of the beanstalk in both hands and lowered myself slowly. Chase watched me, wide-eyed, waiting for a freak-out.

Panic rose and stiffened my limbs. But no. I couldn't freeze. I knew what would happen if Jimmy caught Chase—dragons or the Snow Queen. My foot settled safely on the next leaf down.

"Okay, your turn," I told Chase, clinging to the stalk with both hands. My heart beat so hard I could practically feel it hit my ribs. Then I forced myself to look down for the next leaf.

I made Chase climb a little above me. He was careful with the three limbs he could still use, but he had to keep stopping to wipe the blood off his hands. Once, he lost his grip and started to fall backward.

I caught him with both arms, my legs hooked around the stalk. I closed my eyes tight and told myself that there was a safety net below us, that we were only ten feet from the ground.

"You all right?" I hoped that the answer was yes. If he fainted, he would be too heavy to carry, and I couldn't leave him.

"Yeah," he said, but it came out more like a grunt. I felt him get his grip back. "So maybe I'm *not* dying. But it really does hurt."

Carefully, I spotted the next leaf and blocked everything else out. "Halfway there," I said, trying to sound cheery. My mouth was so dry that my tongue felt clumsy.

Chase looked down and snorted. Half his shirt was already red. "Liar."

Lena moved much faster, even with the harp in her hands and the hen and gold coins in her backpack. She kept yelling encouragement up to us—"You can do it!" and "Only seven more stories to go!"—but her voice became fainter and fainter.

Finally, the beanstalk shook under us, so violently that Chase almost fell off again. I had to grab his bad arm to catch him.

Chase winced. "Looks like Jimmy found us."

The beanstalk shook again, under Jimmy's second foot.

I made sure I had a good grip on two separate leaves and looked down, all the way to the ground. Dizziness hovered close by, but I ignored it.

"Lena's almost there," I said, relieved.

"Good for Lena," Chase said sarcastically.

I didn't answer. I noticed squares moving across the green grass of the courtyard below—the T-shirts of the other students.

Falling is the fastest way down, Rapunzel had said.

The Tree of Hope was just a circle of darker green. A flicker of violet looped right above it, and suddenly, I knew what it was.

I couldn't believe what I was planning to do.

"Rory, this is *not* the time to freeze again." Chase looked up. "Feet! I see huge feet!"

"Were you lying about the magic carpet?" I grabbed a handful of Chase's shirt.

"What?" Chase said, staring.

I let go of the beanstalk and threw myself backward, taking him with me.

hase screamed, his voice cracking. "I can't save us now!"

The wind stole all the air out of my lungs. I couldn't breathe, let alone tell him off for thinking I didn't have it under control, but I didn't let him go. I twisted, turning us both and bending my legs under me.

The little bit of color that had been circling raced up to meet us. It hit my knees so hard I got rugburn.

We were fifty feet from the ground.

Chase stopped yelling. "Oh," he said breathlessly.

"Thank you very much, Mr. Carpet," I said, voice shaking.

Chase nuzzled the carpet with his cheek. "You're my new best friend."

"I'm going to have nightmares for *years*."

"*You?*" Chase said. "I think I just developed a new phobia."

Hovering motionless, the carpet rippled a little in a questioning way.

"Take us to the base of the beanstalk, please," I said.

The carpet swooped down, whipping past dozens of students, who watched us go by. At least seven mouths hung open. When it stopped abruptly, I tumbled off and got to my feet shakily.

"Thanks again, Mr. Carpet," I said, as it flew off. Lena was nowhere in sight. "Never leaving the ground again."

Row after row of faces turned to us, but I couldn't make out anyone's features. All the dizziness hit me at once, and the whole scene spun.

"Is that Chase and Rory?"

"They look so different."

"Older."

"Maybe it's the blood."

All the tension in my body drained away, and my arms and legs felt loose and floppy.

We were back. We were safe. No one here would try to kill us. After the last few days, it was kind of a weird feeling.

Chase drew his sword and marched to the beanstalk. He held the sword in both hands and swung. When it struck the plant, he grunted, gritting his teeth at the pain.

Green chips fell into the lake, creating tiny ripples.

"What are you doing?" I asked.

"Chase! You're hurt!" It was his friend, the mean one. I couldn't remember her name for a second, and I wondered if it was shock or my own bad memory.

"Not now, Adelaide," Chase said.

He glanced up, and I looked too.

Jimmy's hairy shins were visible, hanging from the clouds. I dashed over and swung my sword too. We took turns, but we only managed to cut out a wedge about a foot deep. Jimmy's body was visible up to his waist. At this pace, we wouldn't even cut halfway through in time.

"Incoming!" shouted one of the students behind us.

A silver truck rattled around the Tree of Hope, scattering students. The glare on the windshield vanished in the shade, and I saw Lena behind the wheel. She accelerated straight for us. Obviously, she was still in her reckless mood.

I grabbed Chase's good arm and ran out of the way.

The truck hit the beanstalk with a large crack and the crunch of crushed metal. A jolt ran up the plant. One of Jimmy's feet slipped. Then the stalk began to topple, whistling as it fell. When it struck the lake, it threw up at least twenty feet of water clear to the other side.

I didn't dodge fast enough and got soaked.

"Well, that was quite dramatic." The Director opened the truck door on the driver's side and punctured the air bag with a small knife. Lena peered out, stunned but unhurt. The Director turned to the audience of students. "Everyone, clear the area, please. We don't want anyone to be crushed if the giant falls."

Students backed up hastily. Puss-in-Dress was a little faster than everyone else, lashing her white tail.

I tilted my head back, watching Jimmy's legs dangle from the clouds and ready to grab Chase again if I needed to. Finally, one leg disappeared and then the other. Matilda must've been there to help him. I wondered if she would ever tell her husband about the three questers she had let into the house and hid in the bread box.

Lena unbuckled her seat belt and climbed out of the truck, leaning on the door for support, a little wobbly now that it was all over. I grinned at her, and she smiled back sheepishly. Definitely *not* a Failed Tale. Somewhere across the courtyard, a student clapped, and the applause spread out, growing into a roar.

No one whistled louder than George. Jenny ran out of the crowd, crying, and hugged her sister tightly.

"*You* get to tell my dad that you crashed his truck." Chase's voice slurred, and he swayed. I caught him before he fell over.

"Not fainting," he told me, his eyes a little glazed.

"Of course not." I put his good arm across my shoulders again and shouted over the clapping. "Gretel! We need a nurse! Got a kid with a dragon bite here."

"Dragon bite?" Adelaide repeated hesitantly, hovering close to Chase's other elbow. And she did faint.

In the infirmary, Gretel gave Chase something to drink, telling us it would increase his blood production. Then she cut his shirt away carefully and wiped the blood off his skinny chest with steady, practiced strokes. When her cloth brushed over teeth punctures, Chase grimaced but made no sound.

Each cut was a lot deeper than I had thought. He hadn't been exaggerating *that* much.

Instead of watching the blood well up around each tooth-mark, I spread my fingers and examined my hands. They shook, which didn't surprise me much.

It did surprise me to see Chase watching.

I shoved my hands in my pockets and glowered at him, waiting for whatever insult he came up with.

But he just said softly, "It's okay, Rory. We made it."

My voice caught in my throat. I didn't know how to respond when Chase was being nice.

"Your hands? I noticed that before you came in." Gretel unrolled a strip of bandage. "It's nothing. Your body is just letting off some of today's stress."

That actually did comfort me a little. "He's going to be okay, right?" I asked, because he wasn't acting very normal.

"I told you, Rory. Fit as a fiddle." Chase raised himself slightly.

Gretel held him down with a firm hand on his good shoulder.

"He'll be fine. Rapunzel will be here in a few minutes. She's got an ointment that'll heal up this bite in a jiffy, but I'm afraid there's nothing I can do for the broken collarbone, except give him a sling." At the word "collarbone," Chase made a face, and Gretel added, "But you'll have plenty of scars to brag about."

That cheered Chase up considerably, and I laughed a little.

The door banged open, and a man stormed in, so dusty that his hair stuck together in clumps.

"Jack," Gretel said in a dry, scolding way. "I understand your concern for your son, but my other patients need their rest. And I'm sure the infirmary door would like to stay on its hinges."

Chase and I both drew back warily. Maybe seeing us hadn't been enough. Maybe the Snow Queen had won him over.

Chest heaving, like he had been running, Jack stared at his son. "Were you or were you not in the Glass Mountain two days ago?"

Gretel's face looked stuck halfway between laughter and concern. She obviously thought the idea was so ridiculous that Jack needed to stay in the infirmary for a mental checkup.

"I *told* you to stay away from honey mead," Chase said with the same fierce scowl he'd made on the glass ledge, and Gretel's mouth dropped open.

Jack fell heavily in a chair next to Chase's bed. His hands were in his hair, and his shoulders shuddered. He looked so much like Chase had after he accidentally locked us in the giants' desk that I felt a little sorry for him.

There was a knock, and Rapunzel stood in the doorway, looking at Gretel. "You asked for me?"

"You already know what I want." Gretel reached for the ointment in Rapunzel's hands. "You don't need to ask."

"I'm just being polite," Rapunzel said, pulling her long silver braid over her shoulder, but she was looking at me. Her eyes were very dark—so black that you couldn't see the pupils. They were the oldest feature in her face and the saddest.

"You have seen terrible things," she said with a tiny smile.

I saw glacier-pale eyes in a slush-colored face. It shouldn't have seemed terrible, but it did. Mainly because I knew I would see it again. "She had your picture," I told Rapunzel softly.

"Not pinned to the wall to throw darts at," Chase added suspiciously, as Gretel dabbed yellowish ointment on his dragon bite and gestured that Chase should flip onto his stomach so that she could get his back. He turned carefully, favoring his collarbone. "In a *frame*."

Rapunzel only shrugged. "It is an old habit. She is heartless."

Heartless seemed like the right word, but that still didn't explain why the Snow Queen had Rapunzel's picture in the first place. Had they known each other once?

Then Rapunzel looked pointedly from Chase to Jack, who had curled so far forward that his head almost touched his knees.

Chase's fierce expression faded, and he reached his good hand out to touch Jack's shoulder. Jack clasped it slowly, but he didn't lift his head. They looked more like brothers than father and son.

It made me want to see my own mom. Even if she grounded me immediately. After I told her where I had been this week. *If* I told her.

The door squeaked open again. "Chase, you have another visitor," the Director said smoothly.

In the doorway, Lena and the harp in her hands raised their eyebrows anxiously. She walked halfway to the hospital bed but then stopped, eyes wide. "There's not blood, is there?"

"Hold on. Let me clear this away." Gretel gathered up the bowl of water and all the sponges she had used to clean Chase's shoulder. Everything was the same dark pink, just a shade away from red. "I don't think we have room for another fainter."

Gretel shot a sharp look over to the curtained area where Adelaide, two other girls, and one fifth-grade boy were recovering.

The harp sniffed expertly. "The ointment of the witch whose power is in her hair. A good choice. It heals all ills. I can make it, Mistress," she added, and I got the distinct impression that she was trying to impress Lena. Lena just looked a little queasy.

Chase sat up so fast that he winced and touched his collarbone. "She told you, right, Director? About the Snow Queen?"

"Don't tell me Lena went to the Glass Mountain too!" Gretel said, a sling dangling in her hands.

"No, just Rory and Chase," Lena said.

"Yes, I know she was after the harp, but I shall expect a full report from you later," the Director said. "After I speak with your father."

If it was possible, Jack sank even lower in his chair. Then I really did feel sorry for him.

"We had to fight dragons, and Ferdinand, and this guy with a sack," Chase said proudly. Lena and I gave him a look. "Okay, so Rory fought the dragons, and Lena basically turned Ferdinand into stone, but I had pretty much beaten them."

Lena and I both rolled our eyes.

"Ferdinand the Unfaithful?" Jack repeated, suddenly interested. "The guy who studied under Malistair the Vengeful and slew Binio the Brave?"

Chase grinned, despite the pain in his collarbone as Gretel started working the sling on his arm.

"The lists," Rapunzel reminded me softly.

I had completely forgotten about them. Hurriedly, I fished in my pocket and found the papers. "I don't know if Lena told you, Director, but in the Snow Queen's office, we found these— Oh, no!"

The blackened paper crumbled at the edges as if they'd been charred. I tried to remember how close I had gotten to the baby dragon that could breathe fire.

The Director nodded, as if she expected this. "I imagined that Solange would have a safeguard in place in case the lists were removed. Don't fret. The elves might still be able to extract some information from them. Gretel, if you'll provide the bag . . ."

Gretel pulled a Ziploc out of the cabinet and held it out to me. I dropped the paper into the bag and watched black bits flake off, feeling cheated.

"The only thing that remains to be seen is why Solange would want this *particular* harp," the Director said.

Everyone thought. The harp twiddled her thumbs.

"Has anybody tried asking the harp?" I asked.

The harp beamed at me, but when everyone else looked at her, she ducked her head bashfully. "Oh, me?" Lena set the harp down on a shelf with clean bandages so that we could all see her better. "I am but a lowly harp, not fit to sing babies to sleep—"

Chase rolled his eyes. "Don't be modest. It just wastes time."

"Just 'cause you've never been modest a day in your life," I muttered, and both Chase and his dad turned to me with identical scowls.

The harp batted her eyelashes at her audience. "My name is Melodie."

That didn't mean anything to me, but Lena staggered suddenly. Chase and I both reached out to steady her.

Melodie's smile changed. She met Lena's eyes like they were old friends. "Madame Benne was my maker."

"Oh, my gumdrops," Lena said, half-gasping. "Oh, my gumdrops."

I looked between Lena and the Director's stunned face. Jack looked around blankly. Even Gretel's eyes were wide. Chase and Rapunzel were the only ones who didn't look surprised.

"I think I missed something," I said.

"They've been searching for Madame Benne's harp for centuries," Gretel said.

"I told you," Lena said. "Madame Benne invented the singing harp early in her career to help with her experiments."

"I was her *assistant*," Melodie said primly.

"So, you were there when she invented the Table of Plenty?" Lena asked her new harp. "And magic mirrors? And the cloak of invisibility? And perfected the magic ring?"

"Plus the stairless tower," Melodie said, pleased with herself, "and the Glass Mountain, but who's counting?"

"If Madame Benne invented the Glass Mountain, her harp would know all its secrets," the Director mused.

"She wanted you to help her break out," I told Melodie, horrified, which made even the golden harp seem very solemn.

"I bet Jimmy didn't know," Chase said.

"He wasn't the brightest mirror on the wall," the harp agreed. "But General Searcaster knew."

"Extraordinary." The Director folded her hands. "That a counterfeit book would lead us to Madame Benne's harp."

"But the boy Chase said that Lena was in possession of Madame Benne's cookbook," said the harp. "He described it exactly. Bound with wood covers, painted gold, and her symbol on the bottom corner of the first page."

Lena opened her mouth to explain, but then Chase said, in a pained voice, "*Was* being the operative term."

It took me a second to figure out why he would say that, and then I turned to Chase slowly, scowling. "You said it was just a Fey cookbook."

"Well, it was *written* in Fey," Chase said uncomfortably.

"You lied to Lena?"

"Remember, Rory. I'm injured." Chase lay back on his pillows, trying to look pathetic. "And I already apologized."

"Yeah, but you didn't tell anyone the book was *real.*"

"How was I supposed to know she'd burn it? Lena practically lives in the library. I thought she'd never hurt a book in a million years."

I took a step toward him, furious, but Rapunzel rested a gentle hand on my shoulder. "Rory, you two are friends now. Even the Snow Queen knows it."

Lena had to sit down. "I burned Madame Benne's spellbook."

"You *burned* it?" the harp said. "Are we talking a singe on the corner, or burnt to cinders? Just a singe, right?"

"Oh, no!" Lena covered her face. "Were there secrets?"

"Of course there were," Melodie said. "I've been craving her mushroom-chive scones for nine hundred years."

Chase snorted, but when I shot him a dirty look, he didn't say anything.

"Lena has already made a fresh copy," Rapunzel said. "Last weekend, when she was grounded."

"Good," Chase and Melodie said together, looking very relieved.

"Oh. You're the one with the photographic memory, aren't you?" Gretel asked Lena.

"The binding!" Lena turned to the harp. "The covers! Were there spells?"

"No, no, Madame Benne hated enchanting books. She only created the spell for the fairy tale collections—the same one that your librarian uses—as a special favor," Melodie said. "If you have the text, we're fine. You *can* cook, can't you?"

"Well," Lena said uncertainly. "My grandmother doesn't actually let me use the oven. I blew the last one up. You see, in third grade, this science experiment—"

"Looks like we have a happy ending all around," the Director said, so abruptly that Lena looked a little hurt, and both Melodie and I glared at Mildred Grubb. "Gretel, we shall invade your infirmary no longer. Jack, Rapunzel, come with me, please."

Rapunzel gave the Director the same look a rebellious teenager gives her mother right before a lecture. It was a relief to know that I wasn't the only one annoyed with the Director.

Jack dragged his feet as he crossed the room. "Need anything, Chase? A change of clothes?" he asked, and Chase sat up a little straighter, a smile starting. I was glad Jack was doing something fatherly, even if he was only procrastinating. "Your stuffed ele—"

"Dad," Chase said, cutting Jack off and turning red, and I tried not to laugh.

"Now, Jack," said the Director sternly, and the three of them left the room.

"Oh, no—Rapunzel forgot her ointment," Gretel said.

"I'll take it." I needed to talk to her.

It was easy to figure out which way they had gone after leaving the infirmary. All I had to do was follow the sound of the Director's voice. Her angry, *yelling* voice.

"You knew what the children would be facing. Why didn't you tell me?" the Director asked.

I hung back, just around the corner, wondering if I should leave, feeling awkward like I always did when grown-ups fight.

"Mildred, if I had told you, you would not have let them go," Rapunzel said softly, "and there was no one else. Besides," she added lightly, "you probably wouldn't have understood me if I had said something."

"You should have tried." I had the feeling the Director didn't like not knowing everything that was going on. "You know you should've tried."

"And you should have told the children the truth of the Snow Queen," Rapunzel snapped, and I silently agreed. "You increased their danger by ignorance."

Apparently, Mildred Grubb didn't have an answer for that. "After I deal with Jack, you and I will speak again." She stalked into her office, and the door closed behind her so firmly you could almost say she slammed it—in a grown-up, ladylike way, of course.

"Don't mind her, Rory," Rapunzel called out. (It almost didn't surprise me that she already knew I was listening.) "She is afraid. Solange has done much undetected."

"Thanks for the carpet." I stepped out, a little hesitantly, and I placed the light on the silver chain and the jar of ointment in her hands. "And for this." I noticed the red smudges on the glass. "Sorry we got a little blood on it."

"You're quite welcome, Rory." She put it in the pocket of her dress, and her smile was warm. "You wanted to ask me why we couldn't send anyone else."

She had pretty much read my mind. I shoved my hands in my pockets. "I'm scared of heights. Pretty much anyone would be better than me."

"It didn't matter," Rapunzel said. "It didn't stop you."

"It *did*." I'd gotten stuck on the way up the beanstalk.

"Not when it mattered. You learned to fear for your friends and your loved ones," she said softly, "and you feared Solange for how she would threaten them. You're too young now to know what strength this gives you, but this—" She touched the hilt of my sword, still hanging from my belt. "It would not have worked nearly so well if you hadn't wanted to protect the others so much."

That wasn't all that comforting. "It's a magic sword. It didn't have anything to do with me."

"It *is* magic. I am trying to explain how the magic works, and it seems I have done a poor job," Rapunzel said wryly. "That sword will protect whoever and whatever the wielder wishes. There is a reason that it found its way into your hands. Had another student wielded it, she may not have been able to defeat nine dragonets to help her friend reach safety." She smiled. "Poor Rory, you have no idea who you will become."

My stomach knotted. We both knew she was still talking about Solange.

"Are you afraid, Rory?" she asked.

I thought of the Snow Queen—the way she had spoken to Jack, her terrible smile. It was a different kind of fear. It was the kind that made me look over my shoulder in dark places, and Mom's shoulder, and Amy's, and Chase's, and Lena's. I nodded.

"Good. Keep that fear," she said. "You'll need it, and you will do what must be done."

I didn't realize how much I had been waiting to hear this, but a load lifted from my shoulders. Rapunzel could see the future. She would know.

Maybe she could help with a few other things too. "Should I tell Mom the truth about EAS?"

Rapunzel laughed. It was a much deeper and louder sound

than I expected to come out of such a young-looking person. "I cannot make those decisions, Rory. Only you can. But I would be honest about the photographs."

What photographs? I almost asked. But since it was Rapunzel, I figured I would find out soon.

"You should go back," Rapunzel said. "Chase is about to come after you, and he will be in a good deal of trouble if Gretel sees him out of bed."

I ran back to the infirmary and found Chase with his covers flung off and one foot on the floor, and I shooed him back in just before Gretel came around the corner.

During the ride back, I watched the neighborhood flash by through the car window with half-lidded eyes. It was dark, and Ellie had made me take a shower after she briefed me on how EAS had handled my mother—Gretel had performed a simple enchantment so Mom would believe that I'd gone on a field trip to the capital for five days. "But you're a little dusty. And sooty. And your clothes are completely covered in blood," Ellie had said, handing me a towel and guiding me to a bathroom I had never seen before. "Your mother can't see you like that. There's only so much a spell can do." Being clean and warm had made me sleepy.

I was too tired to open my eyes any wider, but I wanted to see the sights. There was the grocery store where Amy and I had picked up dinner on the way home from the Fairie Market. The dry cleaners where she had dropped off Mom's dresses on Monday morning. The telephone pole that Mom had accidentally nicked while she was parallel parking. She'd made me promise not to tell Amy, but you could still see the chunk that the car had taken out of the wood, right at bumper level.

A smile curled around my mouth. It was so ironic. A week ago, they had seemed as familiar as my mother's face, but right then, I had to dredge up the memories that went with each place. It seemed like I had been away much longer than a week.

"Everything seems smaller," I said quietly, more to myself than to Ellie.

"Happens a lot with giant Tales," she replied. "It takes the Characters a while to get used to human-size things again."

That wasn't it. It wasn't what I had seen. It was how I felt. I had changed up the beanstalk. I didn't feel bigger exactly, but more solid—as if I took up more space. We had done something important—something that really mattered.

I wondered if Mom would notice, if she would ask me what happened. I wondered what I would say.

I didn't like lying to her, and I had run out of reasons not to tell her.

But I wasn't so sure that the truth would be helpful. I knew how she would react if I told her everything. She would pull me out of school, break her filming contract, and move us far, far away. She would do all she could to protect me, and it wouldn't be enough. She couldn't save me from this, or even understand it very well. It would only scare her.

So, if I explained, would I be telling her to do the right thing? Or just to get it off my chest?

Or was not telling her the easy way out?

It would've been nice if Rapunzel had told me what to do, but I guess she was right. It was my decision. I was in charge of my own life story. That could be comforting too.

"This is it, right?" Ellie parked the car.

I stared at the white house and its blue shutters, and after a second, it seemed more familiar. "Yes."

It looked normal. It looked like the farthest place I could possibly get from somewhere giants could eat us or dragons could barbecue us or the Snow Queen could send villains with snowflake-shaped throwing stars.

It looked safe. My nose prickled a little, just under the bridge.

"You okay, dear?" Ellie said.

I nodded. "Thanks for the ride."

As soon as I stepped out of the car, the front door flew open, and my mother stood on the front steps, holding her arms out to me. "Where's my favorite daughter?"

When I saw her there, I started running, and I hugged her around the middle.

"Hey." She covered my face with kisses. "What's wrong?"

"I'm your only daughter," I mumbled into her shirt. "And also," I said, looking up, "I missed you."

She pulled open the door and took my hand. "Now come inside and tell me all about it."

Stepping through the door, I took a deep breath and smiled.

No matter how many times we moved, all the houses eventually smelled the same—like Mom's expensive perfume and the orange-oil spray that we always used to clean. It smelled like home.

I knew right then that I was going to lie. Maybe it was selfish, and definitely dishonest, but it felt too nice to have someplace where there were no villains, no Destinies, and no Snow Queen.

Mom guided me into the kitchen. "Want some tea? Amy's not here. It's her night off."

People lay open on the counter, beside a glass of white wine, and I recognized the figures in the picture: one was the young actress I kept seeing on movie posters everywhere, her red hair in ringlets, half-covering her laughing face. The other was my dad, watching her. They were holding hands.

Underneath the picture, the caption read: *Director Eric Landon with his new girlfriend, actress Brie Catcher, outside café HowPow after a very cozy brunch.*

Of all the things I expected to find when I came down the Beanstalk, this definitely wasn't one of them. The smile fell off my face.

"Oh. That. Trash, I know," Mom said, too cheerfully, flipping the magazine closed, "but my publicist keeps telling me I have to keep up with the gossip."

It hurt her. Of *course* it hurt her, and she was just going to pretend she wasn't upset—like she always did.

Well, if I was going to keep quiet about the Snow Queen and whatever Destiny EAS refused to tell me about, I wasn't going to keep quiet about anything else. Not anymore.

"You know," I said quietly, "it's okay to be sad sometimes, Mom."

She became very still, taken aback, and then concern crossed her features. "Are *you* sad?"

You should be honest about the photographs, Rapunzel had said.

"No." I was surprised to realize it was true. "No, I'm *angry*. I could've *guessed*—he kept talking about her, wanting me to meet her. Why couldn't he just tell me?"

I scowled at the magazine, furious at Dad for being so spineless. I mean, he wasn't the *only* famous person in our family. To make sure my parents wouldn't have to deal with the Snow Queen and whoever else knew about me, I had willingly gone into a giant's dragon-infested home. The least that Dad could do was call and give me a heads-up that he and his new girlfriend were in a magazine. He had no idea how his life affected mine.

I was dialing his number before I realized that the phone was in my hand. He picked up on the second ring.

"My princess! When did you say you got out of school again? I need to get our flights worked out for Oxford."

"I'm not going, Dad," I said coldly.

"Okay." He sounded so disappointed that guilt mixed with the anger, and my next words got stuck in my throat. "Are you sure? Because Brie and I were—"

Anger flared again. I remembered Chase in the Glass Mountain, yelling at his father. I could do this much.

"Dad, I know you're dating her."

He was quiet for a moment. "Did your mother tell you?"

"No, a magazine told me."

"*People*?"

He even *knew* about the article, and he hadn't bothered to call me first? I breathed in so sharply that Mom tried to grab the phone. I stepped out of her reach.

He sighed. "Rory, I know this is hard for you. Brie's the first—"

"I'm not mad about that. Why didn't you tell me? I had to find out from a magazine." Now that I was talking, it all came flooding out. "What if I wasn't at home when I found out? What if I was at school and somebody else had read about it and asked me what I thought? That happens, you know. That's how I found out about your last fifty gazillion movies."

I might have exaggerated slightly, but it didn't make the rest of it any less true.

"Rory, I—I'm sorry—"

He did sound sorry. My fury started to escape, which was bad. Without it, Dad might be able to smooth things over. I *wanted* him to feel bad for a little while. I wanted him to remember not to do it again.

"Fine. Just spare five minutes out of your busy schedule next time." I hung up.

The kitchen was silent for a little while, and then Mom recovered from her shock.

"You are one sweet, brave little girl, did you know that?" Mom stroked my hair. "What did I do to deserve a daughter like you?"

A daughter who lied to her mother and told off her father. "I'm not very sweet right now," I said.

Then Mom sighed. She pulled the magazine toward her and opened it to the next page, with a picture of my father by himself. It wasn't obvious—her mouth didn't tremble, her eyes didn't tear—but sadness filled her face.

"I don't want you thinking that I miss him, or that I wish it was me in that picture," she said quietly, without looking at me. "But for many years, I dreamed of a life that I could share with your dad—a life I imagined we could build together. I grieve for that as much as anything else, and it doesn't feel good to know that he's started his new life before I got a chance to start mine."

I hesitated, just for a second. "But, Mom, is moving every few months building that new life or running from it?"

She looked up, eyebrows raised, and I knew we would both have to get used to my sudden outspokenness.

Then she smiled, a more subtle version of the too-cheerful look. I had crossed into *Oh-Rory*-I'm-*the-mother* territory. But that was all right. I had still said it.

"Tell me about your trip," she said, sitting down.

I slid onto the barstool next to her and started constructing a Tale.

y golden harp hath been stolen!" Chase—as the giant—raced across the stage after Lena. I remembered my cue.

"Darling!" I cried in a high-pitched voice, running after Chase, my arms full. My face had turned red even before the skit had started, but that was okay. It kind of suited my character. "You forgot your scarf!"

The audience laughed. I almost stopped in my tracks, but then I remembered that I was *supposed* to be the comic relief.

Lena disappeared offstage. I caught up with Chase and wound the scarf around his neck very carefully as the curtain closed behind us. On the other side, I could hear the triplets putting the wire and papier-mâché beanstalk in place.

"Now your coat," I said sternly. As I put it around his shoulders with exaggerated care, a few more parents chuckled.

Scowling at me, Chase looked so ridiculous with the green paint on his face that I almost laughed myself. "Woman, none of your silly fussing," he said, sounding a little less like a robot. "I have to go catch our supper."

"You'll wait, or the only thing you'll catch is a cold," I said mock-sternly. "Last time you had a runny nose, you kept smelling Englishmen all over the place."

The audience laughed again, harder this time. Chase gave me a look that plainly said that he resented me having all the good lines.

"There, now." I patted his shoulders, and we both ran offstage.

Lena stood at the top of the triplets' beanstalk. Her harp hung from her hand, gasping.

For the yearly parents' presentation, EAS had voted on a "Jack and the Beanstalk" skit, but some of those parents—like Amy and my mom—didn't know about the magical aspects of the program. So, the harp couldn't have any speaking parts. Or even breathe onstage.

"You okay, Melodie?" I asked as Chase climbed to the tippy-top of the beanstalk, very nimbly for someone with a sling and a broken collarbone. I pointed at the cardboard cutout of a harp. "Because we have a stunt double all ready for you."

Melodie looked outraged at the suggestion. "I've waited centuries to be in a play. This could be my big break."

The triplets pulled the curtains open, and Melodie held her breath again, her cheeks bulging.

It was hard, but I didn't laugh.

"I'll get you, Jackie!" Chase shook his green fist.

Lena hurried down the rest of the beanstalk.

"Oh, behold!" Adelaide said to the audience, sounding extremely irritated. She still wasn't happy about being cast as Jackie's mother. "My child has returned."

Lena jumped the rest of the way to the floor. "Mother, mother, an ax!"

Adelaide handed her a cardboard imitation. Lena took one swing, and the papier-mâché beanstalk toppled slowly as Kyle pulled the ropes.

Chase screamed, very enthusiastically. His favorite part.

He landed on the floor a little offstage and then let himself fall to the ground, his eyes closed and his tongue sticking out. Then he opened one eye and whispered, "Is it just me, or should we not let Rumpy write the skits anymore?"

Afterward, searching the crowd for my mom and Amy, I overheard Jack telling Chase, ". . . terrible that you weren't a Jack. Terrible. But there's still hope. You could be a Giant-Killer." He had obviously recovered from his guilt.

Chase scowled fiercely, clearly waiting for Jack to move on to another subject, but he was still standing exactly like his dad—leaning against the courtyard wall, arms crossed, and a hand over his chin. I smirked. Chase noticed and dropped his arms sheepishly.

"Or you could be an Aladdin!" Jack cried happily. "There hasn't been one in years. I'll see if I can't find the magic lamp. The Director keeps hiding it—"

Chase didn't take his eyes off his father, but he leaned slightly back to whisper, "Refreshment table in ten minutes. Come get me if I can't get away."

"Ditto." I spotted my mom running toward me in her business suit, her arms spread wide.

A bunch of the other parents and some EASers did a double take, recognizing her as she passed them. That secret was definitely out. It didn't bother me as much as it used to.

We had invited Dad, too, but he said he had a bunch of meetings that day. (Privately, I thought he was still smarting from the talking-to I had given him a couple weeks before.)

Amy followed Mom slowly, throwing wary glances right and left. She gave a particularly sharp look to an older Character with hair down to her knees, leading a line of seven huge white birds.

She hadn't liked EAS much ever since I had come back from a field trip to the capital with a camera full of pictures I didn't remember taking. Which made me think that maybe Gretel had only enchanted Mom, not Amy.

"My little actress." Mom hugged me. "You were so good!"

Even Amy mustered a real smile. "Perfect comic timing."

"Thanks," I said, embarrassed but pleased.

"Really, they should've given you the lead," Mom said.

"Mom!" I shot a significant glance toward Lena and her family, just a few feet away.

"It's in your blood," Amy pointed out.

"And I'm your mother. I'm supposed to say stuff like that. I could tell embarrassing stories about you as a baby instead. This one time—"

"No, that's okay," I said hurriedly. Chase was looking our way, definitely listening.

"Is that your sword?" Amy said, eyeing it with distaste.

It had been a prop too. I had used it to cut a giant-size roll during the performance.

"I didn't expect it to look so real," Mom said, surprised. "Can I hold it?"

I hesitated. It was a magic sword after all, but when Mom took it from me, she didn't seem to notice anything unusual. Instead, she started to swing it, making lightsaber sounds.

"*Mom,*" I said in a pained voice.

"I know that look." Mom sighed and passed the sword back. "That's the look that tells me you're going to be a teenager soon."

"You ready to go?" Amy asked, obviously hopeful.

A few weeks ago, I would've hesitated to mention it. "Chase and Lena and I were going to grab some food."

Mom's face fell. "Rory, you've made such good friends here. That's wonderful."

"Uh-oh." I knew this day was coming. I'd been expecting it. "We're moving," I said flatly. I sheathed the sword and wondered if I had to give it back, if this would be the last time I would ever hold it.

"The shoot finished yesterday," Amy said, "and we have to be in Colorado for another one on Tuesday."

"I'm so sorry, honey," Mom said. "I know you were really happy here."

I nodded, numbly. I had been happy. I had been scared for my life and so mad at Chase that I wanted to hit him and sometimes really confused, but I had also been happy.

"Rory!" Chase waved to me, halfway to the refreshment table. Lena stood just behind him, waiting. "Chow time?"

They didn't know I was leaving. I hadn't told them yet. I hadn't meant to keep it from them, but with all the excitement of Lena's Tale, and the upcoming skit, the right time hadn't arrived.

"Go say good-bye," my mom said. "And get their e-mails! Maybe we can ask them to come on vacation with us."

I trudged off. It wouldn't be the same as seeing each other every day and going on adventures together.

As I crossed the courtyard, a few EASers pointed me out to their parents. Like with their fingers, so I noticed. Those parents must have known about magic, because as I passed them, I caught a few bits of their conversation: "the golden harp" and "the Snow Queen," Lena's name, Chase's, and mine.

Even though I didn't turn to look, my face heated, but there had been a lot of talk like this in the past couple weeks.

This was why it didn't bother me so much when EASers found out about my famous parents.

The Director had asked us to not talk about it at all. So, at first, I'd assumed that Chase couldn't resist bragging. But he had been insulted at the thought. "It wasn't me. Not all the fainters stayed fainted." And once the story was out, *everyone* knew.

When I was close enough, Lena grabbed my arm. I smiled a little when I noticed Melodie in the bag hanging over her shoulder. I hadn't seen Lena without the harp since we'd come down the beanstalk. I was pretty sure Melodie even went to school with her.

"Did you have to bring *her* with you?" Chase asked Lena.

"I'm not taking any chances," Lena said stoutly.

"I may just be a musical instrument," Melodie said in a wounded voice, "but I still have feelings, you know."

"He's teasing *me*, not you," Lena told her harp absently.

I smiled again, and a wave of sadness hit me. I would even miss the bickering.

"You're a thousand years old," Chase said. "Shouldn't you grow a thicker skin?"

"There are plenty of Fey even older than me," Melodie told Chase. "*They're* still touchy."

"Oh, Rory. They have Fey fudge!" Lena cried happily. "We couldn't use the Table of Never Ending Refills, because the refill part might freak out the parents. So, Gretel buys most of the food, and she always gets this big tub of Fey fudge."

I wasn't particularly hungry, but I let Lena hand me a plate and load it up with fudge.

Searching for a place to sit, we passed Adelaide and Daisy, the new sixth grader who'd joined EAS while we'd been up the beanstalk—and Adelaide's new fan club. She had a chubby face on top of a really skinny body, which made me think of a chipmunk every time I looked at her.

Adelaide watched Chase as we walked by. I was pretty sure she still missed him.

I hadn't known what to expect after the Beanstalk, as far as Chase went. But that Monday, he had slid into a seat at Lena's regular table and stuffed himself with snacks, like it was something he did every day.

When he'd noticed me and Lena staring at him, he'd said, "What? Adelaide and Daisy won't stop talking about what color they should paint their toenails. You really can't expect me to suffer through that." He looked at me and Lena fearfully, like girl talk was a contagious disease, and he was worried it would spread across the courtyard.

"What about the triplets?" Lena asked, flabbergasted.

"Geez, Lena—way to make him feel unwanted," I said, mainly because I was afraid he would leave if he felt that way.

Chase just shrugged. "They're brothers. They spend all their time together. They don't really have room for a fourth wheel."

Then Rapunzel had been right. Chase did need more friends.

I'd once overheard Kevin talking about how the three of us were all buddy-buddy now (at least until Kyle noticed me and punched his brother in the shoulder to shut him up). But nobody really questioned it. Apparently, jumping off a beanstalk together did that to old enemies.

When we neared the Tree of Hope, some fifth graders stopped talking and scurried away, looking over their shoulders at us anxiously. They tended to do this a lot when they saw me, Chase, and Lena together—as if now that we'd escaped the Glass Mountain and slayed some dragonets, we were on the prowl to bully younger kids. It was kind of annoying, actually.

Chase loved the attention. Grinning, he dropped into a cross-legged position. "Starstruck. We're famous, you know."

"Yeah, yeah." I sat down on the roots with my plate in my lap.

"I'm not sure everyone's getting their facts right, though," Lena said.

"Rumors abound," Melodie said solemnly.

"It's awesome. You know what I heard last week?" Chase asked me. "That you mortally wounded the Snow Queen in a duel. Also, you smashed all her magic mirrors, and my personal favorite: you threw a cream pie in her face."

"I heard you started that last one," Lena said to Chase.

I rolled my eyes. "What are they saying *you* did?"

"The story is too violent for your tender ears . . . ," Chase said.

"They say he got bitten," Melodie said.

Chase grimaced, so I knew it was true. Then he abruptly changed the subject, which he was good at doing when he didn't like where the conversation was headed. "I talked to my dad about the Snow Queen."

I wondered if it had been the kind of talk that involved yelling.

"Solange. I never liked her," Melodie said in a confiding tone.

Chase licked some fudge off his fingers. "He said that she had more visitors than she was allowed to have. It was the only thing he knew for sure was a no-no."

"We've been spending a lot of time in the Shoemaker's workshop," Melodie said.

"I asked the elves about the lists," Lena said. "They said they only recovered three names so far."

"And I asked Rapunzel about the Snow Queen breaking out of prison," Chase said, sounding a lot more serious. "'Inevitable' was her exact word."

I sighed deeply. As much as the idea had freaked me out, I

would kind of miss the chance at having a Destiny. I hadn't even found out what my Tale was.

"Rory, are you okay?" Lena asked.

"Yeah, you've been sighing a *lot*." Chase was so concerned he even put down his fudge. "Do you have a crush on me too?"

I stared at him incredulously, not sure I had heard him right, and Melodie said, "You are remarkably self-involved."

Chase looked insulted. "Adelaide sighed a lot right before she said she had a crush on me."

"She had to tell you?" Lena said, surprised.

I snorted. "That's totally it. It was the paint on your face. '*My heart awakens in sight of your green skin/as clean and warty as a toad's has ever been—*'" I said in my best reciting voice, and we all laughed.

Even laughing hurt. I already knew that I would miss Chase and Lena the most.

"I'm moving," I said.

Chase and Lena waited for me to say more.

"Oh," Lena said, realizing that I wanted sympathy. "That sucks."

"As in with boxes and moving vans and stuff? I've always wanted to try that." Chase took another bite of his fudge.

"As in leaving North Carolina?" I couldn't believe they were taking this so well. "As in I can't ever come back to Ever After School."

That shocked them.

Chase's chocolate fell out of his hand into the grass. *"Why?"*

"Did your mom find out about the giants?" Lena asked worriedly.

"Oh, yeah, some parents have a hard time with magic." Chase made it sound like that was really difficult to understand.

"You need to find a way to come anyway," Lena said earnestly.

"Your Tale will come no matter what, and they're *much* more dangerous without support."

That wasn't good news. Thinking about facing the Snow Queen alone gave me chills, but I did feel slightly better now that they seemed upset. "How can I? I'll be in Colorado."

Chase and Lena blinked at me, not getting it.

"So?" said Chase.

"Wait. Rory, where do you think Lena lives?" Melodie asked.

That was a weird question. "North Carolina."

"Oh," Lena and Chase said together, like they understood something I didn't.

"I live in Milwaukee," Lena told me.

"I didn't know there *was* a Milwaukee in North Carolina." Then I realized what she meant.

"Rory, this is the *North American* Chapter of Ever After School," Chase said. "We've got a whole continent's worth of Characters here."

I blinked, stunned. "That's a long commute."

"The doors." Lena pointed to the different-colored doors that lined the courtyard. "They're our own Door-Trek system."

"Some of them go places here like Rumpy's library," Chase said. (Both Lena and Melodie gave him a dirty look for using that nickname.) "But most of them go to different cities in the US and Canada."

"The one to Milwaukee is striped green and white," Melodie said.

Ellie had told me that I would always go through the ruby door like it was important. "Ooooh."

"Usually, when Characters move, we just pretend EAS is a day-care chain," Lena explained.

"In a week, the Director or Ellie or somebody will send your mom a brochure with the new location on it," Chase said. "You can act all excited and be right back here."

I wouldn't have to start all over every time we moved anymore. I wasn't going to lose my friends. For a moment, I couldn't speak.

I concentrated on *not* crying. It would freak Chase out.

Lena giggled. "Maybe the Director shouldn't let Sarah Thumb do the orientation anymore. She leaves a lot of important stuff out."

"Well, now that the disaster has been averted, I'm going to finish eating." Chase picked up his fudge and flicked the grass off it.

"Jacqueline!" shouted someone.

Lena turned reluctantly.

Her grandmother waved a handbag at her, gesturing her forward and looking very stern. The first thing Lena had bought with her gold coins—besides repairs for Jack's truck—was a new wardrobe for her grandmother, who couldn't stop showing it off. She looked very dressed up in a suit of eggplant-colored silk.

"I better go." Lena stood up hastily.

"Lena's grounded," Melodie told us, and Lena gave her harp a harsh look, like she hadn't wanted this information shared.

"Again?" I said. "Didn't she let you off the hook for the grocery-money deal?"

"Well, she kind of caught me experimenting in the middle of the night," Lena said uncomfortably.

"The upstairs bathroom currently shows the main terminal of Grand Central Station," Melodie told us. "We haven't been able to fix it yet. I think we used too much rosemary in the formula."

"Wow, Lena—you're practically a mad scientist," Chase said, and Lena looked flattered.

"Jacqueline!" Lena's grandmother called again.

Lena trotted away. "See you in a few weeks, Rory."

"You're going to have to go soon too," Chase said, sounding a little unhappy about it. "The woman who's not your mother keeps looking at us."

I nodded. "Her name's Amy."

The weekend was coming. It would be lonely for Chase—stuck at EAS without any other kids, and without his dad. I knew how hard that was.

"Whose Tale do you think will be next? Yours or mine?" Chase said.

"Couldn't tell you." Of course, feeling sorry for him didn't stop me from getting annoyed. He *always* had to be competitive. I guessed I was stuck with it, now that I was coming back.

"Normally, I would say yours, but I don't know. You've got that Destiny to worry about." Chase stuck another piece of chocolate in his mouth. "It would help if we knew what it was. Your Tale could be part of your Destiny, or it could be separate, or they might even interfere with each other. Hard to tell."

For a second, I saw ice-blue eyes again. "How am I supposed to know?"

Chase sighed deeply. "I asked Rapunzel that too, but she wouldn't tell me."

I didn't mind if my Tale didn't come for years. I wanted a chance to grow up a little. To get better at whatever might help me. I looked at the sword in my lap. Before seeing the Snow Queen, it would've been a huge relief to know it was magic, but now I wondered if it would be enough.

"Don't worry, though," Chase said. "I'll help you. Lena too."

I smiled. That *did* make me feel better. "Chase, I've been thinking— could you make my sword heavy again?"

Chase's mouth fell open. He had chocolate on his chin.

"If the Snow Queen really is coming back, I'm going to need all the extra help I can get, right?" I held out the sword. "I'll practice while I'm gone."

"Right." Chase brushed the chocolate off his hands and drew the sword. He turned it end over end three times and said something in Fey that made the hair on my arms stand up. He handed it back, looking pleased with himself.

"Rory!" Amy called. "Time to go!"

Chase scowled. I was touched that he cared.

"Want my fudge?" I offered, knowing it would cheer him up.

Chase grinned and reached for the plate. "I'll take it off your hands. You might have a good Tale in you after all. Almost as good as mine."

I grinned, ridiculously happy for a second. "You're only saying that because I gave you candy." I waved and headed off to where Mom and Amy were waiting for me, still smiling. For once, I didn't have to pretend to be happier than I actually was. "Onward! To bubble wrap and packing boxes!"

"Are you allowed to take that sword with you?" Amy clearly hoped the answer was no.

"I'm allowed to have a memento." I was already lying to them again. Colorado wouldn't be perfect either. I would have to be careful not to talk about Chase and Lena like I had just seen them, and inviting Lena over for another sleepover would be complicated.

Mom threw an arm around my shoulder, like she always did when she suspected I was putting on a brave face. "You'll see them again, honey," she said, as we went off in search of the right door.

"I know," I said absentmindedly, thinking of my next adventure with my friends. It didn't matter whose Tale it was.

• • •

I had been wrong. At EAS, everyone talks like your life gets started at about the same time as your Tale. But it's not like that.

Even when your Tale starts, you react to what the world throws at you—finding whatever magical object your Tale names, fighting off whatever villains show up. There's no problem with that. Sticking to the guidelines might even help you get a happily-ever-after. But that's your Tale, not your life. With life, you *have* no guidelines. Your life starts when you stop just reacting to what happens, and you start making decisions about what you can do.

Your life starts when you start taking matters into your own hands—no matter how scared you might be.

At least, that's how it was for me. Don't just take my word for it. Go and find your own.

ACKNOWLEDGMENTS

Writing a book is a lot like going on a quest, except you search for the right words instead of golden harps, and you slay plot snarls instead of dragons. But you also get a lot more than two Companions to help you out. Without these people, this book would definitely be a Failed Tale:

Courtney Bongiolatti, editor extraordinaire, whose savvy and vision made this book become all that it could be. I'm so extremely grateful for everything you've done. To the people of Simon & Schuster Books for Young Readers, thank you for giving Rory a home and an enthusiastic welcome! Special thanks to Chloë Foglia, who made the cover *so pretty*.

Joanna Volpe, my rock star agent, who loved and believed in this story from day one. Rory and I would be lost in the cyber slush pile without you and your hard work, and words cannot express my gratitude and appreciation. Sara, Nancy, Kathleen, and Suzie of Nancy Coffey Lit, you guys have been supportive and sweet from Suite 500 to Suite 410. To the extended NCLit crew, your awesomeness knows no bounds. I'm so glad to be part of the club!

Arielle DiGiacomo, old friend, you read it *twice* (and it's not short!), and I only paid you in ginger chocolate chip cookies. Amanda S., Jennifer A., Nikki R., and Trisha L. all read early chapters and gave me encouragement, just when I needed it the most.

Acknowledgments

Professor Beth Darlington of Vassar College, this book would not exist without your Fairy Tale course. (I also want you to know that I read every page of this book aloud to catch typos, just like you taught me.) Dr. Waples, writing wise, you pushed me more than anyone: I once gave you a story, and you read it, declared it fine, and then said that it didn't have enough of *me* in it. That ticked me off at the time, but it was probably the best advice of all—for writing and for life. Angela, I was teetering at the brink of a big change, and when I told you I wanted to leave the city and go write novels, you didn't even blink. "You will, Shelby," you immediately replied, with such confidence that I started to feel confident too. Maria, Jena, Laura, Barbara, and Rosemary, I'll never forget your kindness back when I left to chase a tiny little idea about a fairy tale world.

My family, who supported me and my dream my whole life. You never questioned whether or not it was a good idea to be a writer when I grew up, and I'm old enough now to know how rare that is. (Mom, I know what you're going to ask, and don't worry—Rory's parents aren't based on mine. You and Dad are awesome.) I love you guys.

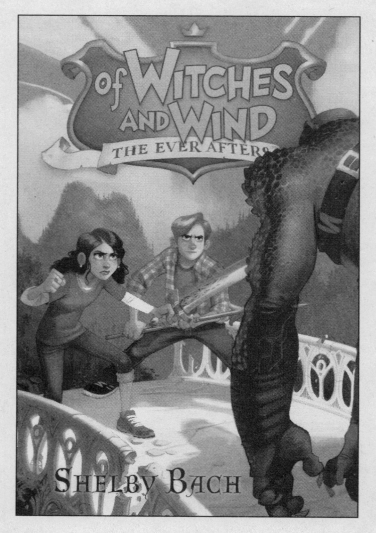

You would think, if you were battling a flock of ice griffins, you would want your best fighters on your side. Or at least someone with experience. These creatures—half bald eagle, half snow leopard—weren't exactly a picnic. Most kids could avoid their giant hooked beaks, the talons on the feathery front legs, and the retractable claws on the furry hind legs, but what you really needed to worry about was their breath. Each griffin could breathe out air so cold that it would freeze puddles into ice slicks under your feet.

But the eighth graders wanted to fight the flock all by themselves.

The ice griffins herded them together in front of the soccer goal. If an eighth grader tried to stab one, the griffin just flapped its wings a couple times and dodged into the sky. Our guys were completely trapped.

"Wow. This is going to end so well," I said.

"We should really follow the Director's orders," said Lena, my best friend. "You know, keep looking."

"Just a sec. Seeing this gives me a warm fuzzy feeling inside," said Chase, my other best friend. His dad, Jack, a big-deal warrior, kept track of how many dragons, griffins, and trolls Chase slayed on every mission. So getting demoted to backup was harder on him than it was on most of us seventh graders.

We all attended Ever After School, a program for fairy tale Characters-in-training, which met every weekday after school left out. We would all survive our own Tale someday, but in the meantime, we trained. Sometimes we even went on missions to make sure magical creatures didn't attack any innocent bystanders. Usually, that meant fighting dragons or ice griffins sent to kill some Character EAS hadn't discovered yet.

Like now. Earlier this afternoon, the Director of EAS had received a report that ice griffins had attacked an all-girls boarding school on Lake Michigan, and she'd given the eighth graders the mission. We lowly seventh graders were just supposed to find the new Character who was under attack.

Seniority was stupid.

A roar thundered across the field. The lion head of the chimera, the flock's three-headed captain, had given an order. The griffins stopped herding, but it didn't matter. The eighth graders were completely surrounded. The snake head wiggled a little, another signal—three griffins straight at the ground. The puddle underneath them turned to ice, and suddenly the tight knot of warriors twisted and wobbled like they were all simultaneously trying on roller skates for the first time.

I groaned. This was actually painful to watch.

Normally, some people from the boarding school might have come out to investigate all this noise on their soccer field, but we were lucky. Lake Michigan was extremely foggy. We only caught a glimpse of their brick buildings every few minutes. If any students or teachers heard all this shouting, then they probably just thought someone was having an extra-epic soccer game. I wasn't sure what they would think of all the roaring, shrieking, and bleating.

Two eighth graders slipped and landed facedown on the ice.

The chimera's goat head bleated. A half dozen griffins leaped into the air and swooped down at their victims, talons and claws outstretched. A few eighth graders screamed.

"Can we help yet?" Chase yelled at Hansel, EAS's sword master. He was also our chaperone for this mission, but, lounging by the bleachers, he didn't look too concerned that the eighth graders were losing.

"Bryan, you're the smallest, fastest, and tastiest. Use that to your advantage," Hansel shouted. The eighth grader whose Tale had turned him into a fawn darted out of the ring. He squeezed between two griffins and cantered as fast as his hooves could carry him. The walking, talking venison was obviously too snackworthy for three griffins to resist. They broke rank and swooped after him, despite the chimera's protesting roars, bleats, and hisses. The eighth graders started fighting their way out.

In all the commotion, one eighth grader in a bright red blazer was too busy not slipping to get his spear up. Seeing the opening, an ice griffin closed its talons over his shoulders and lifted him bodily away from his classmates.

"Crap!" Chase said, and Lena gasped and clutched my arm. My hand closed over my sword hilt, like that would help.

"Go after Ben," Hansel told us, pointing. The kid in red screamed as the griffin carried him across the field toward Lake Michigan. "Make sure he doesn't drown."

And so we were demoted to lifeguards.

We sprinted forward before we lost Ben in the fog. Lena pulled out in front. The grass under our feet gave way to sand. We scrambled down a dune toward the shore.

Ben yelled again.

"Poor sucker," Chase said. "His second day at EAS and he gets kidnapped by an ice griffin."

The griffin kidnapper in question glided straight past the beach and over the lake.

"We can't follow them over water!" Lena cried.

The fog was thicker here. All we could see now was a silhouette of ten-foot wings and kicking legs. Plus one long pointy thing. "Ben! You still have your spear! Use it!"

"Aim for the wing joints!" Then Chase added, much more quietly, "And hope you don't break your neck hitting the lake."

I didn't think of that. Maybe he hadn't heard—

Ben grabbed his spear with both hands and jerked it upward into the feathery chest. The ice griffin shrieked and released him. I gulped hard, watching Ben drop. I hated heights more than most people.

"He has a better chance of surviving that fall than—" Lena winced, interrupted by a huge splash. Ben was in the water. The fog made it impossible to see exactly where he fell in. "—the griffin taking him back to her nest."

"Ben!" I said. We sprinted across the sand to the water. "Ben! Shout back if you can!"

No answer. I put a finger on my nose and glanced at my friends. I didn't want to be the one who went after him. It was cold here.

Lena caught on, her finger on her nose. "Not it!"

"Awesome. Thanks, guys." Chase kicked off his sneakers.

Chase was moving so slowly. I'd seen him muzzle dragons faster than he was unbuckling his sword belt. "Ben could drown, you know. If he's unconscious," I said.

"Nah. He probably just had the wind knocked out of him."

Chase shoved his sword, jacket, and shoes into my hands and waded into the lake.

"I'll check this way," I told Lena, heading left.

She ran right. "Ben!"

For anyone looking for a kid who might have swum to shore on his own, fog doesn't really help. It muffled my shouts, and every slap of waves against sand sounded like Ben splashing back onto the beach. I nearly ran into a boulder, but I didn't find him.

I had just started wondering if the others had had any luck, when Chase called from the water, "Let me know if you've got him!"

"He's not here!" Lena shouted, so far away that I could barely hear her.

"Ben! BEN!" I hadn't meant what I'd said about drowning, but the idea didn't seem so crazy suddenly. Trying not to panic, I listened harder, past the chimera's roars, the griffin squawks, and the waves on the sand.

"Here." The voice came from behind me. It definitely wasn't Ben—it belonged to a girl. I turned around, listening again, and the voice said louder, "Here!"

I ran back, and near a clump of stones I'd searched a minute before, I spotted two figures. But by the time I reached them, only Ben was there—his jacket covered with wet clumps of sand.

"Found him!" I shouted happily.

He vomited water, on his hands and knees, eyes squeezed shut. He had also lost one shoe. His rescuer had disappeared.

"Thank gumdrops!" Lena cried, through the fog.

"So, I got all wet for nothing?" Chase shouted, but he sounded relieved too.

Ben wiped his mouth and drew a shaky breath.

"Anything broken?" I asked him anxiously.

"My lungs, maybe," Ben wheezed without looking up. Then he threw up some more.

Chase splashed out the water beside us. "Sense of humor's intact. I bet this one's going to live."

"Who rescued you?" I asked Ben.

Ben frowned. "A girl. Long dark hair. Great swimmer."

That didn't sound like anyone on this mission. "Did you recognize her?"

"Not precisely," Ben said. "She might be a student here."

"Give him a break, Rory." Dripping, Chase squatted down beside the eighth grader. "The kid was busy drowning."

"Well, that explains the huge splash," said someone behind us. Adelaide, one of my least favorite seventh graders at EAS. "We were wondering."

Four figures marched down the beach, their bows and quivers slung over their shoulders—Adelaide, Daisy, Tina, and Vicky. They were the seventh-grade archer squadron. I liked the last two the best. Tina's dad and Vicky's mom had just gotten married in January. They spent a lot of time bickering over who would be Cinderella and who would be the ugly stepsister. Daisy just did whatever Adelaide said.

"We heard all the shouting and came to see what was up." Tina whirled around suddenly, bow raised, like she'd heard something behind her. But it was only Lena, sprinting along the water.

Chase carefully peeled Ben's red blazer away from his shoulder. "Just two talon punctures, Ben. Your shoulder pads took the brunt of it. Once we get back to EAS, we'll get you fixed up before you get home."

Did you guys find the Snow Queen's target?" Vicky asked.

Lena shook her head and glanced at me. She knew my stomach always flip-flopped whenever that name came up.

The Director had never mentioned it, but every Character at EAS knew: Only one villain commanded armies of ice griffins and dragons—Solange, the Snow Queen. During the war that had lasted half of the twentieth century, she'd almost wiped out everyone who opposed her, including all Characters. She was locked up in the Glass Mountain, but apparently that didn't stop her from sending monsters after defenseless kids.

"Ooooooh! I forgot!" Lena started digging in the tiny electric-blue backpack she carried everywhere.

It always worried me when she did that. Since she was a magic inventor, Lena's bag of tricks was more unpredictable than the average seventh grader's. Once, in the Boston Common park, when we were flushing out the troll that lived under the bridge, she whispered a spell to a painted dragon scale, and a phoenix as big as a limo flew across the sky, a riot of flame and feathers. She told us it was the most beautiful light show she could whip up on short notice. Since trolls can't resist pretty things, she guaranteed that the trick would lure the troll straight to us. Which it did, but every other troll in a ten-mile radius came too.

Humans can't do magic. That was one of the first things the grown-ups told you when you joined EAS.

But every rule has exceptions, and Lena was one of them.

Lena becoming a magician was the weirdest thing that had happened since we'd climbed the beanstalk during Lena's Tale last May. Melodie, the golden harp we took from the giant's safe, had taught Lena a whole bunch of spells, where she could use dragon scales, phoenix feathers, or unicorn hair like magic batteries. Usually, Lena enchanted them to power new inventions.

All Lena's searching woke up Melodie. She stuck her golden head out of Lena's backpack and yawned. "What is it you're looking for, Mistress?"

""Got it!" Lena waved a fabric-covered square triumphantly in our faces. It kind of looked like an e-reader cover, but I knew from experience that the hard casing held a square mirror. An M3, to be exact—the EAS version of a walkie-talkie. "My mini magic mirror."

"Big whoop." Adelaide never missed a chance to criticize us. She had been Chase's closest friend before Lena's Beanstalk Tale, so we definitely knew why. "You invented those back at Thanksgiving. You can't expect us to still be impressed."

"When was the last time you invented something, Adelaide?" I snapped.

"I've been modifying the mirrors." Lena's eyes gleamed behind her glasses. She was obviously too excited to get her feelings hurt. "I'm trying to give them new capabilities, so they can do anything smartphones can do."

"Text?" Tina said, interested.

"Tetris?" Vicky asked, impressed.

"No, not those," Lena said, in a smaller voice.

The others looked disappointed, so Melanie sniffed, "All practical uses."

Lena just opened the M3 and muttered something in Fey. Chase, the only other kid in earshot who spoke that language, burst out laughing.

I sensed a joke. "What?"

"Don't you dare translate, Chase Turnleaf," Melodie warned. "If you do, Lena and I will turn you into something small and slithery. Like a salamander. We just perfected that potion."

For someone about a foot tall and attached to a golden harp

without legs, Melodie could be really scary when she felt like it. Chase abruptly stopped laughing.

"Tell me later?" I whispered to him.

"Do I look like I want to turn into a salamander?" Chase whispered back. "If she'd said frog, I would've considered it. 'The Frog Prince' isn't a bad Tale."

Ben laughed, but then he choked a little and brought up another round of puke. My chest squeezed in sympathy.

"Wow," Adelaide said mildly. "Did you swallow half the lake?"

Lena angled the M3 at Ben and his watery bile. His face was nearly as red as his jacket.

"Geez, Lena." I pushed the magic camera down with maybe more force than was necessary. The paparazzi had recorded enough of my ugliest memories for me to know that it sucked. "Do you have to film this?"

But Ben perked up. "You filmed it? Did you get the whole thing?"

"I wish." With a sigh Lena swung to angle the M3 around, toward the eighth graders' fight. The wind thinned the fog, and past the lumpy dunes and half the soccer field we caught a glimpse of feathers. "I just turned it on."

"How far did I fall?" Ben asked eagerly.

"Fifty feet or more," Chase said.

"Really?" Ben sat up with a wince. He actually sounded pleased with himself.

Adelaide and Daisy both rolled their eyes.

"You're gonna be one big bruise tomorrow," Chase said, with the air of someone bequeathing bragging rights.

"I don't think it's very funny." The voice came from the lake, so soft that you could barely hear it. "He was underwater for a long time."

We all turned. A girl splashed to shore, water dripping from her plaid skirt and jacket. Her long black hair was the kind that got very wavy when wet —but it made her look elegant, not scruffy. She had the beginning of a tan, which gave her skin a golden sheen, and her light blue, long-lashed eyes took up most of her heart-shaped face.

She was beautiful. Not just normal beautiful, but too pretty to feel real. Like a sculpture, or a painting, or an airbrushed photo.

She didn't seem to notice that everyone was staring at her with dumbfounded expressions. Even Ben's mouth hung open. We weren't used to kids outside EAS approaching us on missions, and definitely not ones who looked like models for school-uniform catalogues.

"Who are you?" Adelaide shook her blond hair back. She only did that when she felt threatened.

"My name is Mia," the dripping girl said uncertainly.

"You're the girl who saved me!" Ben burst out.

I did a double take. Mia didn't seem like the rescuing type.

Encouraged, Mia slipped out of the water and glided to Ben's side. She held out something oblong and leather—his missing loafer. "You lost this."

"Right," Chase said. "Because that makes sense. Diving back into Lake Michigan to rescue his shoe."

I personally thought this was a fair point, but Ben shot to his feet in knight-in-shining-armor mode. "She saved my life. That doesn't happen every day."

Poor new kid. After he spent more time at EAS, somebody saving his life wouldn't impress him so much.

"She might be the Character we've been looking for," Lena said distractedly. She was busy glaring at her M3. "It's too foggy. We won't be able to record anything this way."

"Maybe if we got a little closer, Mistress," Melodie suggested.

"Good idea." Lena hurried toward the dunes between the shore and the soccer field.

Adelaide turned to the other archers. "Who has the mirror the Director gave us? For the test?" Tina and Vicky both pointed at Daisy, who pushed her arrows aside and reached into her quiver.

The chimera roared extra loud, and I glanced back toward the battle —all I saw were dunes, fog, more fog, and a soggy stretch of grass.

But Chase tensed too. He took his sword belt back and buckled it on.

"Test?" Mia asked, drawing closer to Ben.

"It's not hard. You just look into a magic mirror and tell us what you see in it," Ben explained.

I was sure Mia would never suspect that he had just taken the test himself three days ago. "We need to know if you're a Char—"

"Incoming!" one of the eighth graders called.

The chimera galloped across midfield as fast as its lion paws could carry it, all three heads focused straight on us.

I dropped Chase's stuff and hurriedly drew my sword.

"Oy! Monster!" cried Ben.

Snorting, Chase unsheathed his blade. "Did you seriously just say that?"

Only one Character stood between us and the charging chimera, and she was too absorbed with her updated M3 to draw her sword.

Lena.

Chase and I erupted forward. The second my hand curled around the sword hilt, my body seemed very far away, like someone else was moving for me. This was normal. I had an enchanted sword. This runner's-high feeling happened every time the magic kicked in.

"I got it." Chase ran so fast he practically skimmed over the sand. "You go cover Lena."

The sword's magic sent me weaving through the dunes to Lena's side, right at the edge of the soccer field. Her eyes were still glued to her M3. "Rory, you have to see this!"

"The image is so clear," Melodie added.

They clearly hadn't noticed the chimera barreling over the grass, twenty-five feet away and closing.

"Lena, we've got company!" I tried to tug her back through the dunes. She would be safer behind the archers.

"No, I can't move—" Then she glanced up and found herself practically face to face with a three-headed monster. "Oh!"

"Don't worry. I'll take care of it." Chase charged out, and, see-ing him on the field, the chimera slowed. Its snake head hissed. "Yeah, you know it's all over for you—don't you, ugly?"

Lena dashed back through the dunes and behind the archers before Chase and the chimera even came to blows. She wasn't the fastest runner in seventh grade for nothing.

When I was halfway to the others, Chase said, "Crap!"

I whirled around and raised my sword, its magic thrumming.

But Chase wasn't hurt. The chimera leaped from the edge of the grass to the nearest dune. It had gotten past him.

He sprinted after it. "I still got it, Rory!"

The chimera glanced at Adelaide, Daisy, and the stepsisters, their arrows notched to their bows, and then closer to the water, where Ben just watched. His mouth was open. Mia peeked ner-vously around him.

The new kid didn't even have a weapon.

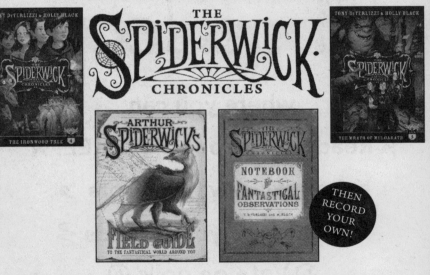